THE KILBEGGAN TOUCH

THE
KILBEGGAN TOUCH

James McAleese

Fieldgate Press

Second Edition

Published in Paperback by
The Fieldgate Press
Kells, Co. Meath
Phone/Fax 046 - 54211
ISBN 0 9534790 0 5

Printed in Dublin by Irish Litho Print

Previously Printed in Hardback by
The Book Guild Ltd.
25 High Street,
Lewes, Sussex

1

He gave her a playful little nudge. It was intimate, cheeky, moving. She felt the slight touch. Both she and the car shivered slightly. She turned sharply to remonstrate. He was sitting insolently in his Porsche which was dark and powerful like himself. He smiled, inviting a conversation. She noted the amazing luxuriant hair, the tanned cheekbones, the wide sensuous lips and those eyes. The superb Magee jacket hid powerful shoulders. He had followed her, perhaps fifty yards behind her ancient but fast MG along the green Welsh roads that led to the port. Now at Fishguard, he had joined the queue of cars for the ferry directly behind her MG. He had moved closer and now she had felt the violation of her car and herself. He had noted the proud toss of her head, the slightly freckled skin, the sexy mouth, a dream on wheels. Perhaps, he thought, I'm making a proper fool of myself. She could have legs like pillars, thighs like a fishwife. But he was wrong. Long golden legs swung out of the MG supporting magical hips. She strolled back, leaned down to the door of the Porsche, showing a sharp silver tin opener in her hand.

'Repeat your action,' she spoke in a divine Celtic accent, 'repeat your action and I'll mark your car from bumper to bonnet.'

Now it was his turn to gasp as she rejoined her ancient shining model. A wave of excitement swept through Milo. This was a real challenge. Once in his last year at Harrow, he had eyed a beauty like this across a bookshop in the town. A glimpse of golden breasts had inflamed the nineteen-year-old schoolboy. They had eyed each other with sudden desire. He had moved around a corner to get closer only to find her claimed by a young naval officer in uniform.

1

But this was a much more promising encounter. What eyes, what sexual come-on behind the fury of her refusal. He decided that come hell or high water they would get closer, much closer on the ship. He followed her more cautiously as the line of cars crept slowly onto the car ferry.

Seagulls screamed and the ship's foghorn boomed as the ferry edged out of the harbour. There is a sense of excitement which is always felt even by seasoned travellers. All around Britain there were ferries moving out to Sweden, Holland, Belgium, France, even to the Isle of Skye. *The Innisfallen* was travelling to Ireland laden with British and Continental travellers, Irish people returning, holiday-makers of all kinds. Sheila parked her beloved MG, locked it carefully and climbed the narrow staircase. She made her way carefully through the crowds to the Purser's office.

'Cabin for Miss Kelly?' she asked.

'Miss who?' he asked rudely.

'Miss Sheila Kelly from London.'

'We have no record of any booking in the name of Kelly.'

'But I booked it personally last week in Tooting.'

'Possibly another ship,' he suggested, 'we have no booking in your name and all the other cabins are reserved.'

He turned away to serve the other clients. The obnoxious young man with the Porsche was next.

'Name, sir?' the Purser enquired.

'Kilbeggan,' said the dark-haired young driver.

'Ah, yes,' said the Purser, 'double cabin booked for the Earl of Kilbeggan. No. 15 on B deck, my lord. Shall I get somebody to carry your cases?'

'Double cabin?' said the young earl, 'single was booked, but I suppose I might as well take it.'

He turned suggestively glancing at Sheila. Hot with resentment at the double insult, she pushed her way to the lounge.

Here in some discomfort amid playing children and some drunken teenagers, she found a seat and brooded on the astonishing coincidence. So this was the young heir to the local big house. At home in her father's little farm in Westmeath, all the gossip was about the person who had

2

inherited the great manor house which stood two miles outside the local village. The historic estate was empty since the death of the last owner, Lady Cynthia Kilbeggan. This eccentric and rich old lady had presided over the country-side for half a century. She had survived political changes, run the hunt, farmed her decaying estate, become a local legend. Country people believed she was the last of her line, that the great family had nobody to inherit. Auctioneers awaited eagerly the sale of Kilbeggan Castle. Local farmers thought anxiously of dividing the estate to increase their holdings. But the county paper, *The Westmeath Examiner*, had printed a bombshell.

'New heir for Kilbeggan estate,' ran the banner headlines. Her father had sent her a copy of the paper. With huge interest she had read the news. A remote ancestor of the Kilbeggan family had left in disgrace in 1894. Now, a hundred years later, a young man of this line had claimed both title and estate. The young squire was returning to claim his own. The newspaper suggested that he had inherited the famous Kilbeggan Touch. This was the fasci-nating 'cure' which the Kilbeggans were supposed to possess. Certain illnesses were curable if the Kilbeggan heir touched you on six specified areas of the body. Neck, chest, elbow had to be touched in order. Next, hands were laid on knee, leg and buttock. Thousands had claimed in the past that this had cured them. Lady Cynthia had been plagued by requests for the cure. Finally she had ordered her elderly butler to refuse all entreaties. She had never had the power, which descended in the male line. Death had followed and then came the news of her young successor.

Sheila sat bemused. So this was the new master of Kilbeg-gan, a man to whom she had taken an instant dislike. What a coincidence. What an overbearing, over-confident and, she thought irritably, over-attractive young male who would be her family's neighbour. How she hated arrogance. As a young nurse, she had refused several invitations from hand-some house doctors who had laid their eyes on this lovely country girl. She had warded off many prying hands, had outstared several surgeons who had more than medical interests at heart. The tilt of her small pert bum in its tight uniform had excited many a young medical student not long out of his exclusive public school. Smiling and happy with her friends, whom she called 'real people', she had an inherited resentment of powerful people, of 'law dee daw' accents, of the over-security of inherited power or wealth. She preferred her own kind. She determined to stick to her own. So this would be her attitude to the new Lord of Kilbeggan. She sat not too comfortably in the overcrowded lounge.

The seas around Britain look very ordinary on a map. Dover to Calais looks a quiet short trip. But many an innocent day tripper has found otherwise. The Irish Sea can be a superb voyage on a calm sunny day. Only occasionally do the strong Atlantic currents sweep angrily between the two great islands causing mighty seas to rise up. So it was tonight. Sheila felt the ferry uneasily shaking as it butted its way across the Irish Sea. Glasses rattled behind the bar, packs of playing cards fell off tables. Elderly people clung to their chairs, children began to cry. The feeling of fear began to grip passengers as the force of the elements increased. Only the drunks found it entertaining. The crowd still remained thick around the bar, the love of beer overcoming the fear of storm. Sheila watched one rowdy passenger calling for two pints of Guinness. He swayed where he stood. With two strong hands he held the pints of stout and began to make his way across the floor. Just as he went past her, a fierce roll occurred in the ship. He very nearly kept his footing but suddenly stumbled. He fell across Sheila and a quarter of a gallon of beer splashed all over her, soaking her from head to foot. The empty glasses knocked against her but thankfully did not cut her. She arose soaked to the skin in the thick smelling liquid. All her dainty instincts were outraged. She felt filthy, depressed, did not know what to do. Suddenly from the direction of the bar, help was at hand. The tall figure which had become so recently familiar

4

to her gripped her firmly. This time she did not resist, felt no resentment.

'Come down to my cabin and clean yourself up,' he urged her.

He took hold of her case and led the shaken beauty down the stairs and into a comfortable, even luxurious cabin.

'I'll ruin your cabin,' she blurted, 'everything will get filthy.'

'Strip off,' he commanded her, 'or you'll catch cold.'

He showed her the little cabin bathroom. She took her case and closed the door. Her skirt fell in a sodden mass to the floor. A quick movement had her jumper over her head and it joined the skirt. A heave of the ship nearly sent her crashing into the corner of the tiny room. She undid her bra and stood naked on the wet floor. She felt isolated and pathetic. There was hot water and soap in the miniature basin and, struggling to stay erect, she managed to clean herself free of the clinging beery liquid. Another roll of the ship nearly sent her flying as her feet slipped on her soaking clothes on the moist floor. However, wrapping herself in a large towel, she managed to dry herself and then take a pair of jeans and sweater from her case. Sticking her unpleasant smelling garments into a plastic bag, she felt no longer like a drowned rat. She brushed her hair and opened the door, presentable again.

The young Lord Kilbeggan regarded her solicitously. 'What a change', he said cheerfully. 'You're most welcome to stay here for the night and take one of the two bunk beds. I can only use one myself.'

She glanced enviously at the slim bunk bed. She would have given anything to take refuge in this quiet cabin, to lie in comfort rather than face the uncomfortable squash upstairs. For a moment she was tempted. This good-looking man, no longer arrogant and high-handed now seemed more like a kindly companion. But caution won out. Her country girl's prudence made her decline the offer. She watched his face express his disappointment as she thanked him for his good natured gesture. But a sudden touch of unguarded feeling swept through her and she kissed him on the cheek. In the confined space it had been almost impossible not to touch.

'Can we meet again?' he asked.

She pointed to the address on her travel bag.

'Sheila Kelly,' he read, 'Drumlerry, Kilbeggan, Co. Westmeath.'

Delight swept through him.

'I've read about you,' she said, 'We'll see each other in Westmeath.'

'I'll need friends,' he said.

'So many differences between us,' she answered.

He looked at her longingly and shook his dark head in denial.

'Differences will be easily overcome,' he spoke in his surprisingly deep masculine voice.

She kissed him suddenly, broke off and left the cabin.

It was not long before he met her again.

2

Kilbeggan is not a sleepy village. It lies on the main road west from Dublin to Galway and is also intersected by another main road from Dundalk south to Limerick. Great lorries heave their way through the ancient streets. An old whiskey distillery, Locke's Distillery, used to provide large employment and sold a famous brand of whiskey. Lately the distillery had reopened inside its grey stone walls. The Kilbeggan Race Course lies outside the town and three times a year the races draw great crowds of owners and trainers and racegoers to the attractive but difficult course. Travel past the race track, take several turns down side roads and you find yourself facing the imposing entrance to Kilbeggan Castle. Gothic-style twin gate lodges stand on each side of tall pillars which hold heavy rusting gates. Behind the gates, the avenue turns hidden in overgrown rhododendrons. The castle is not visible from the road. On each gate lodge is carved the coat of arms of the Kilbeggan family. Two wolves stand erect facing a dark hand and the crest underneath reads *Vinceo quem tango* or in plain English, 'I conquer through touch' – a reference to the famous Kilbeggan touch. Past these gates Sheila drove, humming the words of the old song –

> Westering home with a song in the air
> Light in the eye and it's goodbye to care.
> Laughter o' love and a welcoming there.

It was welcome she got when she travelled further on and drove down the old farm track to her family home Drumlerry. Hens scattered, geese gobbled, a collie dog came flying out from a stable. Her father's face was full of pleasure as he held her, overjoyed in the return of his only daughter.

7

Her mother wiped dough in her apron; she had been cooking to feast the start of her daughter's holiday. Seamus, her sporting young brother, came out from the calf shed where he had been dosing a sick calf. She was lifted from the ground and given a twirl. Roses grew up the walls of the old house. Peat smoke drifted from the chimneystack. A red creeper grew in brilliant colour over a dark cupressus. This had grown from a root given to her granny who had worked as a maid in the big house. 'Tropaeolum' the old Lady Kilbeggan had called it. Two cats purred at her legs – had they remembered her? Seamus looked with delight at her MG sportscar – he hadn't seen it before. He jumped into it, and turned on the engine and revved it hard.

To her father it was only 'Half a car. Shure it's got no top on it. Could you not afford a proper car?'

'Ah! Daddy,' she said and they went into the low kitchen.

Geraniums on the window ledges obscured some of the light, but she felt a pang of pleasure – the sheer joy of being home. She sat beside Daddy's chair answering question after question while her mother, traditional in her ways, made the tea and that wonderful bread which made shop bread taste false. Out from the cupboard came great pots of home-made jam full still of the sweet taste of the fruit. The questions poured out as the old farmer questioned her about the city – London, the hospital, her friends, the matron, her health, the rest of the staff and a hundred other subjects.

Little work was done on the farm that day. Neighbours called, delighted to hear that Sheila was home again. Her mother happily made pot after pot of tea as her school friends heard the news and came in after their day's work. Her best friend, Brigid Horan, she had not seen for a year and what a change they saw as they inspected each other laughingly. Brigid had been a rather clumsy, almost uncouth girl, great at games but shy socially and bashful with others. A transformation had taken place. She had taken a year's secretarial course with some work experience involved in a local accountant's office. Her temporary employers had liked her so much that they had gladly taken her on permanently at the end of the year and now she was secretary to young Bobby Boyle, the junior partner, and it was said that they were getting closer day by day. Bobby had driven her out from the town and had left her there while he went to see a client. Sheila looked at her with admiration as she entered the low farmhouse door.

'Brigid,' she said, 'you look wonderful. Life must be treating you very kindly.'

Brigid smiled warmly, the pair of them embraced and reminiscences began to flow.

'Do you remember when Kitty hid the teacher's gown?'

'What happened to David Kelly – did he ever make the county team?'

'Wasn't it very sad about poor Dervilla? A baby at her age and the lad has left her – gone off to work in Dublin.'

'I hear Mary McGrath failed her chemistry exam.'

'How's the nursing? Do you get used to the work after a while?'

Old Mr Kelly went in and out to the yard doing the essential jobs. Cows have to be milked and foddered. Milking is now a hygienic machine – like exercise, not like the old days when Mr and Mrs Kelly each with a bucket and stool worked in the small dark cow house. Now he had to connect udders to milking machines and the hum of machinery filled the new shed. Certain things never changed. The cats still hovered around looking for the odd squirt in a saucer but hygiene regulations are strict and you couldn't let them too close. Sheila and Brigid came to watch the work and the two of them fed the hens and drove the geese back to the yard. The gander hissed angrily ready to protect his goose and goslings. Sheila had forgotten how aggressive geese can be and she needed the help of a stick to drive them into their sheds. A battered old Peugeot van drove noisily into the yard, the sound of its diesel engine echoing against the yard houses. Seamus's friends had called to take him to football practice. They eyed the two girls across the yard with appreciation. Shyness blunted the expression of their feelings.

'Great to see you, Sheila. Nice to see you home.'

Young Reynolds with the dark ponytail, Kavanagh thin as a rake but a superb footballer, Paul Smith who still drove far too fast despite the car crash – Sheila knew them and smiled her greetings. She would be seeing them at the weekend disco. Seamus came out with football togs in an old sports bag; he squeezed into the van and, with a noisy salute, the lads drove away to practise their skills at the local pitch. It was different skills they employed at the local disco but they enjoyed both exercises.

Sheila and Brigid were called in to tea by Mrs Kelly and the smell of baking still hovered in the kitchen. Mrs Kelly was never satisfied by her daughter's eating habits.

'You'll become an anolectic or whatever you call it.'

All was home-made. She considered 'shop cakes' as a superior form of sawdust. Only her own hens supplied decent tasty eggs, not like the pallid eggs from the battery hens. Rhubarb tarts and apple tarts lay hot on the ancient plates and as usual Sheila disappointed her mother by not finishing them there and then.

'Brigid, you're as bad. You'll both have to eat better or you'll grow into sticks of things.'

The two girls laughed but could manage no more.

'Bobby will be back to collect me at half-six,' said Brigid. 'He's leaving a note for a client. Have you heard about the new Lord Kilbeggan? He's just inherited Kilbeggan Castle from his aunt and has come over from England to live and he's going to farm the estate. The place nearly went to rack and ruin with old Lady Kilbeggan. They say when slates fell off the roof they were never replaced. Paddy Neligan, the butler, is crippled with rheumatism. The pheasant shoot has been poached out of it for years. It's a right mess the new lord will come into. I don't know whether he's young or old but God help him with the place. Maybe he'll be very grand like some of the old gentry and not want even to come near the likes of us.'

She stopped and noticed that Sheila was colouring slightly.

10

3

No warm family welcome awaited the new Lord Kilbeggan as he arrived at the ancient family seat. He remembered the impressive twin gate lodges and the massive iron gates, from an earlier visit as a child. Now the gate lodges stood empty and dismal. Ivy had grown through the broken diamond-paned windows. Milo stopped the car and got out to open the great rusting gates. They stirred unwillingly and he pushed harder until they groaned back through the weeds that fettered them. Young and fit, it was all he could do to force an entrance wide enough to allow his car to enter. He drove through and wondered if he would succeed in reaching the castle. Every few yards laurel or rhododendron hit the car window, showering raindrops over the vehicle. A particularly deep pothole nearly held the front axle but he revved the engine and kept going. He drove over an ancient stone bridge and wondered if there were still good trout in the river below. He passed the famous tulip trees, mighty in size and girth and not yet showing their attractive light green flowers. Through damp tunnels of woodland he passed and several times had to stop the car to remove broken branches. At last he turned a corner and entered a lighter countryside. Meadows turned into lawns and wildly overgrown flowerbeds appeared in front of him. He gasped suddenly as the enormous facade of Kilbeggan Castle towered out of the morning. The great Victorian Gothic pile stood like an illustration from a ghost story. Turrets and battlements gave it a warlike air but the great lime-stone pile had never suffered a siege, although an earlier castle on the site had been besieged by Cromwell. He stopped the car outside the huge pillared entrance where a flight of steps led to the great double entrance doors. Milo

11

took out his cases, trudged up the steps, jangled the bell and waited.

'Madness,' he said to himself. 'What an appalling place to live. Sell it and go back to civilization.'

No reply came. No sound except the cawing of alarmed crows broke the stillness. He peeped in the hall windows. Dustsheets covered furniture in the vast gloomy hall. Again he pressed the bell and kept his hand on the bell. As it jangled in the depths of the house, the ancient butler, Neligan, stumbled across the hall, withdrew the bars on the doorway and opened the creaking doors.

'Welcome home, my lord,' he said hoarsely. Into the damp hall they took the cases. Neligan realized as he bent to take a case that his fly was open and the yellowing woollen combinations were apparent. He turned to the wall for a moment, fastened the trouser-buttons, adjusted his false teeth more comfortably and repeated, 'yes, welcome home, my lord.'

Mrs Neligan had appeared behind him, puffing and panting up the basement staircase.

'You're very, very welcome, my lord,' she said. 'Very welcome and I've set a fire in the library for you and we've been airing the Green Bedroom for days. Patsy will show you up and then we'll have a nice meal on a tray for you in the library. Mr Kinch, the solicitor, is coming to see you at three o'clock and there's a drinks tray waiting in the alcove. I hope you didn't have too horrible a journey on the boat.'

Neligan went very slowly up the wide staircase ahead of him. He stayed close to the banisters and talked to cover up his slow progress.

'Ye'll find the house very comfortable. Old-fashioned it may be, but there's no denying the comfort. It's a great bed in the Green Bedroom. I remember old Lord William had his last illness in it. He suffered from the convulsions, you know, but he couldn't have been more comfortable not if he was in The Kilbeggan Arms or The Greville Arms in Mullingar. And it has a great view over the lake and beyond to the mausoleum where all your lordship's people lie buried. And there's a private staircase down to the library underneath where ye'll have your meals. Mrs Neligan is a great cook and we must find out what food you like. And you must ask for anything you want. We're always at the end of a bellrope.'

He paused on the landing to get his breath back and set off down the dark passage that led to the Green Bedroom. He flung open the door. To Milo's relief a fire glowed in the hearth and a log basket lay nearby with logs and peat. A huge four-poster bed stood in a corner of the room.

'Ye'll find a bathroom down the passage. Turn left and across the long gallery and it's the third door on the right. Packy will bring you up hot water for a bath in the morning, if you'd like a shave. There's the staircase down to the library and wherever you like. Ring the bell and we'll have a meal up to you and again a hundred welcomes to you.'

With that he closed the door and Milo was left in a bedroom which was twice the size of a London flat. Three large windows lit the room and he looked out over a landscape of thick meadows, tall trees and a stretch of water where the river had been widened into a lake. Beyond it a spire broke the line of the trees – the mausoleum where his ancestors lay buried. Faded watercolours by Lady Waterford hung on the walls and some pictures of his forbears, whom he had never heard of. A bookcase held an old set of Ruff's *Guide To The Turf* and numerous sporting books including *Wild Sports Of The West*. A sketch of a long dead terrier hung near the bed. On a writing table lay some damp sheets of writing paper enscribed heavily:

Railway Station   Kilbeggan Castle
Mullingar, Co. Westmeath

An earl's coronet decorated each damp sheet and accompanying envelope. Milo put down his luggage and went down the narrow staircase to the great library beneath.

The library, dank and gloomy, was lit partly by a wide log

fireplace where huge sections of an ash tree flared and then died back. The meal when it came was surprisingly good.

'I hope you like nettle soup,' said Mrs Neligan, 'the gentry round here used to adore it. I cooked you a bit of salmon that Packy caught in the big river, though I didn't know if you'd like fish.'

'Thank you, Mrs Neligan,' said Milo, 'the more fish I get, the more I'll be delighted. Tell Packy I want advice on where to fish around here. I've brought my rods in the back of the car. I don't know what flies to use on the Westmeath rivers.'

'Is it flies you use?' said Mrs Neligan, 'Packy only uses worms, and sometimes a spinner. He's not supposed to fish on the big river. Colonel Burden would kill him if he caught him on his stretch. He takes the shotgun to poachers. But he mightn't mind your lordship fishing there, as you're the same type of people.'

She disappeared and Milo ate ravenously. The nettle soup had a good base and a sharp tang to remind you of its origin. The large piece of salmon was coloured mildly pink as wild salmon are, so unlike the menacing red colour of the farmed salmon. This was a bonus he thought. A good cook to look after you was a rarity nowadays. Up she came again with a tray holding a splendid treacle pudding. His mouth watered.

'Mrs Neligan, you're a wonderful woman and a great cook,' he said.

'Lady Kilbeggan was very particular,' said Mrs Neligan. 'Shure the good food kept her alive. She had no interest in drink. Indeed she hated it, for it killed the old lord – he had a passion for whiskey, God bless him, but it destroyed his liver. There's few would have survived if they drank like his lordship. She locked the cellar door the moment he died and it's never been opened since. If you'd like to see it, I've got the key put away in a safe place and I'll send Packy with you to try to open it. He'll come up to you when you've finished your dinner. He's back from college this weekend.'

Milo ate heartily. He found the treacle pudding reminded him of his childhood and the meals in the school dining

14

hall. Pudding was followed by a very inferior coffee served in a delicate cup. This brand of coffee was the type to be served in a mug and he resolved to buy a decent tin of coffee that would finish off a good meal perfectly.

He met two other people on this the first day in his new home. Packy came in to introduce himself. You would never have guessed that he was Mrs Neligan's son. Packy was thin with long fair hair. His jeans had holes in all the right places. He looked sensitive and intelligent.

'I'm studying at art college in Athlone,' he explained, 'I come home for the weekends.' There was no suggestion of deference or an awareness of class distinction. 'I didn't get your name,' he said, 'and I'm damned if I'm going to "my lord" you. You'll get enough of that from my mother. You're welcome in any event.'

Milo wondered if he was suffering from a chip on the shoulder or severe left-wing tendencies.

'Look,' he said, 'forget the title. I'm Milo Kilbeggan and I'll be glad of your company and of any help you can give me starting off my new life here. I'd like to go fishing with you and maybe you'd come down and we'll try to open the cellar.'

The two young men left the library. At the back of the hall there was a hidden door. Packy switched a light on and they saw granite steps leading down to a great cold and damp basement. They travelled down a passage past ancient servants' quarters until they came to a black studded door almost hidden in cobwebs. Packy tried to insert the huge key into the mortice lock. His thin artist's fingers made no impression – the key would not enter the lock. Milo took the key from him and his firm confident hand pushed the key into place.

'Now to turn it,' he said, but as he spoke the lights suddenly thinned and went out leaving them completely in the dark. 'Christ,' Milo swore, 'what the hell has happened?'

'Hold on,' said Packy, 'we sometimes get a short in the wiring. I'll just twiddle with the switch. It sometimes happens but it comes on again.'

Milo waited uneasily in the black empty corridor, not very confident of his new companion's intentions. But inside a few seconds, the lights came on again and he felt regret for his doubts. He held the key again and pressed it hard. It moved reluctantly and with a sense of triumph he opened the door. It creaked reluctantly back, but he tried to close it as an indescribable smell came out of the cellar. The fetid air rushed into the passage, nauseating and repulsive. After a few minutes it had dissipated enough to allow them to enter. Thousands of empty bottles that once held claret and burgundy, port and sherry, brandy and spirits lay on their sides. Corks had rotted, wine gone to vinegar. Thirty years of neglect had destroyed what must have been a very valuable collection of wine. None of the bottles had been recorked regularly if at all and some thousands of pounds of liquors had gone wrong and eventually seeped out through the rotted corks. A sight to make a drinker melancholy. Only a few bottles held their charge – some brandies and strangely some home-made wine.

'What a sad sight,' said Milo, 'surely she could have sold them, instead of letting them go to ruin.'

They retraced their steps, through the bowels of the great house and up to healthier parts.

'She thought it was poison,' said Packy, 'she felt it had killed her husband.'

Mrs Neligan met them in the hall.

'The solicitor's in the library,' she said, 'waiting to talk to you.'

Milo made an appointment to go fishing with Packy and re-entered the library.

Mr Kinch, thin, cautious and very conventional looked at Milo with some surprise. After a few introductory greetings he commenced to enlighten Milo on the business side.

'Your aunt kept the place together for years on her Lloyds investments. At that period of time, the names in Lloyds made very comfortable incomes. She even went on a world cruise in 1990 and Mrs Neligan got a rise of £5 a month. But with all those natural disasters, Lloyds syndicates began to

16

lose money and your aunt's syndicate had to start paying out. In the old days the cheques flew in. Now they had to fly out. She began to sell land. What's left now is about one hundred and sixty acres mostly in woods and the lake with only about fifty acres of pasture land. I'm deeply afraid,' concluded Mr Lynch, 'that you will not have enough money to keep up this establishment unless perhaps you have a large income of your own.'

His thick spectacles and his silver hair glinted in the firelight. As senior partner of Kinch and Gore, he had looked after Lady Kilbeggan's affairs for nearly half a century and was curious about this strange young man who had come to inherit the place.

'Could I make so bold as to ask you, my lord, have you a private income of your own?'

Milo laughed heartily.

'I haven't a bob,' he replied, 'apart from my car which I saved up for, I have no earthly possessions. I had hoped I was coming into money.'

'You are inheriting the castle and grounds and a load of unpaid bills,' said the solicitor gloomily. 'Mrs Neligan wasn't paid for weeks and that son of hers got quite aggressive on the phone to me about it, the poncy young brat. We shall have to give much thought to this. But I've paid her now up to date. The outlook is depressing. You may well have to sell castle and furniture to some interested party. It would make a nice country hotel or golf club. The tinkers broke in and stole the best furniture and it's never been seen since, so there's not much to sell off. The few fields are let to Mr Kelly for cattle and we get two thousand a year for the grazing but that won't feed you, never mind pay the Neligans. About £6,000 comes in each year from the remaining stocks and shares. I'm sorry to be so depressing but you'll have to think seriously about selling. Come over and have dinner with us next week and maybe we'll have something worked out by then.'

He rose stiffly and Milo escorted him out to where an immaculate Mercedes stood sombre on the gravel.

17

'By the way,' said Mr Kinch, as he climbed into the leather seat, 'would you mind if my wife came to take a few cuttings from the flower borders. She always envied your aunt's blue phlox and there's some double Michaelmas daisy that she'd love to take a root from. She might bring over a few friends of hers – Patricia Daly from the bank and the doctor's wife. They're all great keen gardeners. And by the way, be careful of that young Neligan lad. He'll get into trouble some day. How two decent people could rear such a trouble-maker, it's hard to fathom. Good luck to you.'

He waved and drove slowly off through the overhanging avenue.

Milo climbed wearily up the great staircase – his mind as confused as his body was tired. What a cast of characters to meet in twenty-four hours – the impressive and venerable old solicitor, the effeminate and perhaps sinister Packy, the warm and caring Mrs Neligan. But his mind kept picturing a freckled face with sensuous lips. He thought of her magnificent bold breasts, her air of virginity, and excitement rose in him. He jumped into the great bed for a night full of confusing dreams.

4

Next morning was the start of a perfect summer's day. The sun glittered on the lake. The dome of a classical boathouse pleased the eye and a great cawing came from the rookery among tall beeches near the castle. Milo stood admiring the view and now felt determined to preserve his heritage. Turret and tower were his; he would fight to keep them. Without the courtesy of a knock Packy entered the bedroom bearing two brass buckets steaming with hot water.

'Come on, me lord,' he said sarcastically, 'me mother thinks you should have your bath. I'll show you where the sauna is.'

Milo followed him down the dusty corridors and eventually into a huge gloomy dressing room where an ancient bath stood on clawed feet in the middle of the floor. Packy emptied the hot water into the bath and stood beside it.

'Hop in quickly,' he ordered, 'or 'twill grow cold.' Milo slipped out of his pyjamas and lowered his narrow haunches into the slightly brownish water. Two oak leaves floated in the pleasant brackish soup. 'Well, do you want your back scrubbed or do the aristocracy do without these attentions nowadays?'

Again Milo suffered an uneasy feeling as he felt Packy's eyes taking him in.

'Thanks for the water,' he said dismissively, 'I'll see you later to talk about the fishing.'

Packy took the hint and headed for the door only to turn back again, his fair hair nearly obscuring his face.

'I'd be careful of that solicitor,' he said, 'he'd do anything for money. He had your aunt nearly persuaded to sell the place, only she saw through him in the end. They'll tell you in any pub in the town he has a syndicate ready to take this

19

place over and turn it into a country club. The bastard nearly had me in jail over smoking a reefer. Only the judge did the decent thing and ignored him. Just be careful.'

He left the bathroom reluctantly and Milo was only too glad to see the back of him. He lay back and had a game with the ancient golden sponge which reminded him of something more pleasant. After his wash he went down to a huge breakfast.

'We keep our own hens,' said Mrs Neligan, 'so your scrambled eggs will taste well.'

Milo threw an ounce of pepper over the golden riches and ate the best scrambled eggs he had ever had in his life. Thick brown bread was served with a rich blackberry jam. 'We'll have you a proper weight in no time,' said Mrs Neligan, looking pityingly at the young lord's thin frame. She had the old countrywoman's admiration for a big man, a good fourteen-stone weight, not like this pitiful young lad. 'We'll put the condition on you in no time,' she said. 'Ye wouldn't win a bumper at Kilbeggan Races, the way you look now.'

Milo shuddered at the prospect. He would have to refuse some of her offerings. He did not share her opinion that quantity meant quality in the human frame.

'I won't be here for luncheon, Mrs Neligan,' he said, 'I have a lot of business to attend to in the town.'

But it wasn't to the town that he went. After a few local enquiries, he found out where Drumlerry was located and the dark Porsche followed the rutted avenue up to the white-washed farmhouse. A collie dog jumped up with muddy paws on the Porsche barking menacingly. A dignified old woman with a kind face, grey hair and a blue spotted apron came out to quieten the dog.

'If it's insurance you're selling,' she told Milo, 'you'll want to see my husband who's down in the milking parlour.' She pointed down the cobbled yard.

'No, Mrs Kelly, I'm not selling insurance. I'm your new neighbour. Kilbeggan is my name – Milo Kilbeggan.'

Mrs Kelly's face lengthened with astonishment. She had

long associated the name Kilbeggan with ancient rather arrogant gentlefolk. This healthy and unassuming young man was not what you'd expect.

'Come on in,' she flushed with pleasure, 'my daughter said something about meeting you on the boat. Dadda will be delighted to see you. It's only yesterday he was talking about renting those three fields again. I'll call him up. Seamus can finish the milking.'

She hurried down the yard and Milo sat in an old horsehair sofa near the kitchen fire and took in the atmosphere so different from the damp castle. A warm stove glowed in the ancient fireplace. Cats in a cardboard box eyed him, too comfortable to move. A red light glowed in a dark corner before a holy picture. Impressive tin trophies stood on the high old cupboard. He stood to inspect them. Most were for local football tournaments with the name Seamus Kelly Sportsman of the Year engraved on their thin surfaces. A richer looking silver cup was the prize for Best Friesian Bull at the Longford Agricultural Show. A faded old photograph showed a handsome couple in a horse-drawn trap, drawing away from a country church – a wedding long ago. It was hard to distinguish other photographs because geraniums almost blocked two of the windows. As he waited enjoying the comfort and homely feeling, Mr Kelly came in taking off his Wellington boots before shaking hands with his guest.

'Well, Holy Moses,' he ejaculated, 'you're not like your aunt at all, though mind you she was a good-looking woman in her day. She had a bit of a twinkle in her eye then, just like yourself. Well, it'll be great to get young people up in the castle again – it's half a century since there was much stirring up there. Mind you, you'll have to get a partner.'

'Ah Dadda,' reproved Mrs Kelly warningly. 'You can't be forcing the young man to marry just to fill up the castle.'

'Shure there's many a smart young London lassie he must have had his eye on,' said Mr Kelly. 'However, I'm only joking. Sit down and have a cup of tea and some soda bread and welcome heartily to this country. Sheila's in town doing

21

some shopping and Seamus is milking but they'll both be back soon and delighted to see you.'

They got down to business while they were waiting. Mr Kelly was keen to take the three fields to lease for another year.

'It's a grand handy division, right beside us and I'm carrying more cattle than my own land will feed. Your aunt was very content to rent it to us and I'm hoping you have no new plans about the fields.'

Milo assured him that he would be quite happy to carry on the arrangement. He had no problems with that. He explained his financial difficulties to the Kellys and his hopes for survival.

'Shure we thought it must be a millionaire from London that was coming or one of those property dealers who made a fortune when that Mrs Thatcher was ruling ye all over there.' Milo assured him that there was no money forthcoming, that he was living from hand to mouth, that he was hoping to make money in Westmeath. The old farmer laughed heartily at this notion. 'Faith, it's leaving us they are to make money, rather than coming to make it here.'

Well, the young chap might have no money, but he was all right otherwise – there was none of that overbearing attitude, the superior inherited feelings, the laughable grand accent that drowned other people's conversation. Indeed he was more like themselves, a homely gawson that you could talk to. At this point a car arrived in the yard and then two young Kellys entered the house together.

Sheila had recognized the unfamiliar car in the cobbled yard. A blush of pleasure spread over her animated face mixed with a feeling of embarrassment. She had not explained to her parents that she had met this young man. Her parents were obviously enamoured of this nice young man.

'How are you?' she asked in stilted artificial tone.

'Very well, thank you,' he replied in an equally artificial voice.

Fortunately Seamus was full of enthusiastic comments

22

about the Porsche and the two young men became engrossed in a question and answer session about the car. Seamus was astonished at the low rate of tax and insurance in England.

'Faith,' he told Milo, 'you'd be crucified if you were insuring it over here. The insurance companies seem to think that young people are incompetent savages. My own old Volkswagen costs me £700 a year and it's only that low because we insure the tractors with them.'

Milo, half distracted, kept his eye on Sheila across the room and his mouth almost watered as he looked forward to their next encounter, hopefully just the two of them. In the meantime he replied to the decent youngster, promised him a ride in the Porsche, enquired about his football activities. He heard that Seamus was captain and full forward in the local Gaelic football team. He was invited to watch them play next Sunday and accepted with pleasure, thinking the sister might follow the brother's team. How to get alone with her without making things too obvious – this was tormenting his mind in the tumult of talk.

'Will you stay for dinner?' enquired Mrs Kelly.

He declined politely, telling them about his business in the town.

'Perhaps I might call back and bring Sheila over to see the castle. She seemed very interested when we were talking on the boat.'

The Kellys looked surprised but Sheila replied instantly that she would love to, she would drive over at three o'clock if that suited him. The rest of the family seemed taken aback and tremors of class-consciousness seemed to emerge for a few seconds.

'Well, shure it won't do you any harm,' said her father.

'Don't be coming back with any grand notions,' said her mother laughingly.

'Think about the football,' said Seamus to Milo, 'we could do with a fit full back.'

They crowded into the yard to watch him depart

which he did with some style, although trying to avoid the potholes.

As is always the way, they discussed the departed visitor who had impressed everybody. Mrs Kelly thought that he was a lovely young lad, very unassuming, you'd never think he was a lord. Very sensible and not too towny, thought Mr Kelly. A pity he would not be staying in the country, not able to afford it. Seamus couldn't wait to get his foot on the accelerator of the Porsche. He saw himself picking up his girlfriend in it on a Sunday night and off to Spiders' Night Club in Navan or to the Oasis in Carrickmacross. As for Sheila, she realized now she had gone through three stages in the short relationship – at first a dislike and suspicion, next a gradual acceptance and toleration, and now an eager desire to get closer or, to use the politician's phrase, to 'press the flesh'. She hid her excitement from her mother, turning the conversation towards nursing topics, in case her anticipation was spotted. But mothers have experience and mothers are wise old birds, and Mrs Kelly realized that Sheila's evasions covered a deeper interest. The realization surprisingly made her feel very happy.

Milo drove the ten miles to the country town of Mullingar and the offices of Kinch and Gore, which seemed as dusty as Kilbeggan Castle although fax machines and computers and up-to-date paraphernalia were obvious. Two ancient secretaries eyed him with interest, paying great attention to his title.

'Mr Kinch will see you shortly, my lord,' said the aged brunette with the slight moustache.

'Maybe your lordship would like to read *The Irish Times* while you're waiting,' said the more motherly secretary, with a smile. 'We knew your aunt very well. In fact she used to ask us out to take some cuttings in the autumn and when she was dividing up her plants. I've got a lovely *lobelia cardinalis* that came from Kilbeggan Castle and her phlox were beautiful.'

Milo began to think that all that he had inherited was a pile of herbaceous plants.

24

'Come out any time,' he told them recklessly, 'and collect some more.'

At that moment Mr Kinch appeared at the door and invited him in. Milo went in and sat down opposite Mr Kinch who sat under a portrait of his father or could it be his grandfather? Ancient boxes with faded crests littered the floor around him.

'You probably realize that there are several titles in your family. Along with the Earldom of Kilbeggan, you also carry the titles of Viscount Kilcock in the peerage of Ireland and Baron Ballivor also in the same peerage. When and if you marry, your children will inherit these titles. But to be brief, I'm afraid titles are all that you have got. I have gone carefully through all the documents and the papers that the accountants have made up. You will have an income of perhaps £9,000 per year – all that is left from a previously vast fortune. I'm sorry to tell you that your ancestors squandered huge amounts. The fifth earl won the Punchestown Gold Cup with his horse and is said to have entertained every man, woman and child in the town of Kilbeggan for nearly a week to celebrate the event. He was hugely popular but had to sell off farms to pay the bills. As you may know, there was a great famine in this country in 1845. The sixth earl gave all he had in relief to the starving people and had to live in a couple of rooms in poverty. The family have really never recovered from the blow and have only held on to the property by the skin of their teeth. Your aunt could hunt and keep the place, but she sold field after field to keep going. Now there is only the skeleton of a once vast estate. I had hoped that you might have some private money of your own that might help you to keep the place but you tell me that you have none. I have paid Mrs Neligan up to date as I told you, although that brat of a son seems to acquire money more easily. There is a sum of three thousand pounds to your credit in the Bank of Ireland in Kilbeggan and that is about the sum total of your financial inheritance.'

Milo sat depressed listening to this sad tale. His friends in London would not believe him. Earls have castles and incomes to keep them – this was the popular view – a poor lord was an oddity. Something to be written about in the Sunday papers. How could he keep up a castle on £180 a week. Gloom descended on him.

'Of course there is one way out,' said Mr Kinch. 'Have you thought of perhaps selling the property – not that you'll get much for it – for sporting purposes. It will take a group with capital to make all the improvements necessary, but I dare say that I could contact some business men who might risk the investment. This could leave you safe and sound, with perhaps £100,000 in your pocket instead of a load of debts. I would recommend this very strongly to you. You would need to make up your mind quickly before the property deteriorates further or falls around your ears. I've seen evidence of dry rot and wet rot. Indeed the architect tells me that parts of the castle are dangerous. Insurance could be a problem. Have you thought what might happen if Mrs Neligan slipped on a damp floor and broke her hip? That son of hers would take you to the cleaners for compensation. Think over it very carefully, my lord, and let me know your decision as soon as possible. My wife asked me to pass on her good wishes and she'll be glad to come and look at the herbaceous beds. Come and have dinner with us next week. I'd like to introduce you to some local businessmen who might be interested in the estate. It would be wise to keep them interested. Goodbye, and a very good morning to you.'

Milo ate his luncheon in The Greville Arms – the old traditional type of country hotel. He looked at the tables around him. Hearty families ate hearty lunches. Groups of French and Italian tourists on their way to fish or surfboard in the west, scanned the menus with interest. A county family in town for the day sat in a well-bred pouchy silence. He wondered how many of them had his financial problems. He doubted it. Prosperity was highly evident in the Irish midlands. As he drove back afterwards he passed expensive bungalows of every style. Some had crazy paving as a feature of their front walls – a kind of Jack Duckworth cladding.

The gardens were almost all similar, having a barren lawn in each case with a dull bed of dwarf conifers and garden centre plants. None of the new rich seemed to grow vegetables. No doubt, he thought, the bungalows were all comfortable and centrally heated, unlike his own great draughty barracks of a castle. But he would not swap. Even after a twenty-four acquaintance, even after the unpleasant news from the solicitor, he was determined to preserve his inheritance. The Kilbeggan motto *Vinceo quem tango* would be true in his case. But his thoughts were turning to his next visitor and his head soon filled with pleasanter fantasies.

5

Sheila was in almost grumpy form when she arrived at the castle. Milo changing into sweater and jeans flew down the great staircase when he heard her car.

'I know, don't tell me,' he said, 'you found it hard to open the gates. I should have waited for you at the gate lodge.'

She had dressed in a light pair of figure-hugging trousers to visit the castle and they were spattered with mud from her encounter with the gates.

'You'll have to do something with those gates and clean up the avenue,' she said. 'Otherwise nobody will come to visit you.'

Milo thought of all the middle-aged ladies coming to raid his borders and wished that this might put them off.

'Holy Cow,' said Sheila as he escorted her into the hall, 'it's like living in Saint Paul's Cathedral.'

She smelt a decayed fusty scent and drew closer to the healthy young owner. He gave her a tour of the main rooms. Fingers touched, shoulders brushed each other. Neither resisted the natural attraction. He put his arm around her as they climbed the great staircase. Never had contact been so quick. Sexual encounters previously were nothing compared to this. She too felt it the most natural thing in the world. She knew this was right. She was slightly afraid of the explosion it might lead up to but every touch gave her more confidence. He too was apprenhensive about this very different experience. Like many healthy young men, he had experienced close encounters in cinemas, after parties, in narrow beds in flatland. He was no stranger to sexual pleasures. He remembered the bath he had shared with the glamorous young Jamaican. There were few tricks he had not learnt in the multi-cultural world of Knightsbridge and

Kensington. He would have awarded himself nine out of ten for experience. But this was shockingly different. He was head over heels in love with somebody he scarcely knew and he was pretty sure that she felt the same emotions. The feeling transcended differences. All the differences between them – race, religion, class, education, interests – were forgotten in one overwhelming rush of emotion. They entered the library and threw themselves panting onto the great upholstered sofa in front of the fire.

'Come upstairs,' he whispered, 'in case we're interrupted.'

They scarcely managed to climb the stairs. Shivering, they took off clothes or tried to take them off. Awash with desire, he held her in his arms and transferred her gently into the great bed – a fit setting for courtly love. What a marvellous body he felt and it responded to his touch with tremors of excitement. He kissed her everywhere as the bedclothes heaved over their movements. She too used her hands to explore the exciting body of her lover. How thin, how bony was this wonderful stranger.

Four storeys below, Mrs Neligan was cooking potato cakes on the Aga cooker.

'His lordship is showing Sheila Kelly his property,' she told old Neligan. 'That's the one that went on for a nurse. She went working to London in a hospital there. She has a lovely head of hair – d'ye remember her mother was a lovely blonde until she turned grey? I wonder should I go upstairs and offer them some tea. The gentry always have tea about this time but the Kellys wouldn't be eating until six o'clock like the rest of the people. Maybe I'll wait until he rings down for it. I hope he's not looking down on young Sheila. That's a grand family she comes from.'

Looking down on young Sheila was exactly what Milo was doing. She lay blissfully in his thin yet strong arms. *Vinceo quem tango*, he thought delightedly to himself as he looked at his willing prisoner. Not only was she beautiful but the experience had brought a look of overwhelming happiness to her face. Milo felt strong and masterful. On previous occasions he had felt twinges of guilt as if he had done

29

something not entirely right. But now he knew that this experience had been wholesome and fine and good. He had no doubt that she felt the same. They lay blissfully in the great bed wishing that the warmth, the emotions, the sheer feeling of heart-ease would last forever. He had found such softness, such comfort, such sunshine in this woman that his heart rejoiced. She too exulted in the moment for he was all that a lover should be and she felt a deep sincerity in him. This was no ship that was going to pass in the night. And so the afternoon wore on into evening until dusk enveloped the room and she realized that it would take a lot of explaining to her parents. They dressed, after washing in the jug's cold water which they poured into a great discoloured basin. Then they descended into the library. There Mrs Neligan found them pretending to examine old estate maps which showed the Kelly farm as a tenant farm of the estate. She recognized the position instantly and they knew that she knew that an almost electric feeling of pursuit and desire hovered between the young couple.

'Packy said that he would take you out in the morning to fish the lake,' she told the young lord. 'Would Miss Kelly like a sup of tea?'

Sheila thanked her regretfully and told her that she must not waste any more of Lord Kilbeggan's time, that it had been a lovely experience looking over the castle and that she must fly home to help her mother. Such are the fictions and white lies, the little harmless glosses that make civilization continue. Milo, listening to her ingenuous words, felt a surge of affection for his guileless sweetheart. Passion flared up as he led her through the cold hall and out towards the muddy MG. They kept apart, aware of inquisitive eyes.

'When shall we repeat this experience, or can we repeat it?' he enquired hoarsely.

'Give me a ring tomorrow after you've finished fishing,' she almost whispered. 'Never will I wait for a phone call so eagerly.'

He spoke in a louder voice to impress any listening ears.

30

'Thank you for coming over, Miss Kelly. It was very nice showing you round and I'll make sure that your father gets a copy of those maps.'

He watched the sportscar as it drove down the avenue and with overwhelming happiness bounded up the steps to his ancient mansion.

6

It was a misty warm morning that greeted Milo next morning. He took a pike rod with several traces for safety. He had found a selection of spoon baits in the game room. Most of them looked as if they had been made by the local blacksmith. He found a pair of Wellington boots that fitted him and joined Packy who was waiting carrying oars and pins in the courtyard. They took a track through the woods and arrived at a large decayed boathouse which must have been an impressive stylish building in its day. Packy opened a door and led Milo into the damp antiquated interior. A venerable punt lay rotting at one side, while a more modern clinker-built rowing boat lay beside it.

'Bail her out,' said Packy roughly thrusting an old bucket towards Milo. 'She leaks a fair drop.'

Milo took twenty half-buckets of green slimy water out of the boat and at last was able to step gingerly into the rocking craft. Packy used an oar to push at the sides of the boathouse and the boat slid out into the calm waters of the lake. Disturbed wildlife fled into the rushes. Packy took hold of both oars and his skinny arms rowed them out. This was a much bigger lake than Milo had expected. It was well over a mile wide and perhaps two miles long. Thick woods grew down to the shore except where two gaps opened up vistas – one to the castle now almost hidden in mist and another to a stone mausoleum, a grey depressing temple with steps up from the lake.

'Start spinning,' said Packy gruffly. 'This lake is alive with them.'

They rowed slowly up the lake, Milo casting a gleaming spinner and drawing it slowly back to the boat. On the third cast, a violent tug announced excitement. Milo's line sang out happily.

'Pull him in,' roared Packy, 'you'll lose him.'

Milo decided to play the fish as if it were a trout. The tactic didn't work. The fish went deep and must have wrapped the line around an underwater log because, try as he could, Milo could not get any response. Eventually, trying to draw in the line, he felt it go slack and it raced back minus the pike bait.

'That's what pike do to fucking fools,' said Packy triumphantly and rowed on sourly.

Milo began to dislike him intensely and regretted coming out with him. He fitted on a second trace and bait to his line and cast out again. Again he felt a strong tug but this time he kept a tight line and after some ten minutes had a splendid six or seven pound pike in the boat.

'Not a bad little yoke,' said Packy sarcastically. He stood up. 'Watch out,' he muttered, 'I'm having a slash.'

With that he opened his flies and started to urinate into the lake a few yards from Milo's head. Drops spattered very close and Milo, enraged, decided that this was the last time he would ever associate with such a thoroughly unpleasant character.

'Come over and see where all your lot are buried,' said Packy when he'd sat down.

He rowed over to the flight of steps which led up to the pillared mausoleum.

The strong wooden doors had a stout lock fastening them.

'I keep the keys,' said Packy without explanation.

The lock opened smoothly and the doors opened as though it were an everyday occurrence. Milo stepped in to examine the tombs of his ancestors. A number of stone monuments lay by the dank walls. Some were ornamented with angels, others held effigies of the dead beneath them, others had plain tablets to commemorate their owners. Here lay colonels whose very regiments were now obsolete. Here lay clergymen whose beliefs were now obsolete. The earls were honoured by coats of arms which featured the two erect wolves facing the dark hand and the famous motto. Pomp and circumstance were mocked by the dust and decay. The most recent monument was to his aunt and was much simpler than the rest. As he turned towards the door, Milo observed to his surprise that Packy was removing a loose brick from the wall and had pulled out a small tin from behind it. He extracted something, lit a match and the sweet smell of *marijuana* hung on the fetid air.

'This is where I keep my little hobby,' said Packy. 'Do you want a joint?'

Milo's keen nose detected a scent of cannabis above the mouldy smells of the mausoleum. Canvas chairs lay in a corner. Empty beer cans lay scattered near some of the great marble sarcophagi. Somebody had struck a match repeatedly on the stone hand of a statue. There was evidence of very recent occupation. He put two and two together. Parties were held here or else this was a dealer's den.

'No thank you,' he replied, 'not my scene.'

He walked outside and sat on the steps. The whole morning had been unpleasant; now it had gone completely sour. Packy emerged in much pleasanter humour.

'If ever you want some,' he said, 'let me know. You won't be telling anybody of course, because you'll want to keep your castle intact!'

Was it a joke or did it hold the menace he felt it did?

7

After rowing back in an air of overt hostility, Milo tramped back to the castle accompanied by the obnoxious Packy. As they emerged from the green tunnel of the track on to the wider avenue, Packy again invited him.

'You've only to ask if you want something out of the ordinary. Ye'll get it cheaper from me than you will in the town.'

How had the respectable and responsible Neligans produced such an evil character? He met Mrs Neligan in the hall, wholesome and welcoming.

'There's been a ring from Mr Kinch. He wonders if you could meet him for lunch in Mullingar. He'll expect you if you don't ring back. And there's some letters on the hall-table.'

Milo was surprised to see a plateful of letters awaiting him in the great draughty hall. Apart from a few London friends, few would know he was here. But apparently the word had flown around the social circuit. The first letter was addressed from Kilnacrann Abbey, Raharney, and it invited Lord Kilbeggan to drinks with Colonel and Mrs Baring-Brown and Miss Penelope Baring-Brown on Saturday. Regrets only. The second was from Captain and Mrs Metcalfe of the Old Mill House, Killucan. They were delighted to hear that Cynthia's nephew had arrived in Kilbeggan Castle. They were old friends of his aunt's, had played bridge with her in the old days and hoped Milo would come to lunch with them whenever he wanted. They did not travel out much at nights as they weren't in the first flush of youth. They hoped Milo would not object if they came over some day to dig up some fascicularia. Such an interesting plant. Cynthia had always been promising to divide it and give them a section.

35

Milo felt that he would have to bring a JCB into the garden to lift enough plants to please the Westmeath ladies. A third letter was from the rector, the Reverend Norman Muddock. He regretted that the church inside the estate had been closed down for lack of funds but he hoped to see Milo after service in the town. They were also hoping to tackle the dry rot in the belfry and would be grateful for subscriptions which could be sent to the treasurer, Captain Metcalfe. He asked Mrs Neligan about these local dignitaries.

'Lovely people,' she enthused, 'the old stock and great friends of Lady Cynthia. Miss Penelope is a lovely girl, touching forty and your own class.' She nearly added that she was more his own class than the young Kelly lassy. 'Mrs Metcalfe suffers from arthritis but the captain is a great sport – a very jolly man – you'd hear him a mile away.' Milo shuddered at the description of the hearty military man. 'The rector's very musical. He has half the county at his concerts and his wife's a lovely lady – no nonsense or put on about her. They're a great pair.'

Milo bundled up the letters, rang Sheila to say he'd be over after lunch and set off for the town.

Margery and Connie, the two ancient secretaries smiled at him and almost knocked each other over as they brought him into the solicitor's office.

'I think I've something very promising for you,' said Mr Kinch. 'We'll say no more until we have our lunch. I want you to meet a most important member of our community. Have you heard of P.J. Fogarty?' Milo shook his head, 'Well he might have something that might interest you. We are going to have lunch with him at Medigorge Villa – a lovely place; some of the pictures would take the eye out of your head.'

He continued talking as he brought Milo down the stairs after passing the still smiling secretaries.

P.J. Fogarty was President of the Chamber of Commerce. He had started off in a small way, the son of a local plasterer. He had started to build houses himself, first one, then a couple. Next it was whole housing estates he was building.

He had crossed the water and done some work in London. Now with the building slow and not much demand for new houses, he was diversifying into other interests.

'You'll hear a little more when you meet him.'

P.J. was a big wheel in local politics, a great expert on planning permission. He'd made his money and held on to it. So Mr Kinch filled in a full description for Milo as they drove in his Mercedes through the town and out the main road. They entered a drive lined with conifers and emerged in front of a large house which could have featured in any American soap opera – a cross between *Dallas* and *Falcon Crest*. The doorbell played not just a chord but a whole tune. A well-dressed hard-faced man opened the door and Milo nearly sank in the hall carpet which rose to warm his ankles.

'Milo, I'd like you to meet an old friend of mine, P.J. Fogarty. P.J. this is Lord Kilbeggan, whom I've told you all about.'

Milo, wondering what all this led to, found out more at lunch. Here he met Mrs Fogarty, a compliant woman in awe of her husband and her two sons Wayne and Gary. Wayne was doing business studies at DCU and might come into the business later, but his father was inclined to think that it was better to have two strings to your bow. Gary was reading history and archeology in Dublin but had a summer job in the golf club. Milo admired the huge display of Waterford crystal on the table.

'Here pick it up,' said P.J. handing a goblet to Milo. 'Just feel the weight of that. They presented the set to me when I knocked down the old church at Drumuisge and built that new modern-style church for them. I should have got the Turner Prize for that job.' He laughed heartily and plied Milo with drink. 'A pity you can't meet Sharon today. She'd love to meet you. She's teaching in the convent. There's her photograph.' He pointed out a huge photograph of a smiling young woman with academic gown and parchment. 'You can't beat the education I say. I'm chairman of the board of management of our local school. Takes a business-man to keep them in line. Now when Mammy is clearing up, we'll go into the lounge and discuss a little project which depends on you.'

They left the dining room and sank into easy chairs in the lounge. Milo was quite enjoying the comfort and heat of the room, despite the glitz and ostentation all around him.

'Let's be frank with each other,' said P.J. impressively. 'I'm a straight man and I always talk straight. Now rumour has it that you may not be as rich a person as might be expected from the title and the background. No fault of yours – it could happen to any of us – I'm just one of the lucky ones. Money's a quare lad. It's like health. You're nothing without it. You've heard of the rhyme – Money is honey, / My little sonny / And a rich man's joke / Is always funny. Now don't mind me going on about it, but I've got a little scheme in my head that could make a lot of money for both of us. Money up front for you. You have something that I want and I've got something that you might like. To cut a long story short, although people will laugh at me when they hear about it, I want to make you an offer of money for Kilbeggan Castle and grounds and a chance of a yearly income afterwards, if all goes well. But first of all, before I expose myself and my plans, can I ask you, do you want me to talk on? Just stop me if you're not interested.'

'Carry on,' said Milo concerned by this new idea.

'Now I know more about your castle and your prospects than you might think. First of all, the house is riddled with dry rot, wet rot, woodworm. I know as a builder because I was called in to do some repairs by your aunt. The whole of that roof will collapse on top of you some time. The timbers holding it up have dry rot running along them; they won't support the weight of those thick Bangor slates which will fall in sooner than later. The walls look great; Ardbracken stone was a fine building material but you see it's not stone all the way through. There's a thick lining of rubble behind the cut stone and it has been damp and rotten for years. There is not a window in the place that doesn't need the frame replaced and every one of them would have to be measured and made by an expert joiner, although I'd put in aluminium double glazing myself – a far better job. Just look at me own ones' and he pointed at his lounge windows, 'and they're better against burglars as well. That's another thing. Sure that old pair that looks after your house are half deaf and helpless. If the place was robbed they'd put up no resistance. As for that young ne'er-do-well of a son of theirs, I wouldn't have that pup inside a house of mine – I'll tell you that.'

'I agree with you there,' interrupted Mr Kinch, 'I've told our young friend about him – he's bad news.'

'Another thing,' continued the builder, 'the wiring is dangerous. The place could be burnt down if something goes wrong with the wiring. It's the original wiring and plugs. You'll find round plugs, square plugs, three point plugs, two point plugs and a lot of rooms with no sockets at all. There's some rooms you still have to use candles in. Along with that, the whole house will have to get a proper heating system. It's the coldest house in the county. There's people in cottages used to pity your aunt, especially in the winter. Of course that's why she used to wear those thick woollen stockings and those great tweed skirts. The stables were warmer than the house. There's bathrooms with huge baths and no hot water.'

'I've noticed that,' said Milo ruefully.

'I don't like to knock the house too much,' said the builder, 'but there's a question about the staircase. Have you noticed a slight tilt in it? There was a hunt ball held there years ago, when the gentry would hold the hunt dances in their own houses. Great occasions they were. I remember dances in Ballinlough Castle and in Gaybrook but the best of the hunt balls was in your own house. But the last time there was a bit of an alarm – it was only a slight shift in the staircase levels but it gave a fright to a lot of people. Some of them sobered up very quickly. Apart from that, did you know that the dome over the staircase – the big glass circular dome – always gave trouble? It seems impossible to stop the leaks coming through. As for the Aga in the kitchen and I know Agas are said to be the royalty in the matter of kitchen stoves, but somehow the Kilbeggan one always gave trouble – they said there was a down draught from those huge chimneys but no matter what was done I believe it never worked properly. I hear the planning people were on to your aunt about the drainage system – it goes straight into the Deel River and into Lough Ennel. I hear the Fishery Board was complaining. They're very strict about that sort of thing nowadays, you know. There's a lot of other things need attention.'

Milo's heart sank as he listened to a further recital about the fatal defects in his castle. It seemed that the water supply was polluted. Every single room needed painting. Even the aristocracy nowadays had fitted and expensive kitchens. The farmyard was a disgrace. Doors were hanging off hinges, slates were missing off the cow byres. A calf had drowned in the well in the middle of the yard and people said the carcass was still at the bottom of the well. The gate lodges were all derelict and had been vandalized. The avenues, as he must know, were full of potholes – people thought they were driving through Cavan when they drove up the main avenue. The ballroom had been a lovely room but the damp had got at the plasterwork and there was a crowd down from the Irish Georgian Society complaining about the neglect. There was not a fence on the farm that would hold in sheep. Only old Kelly was a decent neighbour and did not complain about the fencing, there would be trouble about strayed bullocks. On and on went the recital until it seemed to Milo it would never end. He finally decided to interrupt the harangue.

'What I'd like to know,' he said, 'is why you want to buy the place if it is in such a deplorable condition?'

This stopped Mr Fogarty in his tracks.

'Hold on a moment,' he requested, 'I'll get to that point very soon. What I was pointing out to you is the plain fact that it will cost you a fortune to restore that rundown place. Not just thousands but hundreds of thousands of pounds will have to be spent and when you have it restored, you'll have to keep it properly. You'll have over a hundred windows and I don't know how many doors to paint regularly. It would take a team of painters a month to go around it and they would nearly have to start again once they had finished. I'm exaggerating now but you realize what I'm talking about. Unless you have a huge private income, your castle will be a millstone around your neck. It will swallow up every penny you ever had. But to develop my ideas, I'll tell you why I'm interested in the property. Around this area of the Midlands, there are a lot of people with money to spend but nowhere to spend it. They have to go up to Dublin to enjoy life, to join clubs to meet their own kind in a social setting. What I'm proposing to do is to present these amenities close to home, to develop a large country club with every sort of sporting and social activity. It will be expensive to join but also exclusive. There won't be a businessman in the Midlands who won't want to join it. We'll have squash courts, swimming pools, indoor tennis courts, a good fishing lake and a stately home which can be their second home. Don't tell me there isn't still a lot of snobbery in this country. Members will feel up in the world. They can have their daughters' wedding receptions at their club. The photographs can be taken at the top of that great flight of steps.'

(Here Milo wondered how he could talk like this after his allegation that the steps were dangerous.)

Mr Fogarty continued, 'I can supply the building skills and the team to restore the house. I can also put a substantial slice of capital towards the costs and our friend Mr Kinch and some other local men are willing to invest the rest of the money needed. It will take a huge sum, all told. What I'm proposing to you is this. A hundred thousand pounds into your pocket for a ninety-nine year lease of the whole place. But perhaps more important, we want you to stay in the castle and live there as the lord of the manor but working for us, with a substantial income. My point is this – I may be repeating myself. There is still a great deal of class distinction in this little republic of ours. You may have

41

noticed a lot of people paying attention to you and not just for the colour of your eyes. 'Tis pure snobbery. A lord is still a lord in Ireland despite all our ardent republicans. I remember when I hadn't got a bean, people wouldn't bother to say hello to me. Now that I have a few bob, they're very civil indeed. "Would you like to join the Hunt Supporters Club?", "You should join the golf club, Mr Fogarty." They wouldn't have let me in the gate in the old days. Well you haven't got the same advantage of money, but you have another one. You have a title and a good old title, a famous old name. With you as manager, as host at our country club, we'll have a flood of applications for membership. They'll be boasting about their friend Lord Kilbeggan. We have a famous Miley in Glenroe, but this will be another celebrity, Milo in Kilbeggan. To put it bluntly, it will give a touch of class to the club that other clubs lack. You can invite over your posh friends and if they have a handle to their name, all the better. A young, good-looking crowd with the odd title will bring the customers flocking in. That and the historical old building. Keep any postcards you have and any other old pictures – it will impress the clients. Four-poster beds are important and if you haven't got a ghost, we'll invent one for you – a nice one, not a threatening one. We'll need smart staff with classy accents – none of the "how are ye" brigade being too familiar with the customers. Now I've had accountants and financial experts working on this for a long time. Mr Kinch tells me your possession is sound. You have the offer. All it needs is your signature and you're a rich man with a future. Well, what do you say to it?'

Milo's head was full of confusion. A few hours back, he was wondering how he would support himself. Now he had the tempting offer of a large sum of money and a future income and the prospect of his house getting all the expensive repairs it needed. He had noticed other similar properties in ruins, deserted by their owners, too expensive to keep in proper condition. He had noticed a book called *Vanishing Irish Houses.* He would dearly love to see Kilbeggan

Castle repaired, heated, painted, decorated and once more a proud place to live. He would give a lot to see the splendid Gothic pile saved from dampness and decay. It would have to be restored soon or the damage might be irreparable. In many ways the offer was too good to be true. But he also was suspicious of the offer. He needed time to consider it.

'Well, young man,' said Mr Fogarty, 'will you come in with us or do we have to look elsewhere?'

'I am very interested indeed,' said Milo, 'and your offer is strange but attractive. But you will have to give me time to make up my mind. This is all very sudden. I can tell you that I'm very tempted. I don't agree with everything you've said about the property but a lot of what you say is true. You'll have to give me time to think it over.'

'Well,' said Mr Fogarty, 'you will have to make up your mind soon. You're not the only fish in the sea and investors might shift their money elsewhere. Give us a reply as soon as you can and another important thing, don't mention this scheme to anybody. Tongues could wag and it wouldn't do the business any good. Keep the offer under wraps.'

On the way back into the town, Milo listened to Mr Kinch who repeated his praises of P.J. Fogarty.

'He's a good man to be friends with but he'd make a hard enemy. A powerful man to have on your side and a great businessman. I've seen him floor fellows with a string of degrees and diplomas from the Harvard Business School. If you'll take my advice, you'll be a wise man if you accept his offer. P.J. is out to make money and won't fail you. It would be an honour to be associated with him. Incidentally, my wife asked me if you'd like to join the bridge club. She'd be delighted to propose you for membership and there'd be no difficulty in getting one of her friends to second you for membership. Don't forget she'd love to see your garden any time it's suitable for you. But remember to make up your mind quickly on that offer.'

The Mercedes glided down the town through several sets

of traffic lights and pulled into the square near Milo's stylish
and sporting model which now also sported a parking ticket.

When Sheila met him at the door of the farmhouse she
knew that something serious had occurred. After some
necessary chat with the old couple, she proposed a walk
down to see the foal and they set off across a lane. Once out
of view of the farmhouse, he took her behind a beech tree
and they clung to each other longingly. But common sense
and a need not to risk shocking any locals overcame this
and she led him out, still hungering but dejected. As they
walked on, his arms clung around her, but gradually he
calmed down and told her the result of the morning's
meeting. He confided his misgivings and yet admitted to
being attracted by the offer. Within a few days, his lifestyle
had changed incredibly. From being a frivolous young
socialite he had turned to more serious concerns. Now all
he wished for was to uphold the ways of his ancestors.
    'But you see, Sheila, it won't be like living in my own
house. It will be like a holiday village or like living in a Forte
or Hilton Hotel. They'll expect me to earn a living by being
their tame aristocrat, smiling at snobs and humouring their
desire to talk to a lord. It's going to be hard to live an
ordinary life. And I like the house as it is. I don't like the
damp and the loose plaster and slates slipping off, but I do
like the space and the proportions and the outlook across
fine trees to the lake. And I like walking around in jeans and
a T-shirt. I don't want to be dressed in formal clothes every
day of the week.'
    She listened to his outpouring, astonished to find that she
was included in his scenario.
    'How can we be together when there's mobs of people
complaining about the onion soup or that sheep have
strayed on to the golf course?'
    His hand dropped longingly to the cleft in her slacks and
playfully he inserted a finger. She stirred with trembling and

then slapped the bold member. They arrived at the small field where mare and foal stood happy with each other. The lovers gazed at the handsome young foal. Mr Kelly, like many an Irish farmer, supplemented his income by keeping a brood mare. He had sent her to a neighbouring stud at Russelstown where she had been covered by Persian Mews.

'He's a very good sire,' said Sheila mischievously, 'and his grand sire was like yourself, he was a Bold Lad. He's had a fine crop of young winners, so we're hoping for great things from this foal.'

Mare and foal nuzzled each other contentedly in the evening sunlight. The English lord and the Irish nurse did likewise.

'We'd produce a fine one ourselves,' said Milo affectionately caressing her breasts which stirred under the light cotton frock. His fingers sought to undo her bra straps. But she stopped him again. Restraining him was necessary but difficult.

She promised him, 'Later, and we'll have to find a quiet spot. People are very conventional around here. They're shocked very easily and my parents are no exception. So just behave yourself or you'll spoil things.'

They walked back to the old farmhouse, disengaging all the physical parts before they came round the corner of the hay barn. Milo was persuaded easily to have tea – a delightful meal with golden eggs and a splendid brack and strong tea 'that you could walk a mouse across'.

Seamus finished his tea before the rest of them and rushed around looking for his football boots. Milo and Sheila promised to give him a lift to the football ground, where they were going to practise for the big match on Sunday.

'It's a crucial match,' said Seamus. 'If we win this we're into the next round.'

The three of them piled into the Porsche and after traversing the bumps on the farm lane, they sped off to the local GAA field. Here a volley of cheers rang out as Seamus emerged from the Porsche to greet his astonished club mates.

'Have ye swapped it for the bike, Seamus? Have ye won the lotto? Did that old uncle die in America?' were some of the less raucous comments that greeted the popular Seamus. He shyly introduced Milo.

'This is Milo Kilbeggan who's come to take over the aunt's place,' said Seamus. The youths looked puzzled. This was not their idea of a lord. But the Porsche looked genuine.

'You're welcome to this part of the country. Have you played any football?'

Milo confessed to being an inadequate player in two codes – soccer and rugby. They lost interest and went in to tog out. They emerged in an extraordinarily motley collection of sports gear to start their fitness training.

'They keep their smart togs for the match,' said Sheila.

The lads went through a series of PE training which included sprints and muscle building. Some were more enthusiastic than others. Milo noticed that Seamus was remarkably fit, had great speed and handled the ball with confidence.

'Catching is very important in Gaelic football,' said Sheila. 'I shouldn't be boasting about my own family but Seamus can carry the team in a difficult game. The selectors have their eye on him for the county team, when he broadens out a bit. We'll watch the game on Sunday and you'll see him at his best. He loves football.'

Milo looked at her.

'I love you. Let's get off together.'

They waved to the players and sped off. He thought of taking her out to dinner and then remembered they had just had a huge farmhouse tea.

'Let's go to the cinema,' he said.

'Somewhere we're not known,' she replied. They drove over to Navan where the Palace cinema was half empty on this fine summer evening. Later they could not even remember the name of the film and when she went home later she had to rack her brains when her mother innocently enquired the name of the film. Far in a dark corner, they sat like two furnaces, seduced by each other as lovers can be.

8

Milo was awoken next morning by the sound of distant church bells calling the faithful to mass or church service. He lay luxuriously in the vast bed. His mind pondered the stories the bed could tell if beds could talk. Almost all the important events in the lifetimes of his ancestors had happened in this bed, from conception to departure. The bell-pulls reminded him of a time when the castle was full of servants. The past had been very different. When her ladyship tugged at the bell-pull, down in the depths of the basement the tinkle was heard. Down through numerous walls the long rope tightened until it drew the bell below. Scurrying servants instantly dropped all their business and prepared to ascend the servants' stone staircase and then the great ceremonial staircase. Along the Turkish carpets they had padded to answer the imperious call. The lady's maid and the footmen hurried to do their duties. The valet attended Lord Kilbeggan. Her maid waited on Lady Kilbeggan. Below, the crew of servants prepared breakfast. Coachmen worked in their stables. In the distant walled garden, the head gardener laid out the programme and instructed his underlings. The farmyard was busy with activities. Cows were milked, cream skimmed off for the big house. In the three gate lodges, there was stirring. The estate carpenter measured the seasoned timber in his workshop for a new stable door in the stable yard. Laundry maids started to light the boiler in the laundry room while others sorted out the linen sheets. Mr Ennis, the butler, fussed in the dining room. The great house, indeed the whole estate, had hummed with business and activity. Now in the whole vast unheated mansion silence reigned. The kitchen was empty, for the Neligans had got a lift to mass. Packy lay snoring

48

down below stairs in his untidy cave of a bedroom. He refused to bring hot water up the stairs to the young proprietor of the house, in whom he had lost interest. Milo padded down in his dressing gown and filled a brass water container with hot water from the Aga. Upstairs it barely covered the surface of the blue floral wash basin. What would it be like in winter he wondered and the tempting offer from the builder, Mr Fogarty, floated across his mind. He thought of the day ahead and a glow of satisfaction went through him, as he thought of escorting Sheila to the football match.

After breakfast, he put on a pair of gumboots and set out to explore his neglected estate. The farmyard was a sorry sight. Rusted machinery lay in the ancient sheds. Doors had fallen off their hinges and lay where they had fallen. Recent storms had loosened slates and they had crashed into the yard, leaving gaping holes in barn roofs. Nails had rusted, leaving other slates lying flat unattached to the rafters and waiting for the next strong wind to bring them hurtling down into the yard. The farmyard tower still held its bell which at one stage had called the farm workers to and from their duties. Milo walked through the arch, down past an unkempt box hedge to a door leading into the walled garden. He pulled at the door but found it locked. Annoyed, he returned to the house. Mr and Mrs Neligan were still out. He found Packy's room and asked him for the where-abouts of the key. Packy, with his face pale under the blond hair, lay lazily in his bed.

'Hello, darling,' he said. 'This is nice. Are you going to get in with me?' and he motioned invitingly to Milo, who ignored the offer and repeated his demand for the key.

'As a matter of fact, I keep it here,' replied Packy. He thrust out an arm which displayed needle marks and a tattoo and retrieved an iron key from under the bed.

'You'll bring it back to me, my lord,' he said with unpleasant sarcasm, 'I like to meditate in the privacy down there.'

Milo pulled the key from his hand, slammed the door and

49

retraced his steps to the garden. How could he get rid of the obnoxious Packy without offending the two loyal old parents? The mere thought of Packy living in the same house caused him unease. He opened the gate into the walled garden and stepped into a wilderness. He fought his way along the neglected paths. Briars now flourished where nature had once been subdued. Nevertheless there was a track of sorts which led to a gardener's shed. This to his great surprise had been used recently. A bed had been fixed up with an ancient mattress and blankets. The fireplace showed evidence of a recent fire. Makeshift tables and chairs littered the room. Empty beer cans lay on the floor. It looked like a den or a squat in London. But how did it come to be used in this isolated wilderness? He left the building and then had to fight his way past the once splendid greenhouses, now treacherous ruins of broken glass. Neglected peach trees still clung to the walls. He plucked some nectarines to bring to the Kellys and then gave up the struggle to explore the rest of the once famous garden. He contended his way past the herbaceous borders where black-eyed Susan and hemerocallis were being ousted by strong weeds. Milo left the garden and determined to keep the keys himself in future. He drove off to seek Sheila.

Flags hung out from houses and hedges as he drove over to the Kelly farm. Amateur posters shouted good luck messages to Kilsharvan, the local team. Their opponents St Liam's came from the other end of the county but were long-term antagonists. They had had many struggles in the past and this was a match that could produce not only strong play but also emotional reactions. Referees did not compete to umpire the Kilsharvan-St Liam match, for both teams were highly suspicious of the referee and each believed the poor man was secretly in favour of the other side. Scenes had occurred at past matches which local newspapers had condemned as shocking and unnecessary. So local interest was huge, and Milo and Sheila joined a long line of cars, and some tractors, heading towards the village football pitch. They had to park some distance away and walk along the muddy road to the park. Sheila was greeted happily and enthusiastically by neighbours as they walked along. Curious eyes were laid on Milo as rumours had spread quickly about her friendship with the young lord. They noted the flush in Sheila's cheeks and the closeness between the young couple, for Milo brushed frequently against her and each touch made them both feel radiant and happy. The park was muddy from recent rains and they climbed a bank of steps which was already thick with Kilsharvan fans. Sheila introduced him to her friend Brigid Horan, the dark-haired beauty who was engaged to Bobby Boyle, an accountant and friend of the Kinches. They all cheered enthusiastically as the Kilsharvan team ran onto the pitch while some of the younger crowd booed as St Liam's took to the field. As always, the opposition seemed taller and better built than one's own side but Milo noted that Seamus Kelly looked outstanding among his fellows.

Gaelic football has elements of soccer and elements of rugby and elements of its own which make it unique. Even the scoring is different from the other codes. A kick into goal scores three points, while a kick over the net and between the posts scores one point. No team can make progress without an efficient free-taker. Good kicking and catching are essential. Tackling is the problem, as physical tackling in the rugby sense is prohibited and leads to a penalty. This prohibition leads to frustration and often to spectacular fouling. In the first quarter of this game, St Liam's took the lead. Their forwards received a constant supply of the ball which they put to good use. Their corner forward pounced on a good pass early on and drove in a magnificent shot which the Kilsharvan goalie was unable to reach. Next they were awarded a free kick a good 60 metres out from the Kilsharvan goalmouth. When some of the Kilsharvan midfield protested, the referee moved the ball up to ten metres and the St Liam's free soared high between the posts. This was four points down in as many moments of play and the home supporters grew resentful as their side seemed unable to cope. For the next ten minutes they were dominated by St Liam's whose supporters grew raucous and triumphalist as the game went on. Several stunning movements silenced the home side as St Liam's, passing with superb accuracy and outrunning their opponents, swept up the pitch to score several spectacular points. At this stage of the game, it looked as if it was going to be a landslide victory for the visiting side. A beaten side loses heart and takes refuge in fouls and obstruction. But gradually Seamus Kelly began to pull his team together, using encouragement instead of criticism. The start of the Kilsharvan revival came when Seamus rose highest to catch a pass from his midfielder and fired a perfect shot low and unexpected into the back of the St Liam's net. A great cheer rose from the Kilsharvan selectors and Milo found himself hugging Sheila for two quite different reasons. Proudly she watched as a moment later Seamus took another long pass, raced mercilessly past his opponents and scored a second crashing goal, outwitting the St Liam's backs. You could hear the roar at the other end of the parish – a roar of relief and pride. A sea of Kilsharvan flags rose among the spectators. Now the home team took over and it was St Liam's that lost all its confidence and control. Now they looked out of their class as Kilsharvan mounted a steady stream of attack which resulted in two further points. The forwards not only looked menacing in attack but Seamus even dropped back several times to lend his backs assistance whenever they looked in trouble. A clean and sporting player, he projected the image of enjoyment in sport and inspired the team around him. Milo began to share the pride Sheila had in her brother and they rejoiced when half-time arrived with Kilsharvan leading 10 points (2 goals, 4 points) to St Liam's 8 points (1 goal, 5 points).

Several substitutes came on in the second half after an excited conference among the St Liam's officials at half-time. In particular a thick-set red-haired youth came on to the field among the St Liam's backs to mark Seamus.

'That's young Dunn,' said Sheila. 'He was suspended two months ago for dirty play. He's inclined to play the man instead of the ball. He won't be fast enough to mark Seamus properly, so I just wonder why they've put him on in that position.'

They found out five minutes later. But first there was a period of indeterminate play. Both sides missed promising passes, kicking was inaccurate and the crowd began to yawn as the sparkle had gone out of the game. All the agitated advice at half-time appeared to have had no result and Kilsharvan seemed content with their lead. Forwards were left with little to do as play hung around mid-field. A free was awarded to Kilsharvan and their half-back kicked a magnificent ball high up toward their forwards. Seamus jumped like a stag to catch the ball. His red-haired opponent came in with a heavy tackle as Seamus descended with the ball. There was a crunch which could be heard on the terraces as he hit Seamus on the shoulder and the Kilsharvan captain fell to the ground and tried helplessly to get up. His right arm was powerless to help him arise and a storm of booing and invective came from the Kilsharvan supporters as they realized the tactical reason for Dunn's appearance on the field. At this stage it looked as if excited supporters were going to swarm onto the field and some Kilsharvan players were being prevented from attacking their opponents. Seamus was finally removed from the field with a look of agony on his proud face and the referee, who had sent Dunn off the field, finally got the game resumed in an atmosphere where sport was missing and partisanship predominated. Sheila took Milo by the hand and they struggled through the crowd to find out if they could help her brother in the pavilion.

Eventually scuffling across a sea of litter and empty Coke tins, they reached the club-house. Seamus sat white-faced and shocked on a bench while the local doctor examined his shoulder. He squirmed with pain as the doctor's hands probed the bruised flesh. He was also uncomfortable from an old groin injury which he had jolted when he had fallen to the ground. Sheila told the doctor about her nursing background.

'Bring him into casualty immediately,' said the doctor, 'and make sure he gets an X-ray. I'm suspicious of that shoulder.'

The Kilsharvan supporters were still seething with resentment as Seamus was brought through them to the car park. Several wild and possibly drunk supporters assured the hurt player that they would avenge themselves on the St Liam's club. Seamus, despite his injuries, tried to calm down the atmosphere and Milo admired his sporting nature. They eased him into the car and drove gently down the track and turned right for Mullingar. They finally drove into the hospital car park and brought Seamus into the dingy casualty department.

'Take your place on the bench and we will take down your particulars,' said a harassed middle-aged nurse.

A child screamed behind a curtain as two foreign doctors tried to reassure it in broken English. Seamus shivered and Milo fetched in his long wax jacket and wrapped him carefully in it. It was almost two hours before the queue disappeared and Seamus was examined again by a dark house doctor. He was told to join the queue for the X-ray department and they tried to cheer him up as the aching shoulder and strained groin injury made him more and more uncomfortable. An eternity later, he was X-rayed with a pleasant radiographer apologising for the delay. Back they came to the casualty department. Eventually the doctor examined Seamus's X-ray. The shoulder was broken, a tendon was torn, there was evidence of previous damage which had not healed completely. He was equipped with a sling, given some painkillers, told to report back to see the general surgeon and released into the night air. Hungry and tired they drove back to the farmhouse where Milo helped the injured youth out of his clothes into pyjamas and dressing gown, and Mrs Kelly insisted that he go straight to bed where she fed him with warm soup and slices of the Sunday chicken. The rest of them sat downstairs discussing the discomforts that cutbacks had brought in the medical and hospital services. Mr Kelly complained about the government losing all common sense and feeling.

'There's the Beef Commission,' he grumbled, 'millions of pounds going into lawyers' pockets while the hospital service is run-down and the roads are full of potholes. Why should we have to spend hours queuing in casualty departments when the same amount of money could purchase extra staff and proper equipment? Everything is deteriorating while those boyos are running around lining their pockets.'

Milo told him about a similar situation in Britain while Sheila described the difficulties nurses faced in London hospitals. But London was a far-off place to Mr Kelly and local problems loomed largest in his mind. Eventually, Sheila saw Milo out to his car and they were almost reckless in their closeness as the dark farmyard swallowed them up. But respect for the feelings of the old pair prevented any further indiscretion and they parted reluctantly with lovers' promises. Milo drove away and as he carefully skirted the rutted surface of his main avenue, he consoled his sexual frustration with fantasies about their next meeting. The great four-poster bed seemed to mock him with its vast size and he thought it cried out for a partner to console him in his solitude. He determined that it would not be long before flesh was united again. His ancestors in their great frames seemed to gaze sympathetically at the thin forlorn figure in the bed. He turned off the light and was united with Sheila in his dreams.

9

When Milo came down to his breakfast the next morning, he found Mrs Neligan fussing with importance. Miss Penelope Baring-Brown had rung up and had asked her about her rheumatism. Such a thoughtful lady. A great shame she had never married. Those that would have proposed to her would not have been acceptable to the Colonel or Mrs Baring-Brown. Those that would have been acceptable had never asked her. There had been rumours of a most presentable young man years ago but unfortunately there was a religious barrier and this prevented a closer alliance.

'It's not a great success when the two religion mix,' said Mrs Neligan meaningfully. 'Neither of them gets satisfaction.'

Milo wondered at her emphasis. She went on to explain that Miss Baring-Brown would like Lord Kilbeggan to ring her back whenever he found it convenient. And the Metcalfes had rung up and were coming over at eleven o'clock to visit the garden if this would suit Milo. He resigned himself to a morning of meeting elderly conventional people and went to the old black telephone to ring Miss Baring-Brown. A deep commanding voice answered the call. Dogs were causing chaos in the background.

'Down, Nuts,' said the voice, 'Bolts, behave yourself. Mummy, do take them out of the hall while I answer the telephone. Hello, sorry about that. They get so excitable when the telephone rings. Bolts is a positive maniac but a very good ratter. Who's that speaking? Oh! Lord Kilbeggan. That's very good of you. Excuse me a moment.'

There was an uproar of terriers again and the deep voice upbraided them until there was silence.

'Sorry about that. They're great fun really. I could get you a pup if you'd like. Bolts covered Miss Black's little bitch and they're the most gorgeous puppies. She'll let them go at fifty guineas to the right sort – she's very careful whom she sells them to. I'm sure she'd be delighted. I'll ask her next time I see her.'

Milo reeled as the torrent of words continued. He had not uttered a word and yet here he was being promised a terrier he had not even asked for.

'I'll ask you over to see them some day this week. We're all so pleased you've come and hope you'll settle in. If you want any help with the garden just let me know. I can bring over a team to help you prune and clear things up. Di and Ginny would come. You'd love to meet them. Such fun. We'll bring the dogs and have a bit of ratting. At any rate we'll arrange it all over drinks next Saturday. You are coming. Splendid. You'll enjoy meeting some local people. Look forward to seeing you. Goodbye.'

Milo had once seen a film starring Joyce Grenfell and had laughed heartily, not realizing that the real world is full of eccentric people and that life beats fiction hands down. Without any assent on his part he was going to be drawn into a world which sounded extremely bizarre. He rang Sheila and her eager voice gave him a tingle of pleasure. But Seamus was in discomfort and hated being in bed where Sheila was enjoining him to stay. Milo promised to take her out after luncheon and had scarcely rung off before he heard the sound of a car on the gravel. A large old grey Rover, surely a classic model if not a vintage prototype, was drawing up slowly in front of the steps. The sensibly large doors opened and an elderly couple ascended the flight of limestone steps to the hall door. Mrs Neligan forgot her ailments and almost raced past Milo to answer the bell. She opened the tall doors and ushered the visitors into the hall.

'Captain and Mrs Metcalfe to see you, my lord,' she announced triumphantly.

Captain Metcalfe had clear blue eyes which had stared from the bridge of ships he had commanded. But youth had now slipped away from him and he limped forward with the aid of a stick.

'Metcalfe,' he announced himself, 'William Metcalfe and this is my wife, Bugsy.'

Bugsy smiled an ancient well-bred greeting and Milo brought them into the study where Mrs Neligan had lit the fire.

'Mrs Neligan's looking after you, I see. She really is a jewel – not many of them left like her. We haven't a maid in the house ourselves. William polishes his shoes himself, but that's a labour of love, and I keep the kitchen going. It's a struggle, but most of us are in the same boat. But let's not talk about ourselves. Tell us all about yourself and your plans for the future. Oh and by the way, here's a little chutney that I made and I don't know if you drink, but here's a bottle of William's home-made wine.'

Milo tried to look overwhelmed by gratitude. They hoped he would come over to play a rubber of bridge with them and possibly meet some young people, although there was hardly a young person left in the county. Milo wondered, thinking of all the young people at the football match and thronging the town, but realized they were delicately hinting that not many young people of his class were living in the county. They quizzed him gently about his life in London and were disappointed to hear that he had not been in any of the services. Captain Metcalfe still believed that the navy was a great life for a young fellow, gave him a good start. Mrs Metcalfe proposed a dig in the garden if Milo was agreeable and left to return to the Rover. Milo said she was welcome and offered to get her a plastic bag for any cuttings. Mrs Metcalfe told him she had two little plastic bags in the car which she kept for cuttings. She strode off towards the garden.

'She's a great gardener,' said the captain. 'Never bought a plant in her life. Takes roots and cuttings everywhere she goes. Loves digging and dunging, although it's hard to get decent dung nowadays without horses in the stables.'

He continued to give Milo a dissertation on dung –

58

compost was no substitute for it – while Bugsy spent a long time in the garden before returning red-faced, scratched but happy. She told Milo she had put the two little bags in the boot before returning to the study.

'Very fortunate. I just took a few small plants that Cynthia promised me.'

Mrs Neligan brought them coffee. Delicate blue cups were set down on a silver tray.

'Will that be all, my lord?' she enquired.

The Metcalfes beamed at this resumption of ancient standards. They left a little while later with Milo's promise that he would visit them for bridge and some supper. As the ancient Rover wound its way across the gravel, he waved goodbye with his mind full of Sheila and not of retired sailors and their consorts. Back inside the house, he retrieved the jar of chutney and the bottle of home-made wine and decided to present them to Mrs Kelly. He put them on the back seat of the Porsche and sped off towards Drumlerry. But when he reached the front gates, he found Captain Metcalfe's Rover stopped with a puncture in a rear wheel. Some choice naval curses were being uttered as the captain tried to extricate the spare wheel from the boot. He slammed the boot closed as Milo's car came around the corner. Both the Captain and Mrs Metcalfe told him not to bother helping them but Milo insisted, to Mrs Metcalfe's embarrassment.

'We'll manage,' said the captain firmly and his wife cried, 'Do go on. I'm sure you're going out for luncheon.'

Milo persisted and the captain reopened the boot with great hesitation. The huge boot was stuffed not only with the two little bags of roots and cuttings, but with a great tangled heap of freshly dug-up plants and shrubs. These were the 'few small plants' that Mrs Metcalfe had mentioned. Milo extricated the spare wheel and helped to remove the nuts from the flat wheel with a large and powerful brace. The captain was grateful, for removing nuts on a flat wheel is a difficult and painful task for the elderly.

'Amazing, isn't it?' he commented as Milo replaced the

wheel, 'they can send people up into space and yet they can't devise an easier method for changing the wheel on a car.'

Mrs Metcalfe, still blushing at the unveiling of her hoard of plants, thanked Milo and the old pair drove off in an atmosphere of awkwardness. Milo wondered what they would be saying to each other as they sat stiffly in the old car. He turned right out onto the main road and sped towards the Kellys' farm.

Sheila appeared in a figure-hugging pair of white slacks which had an instant effect on Milo. Sheila brought him inside quickly and the tricky moment was over. Mrs Kelly, who had never heard of the word feminism, was cooking happily in the kitchen. She welcomed him fondly as if she had known him for a very long time. She insisted on feeding him with a plate of bacon and cabbage and as much mashed potato as would feed a football team. Like Mrs Neligan, she believed in large helpings.

'The trouble with yiz in London,' she said, 'is that you're only picking at food. You'll have no strength left.' Her hero was Christy Moore, a ballad singer with a fine solid appearance. 'And now Seamus is eating nothing. Go up and see him later. He's not feeling the best.' Milo told her of the Metcalfes' visit and this set her into a fit of laughing until she had to sit down. 'Oh! the poor lady and she so straight! She once sacked the housekeeper because she suspected her of stealing a ball of wool. It's true, the old saying – The Colonel's Lady / And Mrs O'Grady / Are the same under the skin. But sure we're all the same about stealing plants. I don't know how many cuttings I've taken in my time without asking permission. And that young Reynolds man that has the garden at Trim open to the public, they say that he's plagued with the people thieving plants. Now have some more rhubarb tart and Sheila will bring you up to see Seamus.'

The young farmer lay prone and miserable in his bed as they entered his room. A picture of his paragon, the famous 'Gallant John Joe', a long-dead Cavan footballer, hung near his bed and other sporting reminders were everywhere.

'I'm not great,' he answered in reply to Milo's query. 'I

60

can scarcely raise the arm. 'Tis very sore. The other part is nearly worse,' and he delicately indicated his groin. 'Time and physiotherapy will do the trick they say. But it's going to be damned awkward, especially for the work. The milking is nearly too much for my father. If I'd hurt the left shoulder, I could help him with the cows but I've been told not to go next or near the yard. Thank God it's not the shooting season. They'd never have a pheasant in the pot. I don't want the mother to be doing too much farm work. She has a touch of blood pressure you know and she's inclined to do too much.' Sheila reassured him that she would help out and Milo promised him that he would do anything that didn't require too much skill or experience.

'Well that might be a great help,' said Seamus, although the tone of his voice indicated a slight doubt. 'Maybe I'll cure quicker than I think.'

They left him to rest and descended the stairs, promising Mr Kelly they would give a hand with the evening milking.

'Why don't you have a swim and come back later,' he replied. 'You can drive them in from the fields for me. That would be a great help.'

Sheila went in for her swimming togs and then they drove off.

'Let's go to your lake,' she suggested and they drove off through the hot golden afternoon.

After the wet morning, the sun had come out and the country was hazy with mellow sunshine. Milo led her down through the shaded track to the boathouse. They got into the ancient craft and rowed through water lilies over the lake towards the mausoleum. There on the hot steps Sheila started to change.

'Where are your togs?' she enquired.

'I've none with me,' he replied, 'I'll use my underpants. Why wear anything? There's nobody to be shocked around here.'

True to his views, he stripped off. He tore off a large rhododendron leaf to cover his private parts. She ran up behind him and mischievously slapped his narrow rear. The rhododendron leaf fell. In revenge he chased her and grabbed at her swimming suit. She yelled as his fingers pinched the soft melon-like buttocks. He pulled her into the shade and, there, beneath a pinus contorta planted by the second earl, they came together, first standing like figures on a Greek vase and then lying together in amazement at their mutual happiness. She cried softly and he gasped at the jerking climaxes of their sexual congress. Swimming was forgotten in this deserted place. The two handsome bodies were as one, lying exhausted. His hands once more caressed the backs of her legs and moved up to her downy thighs. So the afternoon wore on. It took incredible will-power to pull apart and they rose and plunged into the lake, shocked at the coldness of the water and slipping ashore eventually through the water lilies. There they dressed, still full of desire for each other. With tousled hair and glowing skin they entered the rowing boat and pulled off from the lake shore. They were unaware of the depraved eyes watching them through the narrow Gothic window of the mausoleum. Mr Kelly was waiting for them in the farmyard.

'They're down in the bog field,' he told them. 'Take it easy with the lame cow. She's not great at the travelling.'

They walked down by woodbined hedges amid the heavy scents of the summer wild flowers. The bog field was colourful with furze bushes and they drove the cows slowly up the lane to the yard. There Mr Kelly took the first eight into the milking parlour, while the rest waited their turn. The milking parlour was immaculate and a power hose kept floors and walls in hygienic condition. Milo learnt how to fit the cup to the cow's udder and watched the white liquid run through the transparent pipes into the cooler. Sheila was as competent as her father and the whole operation ran smoothly, although one cow with a sore udder had to be treated and rubbed with ointment afterwards. They drove the contented herd back to the bog field and slowly with arms entwined returned up the lane. Mr Kelly glimpsed them arriving in the yard and felt a pang of envy, remembering his lost youth.

'We'll make a farmer of you yet,' he told Milo. 'I hope you're here for the haymaking.'

He was one of the old-fashioned farmers who preferred hay to silage. He felt, probably wrongly, that feeding silage in the winter tainted the taste of the milk that the cows produced. He loved the scent of hay well-saved, rejecting what he considered the evil-smelling maturing of silage. This prejudice, however, presented problems in a wet summer when meadows were cut and subsequent rain reduced the cut sward to a sad mush. Yet he mostly finished the summer with a barn filled with golden hay. The two lovers followed him inside where Mrs Kelly beamed happily offering them a pot of tea and fresh brown bread with her strawberry jam. They chatted away until the dusk came. Seamus was still sore and in pain in his bedroom, despite Sheila's efforts to ease his distress. She gave him a painkiller and he dozed off. Sheila saw Milo to his car. She drew his attention back to business and to facts he was reluctant to think about.

'Have you thought anymore about the builder's offer for the estate?' she enquired. 'They'll be tightening their grip and looking for an answer. They can see a fortune in it for themselves, so it'll be up to you to give them an answer fairly soon.'

Milo was dismayed at the mere thought of his new paradise being violated.

'Look, Sheila,' he answered, 'all I want is you and me living happily in the old house. I don't think I could bear the thought of living permanently like a salesman in an hotel.'

The first part of his answer thrilled her with pleasure, but she was also practical enough to realize that an income is an essential part of any union. Nor was she happy with the new modern idea of a 'house husband' where the wife worked, while the husband stayed at home amid the Brillo pads and the saucepans. She hoped that some compromise could be reached. She had known him only a short time but knew instinctively that they were made for each other, so what worried him must worry her. His dark good looks must not

63

be afflicted by too much worry. She kissed him passionately and he drove off into the night. The jar of chutney rolled against the bottle of home-made wine. Damn! He had forgotten to give them to Mrs Kelly. He parked the car in the stable yard of the castle and went in by the yard door. In the hall on a tray lay a heap of letters, all addressed to himself. The first was an Electricity Supply Board bill for £340. The second envelope contained the telephone bill which had apparently not been paid for ages. It was an itemized bill with several calls to Holland. He must ask Mrs Neligan about this. Who could be ringing Amsterdam from Kilbeggan? The last envelope contained a final demand for payment from the executors of Lady Cynthia Kilbeggan. A side-saddle bought years ago from a county saddler had not been paid for. What a way to end a glorious day, Milo thought, as he threw them aside and ascended the great staircase.

10

Tyres skidded noisily on the gravel beneath the great house and awoke the young master from a most desirable dream. He lay quietly trying to recall the happy details. Sheila and he were on a Greek Island where nudism was compulsory. They lay entwined looking at Homer's wine dark sea. Attractive Scandinavians and athletic Germans passed up the beach but Milo had eyes only for his Irish beauty. Things were about to happen. Just at this point, his reverie was disturbed by a panting voice at the door.

'My lord, I'm sorry to disturb you but the police want to see you urgently.'

Milo jumped out of bed, into his dressing gown and slippers and looked down from his tall windows. Two police cars were parked outside. Policemen were disappearing in various directions around the sides of the castle, into stable yard and courtyard.

'What in the name . . . is all this about?' he wondered and clattered down into the huge hall. Two uniformed guards and one plain-clothes officer waited curiously for him.

'Are you Milo John Patrick Delvin Clanricarde Kilbeggan?' asked an inspector, stumbling over the words. Milo had to think twice before he answered in the affirmative. He never used the ancient family names which had been bestowed on him at his christening. The inspector continued, 'Milo John Patrick Delvin Clanricarde Kilbeggan, I have here a search warrant to examine your residence. The gardai have already begun to investigate these premises. I must ask you, have you any drugs including cannabis, *marijuana*, crack, heroin or other prohibited substances concealed on these premises? We have reason to believe that in the last week, drugs have been distributed from these premises to dealers in Ballivor, Enfield, Kinnegad, Tulla-more and Mullingar. I may inform you that we have arrested one minor distributor who has informed us that he knows very little about the methods of import, but he believes his drugs had their source in this area. According to our records, you arrived in this country nine days ago. We have checked with Scotland Yard, who have supplied us with information about a number of speeding offences and an incident with a policeman's helmet in Piccadilly Circus on Boat Race night, but they have no record of your involve-ment in other more serious matters. Nevertheless the coin-cidence of your recent arrival and the recent influx of drugs in this part of the country is quite striking and must be investigated. We would like you to lead us to your bedroom and other rooms in this house which you have been using.'

Milo, shaking with shock and indignation, led them past the horrified Mrs Neligan.

'Excuse me, my lord,' she said shakily, 'will I bring up your breakfast?'

The police inspector interrupted.

'We shall inform you, ma'am, when breakfast may be required.'

She sat down weakly as the four figures ascended the stairs.

One policeman investigated cabinets, chests of drawers, wardrobes and other pieces of furniture. The second pulled back the ancient carpet and examined loose floorboards. The plain-clothes officer examined the bed and then Milo's rather shabby-looking clothes. Then came a moment he resented.

'Perhaps you would be good enough to remove your dressing gown and pyjamas.'

Milo removed the garments and stood shivering in the cold morning sunlight. The inspector scrutinized the thin arms which were bare of any incriminating needle marks. The rest of the body was equally innocent of offending marks.

'Thank you,' said the inspector, 'please dress now and I

66

shall talk to you while you have your breakfast. The gardai will carry on through the rest of the house.'

In the library, Milo rang the bell and Mrs Neligan arrived up with the breakfast tray. She was shaking. Cups rattled in saucers and the teapot and milk jug jangled as she set the tray down. She had experienced official visits before. Packy had provoked the law on several occasions, but Lady Cynthia would turn in her grave if she knew that the gardai were interrogating a member of the Kilbeggan family.

'I've brought a cup for the inspector,' she told Milo, 'and your usual breakfast.'

Doubts entered the inspector's head as he saw the porridge and toast and two boiled eggs on the tray. This was not the usual fare for people connected with drugs. Nor did this healthy and fit-looking young man appear like the usual supplier. Still the aristocracy was no stranger to drugs. The inspector read the English Sunday newspapers. The Marquis of Blandford had recently been convicted. Conservative cabinet ministers' daughters had been involved in the trade. Lord Kilbeggan on the face of it appeared to be a most unlikely candidate for the role. Nevertheless a thorough search might reveal surprises. He began to interrogate the young man over his breakfast.

'Have you been in the habit of using drugs yourself? Lots of young men see no harm in it.'

'No,' replied Milo, 'I have many faults and have often indulged myself in other ways, but I have always kept away from drugs.'

'Surely your friends in the London scene have used them. I believe it's considered part of the social custom over there.'

'No,' replied Milo firmly. 'It's not part of my scene. We may drink too much and do other things but drugs weren't on the menu.'

'Do you keep money in the house? We have found very little money. Where do your keep your cash?'

'It may seem strange to you,' said Milo, 'but I have very little money. I came over to Ireland believing that I would be inheriting an income. Instead I have inherited a load of bills. Look at these.' He tossed the electricity bill, the telephone bills and the saddler's bill over to the inspector, who glanced at them casually but then held up the telephone bill.

'Who do you know in Amsterdam, Lord Kilbeggan?' his voice taking on a suspicious tone. 'There seems to be a connection between this house and an Amsterdam number. I would be grateful if you could let me have a truthful answer.'

'Those calls were made before I ever entered this country. Just look at the date.'

'You have not entered this country before? I'm afraid we shall have to check on this. Are you certain this is your first visit?'

At this point, the rest of the police party entered the room.

'Nothing suspicious,' they said and stood waiting.

'Try the car. I believe you drive a Porsche. A very expensive car for a penniless young man. I wonder how you can afford to run it.'

'The car's in the kitchen yard,' said Milo.

'Examine it carefully,' said the inspector. 'Panels, doors, unusual signs.'

His suspicions had strengthened. They waited in silence until heavy sounds on the stairs announced the gardai's quick return.

'There's no car in the yard,' they announced. 'There's tracks all right but the car has gone.'

Suspicion changed into near-certainty in the inspector's mind. Milo spluttered with indignation. First the interrogation and now his car stolen.

'I hope you put equal efforts into recovering my car,' he told the police officers indignantly. 'This is outrageous.'

'We have not accused you of anything so far,' replied the inspector. 'We'll radio the station and have all squad cars look out for it. Give some details to Garda Tehan here and he'll radio through. In the meantime, there are several outbuildings including gate lodges, mausoleum, garden house that we have not searched. I want the keys to all these buildings please.'

Milo rang for Mrs Neligan to sort out the keys and then remembered that Packy had kept the key of the mausoleum. He asked Mrs Neligan if she could ask Packy for the key.

'No, shure, he said your lordship had kept the key after your last visit out there.' Milo remembered with a sinking heart the loose brick in the wall of the mausoleum and the scented cigarette that Packy had smoked. What a fool he had been not to clear out any contraband and lock and keep the key. The inspector was now looking at him with a questioning stare.

'You visit places with Packy Neligan?' he said. 'What is your relationship with that young man? Have you known him for long? I have a feeling that you are holding something back. Ring for Mrs Neligan again until we find out more from her son.'

Up came Mrs Neligan again, more flustered than ever. In reply to queries about her son's whereabouts she almost lost her voice.

'He went off early this morning to go to Dublin looking for work. I think he was getting a lift for I heard the sound of a car in the courtyard. He's doing his best and said that he'd be away for a while. Shure sometimes we don't see him for weeks. Then he'll come back and always have a few pounds for his parents. He's very generous when he's got the money.'

'Where does he get the money from?' interrupted the inspector.

'He gets work and sometimes overdoes it. I'm afraid he'll overdo it completely sometime working too hard. He has to get injections from a doctor to put the vitamins back into him. I've seen the marks on his arm myself.'

'Thank you, Mrs Neligan,' said the inspector. 'Search that lad's room thoroughly,' he told the plain-clothes officer who reluctantly went down again to examine the unpleasant den.

A feeling of hopelessness overcame Milo. The silence in the library lengthened. At last the plain-clothes officer returned with some items in a plastic bag.

'Not much,' he told the inspector, 'but he's obviously got bad habits. There's enough to convict on charges of possession but no evidence of a big supply. We'll try the boathouse and the mausoleum if this gentleman will show us keys and a boat to reach the mausoleum. We'll bring a pickaxe if the keys can't be found. I've sent the two others to search the garden house.'

Milo led the officers down the tangled lane towards the lake. A heavy dew still clung to the leaves and drenched them when they pushed aside the branches. They reached the boathouse where the inspector examined various sets of footprints in the mud.

'These are recent,' he observed. 'I should say yesterday's footprints. Could I just examine your shoe for a moment?'

Milo tugged off his slip-on which fitted exactly a footprint in the mud. The inspector looked more and more convinced and complacent. Milo rowed them across slowly, the boat low in the water with the two bulky policemen in the bow. Drawing up at the little jetty in front of the classical portico of the sombre stone building, Milo hoped they had left no evidence of yesterday's pleasures to be discovered. Footprints led up to the double doors of the building and the inspector examined them carefully.

'Strange,' he said stooping down, 'your footprints seem to head off to the shrubbery.' He walked over to the rhododendron bushes where a few late flowers still bloomed. The inspector picked up a small broken branch and Milo remembered with lost hope how he had used the branch to conceal his rising member. How could he explain all this to the humourless and suspicious inspector? It was impossible to think of either officer in a lighthearted or compromising situation.

'People have been lying down here,' observed the inspector, 'enjoying themselves no doubt.'

'And how,' thought Milo to himself, remembering the

innocent sweetness of yesterday's activities. The two officers marched back to the heavy doors, shook them irritatedly and began to use heavy pressure to open them. Several strong heaves loosened the lock from the door. A final heave proved successful and the inspector almost fell into the damp interior. They gazed suspiciously at the stone vaults and tombs, monuments of the once great and powerful. Each tomb bore the arms and crest of the once-sovereign family. Incongruously, Coke tins and crisp packets lay as if in contempt on top of the stone pillars. A yellow spill of beer, like urine, lay beside a crushed beer can. Somebody had urinated by the tomb of the third earl. Milo recoiled at this contempt for the dead. What ignorant scum could desecrate and profane the last monuments of the departed? The two policemen took in at once the evidence of some kind of party. They examined the alabaster slabs and the figures in niches. Next they went along the brick walls and finally found what they were looking for and what Milo could have told them was there. They had found the right place but the cupboard was bare and the bird had flown. An empty box lay in the recess behind the bricks. The inspector sniffed and looked behind the box. A packet of needles was all he found. He examined the stone hand of a statue which had been struck by matches. He looked at the canvas chairs in the corner and what appeared to be a decaying mattress. At least six people had been using this quiet place as a drug den. Their footprints were clear on the damp floor. There was no sign of condoms; drugs give such a false sense of security that their users often ignore the perils of promiscuous sexual encounters. Milo waited outside in the wholesome morning air and waited for the two policemen to emerge. The inspector addressed him first.

'I feel that you have not told us everything you know. I would be grateful if you would decide to be open and help us with our enquiries. When we get back to the castle, I shall expect full cooperation from you. This is too serious a matter and at the moment I feel that you are being evasive.'

When they got back to the castle, the remaining police-men reported on their visit to the garden house.

'It has not been used for some time, inspector, but whoever used it last left plenty of evidence behind them.'

The inspector led the way up to the library and sat down squarely opposite Milo.

'Now I want you to tell me all that you know about your property being used as a distribution centre for drugs and as a centre for hippy-style parties. Leave nothing out that might be relevant. You may of course say nothing and wait for your solicitor.'

Milo decided that Mr Kinch was unnecessary in this business and he started off his story. He left little out. His suspicions had been mounting about young Neligan. Yes he should have done something straight away when he found out about Packy's drug habits but the inspector must remember that he had just arrived in the country and life was enormously complicated. Besides that, he had not wanted to hurt Mrs Neligan who, having spoilt her son, still regarded him as the golden boy. It seemed to Milo that he had inherited a maze of problems and he had been left very little time to solve them. He admitted being at the mauso-leum for a swim with Sheila but added that they had lain down in the sun afterwards to rest themselves. They had not entered the mausoleum. The inspector agreed with this, having examined the footprints carefully. He advised Milo to report to him on any fresh signs of activity. The gardai would keep a close eye on the place and he should contact them if in any doubt. The inspector also enquired about his bankers and asked his permission to make enquiries from them.

'I do not believe that you're involved in any of this trade,' he said, 'but you have been very naive in ignoring young Neligan's activities.'

He gave Milo his telephone number and the two squad cars pulled off down the avenue.

11

Black depression settled on Milo as he retreated back into the castle. A load of trouble had descended on him, none of it his making. Mrs Neligan who had been watching everything from the hall hurried across to meet him.

'I'm very sorry, my lord,' she stammered, 'I couldn't stop them coming in. I told them that you had only been here a few days but they didn't listen to me. Thank God Packy wasn't here. They'd have turned on him. They seem to have a down on him, poor lad. I hadn't even time to clean up his room before they burst in and if Packy has one fault, it's his untidiness. He wouldn't do a hand's turn to keep his room clean. That young lad that always stays with him – Packy always insists that he shares the room for company – he says that he's afraid of ghosts and wouldn't sleep anywhere else in the castle. But the room hasn't been cleaned out since he was here. I was so ashamed for the gardai to see the state of it. However, I hope that your lordship was not too upset. By the way, there's been two phone calls for you. Miss Kelly called. I told her you weren't available. She was very persistent to find out where you were but I didn't breathe a word. You can rely on me to keep my mouth shut. There's certain parties not a hundred miles from here that couldn't keep a secret but I'm not one of them. Mr Lynch rang up and I told him you were out in the garden.'

Milo thanked the confused housekeeper. The thought passed through his mind that if anybody could be accused of being naive, it was Mrs Neligan whose adoration of her long-haired son hindered her from seeing his faults. He rang up Sheila and asked her to come over and collect him in her car, as the Porsche had been stolen. He walked down the avenue to meet her and had just reached the imposing

73

gates when the old MG pulled up. His heart leaped with pleasure and reassurance. Her face was tender with concern. The mere contact, the brushing of hands or legs or lips gave him such a thrill of delight that he almost forgot his woes.

'Let's go somewhere where we can eat and talk,' he muttered.

He placed his arm around her, like a second seat belt, and they drove off. She was horrified and astounded by the story. They drove to a lakeside hotel, an old building which had once been a nuns' convent. The long bar was full of attractive pictures. Through the windows they could see across the lawn to the broad expanse of Lough Ennel. It was quiet. Business groups came here for lunch. Tourists who stayed in the hotel were out fishing on the lake. Sheila announced with great satisfaction that she had arranged a fortnight's extra leave from her hospital, to help nurse her sick brother. Milo's heart leaped with satisfaction. He was rapidly reaching the stage where he could not do without her and he hoped that if all went according to plan she would transfer to a local hospital – Mullingar or Tullamore. But things weren't going according to plan.

'Packy's obviously been spreading the rumour,' she said, 'that you are the big supplier. That takes the heat off him and makes you into the fall guy. You must have annoyed him, although he was always a spoilt malicious brat. This is a really nasty bad turn he's done you. Did you hassle him in any way?'

Milo couldn't remember any way he might have provoked the lad.

'He's got you into a right mess now,' said Sheila. 'I think you'd better see your solicitor in case the affair goes any further. The big thing is that you're innocent and they can't pin anything on you without evidence.'

The sharing of his worries took some of the load off Milo, and Sheila told him some of her own cares. Seamus was not any better. He was not responding to treatment and was enduring increasing pain. She felt he should have been recovering and now be more comfortable then he was.

Tendons and torn muscles take a long time to heal. Her father was doing more than he ought to and they would welcome any help that Milo could give them on the farm. They went into lunch and sat at a small table overlooking the lake. Their feet entwined under the tablecloth and the well-mannered young waitress guessed that food was only the second pleasure in their young lives. As their legs brushed under the table, their faces blushed above it. The waitress would gladly have taken Sheila's place. How often she served middle-aged people who were so bored with each other that they scarcely bothered to talk to each other. Here was a couple who could nearly devour each other instead of the food. She smiled and served them gladly. They smiled back in a conspiracy of three.

Sheila waited in Mullingar while Milo ascended to Mr Kinch's office. The two refined secretaries both leaped up to attend to him.

'Ah! Lord Kilbeggan. How are you settling in? It's like old times to have a Kilbeggan visiting the office again. I'm sure Mr Kinch will see you, he's just got somebody in about letting a small farm.' She opened the door into the main office and announced in an important voice, 'Lord Kilbeggan is here and wonders if he could have a few words with you?' In the meantime Connie was reminding Milo of his rash invitation to them to visit the garden. She also told him a story of one of his relations, Lord Kilcock, in whose memory a race was run at the annual point-to-point. Indeed he could see the races himself as the point-to-point was being held next weekend. What a good idea it would be if Milo presented the Kilcock Trophy for the six-year-olds and upwards Maiden Race at the meeting. Perhaps Lord Kilbeggan wouldn't mind if she suggested this to one of the joint masters. Milo agreed politely, hoping it would not involve him having to present any money. He was told that there was no money involved, that it was a perpetual trophy to honour his ancestor who was a famous rider in his time. He was also, Evelyn informed him coyly, a great man for the ladies. Indeed he had broken many a young heart. Milo hoped that the hearts weren't as young as the title of the memorial race might suggest. Mr Kinch, having ushered out the previous client, brought Milo in and beamed at him.

'Well I hope you're bringing us good news.'

His face fell when Milo told him that he had made no decision as yet about selling the estate and instead described the alarming events of the morning.

'Oh my, Oh my. You should have rung me straight away. Let me deal with anything further. This is most unfortunate. Refer the inspector to me if there are any further developments. It really should show you that you would be far better off accepting Mr Fogarty's offer and you would have a supportive group to back you up. Really, the gardai should know that young pup has been distributing drugs for years. Right under his mother's nose and she thinks he's the blue-eyed boy. I'll ring the station straight away to see if there is any news of your car. Miss Thomson, would you phone the barracks for me and find out if there is any news of Lord Kilbeggan's car. Thank you, Miss Thomson. Now, do let me know soon if you intend to do business with Mr Fogarty. I can't recommend it strongly enough. Ah, there you are, inspector; Garret Kinch here. How is the poor mother? Well, she'll be better off. They treat them very kindly in there. My own poor aunt, God rest her, was there for three months. I couldn't praise them too highly. Expensive but the nuns do their best. To get on to a less serious matter, I act for Lord Kilbeggan whom I believe you met this morning. Oh, his car has been found? Where do you say it is? At Trumpet Hill? I know it. Just beyond the Silver River. It's in a ditch. Little damage. That's good. I'll phone the garage to get it out. By the way, I wouldn't like to interfere with your investigations but Lord Kilbeggan has never touched a drug in his life and has been dragged into this business in a most unfair way. I believe the other young man has been hoodwinking every-body to clear himself. He has thrown dust in our eyes while he seems to have got off scot-free. You have checked the Porsche for fingerprints. Good. You say you want to have another inspection of it. You are keeping the car until tomorrow? What time can Lord Kilbeggan collect it? Three o'clock at the barracks. Right. I'll pass the message on to my client. I hope your mother will be happy there. Sister Finbarr is a dear. Goodbye, inspector.'

Mr Kinch replaced the phone with a sigh.

'It gets to all of us. Every day I look down the obituary column in *The Irish Times*, it's another one gone. Old clients like your aunt. However, let's not be down-hearted. While there's life there's hope. Now how will we get you home? Do you want to hire a car or shall I run you out? No trouble. You have a friend, you say? A Miss Kelly? Would she be a daughter of Kellys of Drumlerry? – decent people. No, shure I know the ones you mean. They're almost neighbours of yours. They'd benefit if the estate was made into a business. Well, don't be stirring heroin into your tea,' he chuckled, 'and keep in touch and let's get things settled.'

Milo left, said his good afternoons to the two secretaries and went down the shabby stairs to the busy street. Sheila was talking to friends in the car park and introduced Milo. There was chat about dances, about the point-to-point, about football matches, about an old school reunion. But feeling he was not yet an interested member of the local scene, she put her arm through his and led him off to the car park. They could almost hear the excited gossip behind them with exclamations of 'Wow!' and 'Who'd have guessed it?' floating in the air. But he wanted no other company. He would put up with her feminine manner of driving, irritating though it was, for the sake of her warm humanity beside him.

Mr and Mrs Kelly were sitting in the kitchen when they arrived. Mr Kelly was reading out news from the local paper to his wife, while she knitted placidly pretending to be interested in the stories he read out and even sometimes giving a mild exclamation of surprise or interest.

'What is the world coming to?' said Mr Kelly after reading an account of car thefts in the county town. 'Well, here's one nearer home,' said Sheila and she gave them an account of Milo's distressful morning.

77

'Inspector Coughlan,' said Mr Kelly, 'isn't he a first cousin of Fogarty the builder? His mother was one of the Fogartys' of Lisryan. Well, I'm glad they have recovered your car. I suppose they have to explore every avenue when they're investigating the drug scene. Young Neligan was very clever at removing the scent from himself.'

He was interrupted by Mrs Kelly, who said, 'You're wrong, Daddy. It was one of the Fogartys of Tullahady, the gravel people, that married a Coughlan.'

They argued this point while Sheila smiled at Milo and Milo grinned back. At length, the old couple left their dispute over local genealogy and went on to express their worries about Seamus. He had often taken knocks at football. He was a hardy lad and could endure a fair amount of physical abuse. But they were worried about him this time. Mrs Kelly remarked that you could see the pain in his eyes. He was staying in the bed when normally you could hardly keep him in the house no matter how bad he felt. Things weren't right. Sheila talked about getting a second opinion, about trying for a specialist in Dublin.

'Isn't it a great pity your uncle is dead,' said Mrs Kelly suddenly turning around to Milo. 'The old lord had a great gift. I mind the time when Grandad was knocked over by a bullock and trampled. He was in agony with the back until we asked his lordship to use the Kilbeggan touch. And it worked. It gave him great relief. The pain eased off and he was out and about inside a week. We had to put that bullock down; you couldn't rely on him. Your uncle wasn't too keen to use his gift. It seemed to take something out of him but he'd oblige a neighbour who was in trouble. Then he never wanted to take money, but the touch didn't work unless he got something substantial. I believe we gave him a fiver, which was big money in those days. You'd nearly buy a calf with that sort of money. The old housekeeper before Mrs Neligan told me that he used to give the money to the poor and I'd well believe it. He was a well-bred person – a pity there aren't a few more about.'

Mrs Kelly finished off her speech with a sigh. Milo was

interested in this first-hand account of the Kilbeggan touch. *Vinceo quem tango.* He had thought it referred to warlike deeds that his ancestors had performed. But it seemed there was a strong history of benevolence, of curing people rather than attacking them. All the old people around, he was told, remembered the Kilbeggan touch. When the medical treatment failed they went to the big house. The old earl was plagued by people arriving up the back avenue and knocking at the kitchen door. The local doctor was furious and didn't hold with it at all. 'Upper-class quackery and superstition,' he had called it. The clergy weren't very keen either. They were trying to promote Knock and Lourdes and it didn't suit them to have a tweedy old landowner curing people on their doorstep. Lady Cynthia, who had married him, didn't have the same talent. But the males of the family were supposed to inherit the touch. Sheila suddenly started to giggle thinking what happiness their own mutual touching had brought them. Milo read her thoughts and winked at her.

'Why not try it out, Milo?' she said, 'I'm sure your touch would bring great relief to anybody.'

The mischievous suggestion was taken seriously by the old pair.

'If you could try it out, we would be very grateful,' said Mrs Kelly.

They were very anxious. A farm with an only son is very dependent on the good health of the young lad. Besides this, they grieved when they saw Seamus in pain. Reluctantly Milo agreed to their suggestion that he should go upstairs and use the ancient procedure on Seamus. Sheila all the time was hard put to conceal her giggling. Mrs Kelly went upstairs to prepare Seamus for the news. She came down rather sadly.

'He'd do anything to get rid of the discomfort,' she said. 'Go on up and we'll pray that it works.'

Milo for the second time that day found himself in an unwanted role. Mediaeval nonsense, he thought to himself, he would kill Sheila for suggesting this. The sight of the young man lying on the bed changed his attitude and he

79

decided to go through with it in a more positive mood. He tried to remember the old formula. First neck, chest and elbow. The top half of the body. He opened the pyjama top gently. Seamus's freckled face was weary. The strong and muscular body twitched as Milo laid his white townish hands on the boy's neck, then transferred them to the downy chest. As he shifted them to the elbow, Seamus winced.

'Take it easy,' he said, 'the pain travels there from the shoulder.'

Milo left his hands there for a while. He next removed the young man's pyjama trousers and pressed the knees and calves.

'Turn sideways, if you can,' he said to Seamus who found it hard to turn in the bed.

Milo laid his hands gently on the strong young buttocks. He replaced the trousers and lastly, for good measure, let his hand rest on the damaged shoulder. As he did so, to his surprise he found himself remembering verses which he had last spoken in the school chapel.

'Lo, Thou requirest truth in the inward parts and thou shalt make me to understand wisdom secretly.

'Thou shalt make me hear of joy and gladness that the bones which thou hast broken may rejoice.'

Other irrelevant verses flickered through his memory.

'The Heavens declare the glory of God and the firmament showeth His handywork.

'The Lord is my strength and my shield, my heart hath trusted in Him and I am helped.'

These and other verses flickered through his mind and two lines of his school song echoed over the years – 'Feeble of foot and rheumatic of shoulder, / What will it help you, that once you were strong?'

But when he looked down, he saw to his astonishment that Seamus was asleep, peacefully and quietly lying on his side. He tiptoed out of the room and went quietly down the stairs in a different turn of mind. They saw by his face that his disposition had altered.

'He's fast asleep,' he said.

'Glory be,' said Mrs Kelly, 'he hasn't slept for nights with the pain. What a strange thing.'

She glowed with delight and Milo was pleased that they all looked so happy. Mr Kelly rose and went to the dresser. Out of a broken teapot on the top ledge, he took a £20 note and handed it to Milo, who gave it back forcefully to him.

'Please,' said Mr Kelly, 'you must take it for Seamus's sake. It's a very old tradition and we must not risk failure. It will be a cheap price to pay, if the lad gets any improvement. We know you would be only too pleased to help us for nothing. But this is all part of the pattern.'

Milo took the money and felt that he had done something wholesome for once. The spiritual feeling left him immediately. It was soon time to fetch in the cows for milking and the young couple walked out into the late afternoon sun. Smells of honeysuckle and wild roses hung in the air. They brought in the cows for milking and Milo received a busier job and became an instant expert at washing and cleaning. Two hours later they came in. Seamus was still fast asleep, breathing easier and looking better. After tea, Sheila drove him home and they discussed the strange experience.

'I felt something leaving me for a while,' said Milo, 'a sudden emptiness for about a minute. I only hope it will have helped Seamus a bit.'

Oddly enough, he felt convinced that it would be effective. As was usual with them, serious discussion turned into badinage.

'I must give you a bit of my touch,' said Sheila in a most unladylike manner.

'I thought you nurses had an ethical code,' he retorted but retaliated in a most unethical manner.

Such teasing has only one result and as the day had begun unhappily, it finished with much pleasure. Later, he brought her down the staircase and showed her to her car, letting her leave with great reluctance. Nor did she think of her own ancestors who had come in and out through the back door of the castle.

12

Inspector Coughlan was in quite relaxed form when Milo sought the return of his car.

'You're lucky,' he informed Milo, 'there's very little real damage done apart from a couple of dinges. I'm afraid that we had to make sure that there were no hidden frames or panels that would facilitate the importation of drugs. We have to be extra careful you know. I am eliminating you from the enquiry as a suspect. But in future I'll want instant information if you come in contact with any drug dealing on your estate. With such good cover in the woodlands and plenty of empty buildings, the estate is an obvious target for criminals who want to avoid notice. Young Neligan has escaped us. He's supposed to be an art student, but I learn from the registrar of the regional college that he scarcely attended any lectures and is not now on their student list. Apparently he made connections with some Dutch tourists on the Shannon – people who hire out cruising boats – and we feel that he could be anywhere up or down the river. Thank you for your help in our enquiries.'

Milo and Sheila inspected the car. It was difficult to believe that everything from carpets to dashboard had been removed and inspected – the police had done their job very thoroughly and the car seemed perfect. Wheels were covered in mud where it had sunk in the ditch and several scratches marred its dark beauty but Milo was delighted to recover it.

'At least the bastard left the keys in it,' he told Sheila. 'It would have been difficult to get copies of the keys. I have a spare set in London. But they're locked in a cupboard and there would be endless complications. Oh! by the way, did you hear that I'm to present the Kilcock trophy at the race meeting on Sunday? Apparently some randy ancestor of mine presented it to the hunt committee. They've sent me a free car park ticket and an invitation to drinks beforehand at some colonel's – it sounded like Colonel Damdemall. But that couldn't be right, could it? Oh! Colonel Baring-Brown is it, I'd better not call him the other. You'll come with me, won't you? Oh come on, they won't eat you. Of course you'd be welcome. It's not Buckingham Palace. Let's get back now and see how Seamus is.'

To everybody's surprise including his own, Seamus was feeling not strong but much easier and obviously on the road to recovery.

'I'm going to get up after dinner,' he said, 'just to show that the Kilbeggan touch has a permanent effect. Thanks very much, Milo. It was like a miracle the way the relief came on me. I practically slept through twenty-four hours. They didn't want to waken me they were so pleased. I'd say there's a few other lads on the team who'd be grateful for the same treatment. Robbie McGrath got an awful doing in the Raharney match and hasn't been able to play for two months. There's others besides. Do you know you could nearly make a trade out of it? Don't let them hear about it at the race meeting. Half the jockeys in the country are afflicted.'

Milo smiled at the young lad's enthusiasm and assured him that he didn't want to make a profession of it, unless there were lots of female jockeys injured. Sheila, not too pleased at this turn of conversation, brought him downstairs. They helped Mr Kelly in the yard. Milo did a small repair job on the tractor and then he and Sheila went off. She had promised him a tour of some of the famous places in Westmeath.

In a village called Multyfarnham they visited a seventeenth-century school, still flourishing after centuries of pedagogy. Near the village there was a Franciscan abbey where the ancient church had been restored. Here was evidence of an older aristocracy. Tombs of a great Norman family, the Nugents, nestled in dark corners of the abbey

church. Tablets to another great county family, the Dela-
meres, lined the walls. Some had lost their castles in the
tumult of history; others remained. Milo found out that a
seventeenth-century title was almost like an upstart compared with these venerable families.

Milo was surprised to find what beauty nestled in the flat
midlands. They drove down to Lough Derravaragh, a long
lake with steep sides heavily overgrown with trees. This lake
was the setting for the famous legend of the Children of Lir,
who thousands of years ago had been cursed and turned
into swans. They were destined to live on the great midland
lakes until the curse wore off. Sadly, when they were
changed back into human beings, all their friends were
dead and their whole world was extinct. The poet, Thomas
Moore, had written a famous song which captured their
plight. A great drift of swans swam on the far side of the lake
and Milo wondered if they were related to the Children of
Lir.

The idyllic day wore on. They picnicked at Belvedere
House, a small stately home open to the public. Here on the
lawn under the historic Georgian house the sun shone and
the two of them lay looking out on the bright waves of
Lough Ennel. Trout fishermen in their boats grumbled at
the brightness of the weather which did not make their sport
easier. Milo and Sheila, arms entwined and legs touching,
had no grumbles as they lay blissfully together, all troubles
of the world forgotten. Behind them, tourists were given
guided tours. Families picnicking near them meant that they
had to exercise conventional restraints and not disclose too
clearly their obvious intentions. When the lawn got too
crowded, they walked through the old walled garden and
admired some of the great trees on the estate. Milo admired
the compactness of the early Georgian house.

'Now that's the ideal size,' he said to Sheila. 'It's handsome and graceful and once repairs are kept in hand, it
would be easy enough to keep. My house is so vast by
comparison. Troubles multiply with the size of a house.'

But she wasn't listening seriously to him.

'You're the ideal size,' she said laughingly and pulled him on to an old seat behind the garden wall.

They were disturbed by children playing hide-and-seek and once again had to adopt the appearance of a staid young couple. They walked down to view one of the most famous follies in Ireland. The Jealous Wall is a man-made ruin built in the eighteenth century as a result of rivalry between two aristocratic brothers. This was the folly built by the wicked Lord Belvedere so that his neighbouring brother could not look across and send signals to the earl's wife. This was Betjeman country and Sheila found to her astonishment that Milo had scarcely heard of the famous poet.

'Did they not teach you anything in your school, apart from sexy behaviour?' she challenged Milo.

'I was about to ask you the same question,' he protested innocently.

They admired the venerable structure which looked like the hallowed remains of some once famous abbey, but was really a monument to eighteenth-century pride and possessiveness. In the hot afternoon they decided to find some secluded spot as Milo stated, where they could have 'a quiet lie down together', and further along the lake they found a sequestered spot, where love could find expression. Sheila wondered how sensuality which could appear coarse and almost ugly on television or cinema could be so wholesome and pleasing when one was in love.

When they appeared in the yard at Drumlerry later in the afternoon, Mr Kelly noticed their containment with some concern for he loved his daughter and did not want her to suffer any disappointment or disillusion. He felt that events were proceeding far too fast. It had taken himself and Mrs Kelly years of patient negotiating before marriage was finally arranged. But life moved much faster nowadays and old difficulties like class distinction, wealth distinction, differences of creed and colour seemed to pose no trouble for young people nowadays. He was no spoilsport. Times had improved greatly in many ways he felt. He liked Milo but was still suspicious of the sophisticated background he sprang from. He decided to give Milo the benefit of the doubt and later that night discussing the affair with Mrs Kelly, he pooh-poohed her fears as empty and unnecessary.

'She's an educated girl, she's had some experience of life. Give her the credit for making up her own mind and making her own decisions. I've never seen her look so happy and healthy. It would be very bad if we interfered or started to give her advice.'

So wisely they acted as if this union between the great house and the farmhouse outside its walls was a most natural event, which they welcomed. Country memories are long and retentive and this was a major achievement on their part.

After Sheila and Milo had helped with the cows, they had gone inside for a cup of tea. A programme called *Inside Ulster* was starting on the television and Milo hoped that they would not notice his blushing. His first girlfriend had been a girl called Janet Ulster and the title of the programme brought back confused pictures to his mind. His skills had certainly improved since then. They discussed the race meeting and Sheila finally was persuaded that she should go with him to the Baring-Browns. The invitation had greatly amused Mrs Kelly, who was sitting down relaxed under a window full of geraniums.

'So long as you don't ask them back here,' she told Sheila, 'your father would be moithered if she started to sell him a terrier. Old Shep here would get mad jealous if he found another dog in the place, wouldn't you, Shep?'

The collie lying under the kitchen table wagged its tail so strongly that the sound echoed around the room.

'There, he says "yes", so no sale for Miss Baring-Brown.'

They agreed, laughing, and Milo soon decided to take his leave, for he had boxfuls of papers to sort out at the castle. Mrs Kelly was giving him a great account of Miss Baring-Brown who was apparently as good as a man at most things.

'The postman was telling me that he saw her on the roof of Kilnacrann Abbey fixing slates after the big storm in 1993.

There's a terrible steep pitch on the roof of that house and the colonel was terrified she'd fall off. The postman said that she kept shouting at the colonel, "Don't be a fool, Daddy, send up some more nails." There was another time Ned Gleeson was stuck on the road with a puncture. He couldn't shift the nuts on the wheel. Along came Miss Baring-Brown on the way into town. "Give me that brace," she said to Ned and she had them off in no time. Ned was half-ashamed to tell the story. No, I wouldn't like to cross her, that's a fact. But shure you'll meet her yourself tomorrow.'

Milo, laughing, arose to his feet and said a discreet good-night to Sheila in the yard.

That night in the library at Kilbeggan Castle, he opened up some of the boxes of family papers – diaries, account books, ledgers, land records. They were in no particular order and had not been sorted out. Some were dull day-to-day accounts of country life. Items like, 'Michael McMahon came this day at 14 shillings per week not including stamp money.' Later came the sequel, 'Promised Michael McMahon a rise of sixpence (6d) per week and to pay cost of new breeches for him.'

These were written in the agent's year book, for the agent, in this case, a Captain Balfe, who seemed to control the large staff. In another record, written by the fifth lord, he came across a note saying 'Watch Balfe' – which suggested a lack of confidence of the earl in his agent.

Rent books disclosed substantial sums of money coming in from farm tenants and also from shopkeepers in the town, whose ground rents were owed to the earl. After 1903, this had mostly ceased for the great Land Act, The Wyndham Act, had transferred land from landlord to tenant. Ledgers disclosed huge sums of money spent on horses and hunting. The fourth earl had been master of the Westmeath Foxhounds. There was payment for railway carriages, indeed an entire train to transport horses and the dog pack to a meet near Moyvalley. Uniforms for huntsmen and whippers-in were paid for. Relationships were extremely close and obviously affectionate between the earl and the hunting staff. Christmas presents were given. Visits were paid to sick children. A death was noted with dismay.

Another record puzzled Milo for it produced a list of moneys received in a particular year. He wondered if this was rent money or sales of horses or of timber or hay. But there was no obvious reason why different amounts of money should be received by the earl. They varied from quite large sums to small sums like 6d. The names also were not the familiar names of tenants. There was one entry '5/- from Mayo man'. It was only when he found a soiled and torn piece of paper recording a payment that he realised with a shock the reason for this income. Written in poor script on the piece of paper was the message, 'Much thanks to yr. Ldship for cureing me of the Pains. Bart. O'Conner.'

The book was a record of moneys received by a nineteenth-century earl for using the family gift – the Kilbeggan Touch. Another note said, 'Told Hickey (South Lodge) not to admit supplicants at Christmas and to let that message be public.'

Milo was amazed. He went thoughtful to bed.

13

Kilnacrann Abbey was in no sense an abbey but a venerable country house. It took its name from a small abbey which had been closed down in the sixteenth century. Much of the stonework had been removed by a later plantation landowner to build a great house for himself. The name, Sheila told him, could be translated as the church among the trees. The house stood imposingly among its guardian beech and lime trees. Cars sprawled untidily on the gravel sweep in front of the house and Milo and Sheila found a place to park in an old yard at the side of the house. They came around to the front of the house and climbed the flight of steps to the massive hall door which was slightly ajar. Inside a babble of voices sounded. Two terriers suddenly flew out from the hall and barked furiously at Milo and Sheila. Impersonal upper-class faces looked out at them from the hall and turned back unconcernedly. The terriers lost their interest in Milo and Sheila and began to fight each other. A very elderly Labrador lay snoring in the porch completely oblivious of the human and canine din. They stepped over the sleeping gun dog, skirted a job-lot of polo sticks and dusty hickory golf clubs and entered a large square hall almost full of hearty people. A tall shabby middle-aged woman spotted them and came across.

'If it's the tent poles, bring them around the back and drop them near the hayshed. Thank you. Gerry's in the yard. He'll look after you. Oh Maud, I must talk to you about some Muscovy ducks.'

She turned her back on them before they could say a word and was deep in conversation with another weathered-looking female. Sheila and Milo spotted a table with some drinks and ignoring the previous directions went to collect a drink.

'Sheila,' said the maid behind the drinks table, 'what are you doing here?'

Sheila laughed at the girl's astonishment. She had been to school with the girl, who not academically bright, had left half-way and found a job cooking at Kilnacrann. Sheila made her even more astonished by introducing her to Milo and they chatted happily until the tall middle-aged woman came up behind them with an exclamation of, 'What on earth?'

Milo explained to her that they weren't with the lorry carrying the tent poles but instead had been asked to drinks.

'My name's Kilbeggan,' he said, 'and this is Sheila Kelly.'

Penelope Baring-Brown let out a shout of, 'Good heavens. How nice to see you. Come along. There's lots of people who'd love to meet you and Ginny has kept a splendid pup for you. Mummy, here's Milo Kilbeggan.'

She hurried Milo away through a throng of people, leaving Sheila ignored in a corner. Milo was introduced to a bewildering number of people, many of them retired military men who had reached the rank of colonel and stuck. Their faded wives showed a gleam of interest at the sudden appearance of the handsome young earl and made him promise to come and lunch with them whenever Emma or Brigid or Lavinia or Sophie or Sonia was home. Almost all had nostalgic memories of his family and Milo realized that his ancestors had held a distinct social presence in the county and that an invitation to Kilbeggan Castle had once been highly desirable. The famous novelist, now a local squire, was rather more aloof. The Metcalfes were most friendly, having got over their embarrassment at the car boot loaded with plants. Two elderly men who lived together were discussing cooking with some friends, but were very interested at being introduced to Milo.

'Do come over some night and eat with us,' they said.

A dowager lady, widow of a famous baronet, was extraordinarily languid and distant. Penelope kept him to herself for a moment.

'I must tell you about Di and Ginny. They've hardly got a bean, they're so poor, so they make a few bob from their breeding. But no matter how poor they are, they wouldn't let a pup go to a bad home. So I'm delighted that you're buying one of their pups. Clare often covers for them and they really are splendid ratters. Great fighters too. If you have tinkers driving into the yard, they won't get out of their vans while the terriers are out. Do have another drink while I catch Di and bring her over.'

Milo had a moment to recover his equilibrium and try to find Sheila. He found her near a doorway talking to a vet whose voice rose steadily the more drink he consumed.

'I warned your father about that mare,' he was saying, 'once a crib biter, always a crib biter. The foals always pick it up.'

Sheila was relieved to be diverted. Milo steered her away but was borne down on by Ginny and Di. Although they looked half-starved and shrivelled, their voices were strong and kept trying to eclipse each other. They were so glad he wanted a terrier. They would have a splendid little dog ready in a few weeks, beautifully marked and with a most amusing trick with an ear. Very like the father. Did he know Tiggy's terriers? Well, they weren't the same line but Di felt there was just a tiny tiny hint of Tiggy's breeding, some time in the past. He was to realize that this was a working breed, none of your Cruft-type champions. They laughed heartily at the idea. No, they liked their terriers to work for their living. They would bolt anything, were quite fearless and would take on something three times their size. They hadn't had a rat in Kilsallagh for years. So nice to get him into a nice home. They wouldn't let a terrier go to anywhere near a main road – far too dangerous with the milk lorries and every young brat of a boy seemed to have a car nowadays. Where did they get the money from? Then some people locked up their terriers. You couldn't expect a dog shut up all day to have any character or energy. So they wouldn't let a terrier go to the wrong sort of people. They were sure Milo would know what they meant. Milo and Sheila stood overwhelmed by the torrent of words. Behind them, the vet was beginning to swear enjoyably, as his visits to the drinks table increased. Penelope was whispering to the girl at the drinks table to tidy away the whiskey bottles and some of the guests were leaving. Many of the guests repeated their invitations to Milo while ignoring Sheila pointedly. Mrs Metcalfe, who had an unerring social instinct, wondered what Sheila was doing at Kilnacrann; perhaps she was helping Penelope out. The member of the famous brewing family gathered his various children together. Milo and Sheila left, followed by curious glances.

As they drew nearer the racecourse, traffic began to slow down and a steady procession developed. 'No Parking' signs appeared on the ditches. Programme sellers began to assault the racegoers. The stylish Porsche was, as always, a focus of admiration. The car which was commonplace in Knightsbridge was a rarity in the Irish countryside. Landrovers and Range Rovers were almost the trademarks of the wealthy farmers and Milo reflected on how incongruous his Porsche was on potholed roads and now on muddy fields where the car parks lay. 'Going soft' was the official description of the track that day. It also applied to the car park. They skirted the muddy patches of field and made their way up to the racecourse enclosure.

A very warm welcome awaited Milo when he presented himself to the honorary secretary. He was introduced right left and centre to various important people, many of whom were known to Sheila.

'Well, it's great to see a Kilbeggan again at the Kilbeggan Races,' said the chairman, a local auctioneer. 'Your whole family knew this little track. The old lord suggested several improvements to us and Lady Cynthia came to every meeting. We'll be very grateful if you'll present the cup that your uncle gave for this meeting. It goes to the winner of the second race, the Viscount Kilcock Maiden Hurdle. Come and have a drink and meet some of the committee.'

Milo had to keep refusing offers of drinks pressed on him by the good-natured crowd or he would not have remained sober. The course was small and the attendance large, with a higher proportion of genuinely horsy people than was usual at English race meetings which often tended to be social events where faces were posed for pictures in *Harpers and Queen*. The first race was also a Maiden Hurdle – the Brusna Maiden Hurdle of £3,250, of which the second was to receive £552.50, the third £260 and the fourth £165.50. This was a hurdle race for five-year-olds only, maidens at starting; the distance, two miles and about three furlongs. The Bridge House, Tullamore, was to present a champagne dinner for two to the winning owner. A fair number of the entries were owned by ordinary racing people, farmers with a horse or two, and were ridden by members of the family. But Milo noticed quite a few entries from the big names in Irish racing: A.L.T. Moore, Michael Cunningham, Francis Flood, Christy Kinnane and other prominent trainers. The racecard gave descriptions under each entry. Some descriptions were quirky, some less than complimentary. One filly was described as 'promising and improving, could be in the shake-up'. Another, a gelding, had 'tailed off at Clonmel. Nothing worth considering in recent form.' Another gelding had, 'not a lot to recommend this gelding, although the stable can be dangerous at times'. Although over twenty horses were on the card only fifteen entered the ring. There are no starting stalls at this course as flat-racing was abandoned here some years ago. There are two fairly sharp bends on the course possibly not very suitable for flat-racing. But jump-racing attracts big crowds and the Kilbeggan course has thrived. After some difficulty getting the runners into line, the starter's flag was raised and they were off. After a fairly fast first round of the course, there were a clear five horses well ahead of the field. Passing the stand, a chestnut filly from a distinguished stable had established a sound lead. It maintained the lead with no difficulty and ran uphill to the finishing post amid cheers from the large number who had backed it.

The second race was the Kilcock Maiden Hurdle. This race was for six-year-olds and upwards, maidens at starting

93

which had run at least three times over hurdles and had not been placed second or third in a hurdle race. The value to the winner was £2,245 together with the Silver Challenge Cup presented by the fourth Viscount Kilcock, who had also presented a fund to provide a replica each year to the winning owner.

'We are delighted to have with us,' the announcer informed the crowd, 'the great nephew of Lord Kilcock who has come here to present his relation's prize. Lord Kilbeggan has inherited Kilbeggan Castle and we are honoured to have him here as we were delighted to see so many members of his family throughout the years.'

Sheila nudged Milo and enjoyed his discomfiture over the publicity.

'I hope my little maiden will behave herself,' he whispered to her as they ascended the stand to watch the race.

This race seemed to attract even more of the family combinations where the owner was also the trainer and a son or nephew rode the horse. Most interest centred in the mount of a very well-known jockey who had entered the winner's enclosure on some very celebrated runners. The bookies seemed nonplussed by the fame of the rider and the poor record of the horse. The starter got them away easily this time but there was a crashing fall at the first fence which sorted out the runners. The large field separated into three different groups with the leaders going well out in front. Coming up in front of the stand, a dark mare owned by Mrs McCarren of Cavan, was clear of the field and was followed by three fast horses which were almost neck and neck. Once again the crowd was enthusiastic. There was a lot of money on the McCarren horse.

'Come on, you beauty.' 'Can she keep it up?' 'She's tiring.'

Shouts echoed around the stand as they rounded the final corner and raced up the hill for home. The dark mare, tiring up the last stretch, just held her speed to win by a head from the pair behind her. A photo finish was needed to decide which was second and third.

94

'Winner all right,' came through the microphone and it was announced again that the Earl of Kilbeggan would present his grand-uncle's Silver Challenge Cup to the winner of the Kilcock Maiden Hurdle. Backers applauded enthusiastically. Milo and Sheila made their way down and were led by committee members to the winner's enclosure. The attractive young owner accompanied by her husband, who had trained the winner, was delighted by her success. Milo had to present the cup three times as photographers from local papers and *The Irish Field* wanted to project a human interest story. 'Young Peer Presents Uncle's Trophy.'

The winners told Milo that it was always nice to win a race but they had always admired the Kilcock trophy and were delighted to have it for the year. They asked Milo to come and have dinner with them at Lough Sheelin. Milo found himself being introduced to dozens of people. He was escorted by the captain, a member of the committee, who rescued him and brought him away from the crowd.

'Here's a young chap who wants to meet you,' said the captain. Milo turned to find a thin young man with a pale rather pained face. He was leaning on crutches and forced a smile as if he found it difficult. 'This is Ted Fitzpatrick,' said the captain, introducing him, 'famous son of a famous father.'

Although not a racing fan, Milo had heard a lot of this celebrated racing family. Ted Fitzpatrick, the father, had won almost any race worth winning in Britain or Ireland. There was almost a psychic partnership between himself and any horse he rode. Falls he had in plenty, for none can avoid them who work in this riskiest of professions. But he had now retired to train and his son Ted had taken on the jockey's role. As brilliant and instinctive a rider as his father, he had soon achieved almost equal success and trainers and owners kept looking for his services. Like his father, he had little need of the whip; horses seemed to want to win when Fitzpatrick was aboard. He was one of the few to ride between the two outriders in hunting pink after victory in the Cheltenham Gold Cup. But he had met disaster at the same course. When you reach the final fence at Cheltenham the course narrows and you enter a noisy distracting and uphill straight. In the Coral Handicap Hurdle, Ted, with a clear lead, had taken a crashing fall. His mount had risen quickly to his feet, but Ted was unable to stir and even after the thundering hooves had avoided him and gone on, he lay with leg useless on the ground. The orthopaedic surgeons had seen shattered knees before, but when Ted had reached the local hospital, he was X-rayed twice before they told his family the bad news. It would take months, perhaps longer, before any normal exercise could be resumed. Repeated surgery was followed by repeated physiotherapy. The best treatment, the most expensive treatment was procured, yet six months later he was still unable to walk. Painful sessions of physiotherapy produced little change. Discomfort was constant and a bright and happy young man was sunk in frustration and a feeling of failure. Once flushed with success, he had now literally bitten the dust. He was reduced to hobbling around on crutches, giving advice to jockeys, to whom he had once shown a clean pair of heels.

'I wonder if I could have a word with you. Come over to my car; it's right behind the tent.'

Milo followed the stricken jockey behind the bar tent and into a Subaru Legacy which Ted had been allowed to bring close to the ring. Milo hoped that the jockey was not developing a new interest in herbaceous borders and was about to spring a request for some blue phlox or a root of tropaelium. But the request was much more serious.

'Look,' said Ted, 'I hear them all whispering that I'll never ride out again. At the moment I'd nearly agree with that. I can't bend the knee without getting into agony and it's getting worse instead of better as time goes on. I can tell you I don't sleep at night. Even the pain can be banished with painkillers but the depression is harder to avoid. You've heard of the Black Dog – that's what Churchill called his attacks of depression. Well, the Black Dog sits on my shoulders all around the clock. I'd try anything to help cure my problem. That's why I'm talking to you now. They say that Seamus Kelly is on the mend after you laid hands on him. I often heard my granny talk of the Kilbeggan touch. Look, for pity's sake, if you can do anything at all to relieve me I'd be very very grateful. You must know yourself. If it's all a gimmick, just tell me and leave me be. But if you think you have any power in you that might help me, please give it a try.'

The young man sat back miserable and dejected, slunk in the car seat. Milo considered the request in silence for a minute and at last gave a reluctant answer.

'Look,' he said, 'this cure thing has been sprung on me in the last few weeks. I never dreamt that I might have some influence or power that would be useful to others. It's like being able to dowse for water like a water-diviner – you might never know you had the power until you tried it out. I'm still not sure that I have any gift like that although it seems to have worked for Seamus. Certainly I know my family had the gift and used it. I've found papers that suggest that they helped people through the centuries. Now I still have little confidence in myself. I have doubts about my ability. But if there's anything I can do to help you, I'll do it. Come over and see me tomorrow and we'll both of us hope that it will be successful. But please don't place too much hope or reliance on me. It would hurt me a lot if I plunged you into more depression.'

Ted's face had already brightened. He was already buoyed up by the raised expectation.

'I'll be there with you tomorrow morning,' he said, 'would ten o'clock suit you? We're staying overnight and looking at a horse tomorrow morning before heading back to Tipperary. Just give me the directions and I'll see you sharp at ten.'

Milo gave him the directions and said he'd expect him at ten. He left the young jockey in his car and strolled back to meet Sheila who was chatting with a crowd of young friends including Brigid Horan and her boyfriend, Bobby Boyle. They later piled into their cars and promised to see each other at a pub in Tyrell's Pass, which was the great meeting-

97

place for that set. But Sheila and Milo excused themselves. It had been a long day and she wanted to be home to 'keep an eye' on the old pair. So, they finished the evening describing their day to the old pair. They delighted Mrs Kelly with their descriptions of the two Misses Black and their quick sale of a terrier to this 'very suitable' person.

14

Next morning early, Milo was in energetic form. He rose early and was on the main avenue by seven o'clock armed with scythe, saw and shears. Summer growth was making the avenue hard to traverse and low branches, especially on rainy days, scraped the roof and sides of a car. Milo had almost lost a wing mirror on his return from the Kellys so savage pruning was called for. Despite his towny appearance, Milo was fit and had little bother clearing both sides of the avenue for several hundred yards. He discovered little surprises. Between two wild azalea bushes, his shears struck stone. He clipped more carefully and uncovered a Roman god whose limestone beard was almost hidden by a green moss. Feeling deductive, he crossed the avenue and soon uncovered a mate for the woodland god. Ivy had hidden a stone goddess whom he released from her long exile. Now unveiled, her classical eyes stared across at her lost mate. He uncovered a woodland path which led he knew not where. Down near the bridge behind a green tapestry of creeper stood a grotto with a marble basin. An inscription was covered in moss. Above it was carved grotesque stonework in the form of stalactites. Across the avenue, he found a great rusty iron seat which he cut free from its entangling briars and creepers. It stood on a green mound where elders had obscured it for countless years. Its tall crested back held an earl's coronet in the centre. Milo felt that he had earned his breakfast by now and trudged back to the castle, kicking the cut briars into the side as he went along. This discovery of added possession gave him a feeling of satisfaction and an appetite for his breakfast.

He had acquired the bad habit of reading over his breakfast. Now as he went through yesterday's *Times*, the cheapest paper in the country, he switched a page and saw advertisements headed, 'Porsche Wanted'. He read with interest –

30,000 miles or under
Best prices paid for all Low Mileage
Porsches with full service history.
Collect anywhere.

and another more specific –

Wanted Carrera 911 sports coupé 1988 upwards. Must have air conditioning, full electric seats, Porsche remote alarm, FPSH Porsche warranty. Up to 35,000 miles. £25,000 offered for exceptional condition car.

Garage after garage (from London to Glenvarigill) was offering good prices. Milo felt justified now in saving up for his one extravagance. As he finished his breakfast he heard the crunch of a car on the gravel below the massive walls. Looking down, he saw the lame figure of the crippled jockey limping across to the steps. There Ted halted, waiting for his father. Milo ran down the great staircase. This was one difficulty which now seemed very obvious but had not struck him when he had invited the young man over. All the living rooms of the castle had to be ascended to. The grand flight of steps rising to the hall door presented huge difficulties to the lame or the crippled.

'Hold on there, Ted,' he called out.

They held a council at the base of the steps. Eventually Milo took one side of the jockey; his father took the other. Together they lifted the pale young man up the steps. He gingerly crossed the threshold, afraid that his crutches would slide on the flagstones of the hall. Milo called Mrs Neligan and asked her to show Mr Fitzpatrick into the library and to bring him some coffee.

'You and I, Ted,' he said, 'will go into the small sitting room here and see what we can do.'

100

He led the jockey into the adjoining room, where he sank onto an ancient chaise longue. Milo, who was about to joke rather defensively about his pretence of a cure, was silenced by the look of tension on Ted's face. This was no cause of frivolity to the young man. He would have found it hard to summon up a ghost of a smile, such was his dejection and his constant physical pain.

'For God's sake, do your best,' he muttered.

Milo helped the jockey remove his sweater and T-shirt. The next part was more difficult. He pulled Ted's cords gently down over the crippled knee and at last slipped them over the ankles and hung them on a chair. The jockey, like his fellows, showed the physical effects of competitive riding. The collar bone had been broken twice, various bones dislocated, muscles pulled and torn, blood vessels bruised and injured. Milo marvelled at the courage of jockeys and eventers, of show jumpers and hunter trialists. They really paid for what they got out of the sport. From steeplechase to the flat, the risks were enormous. Yet many young men (and women too), craved for the satisfactions that riding brought them. Milo tried to remember the order in which he should lay hands. The six specified areas were neck, chest and elbow followed by knee, leg and buttock.

'*Vinceo quem tango,*' he thought and laid his hands gently on the back of the young man's neck. The patient lay staring with a helpless look. Milo left the neck and went on to the thin chest. His hands manipulated the frame and then felt the elbows which he massaged with care. Next came the lower part of the body. He placed both hands sensitively on the injured knee and immediately the jockey shuddered at the touch. Milo let his hands linger on the knee and felt a spasm of pain or anxiety pass through the suffering youth. Milo left the knee and rubbed the jockey's legs. With immense care, he helped Ted turn on his side and he massaged the lean buttocks. But he returned to the knee, laying his hands again on it, and now he himself felt an acute sense of weariness, almost of distress, as he felt the tormented body of the jockey.

101

Once again he began to pray without meaning to – 'The Heavens declare the glory of God and the firmament showeth His handywork. If Thou, O Lord, wilt mark our iniquities, O Lord, who shall bear it?'

Half-remembered verses and prayers went through his mind and the Lord's Prayer was repeated. A great feeling of pressure and tiredness came over him and nearly overcame him. He removed his hand from the youth's knee and looking down saw with amazement that Ted was sleeping peacefully, had forgotten all about him. He rose and found two rugs which he placed over the sleeping jockey. He tiptoed out the door and climbed shakily up the stairs to the library. Half-way up the staircase he had to stop as a fit of trembling seized him. He clung to the railings and waited until it subsided before he restarted the ascent. When he opened the library door, Mr Fitzpatrick looked up at him in amazement. He was pale and unwell looking.

'What has happened?' said the trainer. 'Is Ted all right?'

Milo explained that Ted was asleep down below and the father could hardly believe it.

'He hasn't slept soundly for months,' he said. 'I must go down and check that he's all right.'

He left the room and Milo sat down thankfully and drank some coffee. After a short while, the trainer came back looking jubilant.

'I didn't disturb him' he said. 'I haven't seen him look so peaceful and undisturbed for months. Let's leave him where he is for a while. It can do him nothing but good. What an extraordinary effect you have had on him. The illness seems to have passed from him to you,' he continued, looking at Milo with concern.

But Milo was recovering, although puzzled by the effect the weakness had had on him. He remembered the same effect happening to Seamus, where the young man had fallen into a deep sleep. They chatted together for a long while and the trainer expressed sympathy with Milo on the burden which the possession of a huge castle imposed on him.

'Our own place is pretty big,' he said, 'and I'm perpetually replacing loose slates. Every time the roofer goes up, he tells me that I should be doing a major job, that the lathes are rotten and we need a new roof. I tell him I'm not a millionaire and to do his best. Last year we found a lot of wet rot in a bedroom and they warned me to have it tackled or it would cost me dearly later. But I look at it this way – I'll be dead and gone and the house will still be standing. It's the cursed rain that does all the damage in this country, from ruining race meetings to making houses damp. If I was you, I'd just do the essential repairs. I've known friends who've put new central heating systems into old houses and before they knew where they were the furniture was cracking and flowers appearing on the plaster.'

It was nearly lunchtime before the trainer stopped his sermon on the vagaries of old houses. He suddenly looked at his watch and rose from the chair. He took two £50 notes from his pocket and pushed them at Milo.

'Get a load of gravel with this and fill in some of the potholes on your avenue,' he instructed Milo who had tried vainly to resist taking the money.

They descended the staircase and went to awake the sleeping jockey. Young Ted lay where Milo had left him. Colour had returned to his cheeks and he slept easily like a child. It was a deep sleep and they found it difficult to rouse him. Mr Fitzpatrick had a sudden thought.

'Could I leave him with you until tomorrow?' he asked Milo. 'We'll be sending up the horsebox tomorrow with a mare for Russelstown – that's close to Mullingar. Ted could be collected on their way back. It seems a great pity to disturb him now when he's sleeping properly for the first time in months. I'll settle with you of course and if this is a permanent cure, you can ask what you want.'

Milo agreed to the proposal and asked Mrs Neligan to keep an eye on the sleeping jockey while he saw Mr Fitzpatrick to his car. He then rang Sheila and asked her to drive over. 'As well,' he thought, to have a nurse to back him up. He then settled down with some paperwork in the sitting room, while the young Fitzpatrick continued in deep slumber.

'Wisha the poor lad,' said Mrs Neligan softly as she brought a tray of lunch for Milo. 'I saw him on the television once after some famous race and he was talking to the Queen Mother as if she was his own mother. What a pity to see him afflicted like this, but shure maybe your treatment will do him good. I remember the days when there would be a queue of people lining up and the yard full of cars. They were all hoping your uncle would lay his hands on them. There were times when his lordship grew weary with them. Many's the time he would say to me. "Mrs Neligan," he would say, "I'll have to employ an assistant." That was his sense of humour. Then there was a crowd that would take advantage of him – coming day after day when it wasn't necessary. Those Maguires from the bog would be running across with a cut finger or a toothache. It made his lordship so sour that he eventually nearly gave it up. But he had a good heart and did his best for people. Now should we wake the young gentleman to give him some lunch or should we leave him be?'

Milo was loath to disturb young Ted and Mrs Neligan left a plate of cold meat and salad in case the jockey woke up.

Sheila arrived and kept him company. She took Ted's temperature and declared it normal, felt his pulse and gave it the same verdict. They sat whispering together, coming closer together on a small sofa until the proximity made Milo's temperature rise to an abnormal level. He again called Mrs Neligan to keep an eye on the sleeping jockey while he told her that he would show Miss Kelly some books in the library. They filed formally and singly out of the room and ascended to the library but walked straight through this room and ran almost childishly to the top landing where they dashed into Milo's bedroom. Patience was forgotten and clothes soon lay in untidy carelessness on the floor. The two young bodies gratefully offered feel and touch. Sighs of contentment soon came from the huge bed. Guilt was missing. There was no feeling of awkwardness. As before, it

104

seemed to be a natural event, a loving and gracious congress, the healthiest of all unions. One must not intrude on the privacy of intimate moments. Phrases like 'the earth trembled' are vulgarisms to describe such physical bliss. Music can echo such moments but is really inadequate to convey such profound sexual ecstasy. But it is not merely sexual, otherwise any stray encounter would offer equal rewards. This was a personal triumph, the summit of such achievements. Many who desire such moments rarely achieve them. So the play *Romeo and Juliet* appeals in a special way even to those who have never attained such closeness; they get a vicarious satisfaction which life has not afforded them. Milo and Sheila lay together, longing for an eternity of such happiness. They felt wrapt in blessings and goodness. How long they lay together was forgotten until both of them recalled the wounded jockey left in their charge. Reluctantly they disentangled from each other. They descended the staircase and tried to conceal their glow of happiness as they entered the library where Mrs Neligan pretended not to notice their obvious enchantment with each other.

'Well, Miss Kelly,' she said, 'you'd know better than me but the young gentleman seems to be enjoying a very healthy sleep. Not a sound out of him. I've put on another rug to keep him warm but should we not wake him up to give him some food. He must be starving, poor soul. What do you think, Miss Kelly?'

'If you'd make some scrambled eggs, Mrs Neligan, and some toast, we can wake him up and then let him sleep again. Milo tells me that you make superb scrambled eggs.'

'Who?' asked Mrs Neligan. 'Oh, it's Lord Kilbeggan you mean. Yes, his lordship enjoys his scrambled eggs. Well, I'll go below and see what I can do.'

With that she left the room. Milo had enjoyed the housekeeper's little snub to Sheila.

'Yes, we aristocrats enjoy our scrambled eggs. My lordship often indulges in a dish. Indeed my lordship wouldn't mind a little refreshment after pleasuring Miss Kelly in my lordship's bed.'

105

Sheila threw a cushion at him and only the thought of Mrs Neligan's return prevented a spot of argy-bargy in the library. They found it hard to awaken Ted from his deep sleep and eventually he opened his eyes and looked around with surprise at the ancient library, heavy with books and portraits and the flushed young couple watching him. Then he remembered what had happened.

'The pain has gone,' he said, 'even if it's for the moment. How long have I been asleep?'

He looked out the window at the gathering dusk. They explained that they hoped that he would stay the night. Mrs Neligan came in carrying a wooden tray full of wholesome food. Ted almost wolfed the heap of scrambled eggs and toast.

'I haven't eaten properly for months,' he explained, 'nor slept either. It's hard to do either when you're in constant pain. This is the first relaxation I've felt, apart from filling myself with sedatives and somehow only extreme pain drove me down that road. You wouldn't do me a favour? If you've got a transistor could you let me have it for the race results. The brother's riding at Clonmel today.'

He sat up contentedly with a cup of tea in his hands.

Sheila started to organize things in a business-like way. She got Milo to bring down a spare pair of pyjamas and she helped the young jockey into them and examined the knee while she did so.

'That looks quite healthy,' she said, 'now comes the moment of truth. See if you can rise and try to walk, using your crutches if you like.'

Ted swung slowly off the sofa and placed his legs gingerly on the floor. He arose and took a few faltering steps.

'It's still very stiff,' he reported, 'but that damnable pain has gone.'

Milo escorted him across the hall to the gunroom which had a lavatory off it. They heard him return across the flagstones and watched him enter the library, still walking gingerly but without strain or suffering.

'I'm off the rack,' he said with delight. 'How long will it last?'

He eased himself onto the chaise longue and they covered him with rugs to keep him warm.

'Your father or somebody is coming to collect you in the morning,' said Milo.

'Would you do the same for me again before they come?' asked Ted.

Mrs Neligan who had come to collect the tray intervened.

'It often took three or four visits to the old lord before difficult patients were fully healed. I'm not suggesting that your lordship hasn't got an equal gift. But it might be no harm if Mr Fitzpatrick visited you again to make sure the cure is complete. I hope you won't think me interfering.'

With that she left the room. Milo winked at Ted.

'Whatever you think,' he said, 'let's see how you are in the morning.'

Milo and Shelia left him happily fiddling with a transistor, and they chatted to each other on the steps.

'Seamus is able for the milking again. That's at least one success you've had. If Ted recovers satisfactorily, you'll find half the country in on top of you. I shouldn't be encouraging you. We nurses are not supposed to believe in alternative medicine. Despite that, I know some of the surgeons do – they'd nearly sneak off to a quack if they got a bad back themselves. See you in the morning.'

Reluctantly they parted and she drove back to Drumlerry.

15

Next morning saw Milo out again on his front avenue where the work of civilizing the drive continued. He used the saw on the heavier branches which had impeded traffic. The lighter laurels and rhododendrons yielded to a slash hook. He found the entrances to several hidden paths which in the old days had led to green vistas and secret places. On several occasions he blunted the blade of the slash hook as it encountered stone ornaments under a green canopy. Again he found that the ornaments came in pairs. The first of his encounters was with a stone wolf. When he had stripped the creepers and weeds from around its handsome but scowling features he crossed the avenue and encountered its fellow smothered by brambles on the far side. He recalled to mind the wolves on the coat of arms and wondered if the hand they enclosed referred to the Healer's hand. By nine o'clock he was nearly down to the front gates and glowing with the exercise. He picked up his tools and walked up the now wider avenue to the castle. A figure stood in the sun at the entrance to the castle and he saw to his surprise that it was Ted Fitzpatrick grinning from the steps. The smile told the story. Pain had left the young jockey and the relief appeared on his face.

'I still need the crutches,' he shouted, 'but I feel infinitely better.'

He hobbled inside ahead of Milo and they had breakfast together. Ted gobbled down a second helping of bacon and egg to Mrs Neligan's satisfaction and chatted away without strain. He offered Milo several racing tips which were to bring him good fortune later on. They discussed the world of racing which Milo learned was not quite so straightforward a business as the outsider might expect. It was a

108

world which the jockeys took very much for granted but which presented occasional coups and happenings that in ordinary business life might appear to be fraudulent. The risks both personal and financial seemed huge. Milo was left wondering why anybody ever bought a racehorse. After breakfast, at Ted's request, he brought him into the library where a second time he stripped shirt and trousers from the jockey and laid hands upon the six parts of the body. Was it imagination or did the young body seem healthier and less wounded? When he reached the wounded knee, there was no shudder this time at his touch. Indeed the jockey seemed to have little reaction to the touch, although once again Milo felt a sense of tiredness himself, even of loss, as he massaged the lean limbs. This time Ted did not fall asleep but rose happily from the sofa, while Milo sat down wearily.

'Now I'll ask you for a razor,' said Ted, 'and I'll be able to get back to work when they call for me.'

He shuffled across to the washroom beside the gunroom and came out later beaming with pride at having done everything for himself.

'Now before I go,' he said, 'I want to settle several things. You've set me well on the road to recovery but I'll not feel confident unless I can contact you if I'm in difficulty again. You may not want to feel bound in that way, but I would be very grateful if you'd oblige me. As regards money, I don't mind telling you that I've made a lot of cash in the last few years and not much of it has appeared for the taxman. I'll be glad to pay you a retainer – name your price – if I could feel free to come to you when I'm in trouble. I've no cheque book with me now, but you'll get a cheque from me in the next few days. Are you willing?'

Milo tried to explain that he had some difficulties himself and might have to sell the castle.

'Look,' said Ted, 'forget about that. There's myself and a few of my friends like me who might make you reconsider. Is that my driver outside?'

They heard the crunch of Landrover and horsebox on the gravel below them.

'Goodbye,' said Ted, 'and remember what I've said. I'm very very grateful to you. Would you throw this tenner to Mrs Neligan for me?'

With that he manipulated his way down the steps and was in the Landrover, waving as he left.

Milo went back inside. He rang Harton's, the gravel suppliers, asking them to send a load of small aggregate for the avenue. Mrs Neligan brought up the letters which the postman had just delivered. She was delighted with the tenner. The first letter Milo opened was a rather cross letter from P.J. Fogarty asking for a prompt reply to his offer for the property. Mr Fogarty was surprised and disappointed that he had received no communication from Lord Kilbeggan. There was a hint of a suggestion that an 'improved' offer might be available if a quick reply was received. The second envelope which he opened contained a curious message. It had been posted from Carrick-on-Shannon and contained the words, 'Might be nearer to you than you expect. Maybe we might get together again.' It was signed simply "P". It didn't take Milo too long to connect Packy Neligan to the "P" in the message and it was not a pleasant sensation for him. He decided to inform the inspector about the cryptic message. A third letter was from the Black sisters. They were keeping a sweet little dog for Lord Kilbeggan and hoped to bring it over to him in three weeks' time. A small premium of £100 would pay for the terrier. They were so pleased the dog was going to such a good home. A fourth letter informed him that Penelope Baring-Brown was running a sale for the hunt and she would be grateful if he could gather together some stuff for the sale. Small pieces of furniture, pictures, bric-a-brac, old plates, ornaments, plants etc. would be most welcome. She would call to collect them and could help Milo select a few items for the sale when she called. His aunt had been such a great supporter and of course anything that came from the castle went for 'silly prices'. Indeed even members of the committee were quite keen and often bought nice items before the sale. Another letter was from somebody called Rory Vaughan with an address in Navan, Co. Meath. The gist of it was that he had received cracked ribs in a provincial rugby match. He was a cattle dealer and the cracked ribs were causing him irritation and pain. He'd heard from some friends that Milo had healing powers but could not find his name or number in the telephone directory. He asked if Milo could contact him by phone and arrange an appointment. He would come over straight away if Milo could see him.

On his way out of the castle he encountered the old butler making a rare appearance above stairs.

'Could I disturb your lordship for a moment?' Maybe we could sit down inside for a moment. I just happened to see your lordship's letters when the postman delivered them this morning. If I'm not mistaken, my son's writing was on one of them. I'm very anxious, indeed so is Mrs Neligan, that he gets into no more trouble. He's had us heart-scalded for years and it's not doing herself any good. Could I ask your lordship to use your influence if anything can be done to change his ways. Was there any information in that letter of his? If so, we'd like to know. I hope you won't think me too pushy or offensive in asking your lordship's help.'

Milo did not know how to reply to him. The slightly sinister card suggested that Packy might be arriving in the neighbourhood.

'Just a card,' he said to old Neligan, 'he seems to be in Carrick-on-Shannon.'

'Well, I hope he stays there,' said the old butler sourly. 'We had high hopes for him once that he might rise in the world. Mrs Neligan was delighted when he went to college. But he seemed to get in with a crowd of foreigners, Dutch people who had rented a boat on the Shannon. They seemed to like him, always throwing their arms around him the way foreigners do, but I believe they started him on the drugs – he began to smoke those funny cigarettes. But I'll not hold up your lordship. We just hoped that you might be able to do something. I believe the avenue looks great – more power to your elbow,' and with this final irrelevance he walked stiffly away.

111

Milo arrived in Drumlerry to find all four of the family having a cup of tea in the warm kitchen. Seamus was almost his old self – strong and happy looking. Milo told them about the letter from Rory Vaughan and the old couple was very interested.

'Begod, you're attracting the right ones now,' Mr Kelly told Milo. 'Young Vaughan is one of the biggest names in the cattle trade. I'm surprised you haven't heard of him. There was a bit of scandal concerning the father a while ago – the newspapers were putting it about that he was getting preferential treatment about export licences and how friendly he was with some government ministers.'

Mrs Kelly interrupted him.

'Ah, Daddy, don't be repeating such scandalous talk. Those Vaughans always had money. Isn't his mother one of the Dalys of Clandelver and didn't they always have money running out their ears? A great wedding that was. I remember the photographs in *The Independent*. They had a sister joined the nuns. She was mother superior in Clonmellon for years, a very stylish lady she was – could have had her choice of some fine men.'

Sheila winked at Milo as the flood of information continued.

'Ring him up in any event,' said Mr Kelly. 'If you're going in for this healing business, you couldn't get a more important customer. Certainly the job you've done with Seamus is remarkable and everybody around here is singing your praises. It's amazing how the news has spread. I was getting the hair cut the other day in Mullingar, the only place you can still find a decent old-fashioned barber, and they were telling a lot of exaggerated stories about you.'

'Daddy won't go into one of these new unisex hairdressers,' said Mrs Kelly, 'and I can't say that I blame him. Somehow it seems unnatural. This sex thing is getting out of hand.'

Sheila gave a huge wink at Milo and Seamus laughed.

'Well, you're the old-fashioned pair. Wait 'til we get one

of these new women priests on the altar on Sunday. That'll settle you.'

'Never,' said Mrs Kelly vehemently. 'That's the day I'll leave the church. If God had wanted women priests, the twelve apostles would all be feminine. I never heard such nonsense. It's a sad state of affairs when women are trying to become men and some people are encouraging them. Indeed, I know some not a thousand miles from here,' she finished with indignation.

Milo told them about the letter from Mr Fogarty.

'Keep him on the hook,' said Mr Kelly. 'If he wants it that badly, he'll wait. I may tell you that he's not renowned at paying up quickly. We kept a pony for a daughter of his, gave it grass for months and it was a devil trying to extract a few shillings from him. In the meantime, if you can work up a business in the healing line, all the better for you. Go and ring Rory Vaughan now.'

'Mr Vaughan's secretary,' said a sensual voice at the number he had been given. 'Mr Vaughan is at a meeting. He's unavailable. Who did you say is speaking? Oh, Lord Kilbeggan. I beg your pardon. I thought you said Myles something. Mr Vaughan said to put you through immediately. Just hold on please. Mr Vaughan, it's Lord Kilbeggan. You're through now. Go ahead.'

A deep voice greeted Milo. They agreed to meet at the castle at five o'clock that evening.

'It couldn't come too soon for me.'

Milo felt that life was getting faster. He asked Sheila to return with him. By this time Mr and Mrs Kelly were well aware of the strange mutual attraction between the pleasant young lord and their daughter.

'Behave yourselves now,' said Mrs Kelly but there was a twinkle in her eye and she was almost hoping that something would emerge from the liaison.

When the young couple arrived at the avenue gates, they were held up by a huge lorry carrying gravel which lurched slowly up the avenue ahead of them. As it slowed uncertainly near the yard Milo asked them if they could drop the load in three areas – at the top, middle and start of the avenue. He signed the grubby invoice and was given a receipt when he proudly paid the cost of the load in notes.

'Seamus will fill the potholes. He can bring over the tractor and transport box and we can shovel the gravel when he distributes it up and down the avenue,' said Sheila.

But Milo had other ideas for the day.

'Come and see my etchings,' he said with a leer and they set off up the steps. It became a race to reach the top of the stairs and the same inevitable result took place.

'I'll sue you for peer abuse,' he threatened her. 'We threatened minorities must not be attacked.'

They wriggled down happily between the sheets. The two bodies clung together and once more it seemed unbelievably natural and inevitable. Afterwards they lay chatting. He told her of the strange weakening effect that the use of 'the touch' produced on him, as if all strength ebbed out of him and into the person who was being helped. They agreed that it was essential that he should only see people by appointment and at the most once a day or it could have an unhealthy effect on him.

'Not only on you,' said Sheila. 'I won't be too pleased if you're not able to perform properly, because all your strength is going to others. You can save a bit for me.'

She need not have worried – the mere suggestion led him to initiate another performance which left her in no doubt about his unquestioned virility.

As they lay side by side in the great bed they both believed they heard footsteps in the corridor outside and the door shutting itself. Milo slipped on his trousers and slip-ons and went out to investigate. But there was no sign of anybody on the long corridor. When he returned, Sheila had dressed.

'Old houses are noisy places,' he told her, 'and this one is supposed to be haunted. I often heard my mother tell stories of visits here when she was a child. There was one room in the turret where lights were seen going on and off. That was in the days of oil lamps and candles. But I don't believe in any of that piffle. Electricity exposed all the ghosts

114

for what they were – imagination and superstition. If a calf knocked over a bucket in the yard or a cat jumped on a table in the drawing room, you couldn't see what it was because you couldn't switch on a light. It was all fumbling with matches and candlesticks. My mother said ghosts lost their status when the house was connected with electric power.'

Sheila was not entirely convinced.

'There are some things that are hard to explain. My uncle had a saying – "There are more things in heaven and earth, Horatio, than are dreamt of in your philosophy." I must say I'd find it difficult to sleep on my own here at night. I don't know how you do it. Every time I heard a door creak or a window rattle, I'd be feeling anxious.'

Milo hugged her with a sudden wave of feeling and they retreated down to the library.

'Was there anybody upstairs?' he asked Mrs Neligan when she came in with some tea.

'Divil the person,' she replied, 'unless it was your Lord-ship. I'm sure Miss Kelly wouldn't find her way around upstairs and I'm sure she wouldn't want to. Isn't that so, miss?'

Sheila did not reply to this inference and they dropped the subject. Shortly after they had had some tea, a large and powerful Mercedes drew up beside the Porsche outside.

'That must be Rory Vaughan,' said Sheila. 'I'll read the papers here while you see him in the sitting room.'

Milo slipped out and found Rory Vaughan admiring the slimmer racier model beside his own large car. He was a strong, broad-shouldered, athletic type of man who should have been at the height of his powers.

'Jesus,' he said, 'with the way my ribs are, I'd never get in or out of your model. I have to open my own door fully, sit facing out and gradually slide myself round to face the steering wheel. It nearly takes a surgical operation to get in and out of the car, not to talk of the lavatory or the shower.' He broke off and looked at the castle. 'That's some house you have there. I wouldn't buy your land. It would take years of fertilizing before it got right. But that is one fine house,' and he looked up at the Gothic pile with admiration. 'And you have a light on in that turret already. Electricity must be cheap around here. Or maybe it's the sun reflecting on the window.'

He stared up at the turret which stood beyond Milo's bedroom.

'Just the sun, I'm sure,' said Milo rather doubtfully, remembering the noises they had heard a while back. 'Come on in and we'll see what I can do for you.'

The strong body that lay on the sofa before him was in remarkable contrast with the thin body of the jockey that morning. Here was a powerful muscular and well-fed specimen of humanity. Strong chest, thick arm muscles, powerful torso gave evidence of a healthy lifestyle, of regular hard work and exercise, of no lack of feeding. This was a farmer, still at the height of his body powers, but plagued by injury and pain.

'I've a weakness on this side,' said Rory. 'I was nearly crushed by a mad bullock at Carnaross Market when I was about eighteen. It got me in the ribs and that's where I've been having trouble ever since. I play number eight for North Kildare, in fact their whole back row consists of cattle farmers. I was doing fine until this year. We were playing Edenderry in the first round of the Provincial Towns' Cup. I went down on a ball near our line and it felt like all sixteen forwards piled in on top of me. I couldn't breathe and felt things cracking. I was carted off to hospital. I've had endless treatment, the best of advice and specialists, but as time goes on it gets worse instead of better. They're nearly telling me now it's psychological and not physical. Well, fuck them, if they had the pain that I'm enduring, they wouldn't be telling me that it's all in the mind. I tell you how bad I am. I was trying to climb a locked gate to look at some beasts in a field near Batterstown this morning and I nearly fainted. Jesus Christ, it disgusts me to be so hopeless.'

The strong feel it the most, thought Milo, as he gazed at the frustrated and angry-looking cattle dealer. For the

116

second time that day, he started to lay hands on the six specified areas. It seemed almost ludicrous to lay hands on the strong neck and arms that lay beneath him. But he felt the chest and ribs where even the slightest pressure of his fingers produced a twitch of pain. Rory winced under him as the palm of the hands touched his ribs. The suffering was obviously tormenting him and he only relaxed when Milo passed on to the other parts of the body. Knee, leg and buttock were all massaged without any difficulty. Then Milo returned to the chest. Sweat poured through the body mass of hair as his fingers felt the sides of the young farmer. Again Milo felt fatigue setting in on himself as he gently felt the racked body under him. Flagging and almost drowsy, he kept up the treatment. Once again forgotten prayers and lines from psalms and hymns came to his mind – 'Thou shalt not be afraid of the terror of the night or the thing that walketh about in the dark,' and 'Now praise we all our God with heart and soul and voices Who wondrous things hath done in whom the world rejoices.'

Gently touching the sensitive skin, he continued and almost fell over onto the patient when tiredness overcame him. But looking down, he observed with renewed surprise that Rory was relaxed and almost asleep and rose, leaving the room to find a towel.

Sheila was sitting by the library window reading by the declining rays of the sun.

'Lord, you look desperate,' she said and held him to herself as if to protect him. 'You need a break,' she said. 'Don't see anybody for a while. Twice a day is obviously too much strain on you.'

He lay in her arms for a short while and then returned to his patient. Rory was lying still, looking relaxed and happy.

'I wouldn't believe it possible,' he said, 'but it seems to have worked. It's marvellous just to lie here without being afraid to turn sideways. Let's try upright.'

He arose a little fearfully and walked the length of the room. He sat down by the table, still apprehensive that it was only a moment's miracle. But most of the pain seemed to have gone. A huge burden had slipped off him.

'Now for the pay-off,' he said. 'I may be naive thinking this improvement is going to last. But I have a strong impression that this is not just temporary. Now I want to be able to return to you whenever I need you. You have no idea how much this is worth to me.'

He sat down and wrote a cheque for £500. Milo tried to refuse the cheque; he protested that this was a ludicrous over-payment for a few minutes' work. His protests were in vain.

'If you have got me back to a normal life where I can walk across a field without discomfort, push a yard gate without pain and go to bed with a woman with pleasure, then no money is too great for it. I'll be off now and I'm relying on you to see me quickly whenever I need you. You're my new consultant. I just hope you'll stay in the country without hopping up to Dublin or going back to London. Good luck and thanks.'

With that he took off almost jauntily, descended the steps and sat into his Mercedes without difficulty. Milo wearily climbed the steps. Sheila was preparing to go home and she advised him to get a good night's sleep to recover from his day's work. They parted again reluctantly and he went up to bed.

16

It is one of the commonest experiences of life that when you most need sleep, you find it hardest to relax and doze off. Often the mind is to blame, bringing up difficulties or guilt feelings – accusing figures that oppress the spirit. Sensitive people in particular are subject to uneasy nights. They turn on one side to escape from their imaginings only to find a new flow of thought confronting them. Alcohol, instead of relieving the situation, often deepens the anxiety. How many of us have woken up in the morning with our attention concentrated on what we might have said or done the night before? Now Milo was not one of these over-anxious people. His sleep was normally as calm and pleasing as a blameless young person should enjoy. Dreams he did have, but they were often of an agreeable kind which he was almost unwilling to relinquish in the morning. But tonight he felt strangely uneasy and the memory of the footsteps in the afternoon preyed on his mind, until tiredness prevailed and he sank almost unwillingly into sleep.

Fantasies often centre around women and hours later he was dreaming happily of Sheila and himself being in bed together. He was indulging in a happy fantasy of halcyon nights, of bodies joined together, of hands happily feeling in sensuous softness, when a most extraordinary and alarming perception jerked him awake. Still confused and unprepared, he turned over and put on the bedside lamp. Sprawled along the other half of the bed was a thin figure. The long blond hair and unshaven face revealed Packy fast asleep beside Milo. A shiver of disgust ran through Milo. He threw aside the pock-marked arm with revulsion and jumped out of the bed. A string of expletives and curses woke the young drug addict. Milo could scarcely contain himself with rage. He flung Packy out of the bed and onto the carpet where his squalid clothes were lying. Milo was not a violent man, but he felt like battering the young Neligan into the wall. He felt unclean from his physical contact with Packy.

'If this ever happens again, I'll knock your teeth out and your nose off,' he snarled. 'Now get these on and go. If I ever see you or hear of you near this house again, I won't be responsible for myself. You're a foul bastard and bring trouble wherever you go. Only for your decent parents, I'd ring the police immediately and let them know your whereabouts.'

Packy sulkily started to dress himself.

'I suppose I'm not good enough for you. Just because I won't "M' lord" you like my servile mother, you think you can look down on me. Well, I'm the one who was reared in this house. I know every room and passage, every tower and turret. They're more mine than yours. You could change every lock in the place and I'd still get in. There's passages into this castle that you'll never know about, you with your upper-class accent and show-off car. So, don't think you can look down on me with your snooty airs. I seen you with the Kelly one at the mausoleum. You're not the all-pure high almighty you pretend to be.'

'I'm not responsible for the chips on your shoulder,' said Milo, 'nor your drug taking. If you want to live in that miserable way, don't blame anybody else. There's nobody – father, mother, school or anything that's made you such a burden to yourself. It's your own miserable decision and I don't want to be part of it in any way. Now I'm offering you alternatives. I can take you to the police station or I'll drop you on the main road and you can hitch-hike back to your lousy friends. If you come near me again, I won't hesitate to shop you.'

They set off to the main road, where Milo dropped him where the sign said Galway 120 – Dublin 50. Not a word was spoken during the journey, but as Milo left him he asked for a fiver to get something to eat when he reached a transport cafe. Milo gave him £4 and drove back through the wakening countryside. A fox crossed the road ahead of him; all nature seemed bright and fresh. But not until Milo had taken a cold bath and stripped the sheets did he feel clean after the unpleasant encounter. Then between the warm blankets he fell asleep.

There Shelia found him later in the morning fast asleep.

'Up, you lazy aristocrat,' she shouted, whipping the blankets off the bed, 'and now you're not even using sheets. What's the upper class coming to? Seamus has brought the tractor and the transport box ready to shift the gravel and we've a couple of shovels for the labour force. Up you get.'

Milo stopped her flow of speech and told her how right they were in suspecting footsteps the previous afternoon. She listened astonished while he told the story of the youth in the bed.

'Not a word about it,' he told her. 'This would give such a shock to the Neligans that the old man could have a heart attack. Not to talk about the embarrassment to myself. No smoke without fire, they'd all be saying and some of the mud might stick.'

He stopped, flustered by his own mixed metaphors.

'Let's get out into the open air,' she said, 'and hope the bastard never comes back.'

They heard the sound of the tractor moving outside and soon they were working beside it, levelling off potholes and making their way gradually down the avenue. The change was astonishing. The rutted track, dark with overhanging branches, was being transformed into a wide avenue with several fine ornamental features. Trees which had been smothered and hidden by creepers and scrub rejoiced in their colour and freedom. Potholes which had nearly ruined the shock absorbers of cars were now filled and presented no menace to the driver. Milo realized that the avenue had once been planned. It had been designed, not as a straight line between the road and the castle, but as an interesting feature. You could now make out its winding nature, its vista of trees, its sudden view of the lake and then the last turn round a stand of trees where it suddenly proffered the dramatic first glance of the towering castle. The avenue was itself a work of art which had taken advantage of the natural features – water, trees, hills and hallows. By lunchtime, they were weary. Seamus got off his tractor and walked with Milo around the yard, inspecting sheds and outhouses.

'Not much use for modern farming,' he said. 'It's difficult to get big modern machinery through these narrow stone entrances.' He came up to the house and had a pint of beer in the sun on the steps before he had to go back to do his own farmwork. 'Still not a bother on me,' he said. 'Your touch seems to have done the trick.'

Milo thanked him for the help and they watched him drive down the avenue in a flurry of diesel fumes before they went inside.

'There were three phone calls while you were down the front avenue, my lord.'

Mrs Neligan had written the callers' names in a curious old-fashioned style on the telephone pad. Two of the callers were looking for help from Lord Kilbeggan. Mr Kelly had been correct; the news of his curing ability had gone the rounds like wildfire. Milo rang the numbers involved and agreed to see them on two successive days. The third call was from his solicitor. He rang Mr Kinch who told him that he was worried about the insurance aspects of the cure. There had been a spate of compensation claims on medical persons lately; he had dealt with some of them himself. Many of them involved unscrupulous people who claimed that they had been injured during a course of medical treatment. They had put in huge claims for compensation and were often successful in obtaining money.

'They have no conscience,' said Mr Kinch, 'and courts are willing to listen to them and give them the benefit of the doubt. I've seen claimants playing football a few weeks after they had claimed to be unable to walk. It's quite immoral but you can't ignore it. I would very seriously suggest that you take out insurance against such a claim. It would put your mind at ease. I have a son in insurance who could very easily look after it for you. Let me know what you decide.'

Milo consulted with Sheila who told him that insurance would be a wise plan. She said a wave of compensation claims had hit the medical profession and hospitals lately. The 'victims' saw it as an easy way to make money and some of the shadier solicitors were encouraging the practice. The notion of honesty seemed to have disappeared. Children who fell in school playgrounds didn't go home and put on an elastoplast – they were taken to a solicitor by their parents. If you slipped on the floor of the local dance hall, instead of regretting your own clumsiness you sued for compensation. Milo, alarmed by all these stories, rang Mr Kinch back and asked for him to arrange cover with an insurance company.

'Better be safe than sorry,' agreed Mr Kinch. 'I'll arrange cover for you straightaway.'

Mrs Neligan brought in a pile of letters with the cold lunch that Milo had asked for. Ted Fitzpatrick must have posted a letter the moment he had got home. There was a cheque for £200 and a scribbled note of thanks. Milo was overwhelmed by the sudden arrival of money in so short a time and began to think seriously about using the gift to secure his future. Another letter was from a body called the Lough Sheelin Musical Society and invited him to a concert of chamber music at another local great house. A third letter was from the Westmeath Branch of the Irish Society for the Protection of the Red Squirrel. It contained a wad of literature including maps showing areas where the red squirrel had once flourished, maps showing the present crisis situation, car stickers with a picture of a rather twee red squirrel with the legend – 'Save a squirrel for your country's sake', application forms to become (a) a full member, or (b) an associate member, or (c) an affiliate member (not entitled to badge). There was also an application form to order the following books – *Starka the Squirrel* by Stella Entwhistle-Bayley, reduced price £17.50; *My Long-Tailed Friend* by Aubrey Hutchinson-Beauchamp (not suitable for children) or *Tripping Through the Woodland* by Hilda Prance-Nicholson (very suitable for school prizes). If Lord

Kilbeggan would like to join the Westmeath branch as a patron, he should send a cheque for £15 to the Rectory, Drumcree and this would speedily be arranged. In the meantime he could put out nuts.

'Make sure you're insured for that,' said Sheila mischievously. 'You might choke them accidentally and then where would you be?' They continued eating their lunch while Milo opened his correspondence and read it out to Sheila. Lord Kilbeggan was requested to open his house to the public in aid of the Mullingar Rescue Mission to Rwanda. Audrey and Louise Doyle invited him to ask them to inspect his castle so that they might suggest new schemes of interior design and restoration. If he liked, he could visit them by appointment at their gallery in Ranelagh, Dublin, where he could peruse some of their work and order wallpapers, tapestry, curtains and some furniture which might be suitable for Kilbeggan Castle. The next letter contained some type of bingo card. You could play for twenty weeks if you sent them a cheque for £20. A letter from London contained a note from an ex-girlfriend of Milo's containing several naughty suggestions which he tried unsuccessfully to hide from Sheila.

'Wow, what a bitch,' she commented laughing as she read the large feminine epistle. 'So you're not quite the innocent young man you make out to be. Goodness, how did she manage that?'

Milo tried to snatch back the letter. Fiona was now married to a stockbroker and had a baby and a Dalmatian. She should not even be thinking of such things nowadays. Was she getting bored with her marriage?

After lunch they sat down together on a narrow sofa.

'Now,' he said, 'I want to talk about us.'

'Before you say anything,' she replied, 'let *me* talk about us. I cannot take any more leave from the hospital without losing my job. I don't want to do that. It's excellent training and I am probably on the road to promotion. The big drawback is that it's so far from here and at heart I'm a country girl. The other drawback is you! The last few weeks have been like paradise to me. Now I know they say that it takes months or even years to know a person properly. But I'm afraid that I've fallen head over heels. I'm probably a terrible fool and we may both regret it.'

Here he interrupted her.

'Please don't talk like that. I've got to tell you. I couldn't bear it if you left me. You know almost nothing about me whereas I know a lot about yourself and your family. But I don't think you'd find out anything terrible about me if you made enquiries. People will tell you that I'm a bit of a lad and have been a bit of a wild one. But life has sobered me to a great extent and I don't think I'd be a bad prospect for any woman. I can tell you straight that I can't do without you.'

'There are so many differences,' said Sheila. 'I'm astounded how we've come together. There's the class difference. Now no matter what you say or think you've got to admit that there's still a huge amount of snobbery left. You can even see it in Mrs Neligan. She doesn't convey it but she obviously thinks I'm out of place in the big house. Do you remember those people at the drinks party? They really thought it curious that I was with you. The old gentry have long memories. They still think that the rest of the people are not completely civilized. They'd be looking at the way I hold my knife and fork. They'd be listening to my flat "a's" and saying to themselves, "Her grandmother was one of Cynthia's maids. She's related to old Byrne, the blacksmith." Then there's the religion factor. My own side would be worse on this one. "What's she doing going out with him when there's plenty of young lads on her own side of the house?" Now you and I might think nothing of that but we've got to be serious and it does represent an obstacle. There's still a lot of bigotry left behind the externals. They're all smiles and civility to your face and they'll go to ecumenical services, but scratch them and you'll find the old suspicions. The beliefs of centuries are hard to change. The young people are changing but there's a great number of old-fashioned people about. Then there's a lot of people will say that I'm after your money, not knowing that you haven't a tosser. There'll be plenty to say that I'm after a title, little social climber, that sort of thing. How will we overcome those difficulties?'

'I seem to be more used to these difficulties than you are,' he replied. 'I've encountered snobbery all my life, even at prep school. There was a guy whose mother was a famous film actress and the rest of the school was always hanging around him, sucking up to him. My own mother preferred a bit of the rough trade. She used to turn up on sports days with different fellows. This got me a bit laughed at. "Who's going to be Milo's step-daddy today?" One cricket match she turned up with a chap who looked about eighteen years of age. I kept pretending he was a cousin of mine. Some hope! A lot of the time it was just a bit of fun but the fellows who didn't like me used it as a weapon to attack me. I used to hear them talking about Milo's step-toyboy. My proper father had been dead for years at this stage. He died when I was four. I knew that I had some grand relations in Ireland. I never met them. They didn't want to know us for a long while. When it seemed likely that I might be in line for the earldom, they asked us over to stay. My mother was quite clever about it. She didn't bring over any of her boyfriends but behaved like a sober widow. I still had no idea that it might be me who would inherit the castle. So I'm no stranger to difficult relationships. You could produce little that would upset me.'

'What's to happen to the pair of us?' she said.

'This is one of the few things that would make me tongue-tied,' he replied. 'We cannot allow ourselves to drift apart. This is too deep, too loving. I would give anything to have it continue. I have thought about it every day for weeks. Physically, mentally, emotionally we're made for each other.' He took her fiercely into his arms. 'Will you marry me?' he said. 'Will you have me for ever?'

Her heart soared. She could not speak. She sank onto his chest. She spoke not a word. He pressed her again.

'Will you have me, Sheila?' he said longingly. Again not a word could she utter. She kissed him instead and he responded. This time his tongue asked the question in a different way.

Only minutes later, blushing and extraordinarily beautiful, was she able to nod and whisper, 'Yes.'

He took her on his knee and held his golden prize. Here in a state of complete tranquillity, softly she lay and 'let the cares of the world go by'. He too felt calm and stupendously happy. Truth to tell, he was triumphant as well as happy. He had achieved what he had never encountered before – the genuine love of another person. Nobody should ignore the effect of real love on those who have never encountered it. Hours later, Mrs Neligan found them still in the library.

'Oh excuse me, Nurse Kelly,' she said dryly, 'I didn't think you were still here. Shall I bring some tea, your lordship? And will Nurse Kelly be staying for tea?' They disentangled and sat up dishevelled on the sofa. Typical of the gentry, thought Mrs Neligan, do it anywhere, any time. But that young Kelly girl should know better.

After tea, they explored the walled garden. After the avenue, Milo had decided that the walled garden should be cleared and the pathways opened up. They would clean out the garden house, burn the sordid mattresses and remove the empty cans and the grot left behind by Packy's friends. There were splendid things here that had run wild and were almost smothered by jungle. Great box hedges had once been trimmed yearly. Huge rambling roses had pulled the nails from the high walls and were infiltrating the lower plants. Peaches were attracting the wasps. They came across some ancient strawberry beds and, delving deep amid the tangled leaves, they found some charming strawberries with a luscious old-fashioned taste. They tasted them and collected some others in a couple of huge rhubarb leaves to bring as a present to Mrs Kelly. The shadows of evening fell as they made their way up the long walk and came out under the towering front of the castle. They had agreed to keep the engagement a secret between them until they decided on how to announce it to their two separate worlds. Sheila was glowing with pleasure when she finally drove away from the castle, leaving her lover blowing kisses behind her.

17

By ten o'clock the next morning, Milo had scythed the path to the walled garden. After his work you could travel down a pleasant green walk to the old doorway which opened into their hidden world. Despite gloves and boots, he was scratched and bruised by the numerous briars and thorns he had cut. Ancient birds' nests had fallen on him; disturbed insects dropped into his open shirt. Again he had uncovered stonework and ironwork, long concealed by creepers. A long iron seat bore the escutcheon of the Kilbeggan family. A stone crest over the garden doorway revealed the familiar wolves when the tangle of ivy over it was lopped off. A naked Adonis faced an arbour where possibly the ladies of the house had sat in the shade on long hot summer afternoons. Here was evidence of a more leisurely age where ladies of the upper class diverted themselves. Milo retired to the castle where already his next patient, an elderly lady, was being entertained by Mrs Neligan. He went to wash and change before coming down to treat the client.

Now came his next problem. The tradition was that hands were laid on neck, arms, chest, knee, leg and buttock. So far he had only dealt with his own sex, where there was no embarrassment. Now he had to deal with a woman and an elderly woman at that.

'I'm crippled with arthritis,' she said, 'pains in the knees and arms and look at my hands.'

Milo looked at the crippled and twisted fingers – a parody of a hand. It must be hell, he thought, to live in such discomfort by day and to endure pain at night. Pity removed embarrassment from his mind. He decided to modify the process. He would not require clothes to be removed except from the afflicted parts. He pressed his hands lightly on the six parts of the body which the tradition required and then asked her to raise her dress slightly to uncover the knee. Here he felt the instant twinge as he laid hands. The lady gripped the side of the chair and winced as the shooting pains ran through her. Gradually the twinges eased and Milo could almost sense the relief in the limb. He held the poor afflicted hands in his own and once again the weariness came over him almost as if the pain was passing from her hands to his. Gradually her trembling ceased and the tortured fingers lay at ease in his. Similarly for the elbows which were also afflicted by the torment of pain. After fifteen minutes of quiet massage and silent invocation from Milo, the old lady lay relaxed and happy while Milo felt exhausted and drowsy. He wanted to lie down but could not. Shortly after, his client left full of gratitude and pressing a note into Milo's hand. Her family waiting for her in the car looked with surprise at the new-found zest in her movements and the look of palpable relief in her face. Milo retired to his bed for an hour to get over the experience.

Sheila arrived all pink and happy and they kissed passionately in the hall, overlooked by a scandalized Mrs Neligan. The rest of the morning they spent in the library, which the housekeeper was almost afraid to enter. She need not have feared, for they were discussing their future in its most mundane aspect – how to keep themselves. Sheila believed that she could get a job in either of the two local hospitals – Tullamore or Mullingar.

'I'm well-known and I'm well-qualified,' she said. 'There should be no bother picking up a job in either hospital. They'll be glad to get somebody so experienced.'

They both believed that Milo could earn a substantial sum from the Kilbeggan touch. The two major sectors, racing men and footballers, would nearly keep him busy through the year. He was determined to treat only one patient a day or he would find himself getting into ill health. Sheila gave him examples of other faith-healers, especially Finbar Nolan who attracted huge crowds.

'He'd nearly fill a local hall and he'd get through a fair

number in a morning. He even went abroad and large crowds turned up in the belief that he could help them. I don't know whether he found it as tiring as you do,' she said.

They discussed other methods of making money. Opening the house to the public and opening the gardens to the public were other possible sources of income. It would take months to have both areas ready to view and then there was the question of insurance – public liability was essential. Other great Irish houses were attracting a lot of visitors and they decided to visit Newbridge, Mountainstown, Westport or any of the places on the tourist trail.

'What about fishing visitors?' she said. 'There was always supposed to be great pike in that lake. The coarse fishermen from England used to love coming here, until your aunt closed up the place. She didn't want her privacy disturbed. When we were kids, we used to come up and fish for perch. Get in touch with some English fishing club and offer them exclusive rights to the lake – I'd say they'd give their eye-teeth for the privilege. Or else what about an advertisement saying, "Stay in an Irish castle, haunted by ghosts. Four-poster beds. Antique furniture." The Americans would surely pay a fortune to be uncomfortable for a few nights.'

Milo suggested a visit to the gate lodge or gate lodges at the entrance to the main avenue. They took the rusty keys off their hook and set off down the now sunny avenue. The two Gothic lodges appeared to be of similar size but in fact this was an architectural trick. The main lodge was on the left and of quite substantial size with mock battlements surrounding its roof space. The lodge on the right hand side appeared to have the same proportion but was in fact merely a facade to balance the building on the other side. They opened the creaking hall door of the main lodge and saw a damp flagstone floor. In the kitchen was a rusty Stanley range. Hooks were suspended from the ceiling and blurred religious pictures hung on the discoloured walls. They stumbled over broken pieces of lino. The sitting room was opposite; this had a slight air of grandeur due to its vaulted

131

ceiling and decorated door frames and shutters. There was an unpleasant-looking downstairs bathroom, a dripping bath tap still leaked disconsolately onto the brown surface below it. The lavatory bowl smelt as evil as it looked. They climbed cautiously upstairs and had to skip several steps which would not have held their weight. Three reasonably-sized bedrooms each had its little black fireplace. Two faced out over a wilderness that had once been a garden. The third room faced the road and had had its windows smashed by vandals, who even in remote places enjoyed breaking glass. Two dead crows lay on the floor. Rain had driven in through the broken windows and lay in pools on the lino.

'First thing to be done,' said Milo, 'is to get some glass for that window.'

They picked up mouldering copies of long-forgotten magazines. Sheila turned over pages of *Ireland's Own* – a copy from May 1949. It was open at a ghost story "Kitty the Hare", which long ago had kept children from their beds. The electricity had long been cut off from this gate lodge.

'It wouldn't take an enormous sum of money to renovate this,' said Sheila. 'The water is connected and the electricity can be reconnected. The roof looks sound. Let's get that range cleaned out and the chimney swept and see what effect some heat will have on the house. We'll need a load of turf for the Stanley range. There's enough fallen trees on the estate to give us fuel for years. You can also advertise trees for firewood and that will bring in extra money.'

Hand in hand and with a feeling of optimism, they retraced their steps up the avenue. Sheila had a brainwave.

'Seamus has a friend, Jack Brennan, who's studying civil engineering at Galway. He'll be home next week. Now he's very good with his hands – a real case of liking the job he's doing. Why not ask him would he do up the lodge, make it habitable, dry and all the services in running order? Then you could let it and start getting in a small regular income. Jack wouldn't cut corners but he wouldn't charge much either. That could be a most attractive house for somebody who liked living in the country.'

Milo thought this an excellent idea. As they neared the front of the house, a large and indescribably dirty station-wagon jerked to a halt on the gravel. A figure in a headscarf and dusty jeans appeared and removed boxes and bags from the back of the vehicle.

Penelope Baring-Brown ('call me Penny') waited for them to reach her.

'What a cracking morning,' she said, 'Daddy's rheumatism has disappeared, a real sign of good weather. Now come along inside and we'll select some things for the hunt sale.' She swept ahead of them up the steps. 'Now we'll start with the hall. Cynthia was always going to give us that rather gloomy little watercolour – she said it might fetch a few pounds. What do you think?' Milo felt obliged to nod and the landscape by Douglas Alexander was deposited in the first box. 'Oh look! What a silly little thing. Somebody might buy it.' A china shepherdess and dog joined the watercolour. 'Miss Kelly, I hope you'll give us a hand if you're at home. We'd be very glad of you on the produce stall. A few bags of potatoes and anything fresh sell very well. The townspeople never grow anything themselves these days and they're so pleased to get fresh anything. Your mother used to have great loganberries – I wonder would she pick us some?'

She continued talking non-stop as they went from room to room, she leading the way, as she seemed more familiar with the house than Milo.

'We must try the pantry. Always a good place for odds and ends.' Here she met Mrs Neligan and overwhelmed her with a torrent of talk. 'My dear Mrs Neligan, how are you? I hope poor Neligan's hip isn't playing him up. Mummy said to ask you especially if you could make some rhubarb tarts for the hunt sale. Nobody can make a crust quite like you. Really, there are so few decent cooks left. It's no use sending girls to college to learn. A few months learning from you and copying you in your kitchen would have far more effect. And if you could make us a few bracks, it would be wonderful. The colonel asked especially to be remembered to you.'

Mrs Neligan blushed before the flow of compliments and said she would be delighted to help out Miss Penelope again. Milo asked her to bring some coffee to the library where Penelope, with nearly full boxes, was content to relax at last.

'Well, I must say it's great to have a Kilbeggan in Kilbeggan again. We were despairing about the future. Thought it would be another damned golf club. Another blow to the hunt, they hate hounds across their greens. Well, I must say you've done wonders to the avenue. It's as good if not better than the old days.' She looked around her with curious eyes. 'Do you know, there's still some very fine furniture in the house, despite everybody saying that the good stuff had all gone. That desk is a little cracker. Flopsy had one like it and sent it over to Phillips. Of course, all those auctioneers charge high commissions but she did very well from it – had a month in Jamaica with Bingo and had the conservatory repaired. And I noticed that credenza still in the dining room. You ought to insure that. Lovely walnut, always admired it. The Nugents had one like it but not as good. Good thing about this house – it was always damned cold. The central heating was always a washout. Funny thing, that's great for furniture. Central heating, if it's very warm, damages old furniture. I've seen tables that lasted for years suddenly get splits and cracks when central heating was put into the house. It was quite a disaster for people. They suddenly found the house warm and their furniture spoilt.'

The flood continued. She asked Milo what packs of hounds had he hunted with in England. They were getting it very difficult she believed with those hunt saboteurs, crowds of lefties and socialists. It was all 'rent-a-crowd'. They paid students to come out and demonstrate and then fed them with drink afterwards. What a world it was turning out. They wouldn't have dared do it in the old days; they would all have been arrested. The police were getting far too soft. Some of the police seemed to be secretly sympathetic to the saboteurs. Her cousin, Nigel, from Cheshire had been arrested himself for using his whip on a demonstrator. Instead of arresting the culprits, they were stopping decent people from controlling them. Thank goodness there was very little of that sort of thing over here. People wouldn't stand for it. She was disappointed to hear Milo had little experience of hunting. She would mount him next season for a few rides. (Sheila nudged him conspiratorially at this piece of news.) Miss Kelly's father always bred a sensible type of horse. She expected to see them both at the hunt sale and hoped that Milo would come to dinner some night. Still chatting all the way, she led them down to the entrance hall. She mustn't stay wasting time. There was a shed needing re-roofing and they must repot the cinnerarias some time. Her car took off laden with boxes and bags and promises. Sheila kept her gravity until the station-wagon turned the corner and then they both laughed with relief.

'She's taken half the house with her,' she said.

'At least,' returned Milo, 'she hasn't taken the bed. This calls for a spot of sex, I think. Come on, race you up the stairs.'

They set off up the stairs, each trying to hold the other back. Mrs Neligan, coming to bring down the coffee tray, watched them with growing indignation. This was getting blatant. What did the young Kelly one think she was getting up to? It was all right for the gentry. They didn't observe any set of rules. They did what they liked. Mrs Neligan remembered as a girl being cornered by the old lord. Despite a flurry of evasion, she had felt a slight touch of vanity. But the young Kelly one came from a very decent family. She ought to know better. The gentry would only use her and then drop her if she became a nuisance. She went down below to tell old Neligan the touch of scandal.

While the young couple were dozing in each other's arms, a Landrover had arrived at the front entrance to the castle. The driver, in working clothes, climbed hesi-tantly up the steps and rang the bell. After some minutes, Mrs Neligan padded across the hall to open the great hall door.

'Ah, Hughie,' she said. 'What brings you here?'

'I won't come in,' said Hughie. 'I wanted to see the young

lord and ask him could I buy a few trees off him for firing. Is he about?'

'Well, he's upstairs,' she replied, 'but I don't know if I could find him. He doesn't like being disturbed,' she added.

She might have added that it would embarrass her mightily to climb the stairs and disturb the young pair at whatever they were at. How could she knock at the bedroom door to tell her employer that there was a neighbour looking for firewood? This was a problem that she had never had with Lady Cynthia. She hit on a happy solution. The great bronze dinner gong stood in a corner of the hall. It was dusty and had not been used for years. Mrs Neligan took hold of the baton and smote the gong as hard as she could manage. Like a cathedral bell, the gong gave out a great sonorous call which echoed across the hall and could be heard in remote bedrooms in distant wings of the castle. It woke the young couple and Milo, thinking there was some emergency, arrived quickly down in the hall.

'Hughie Quigley from Balrath, my lord,' said Mrs Neligan and left them to their business.

Milo and Hughie left the house to inspect some trees that Hughie wanted to purchase. There were two large beech trees near the back avenue which had fallen in the previous autumn gales.

'These would be grand and handy and near enough to get the tractor and trailer up to them,' said Hughie. 'The back avenue is in very poor state but if you agree, we can do some bartering. I'll bring up two loads of gravel and spread it out for you.It'll turn out as good as the front avenue and it will cost you nothing except for the two beech trees. Now, there's a stand of ash down near the back of the garden wall. It's fit for cutting. I'll offer you £500 for the whole lot – money up front. Let's go down to see them.'

They had to fight their way through briars to inspect the glade of ash trees. Milo, who had the landowner's view of trees, a belief that it was somehow immoral and bad form to cut down a tree, now was confronted with the countryman's

136

common-sense view that trees were a crop, to be cut down and used when mature.

'They'll damage the garden wall if they're blown down in a wind,' said Hughie. 'I'll make sure when we cut them that they'll fall the other way.'

Milo enquired how did he know where the ash trees were.

'I know this whole estate like the back of my hand. The grandfather worked here off and on. I don't mind telling you that we did the odd bit of poaching in the old days when they reared plenty of pheasants here. We had to know every path and track and especially the gaps in the wall, for the old lord would really go for you if he found you poaching his pheasants. It was rough justice in those days. Well, I won't keep you, Milo, isn't that your name? Some of the young lads were saying that there's no side to you at all – none of the old snobbery that there was in the old days. Well, that's a good thing. Now, I said money up front and here it is.'

He reached into his pocket and took out a dusty wad of notes. He counted out twenty-five notes, each for £20 and pressed them into Milo's hands.

'Now that's the first deal I've had with you. Wasn't it painless? We'll start work tomorrow and get the back avenue ready for use. And by the bye, get young Sheila Kelly to tell you about luck pennies. You don't seem to have heard of them.'

He drove off shortly afterwards in his Landrover.

'What is a luck penny, Sheila?' he enquired from his beloved one.

Sheila told him that it was a custom when buying or selling cattle or other goods, that the recipient of the money paid back the buyer a small proportion of the price as a 'luck penny'.

'You should have given him back a tenner,' she said. 'However, he's probably had a good bargain from you with the trees. Hughie is a cute businessman. If those ash trees are sound, he'll probably be selling them on to make hurling sticks. I should have gone out with you. There's a shortage of good ash trees at the moment. You'd think looking at the ditches that every second tree was an ash tree, but in fact a lot of them are poor specimens. However, Hughie will be back to make other deals and trees are things that you've no shortage of.'

Milo felt quite happy with the money in his pocket and decided to visit the bank and the solicitor next day.

They sat down in the library and Milo unlocked more cases of family papers. Old bills, receipts and wage deals would have been fascinating to the social historian.

'Not a bad lot at all,' said Milo approvingly, 'they certainly didn't screw their tenants. Here's one woman who was let off rent for a year because her husband died. And my ancestor even paid for the coffin!'

They continued searching through the papers. Sheila came across details of the third Viscount Kilcock whose main income seemed to be derived from the use of 'the touch'. At the age of twenty-three he was seeing twelve clients a day. Then there were great gaps and details of high life across the continent of Europe. Money had been paid out to a Signorina Verso in the town of Modena and later there were demands for help with education.

'If I'd read some of these beforehand, I wouldn't have agreed to marry you,' said Sheila severely. 'What a crowd of scamps, even if they were aristocratic scamps.'

Milo pointed out a picture in a dim corner of the library. This was a portrait of a thin young man with pronounced saturnine features and a somewhat depraved appearance. 'Myles, 3rd Viscount Kilcock' read the enscription.

'Like a debauched version of yourself,' said Sheila, 'I've caught you just in time.'

Milo pointed out a larger portrait of a corpulent and rather repulsive gentleman.

'That's the same chap later on in life. He inherited the earldom and died of a fierce attack of gout which brought on something worse.'

Presently they came across something more interesting. It was an entry for June 1st 1756 – This day came the surveyor to survey my land, it being rumoured that zinc and silver

138

hath been found in the soil in previous centuries. The same that hath been at Ardbracken with My Lord Bishop.'

In subsequent entries, there were details of payments of men to attend the surveyor. A lot of the results of the survey were incomprehensible to the modern reader, but what did seem evident was the resulting and heartening news that the surveyor felt that with more detailed examination, satisfactory amounts of silver and zinc could be found on the estate. The surveyor departed in August. The next information was in a different hand – 'My Lord sickening. A sudden swelling in the neck hath made it difficult for him to breathe.'

Entry after entry recorded the deterioration in the earl's condition. A query from the surveyor was answered with the information that 'my Lord's sickness hath made it impossible for him to stomach any dealings.' Line after line dealt with the grievous illness until the final decline. The ultimate details dealt with the wake, the funeral, the huge entertainment that followed the earl's obsequies and no more was heard of surveyor or mining on the estate. The next heir lived abroad and had none of the traditional interest in his Irish estate, leaving all dealings to his agent, Captain O'Malley. After the sudden death of the lord when his coach overturned in the Aosta Valley, his brother inherited Kilbeggan and the first entry in his papers read – 'Got rid of O'Malley who hath grown great in my brother's absence. Tale after tale of his oppression of the tenants. Delegation led by the parish priest Mr Flynn to thank me for ridding the county of a tyrant.' This earl seemed to specialize in a different form of harassment, as the countryside found out. Complaints came from tenants not about rackrenting but about their womenfolk.

'Impudent complaint from James Daly about my usage of his daughter, a forward wench yet interesting. Sent them two guineas for baby clothes.' Another complaint read, 'What a to do. As I rode past the gate lodge, Mrs Gannon ran out crying that her daughter was with child. "Tell me who is responsible?" quoth I, "and I will see that he be horsewhipped." But she stopped me, crying, "Oh! my Lord, the child will be of noble blood." Now it comes to my mind that there was a dalliance once as the wench hung out the clothes in the drying yard. She made a pretty run for it all the while protesting but most loving and obliging when I came. Now it appears that her time hath come. Ten guineas paid. She is a good lass and will look after the brat well.'

Some time later was another entry. 'Walker, the parson, came to reproach me for, as he termed, my evil ways. He complains that I have got the whole country with child. Every cottage from here to Mullingar apparently hath a dark-haired brat playing in front of the door. My reply being two-fold. Firstly that it be a noble thing to populate a countryside with decent blood and none of your foolish and feeble peasant stock. Hath not his master and mine proclaimed, "Multiply and fill the ends of the earth"? Secondly that it was I whom he reproached, that hath appointed him. Did he wish to leave the parish with his own large brood of children and whey-faced wife that none but he would touch? Had I not a cousin who was highly desirous of taking orders and would be seeking a parish and should I not oblige my own family? Was there not a commandment to render to Caesar? And was I not the Caesar in his parish? I growing hot and furious pushed him to the door. Civility would become him better than those obnoxious ways.'

'That's him,' said Milo, pushing back his chair and leading Sheila to the end of the library.

A heavy golden frame contained an oil painting of a strikingly handsome youth with an arrogant and petulant stare. Lord Ballivor, as he then was, had two obedient-looking spaniels standing beside his riding boots. Behind him was the outline of a stately early Georgian house.

'That was the old house,' said Milo, 'that they pulled down later to erect this present house. It became the great fashion to Gothicize your house or knock it down and erect a castle.'

'There's my ancestor,' said Sheila, laughingly pointing to a dim figure in a field in the background of the picture. An elderly woman was stooped, obviously gathering faggots for her fire. 'I hope she wasn't got at.'

'Only saved by her age,' said Milo. 'Morals were not so strict in those days. It was considered a bit of an honour as well as a misfortune to be caught by a son of the great house. The Duke of Wellington was said to have populated a countryside and I believe your own Daniel O'Connell had quite a reputation. And isn't there a Taoiseach who had quite a sporting reputation as well?'

'Don't talk like that to my father,' said Sheila, 'he's a great fan of the man you mention.'

They went back to the family papers and read a further account of the promiscuous earl. There were reports of his journeys seeking a wife. He had visited the Cobbes at Newbridge and found the daughter 'distant and proud as if she carried a great dowry'. At Clonalis was the very pretty Miss O'Conor 'of the greatest blood in the country but the Don wisheth her to marry a Papist'. There was a fruitless visit to Sligo to the O'Hara's where once again the young ladies were 'most obliging' but hadn't got a penny to their name, the family money having all been exhausted on 'coaches and horses and high living, for they entertain each other mightily'. A Miss Forde from County Down had a 'severe countenance, being very religious, reads many great thick books, speaketh few words on a Sunday and would be a great catch for somebody not such as I'. As the search for an heiress continued, the lord had the fate of being rebuffed for the same reason as the parson had rebuffed him. He had to travel far to escape from his own reputation. Eventually in the south, he had found a Miss O'Brien, young but 'very promising and a most pleasing countenance'. She also carried a 'most handsome' dowry and was furthermore carried away by the lord's fine appearance and yielded herself very easily to the blandishments of the sonorous title.

'Now,' said Milo, 'you see the type of man you will be marrying. Sensitive, thoughtful, generous and kind.'

They kissed with sudden passion and the estate papers went flying all over the floor.

18

Sounds of tractors and chainsaws awoke Milo in the morning. After breakfast he awaited his client for the day. The well-known professional soccer player was English but had relations in County Westmeath who had informed him of the existence of the healer. He had suffered a groin injury in a collision against an attacking forward in a match against Southampton. The seemingly innocent injury was expected to heal within weeks but months later was still sore, uncomfortable and slowed down his speed drastically. He had tried every cure from acupuncture to reflexology but was losing hope that he would ever regain his fitness or his place on the team. Despite this, many would have envied the possession of a body such as lay on the couch in the sitting room. Only when Milo began to touch his groin did a shudder of pain travel through his body.

'Take it easy,' he advised Milo, 'I don't know why it's so sensitive.'

Milo's probing fingers seemed to bring him more pain. As the familiar weariness came upon Milo, so the patient seemed to get more relaxed. Milo eventually had to pause for a moment and sit down. As if he had run a marathon, such a heaviness hung upon him. The soccer player lay half-asleep on the couch. Milo had to rouse himself to restart the process, tiredly laying hands on the six areas and once again on the afflicted part. This time the soccer player was sound asleep on the sofa. But when Milo returned from cooling himself and wiping away his sweat, the player was sitting up, very much at ease. He swung himself off the sofa, walked around the room and then tried a few easy press-ups. The feeling of hope lightened his face and he dressed happily, paid Milo by cheque and left in great satisfaction. He was

142

staying with his relations for a week and asked Milo for a second appointment some time.

Milo walked around to the back avenue and saw with satisfaction that its large potholes and craters had been filled in. Every day improvements were happening and the resurfacing of both avenues gave him a feeling of achievement. He talked to Hughie who was hauling logs to the edge of the avenue for collection.

'Hughie,' he said, 'I've learnt what a luck penny is,' and he handed over a tenner to the surprised woodsman.

'Nice doing business with you,' said Hughie. 'Let's talk again after we have cleared the present deal.'

Milo took off and drove to the town. First he went to the bank where his current account was considerably increased by the cheques and cash he deposited. He then drove to Mullingar to Mr Kinch's office where he was welcomed as warmly as ever by the two secretaries.

'I've been intending to have you both out to see the garden,' he told them recklessly. 'Would Saturday suit you about three o'clock and I hope we'll be able to give you some tea?'

The offer was accepted with great pleasure –

'So kind, so very kind. It will be wonderful to see the place again, even if the garden has been neglected.'

Mr Kinch was not quite so effusive. There was little twinkle behind the heavy spectacles.

'I wonder could I press you a little on Mr Fogarty's offer for the place? He's getting impatient and beginning to look at other estates, although yours seemed the best prospect in his view. I must say that I think it would solve many of your problems, financial and otherwise. It also offers you a guaranteed job on your place. What could be fairer? Shall I tell him that you'll accept? We can draw up agreements and contracts in jig time. A few signatures would then complete the deal. Does that make sense to you?'

'I'd be grateful if you'd tell Mr Fogarty that I shan't be accepting his offer. Perhaps you'd also tell him how appreciative I am for the thought and effort he has put into the scheme, but I shall not make any decision on the future of the property for at least a year. After that time if he is still interested, there might be another chance of a deal.'

Mr Kinch's face darkened with disappointment. He could scarcely conceal his annoyance. A carefully arranged plan with investment money promised, he himself had hoped to be part of the syndicate, was being scuttled by this volatile young man with torn cords and a shirt which was missing two buttons. He was scarcely able to retain his composure with his client.

'Well, we must all think very carefully about the offer. You may never receive such an excellent offer again. There's many a derelict country house in this area.'

Milo realized that his refusal of the offer had offended the solicitor more than the setting-out of a contract could justify. He wondered if the solicitor had a deeper interest than was apparent to him.

'That may be so,' he replied, 'but I have decided to postpone any decision for a year. Now having got that aside, have you fixed up the public liability policy with the insurance company?'

Milo signed and paid the premium for the policy which would protect him against claims in connection with his curing touch. He left the beaming secretaries and the scowling solicitor, who used slightly less formal language as he rang P.J. Fogarty to tell him that the deal was off. Indeed some of his clerical clients would have been surprised and shocked at the language which the venerable solicitor used in his telephone call.

Milo next visited the county library to get more information about his property and the town of Kilbeggan. He found in one ancient history book that his lake was famous for eels and that the writer believed there were mineral springs in the lake. This was how the seventeenth-century writer described it –

I rather imagine there may be some mineral springs in this water, that may have secret and undiscovered vents. These

144

springs, probably are not without gravel where they rise, in which this sort of fish is known to delight. But this supposition of mineral springs, being but a mere conjecture, I shall not enter into the enquiry how far the feeding of the fish in such springs, might alter their nature, and make them from an wholesome food, to become a medicine; and yet the same gentleman farther adds, that the eels found in this pool are exceeding good, and have no such operation, which if we could lay any stress on our former guess, might not be held inconsistent with it, for that it is known eels delight most in mud, and consequently frequent not the supposed mineral springs.

In Wood's ancient and modern sketches he came across a description of another Kilbeggan title – this one a titled innkeeper, John Cuffe, who received his title in a most peculiar way. When Lord Townsend was viceroy of Ireland he often travelled to the west of Ireland and his stop in the town of Kilbeggan produced a very odd result.

Some assert that the viceroy was a man of dissolute habits, who, surrounded by companions as abandoned as himself kept the metropolis in a blaze with their buffooneries and extravagances, and their exploits were duly recorded by the satirical writers of the day. Lord Townshend, accompanied by four kindred spirits, during one of his excursions to the west, claimed the hospitality of plain, honest John Cuffe, the Kilbeggan innkeeper, and had his claim allowed. It was a godsend to the humble owner of the modest wayside inn to have such distinguished visitors and lodgers under his roof; and it is almost needless to say that he treated the semblance of royalty right royally, and the viceroy, in the exuberance of generosity, conferred the honour of knighthood on the unassuming Tom in recognition of the kindness he and he friends had received. Never did the Fountain of Honour play off so ridiculous a prank as when it showered its spray on the head of an innkeeper.

In those days whiskey was better than it is now and the contents of Cuffe's cellar was all that could be desired – so much so that it had pleased his excellency's palate, and the good man, whilst in a half-drunken state, requested to see his kind host, who had provided such good things for the noble party. Cuffe, on making his appearance, was complimented by the great man, after which he ordered him to kneel down and, taking a sword, he flourished it over the head of Cuffe, exclaiming, 'Rise up, thou mirror of innkeepers, and be henceforth Sir Thomas Cuffe!' The astonishment of the innkeeper may be well supposed, as he returned to his wife to inform her of the title conferred.

The vice-regal party, as usual, retired to rest well saturated with whiskey punch and utterly reckless and regardless of what had happened and rose in the morning forgetful, till reminded of the transaction, at which he was not a little annoyed. But, plucking up courage, he said to his aide-de-camp, 'It certainly was carrying the joke too far, but curse the fellow, sure he will not take any advantage of it. Call him before me, and I'll persuade him to hush up the matter.' Accordingly the man was introduced.

'Mr Cuffe,' says his excellency, 'a circumstance occurred last night which I am sure you understand in its proper light. It was, it is true, carrying the joke too far. I hope, sir, you feel as becomes you, and that you will say no more about it, nor let the thing get wind.'

'Oh, indeed, my lord, the honour you have conferred on me, though I am right sensible of its importance, is still what I, for one, would have no objection to forego, under a proper consideration; but, please your lordship, what will my Lady Cuffe say?'

The innkeeper and his wife were sir and madame all their lives. Some say that Lord Townshend gave them a large sum of money to abandon the title. Lady Cuffe survived the knight some years, and many tourists visited Kilbeggan for the purpose of seeing the recipient of vice-regal honours.

From the library Milo drove to the Kelly's where he told Mrs Kelly the story of the Kilbeggan publican who had become knighted for his efforts. Mrs Kelly was very entertained by the story and nearly had tears running down her face as she told the story to Mr Kelly who had been out changing batteries on a tractor.

'What a silly thing,' she said, 'I've heard of those Cuffes. They were cousins of Tom Kennedy of Loughduff. Did very well out of the cattle trade after the war.' She rambled on about the genealogy of all and sundry in the county while they supped tea in the warm kitchen. Mr Kelly rose suddenly and, taking hold of *The Westmeath Examiner*, made a furious yet fruitless onslaught on a loudly buzzing fly near the bread bin. Several heavy smacks of the newspaper still left the fly alive and buzzing.

'Ah! Dadda, you're losing your touch,' said Mrs Kelly. 'You very rarely missed in the old days. Oh, watch the geranium, please.'

There was a loud crash as the pot plant hit the stone floor. Sheila cleaned up with dustpan and brush, Mrs Kelly went outside to repot the injured plant, and the fly buzzed drowsily around the bread bin. Seamus came in.

'That calf doesn't look right,' he said. 'Milo, we'll have to get you working with animals.'

They discussed this possibility with a lot of imaginative suggestions.

'Luke Curtain has a greyhound with a strained back. You'd want to muzzle him before you lay a hand on him.'

'There's pig fever up in McAuliffe's. Watch the boar. He's a savage.'

The suggestions grew quite hilarious, but then Mrs Kelly was reminded of something and grew serious.

'What a shame we won't be having fun like this next week. Poor Sheila will be back in London. Ah well! Life must go on.'

She sighed at the thought. Sheila and Milo left to go back to the castle, leaving her to her reveries.

'We'll have to tell them some time that we're engaged,' said Sheila, snug in the comfort of the Porsche. 'It's going to be difficult. They like you but it's going to seem very, very strange. They'd enjoy it if I was going to marry a doctor. That really would make them very proud. But this will be outside of their world. It will take some getting used to.'

147

'Well, I have some stiff relations who will also be very curious,' said Milo, 'but most of my family won't care a damn either way. In any event, there are really only two people whom we want to satisfy and that is ourselves.'

They pulled up for petrol and the garage owner admired the car while deprecating the amount of fuel that it used.

'A big slice of tax for the government,' he said when Milo paid for the fifteen gallons. 'That's the lad that does the healing,' he told his mechanic as the Porsche left the station. 'He'd want to cure a big number to keep that on the road.'

They stopped for a beer at a pub in the town and listened to the barman telling another customer about Milo.

'He doesn't come in here. In fact I've never seen him, but I hear he's doing great cures. They say there's no side on him at all. He dresses scruffy, not like a lord at all – torn old jeans and a shirt that needs a bit of a wash. Very likeable, they all say. He was at the races and intends to play some football when he settles down. A lively lad and found some of the local women to his taste.' Sheila blushed and looked annoyed when she heard this description. 'He has the front avenue cleaned up and all the potholes filled in. Hughie was in last night and told me he got a good bargain with trees from the young fellow. Amazing when you think that family used to employ half the countryside and now there's only the Neligans left. I believe the guards are keeping an eye out for young Packy Neligan – that's the foolish lad. He never grew up and got sense. Talking about drugs, I hear Athlone is the place that's full of them. I could tell you a pub down there where you'd have no difficulty buying anything you'd want.'

His listener nodded and told him that a couple of pints of Guinness was all the drugs that he needed. Milo and Sheila happily discussed their future. There are hundreds if not thousands of problems and questions and other items to be resolved by those who are contemplating marriage. Announcing an engagement is one of them.

'I know what they'll all say – aunts and uncles, even distant cousins,' said Sheila. 'They'll all be saying when they hear

148

about it, "How can they know each other well? They've only been together a few weeks." What do we reply to that one?'

'Well,' said Milo, 'we can say that we've no plans for an instant marriage. I can say that I certainly will be more than happy to be engaged to you and with a few arrangements such as they are to relieve pressure, we should have a very enjoyable time. A longish engagement should satisfy them and will leave us quite happy, so really there's no problem.'

This was a decision they agreed upon quite happily and they decided to inform the Kellys the next day. They discussed finances again and Sheila decided to ring around the local hospitals to find out if they had any openings that would suit her. They talked about the castle and how to make it more comfortable. Sheila suggested that a modern bed might be more comfortable, although Milo argued that they had found wonderful comfort in the historic family bed. He didn't tell her about his uncle having died in it, and possibly others of his ancestors as well.

'Aah,' she said, 'every time I think of Packy creeping in beside you, I get the shudders. Let's order a good double bed from Kellets of Oldcastle. And do it discreetly. It's early days to be mentioning me in connection with a double bed. I know the country is modernizing and people are changing their ideas, but we're still a bit old-fashioned.'

They discussed setting up a booking system for his healing process so that they could plan ahead and take some days off together. They discussed arrangements for advertising fishing holidays and starting off on a small scale. They talked about some of the large bills they would have to face – problems like modernizing the heating in the castle, rewiring the house, replacing deteriorating parts like window frames and sections of the roof. Milo believed that if they brought an engineer to the house or a surveyor, the existence of dry rot, wet rot, woodworm would soon be discovered. He remembered P.J. Fogarty's warning about structural deterioration in Irish houses and hoped that too many difficulties would not be encountered.

149

'I can see why the gin and Jag set prefer modern suburban houses,' he said. 'They mightn't have the grandeur but they have the warmth and the knowledge that they won't have too many builders' invoices to face. Mind you, I could live anywhere. I'm not used to castles, no more than yourself. A small flat was good enough for me.'

This last statement nearly alarmed her.

'No flats,' she said, 'we're going to restore that castle between us and make it a beautiful place to live. Why should the rich have all the nice places?'

He recited the words of old school and football club songs to her –

> 'It's the same the whole world over.
> It's the poor what gets the blame.
> It's the rich what gets the pleasure.
> Ain't it all a bleeding shame.'

and

> 'Blow the bloody trumpet.
> Beat the bloody drum.
> We'll blow the bloody upper class
> To bloody kingdom come.'

He also whispered the words of a few other rugby club songs to her, words which would not have been suitable for recitation in most civilized places. She enjoyed them but warned him not to recite them in front of her parents or else approval of their engagement would go astray.

'In any event,' she said, 'I've been to a Guy's Hospital party where some of the songs would have set your ears aglow. Medical staff are not always the demure professional people that we have to appear in hospital life. If you watch *Casualty* on BBC, you'll get some idea of the reality. Most nurses think it's a very realistic programme. On the other hand, none of us think that *Carry On Nurse* is anything else but a caricature of hospital life.'

150

19

The appointment next day was for Leslie O'Dwyer. Mr
Neligan had received the call on the telephone. Although
slightly deaf he had given the caller a ten o'clock appointment. Milo heard the crunch of tyres on the gravel and went
down to receive the patient. To his surprise and secret
gratification a very attractive girl was at the hall door. She
was dark-haired and had very sparkling eyes which gave her
a sporting look. Her voice was deep and seductive. Her
clothes worn carelessly and nonchalantly revealed the curves
of her body which were sensual enough to revive even a
dying hermit. Milo took in the charming smile, the pleasing
curves and wondered who this was.

'I'm Leslie O'Dwyer,' she said, 'and I have an appointment
with Lord Kilbeggan. I wonder is he in?'

She was astounded to hear that Milo was the person who
was to deal with her; she had expected an elderly gentleman.
Her eyes dwelt with some alarm on this sexy-looking young
man who was eying her with appreciation.

'Come along in,' he said, 'and tell me your problems.'

She coloured and followed him in with mixed apprehension and anticipation. Milo was also apprehensive. How can
you keep a professional feeling about a meeting where two
good-looking people are already feeling slight tremors of
desire. She found it difficult to be articulate and to explain
her predicament.

Her sport was hockey. This game used to have a lady-like
image but in fact it is one of the fastest and most demanding
of team sports. In first-class hockey, you require absolute
fitness, good movement skills, a huge degree of agility,
plenty of strength and a killer instinct. The 'jolly hockey-
sticks' Joyce Grenfell type image does not apply to really

151

competitive hockey. Similarly, croquet has an old-fashioned genteel ambience. But you would be astounded at the savage if restrained ferocity displayed in competitive croquet. Leslie was an all-rounder but most famous as centre forward in a top-class Dublin hockey team. Her problem was simple. She had pulled a hamstring when she used her long stretch to snatch the ball from an opponent's feet. For a start this was painful and annoying. She was annoyed because she missed several league matches and the team suffered with an inadequate replacement. Annoyance increased when she went to practise after a month and found the same hamstring sore and hampering her speed.

'Give it time,' she was told. 'An injury like that needs time and rest.'

So she took it easy and gradually it seemed to heal. At last it seemed safe for her to resume her sporting interests. She went out on a tennis court and had no difficulty in the first game where her opponent served. At the start of the second game, she stretched to smash her usual service and felt the same disabling pain in the same part of her leg. She had to apologize to her opponent and limp off the court. For a sports' fanatic this was too much. Physiotherapy, acupuncture, reflexology – she had tried them all and got little satisfaction. Sometimes she had got a false sense of relief only to find the same nagging pain dogging her movements. Certain actions brought pain automatically. Most embarrassingly, when she sat on the lavatory, a cramp-like feeling attacked her. She envied the opposite sex where, so to speak, you could fire from the hip. A friend of a friend had told her of an old Lord Kilbeggan who was a well-known healer and she had taken a day off work and travelled down to receive the Kilbeggan touch.

Now she wondered if she should make some excuse and escape from this unexpected predicament. Before she could articulate any plausible reason, Milo interpreted her fears.

'You're probably going to feel some embarrassment and so am I. You obviously didn't expect to have me dealing with you and, for my part, I thought that Leslie was the masculine name. So any embarrassment you may be feeling will be shared by me. I will have to ask you to strip, certainly down to bra and pants, and this you may not want to do. If you want to cancel the session and leave, I shall not feel offended and will understand your reasons.'

Leslie blushed. Her eyes fascinated Milo and he was almost hoping that she wouldn't change her mind. He was also hoping that Sheila wouldn't arrive and walk in while he was massaging this very good-looking woman and certainly, if it was the reverse circumstance and it was Sheila and a young man, he would feel very uneasy. However, Leslie was smiling and trying to display a confidence that she didn't really feel. She had decided to chance it.

'Right,' said Milo, 'if you'd like to strip off some of your clothes you could lie down on this sofa.'

She hadn't told him that she was not wearing a bra beneath her black woollen jumper and he swallowed as she removed this garment to expose breasts to dream about. They rose and fell gently indicating her nervousness. The superb nipples hardened slightly and he found it difficult to restrain his own excitement. He watched hungrily as she began to undo the buckle of her belt. As she slid her jeans down over black skimpy pants she became aware of the intensity of his gaze. She lay back on the sofa, half in dread and half in a delicious feeling of expectancy.

'Are you not taking off anything?' she asked mischievously. He wondered was this an invitation or a signal. But she was smiling slightly . 'Only a joke,' she said nervously.

Milo gulped in relief. He sat down beside her breathing heavily and almost forgot the sequence of the cure. He touched the sweet curve of her neck, fingers feeling her tremors underneath them. Similarly with her arms, soft yet with the muscles of the athlete. When he touched the chest apprehensively she almost responded with a sensation of warmth. Those glorious breasts moved beneath him and she panted with excitement.

'Easy, relax,' he said to her as her eyes sought his.

Down he went to the knees. Touch was still exciting but at least there was small temptation at the knees. When he came to the curve of the legs below the entrancing buttocks, a new element entered the proceedings. The sultry look left her eyes and pain clouded them over. Suddenly the sexual feeling was dead and a medical perception sharpened. She cried out slightly as his fingers kneaded the hamstrings. He prayed with relief that he had not disgraced himself and that he might retain some healing credibility. The dangerous moment had passed. The serious moment had begun. Weariness stole across him as he continued to lay his hands on the muscular leg beneath him. He touched the buttocks slightly but returned to the curve where pain had its seat. Almost exhausted, he stroked the afflicted part and nearly felt the harmony being restored to the leg. He became conscious of health returning where ailment had been. The belief in his own powers became stronger. Leslie now lay almost comatose on the sofa and now pain seemed to have left her. Virtue had triumphed. The climax had been in the healing. He continued for several more minutes. She was now asleep, relaxed as she had not been for months. He left the room to towel himself down. When he returned, he woke her up and reluctantly she sat up and dressed herself. His actions were understandable, for he feared the arrival of Sheila and the suspicions that might cloud over their relationship if she entered and found an almost naked girl lying on the sofa in Milo's library. Leslie took out an envelope which she handed to him. Already almost returned to active health, she was grateful. A cloud seemed to have passed and danger averted. She gazed at Milo with admiration and fondness. Without speaking they both knew that innocence had not left the earth, nor decency been eroded. He escorted her to the top of the steps. As she moved freely and happily to her car, a second car drew up and Sheila jumped out. The two women's eyes met as they went in different directions.

'Friend of yours?' asked Sheila, as she entered the hall, 'or somebody just spending the night here?'

She kissed him without much enthusiasm. Milo found himself on the defensive.

'Another client,' he replied, 'called Leslie O'Dwyer. Mrs Neligan took the call and made the appointment. I thought it was a man but of course Leslie is a girl's name too. She's a hockey player from Dublin. She had a hamstring injury.'

'That was nice for you,' said Sheila brightly. 'It must be rather pleasant to have such a sexy-looking patient when you have to keep touching her hams. She seemed very pleased with herself. In fact, she looked positively glowing as I passed her by. I'm sure the word will spread and you'll have sex-kittens queuing up to be treated. Why not start a massage parlour and be honest about it? Everybody would be happy then. Or you could go into partnership with Packy – he could take the young men and you look after the girls. No place for me on this scene.'

She turned around sourly and headed back towards the hall door. She reached it and slammed it in his face. Fast as he was, she was faster.

'Sheila,' he called from the steps as she ran towards her car. 'It wasn't like that at all.'

'Go to hell,' he heard her say and the MG left skid marks on the new gravel as it took off down the avenue. The way a car is driven can indicate the emotional state of the driver. Old maids driving to church on Sunday mornings drive placidly and slowly, indicating their temperaments. Sheila drove resentfully and the sound of the car engine echoed her state of mind, which was full of suspicion. Any fool could see that something was afoot. That hockey player had looked too pleased with herself. Asking her to marry him one day and then getting intimate, no other word for it, with a lustful-looking lassy the next day. What a rake! Well, he could pick up as many loose fish as he liked. He was just like his ancestors. He could treat the entire Olympic women's team, if he wanted to. Thank goodness, she had learnt her lesson in time. Some guys were too virile. They would never be satisfied with just one woman. Had he been to the same school as Alan Clarke? Sex was all they were after. She remembered the way he had behaved when she had first met him. She was a bit naive. Her friends were now envious of her. Well, they might be pitying her if she went ahead with the engagement. Kilbeggan would be full of female tennis players and badminton players and international swimmers all looking for treatment from a handsome young quack. Her mind conjured up images and fantasies and circumstances. She almost hit the milk lorry as she drove down the road to Drumlerry. A cat had to use one of its nine lives to escape from between her wheels.

Milo was left nonplussed and worried. Also, if the truth be told, he felt a slight feeling of guilt. Could he have restrained himself if the treatment had gone differently, if the hockey player had been a bit more forward? A certain twinge of doubt remained. One thing was certain. He must not subject himself to the same temptation again. No red-blooded male should have that offering put in front of him. It was like the stuff of fantasy, the dreams of an adolescent where naked women begged to be touched and fondled. No, he would only treat the rougher sex in future – very boring but at least safe from temptation. He sighed but resolved to avoid the impulse in the future. His big desire was to avoid hurting Sheila. The realization that any arousal on his part could change the relationship with Sheila was enough to steel his determination. No more women patients. He went down to tell Mrs Neligan not to take any bookings from female clients as he would not have time to treat them. Was he mistaken or did he catch the old couple winking at each other when he gave her the instructions?

'Of course, my lord,' she said, 'sure it would be much wiser. Women should have their own lady doctors. That's what I always say. Was that Miss Kelly that I thought I saw driving away? She didn't stay long this morning. Shure, she'll be going back to her hospital soon. They say she has a fellow in London. Ah well, I've bread to bake.'

She turned back to the Aga, after delivering her mischievous announcement. Milo returned upstairs with a depression settling on his mind. The line from the old jingle about women kept going through his head – 'uncertain, coy and hard to please'.

Efforts at reconciliation met with a rebuff. He rang Drumlerry to be told that Sheila was out with some friends and they weren't expecting her back until later, perhaps that evening. He went out to the walled garden and did some savage work with the hoe. When he came back to the house, Mrs Neligan informed him that the two Miss Thomsons from Mr Lynch's office had rung to say that they'd be out to see the garden at three. She didn't know if she should put them off, seeing that Lord Kilbeggan didn't want to see females. But she felt that the Misses Thomsons might be an exception to the rules – poor things, there wasn't much excitement in their lives and Lady Cynthia used to ask them out.

'"Pull out all the stops, Mrs Neligan," she would say, "or the Misses Thomson will be telling everybody about us." She used to load the Misses Thomson with cuttings and roots and that did them for another year.'

Milo swore savagely under his breath at this prospect for the afternoon. At half past two, he rang Drumlerry again to be told with some surprise that Sheila was out with her friends. Had she not told Milo where she was going? He passed on that one.

'How are you?' he asked the Misses Thomson when they arrived and regretted having asked the question.

A positive deluge of information about their ailments greeted his question as they walked to the garden. Margery, the older and slightly moustached sister, had been suffering from angina on and off, mild enough but disquieting at times. They had both had a bad time with the flu, fortunately not at the same time. Connie was waiting for a bed in the Mater Hospital to have her veins done. She preferred going to a Dublin specialist, better to be safe than sorry. Your health means everything. Wasn't it sad about Mrs McNeill? He didn't know her? What a pity. She'd been a great gardener in her day while she was able. She'd been president of the bridge club last year. No, it wasn't last year, it was two years ago. No, sorry, it was last year. That was one off the Christmas card list. A great loss to the church; they didn't know how the canon would survive without her. Still, life must go on. Oh! look at the wisteria. One of the old-fashioned ones. He was so lucky to have such lovely things. And there's the tree peonies. They hoped he wouldn't mind a teeny-weeny suggestion. Lady Cynthia had always kept that bed very clear of weeds. Tree peonies hated being crowded. Let's all pull a few weeds now. Angina or not, they set to. Milo had to promise them that he was getting a young person to help with the weeding before they desisted and passed on to inspect heavily overgrown herbaceous borders with disapproving eyes. Yes, he had a big job on his hands. They were afraid that the place had got very out of hand. Oh dear, the ceanothus had been blown down – very soft, poor things. A great pity about the greenhouses – they could remember when old Crowley looked after them. The grapes were exquisite. If ever there was an example of green fingers, that was old Crowley. His children had no interest in plants. Never took a spade in their hands. And talking about spades, they had taken the liberty of bringing a small spade in their car as some of his plants might need to be thinned. Milo told them not to bother, that he had a very good spade in the garden shed and some plastic sacks if they would like to take away the thinnings. At this news they hopped agilely over the box hedge and began their attack. Margery ignored her heart condition and reduced a large flourishing hosta to a small shivering plant. Connie seemed to change character. Cuttings were nicked skilfully from overgrown plants. Her eyes gleamed as she spotted where an azalea had foolishly bent a branch, rerooting itself. Up came the layered shoot and into the bag. Like intrepid explorers in the South American jungle, they found their way through green tunnels, until panting genteelly they stood again on the paths with full bags.

'Well, that should help you,' said Margery surveying the gaps in the greenery.

Milo lifted the heavy bags back to the immaculate Fiesta. An invitation to tea was joyfully accepted and, eyes darting everywhere, the two ladies entered the hall. Mrs Neligan had trays ready and soon there was a scene of refined jollity as the ladies forgot their ailments and ate heartily.

'Always a very good seed cake Mrs Neligan makes,' said Margery, bearing strong evidence of this on her upper lip where some stray seeds had been caught en route.

Crumpet and muffin, sandwich and teacake were consumed with great satisfaction. Milo sat with his mind far away as the reminiscences flowed. The talk ran on, the sisters vying with each other, overtaking each other in their stories, correcting each other about details while Cynthia's handsome young nephew listened as they thought enthralled. But even 'the weariest river winds somewhere safe to sea' and Margery and Connie finally rose and were escorted down the wide steps. Full of compliments and thanks and invitations, they entered the Fiesta and drove off waving happily. With a weary heart and worried mind Milo went back inside to ring Drumlerry.

20

There was no reply from Drumlerry. He let it ring on but they must all have gone outside, as sensible people do in warm summer weather. Milo swore and sat down in the cool library. Everything had been going so happily and now this accursed incident had blighted it. Why were women so touchy and suspicious? God, nothing had happened. There was no reason for her to be so angry. Who the hell was she with now? That red-haired lad from the football club was always eyeing her up whenever they met. The telephone rang and he rushed to answer. A call from Ratoath, another racing personality who was suffering from gout. Milo fixed an appointment for him in a week's time. Mrs Neligan peeped in and realized that something was wrong. The young lord was in a very sour mood. The gentry got contrary at times. If they had to earn a living like everybody else, they might change their ways. Milo paced up and down on the threadbare carpet. The telephone rang again and he rushed to answer.

'Sorry, wrong number,' said a thick voice at the far end.

He resumed his pacing. A sudden noisy fall of soot in the grate signalled a family of crows at the top of the chimney. He sat down and took out more of the family papers. He chose one box at random and opened another eighteenth-century folio. The diary recorded a year full of disasters, personal, emotional, economic –

This day hath seen the sudden death of my son and heir. Dear Milo was riding hard across the deer park when his horse stumbled and now both rider and horse are dead. He was brought to the house on a door and the yard and countryside are full of such crying as I haven't heard since my poor father's death. The keening of the country people hath an eerie sound and there is a piper hath come to play the Lament of Kilbeggan, an air which tugs the heart strings. Ah me, what sadness. His mother hath taken to the bed and stays silent as if her tongue could not speak. My uncle Kilcock, who was riding with him, swears it was an infernal rabbit hole for these creatures are flourishing in spite of dogs and nets.

The rest of the diary read not much more cheerfully. Crops had failed, cattle fallen into sickness, a tower had fallen in the wind. Then came a curious entry –

This day my wife hath left me and travels to Limerick to her sister where she swears she will abide. All on account of May White.

Milo had to retrace the diary to find out the cause of the lady's departure. Some months further back he came across the name May White. The earl had been using the touch to cure many of the ague. Crowds, ranging from rich to poor, had come seeking the healing touch. The earl had been repaid with offerings. Thady O'Hara had offered some acres of woodland if the cure was effective. Peter McMahon brought four pigeons, 'two of them as old as himself and as uneatable'. There was a piteous message from a Thomas White to ask the lord to heal his daughter. The message acknowledged that Lord Kilbeggan used his touch only on men whom it seemed to cure but begged him to see his sick daughter, a girl of nineteen whom he doted on. Some pages later the reader found that the earl had answered the plea and was seeing 'poor May White'. There were references later to 'May White greatly revived, no longer skin and bones'. Thanks and presents were showered on Lord Kilbeggan, who now saw May White regularly. 'Poor May White' became 'dear May White' in the diaries. The entries became more frequent – *'Brought May White sailing on the lake which hath made her most cheerful.' 'Roses in May White's cheeks. She scarce hath need of my touch, though none seeks more to enjoy it.'* A

161

few pages later came the sentence, '*My Lady hath taken to her room and bars my entrance to it.*' The naive narrative continued.

> *May White very loving and grateful to me. 'For what?' quoth I. She is a sweet lass and well bred. None better.*

A few pages later came the entry –

> *May White now got with child. Tales wagging with the malice mongers. Young Shaw acknowledges the charge but I fear the spiteful and the common herd will not believe him.*

Shortly after this came the entry which proved that Lady Kilbeggan did not believe the story. As far as the earl went, it was one touch too far. Horses were brought out of stables and a sad entourage had travelled south, leaving the earl alone in his castle.

Milo finished reading the entry and sat thoughtfully in his chair. Could similar causes have similar effects? Human nature remained the same in spite of scientific progress. What started out as human kindness could end as temptation and disaster. You either accepted the risk and took the consequences or else avoided such situations. He determined that never would he land in a similar situation and he would tell Sheila so. One mistake was enough. He would have to convince her of his sincerity. If she felt she could not trust him, there would be no question of marriage. Only a fool marries a philanderer and Sheila was no fool. He must convince her that he would not stray or desert her for any attractive girl who crossed his path. He realized it was going to be difficult. He had been used to roving sexual experiences. Most young men that he knew took the pick-up as automatic. He had met few refusals; his success rate was phenomenal. Even travelling in the tube brought him some pleasant experiences. A brush of fingers on the same holding strap might bring an encounter with a stunning foreign au pair. Eyes had smiled invitations at him and he had got off at unaccustomed stations. He could have written a book about his encounters. Fifteen minutes after spotting an Australian blonde on the tube, he could be in a box-like room in Earl's Court having the time of his life. There was scarcely a European country whose wares he had not sampled. Youth was amoral and he had had some glorious times. Sensible enough to take precautions, he had not suffered from his experiences nor caused any suffering. He had taken pleasure and given pleasure from Edinburgh to Ascot. They were casual encounters certainly. He had no strong desire to set up house with any of them, no matter how desirable. Now he had somebody very desirable and he wanted to set up house with her. Had he lost the opportunity? A strong resolve to avoid the temptations in order to gain the greater fulfilment was necessary. He would not only have to make and keep the resolve but also to convince Sheila. He went out and telephoned again. No reply. He ran down to the Porsche and took off. From the basement window Mrs Neligan watched the car take off in a flurry of gravel.

'Where's he off to now?' She turned to old Neligan. 'That young man is crazy about the Kelly girl. There's been a row for certain. There won't be any gravel left on the front if they keep this up much longer.'

Sheila had certainly scattered the gravel in her temper earlier on but it was not all emotion that propelled her angry exit. She too was determined in her resolution. She would show Milo that she would not share him. She felt that his sexual appetite which made them both very happy might be their downfall if it was extended to others. She also felt that if he had a weakness this was it. She would have to make a stand at the beginning or their life together could be dogged by his infidelity. So it was important to let him know that there could be no deviation from their loyalty to each other. But she was genuinely angry as well and not a little jealous. Her one glance at the hockey player had told her that this was a very sexually alert young woman who wouldn't be backward at accepting an invitation. Those very bright eyes and the blushing skin told a story. There had been a state of excitement. So Sheila decided to keep Milo on the hook for a while to emphasize her distaste.

'Double-cross me at your peril,' would be her motto. She went off for the day with some friends. Shopping and window shopping in Mullingar, having a meal out in the golf clubhouse, they had a most enjoyable day, although she felt a slightly guilty twinge about Milo and a longing for him was not far away.

It was dark when she finally pulled up at Drumlerry and felt her heart beat when she saw the Porsche parked outside. Not to appear too eager, she delayed her entrance, getting her shopping bags together and at length opening the door with an unconcerned look. She greeted them all as if everything was normal, showing them a jumper she had bought in the expensive shop in Mullingar. She scarcely glanced at Milo but when she did it was almost unbearable – misery was written across his face and an equal longing. Emotion spoke to emotion. Her chatter seemed false and forced. She kept on talking, telling them about Siobhan, a friend of hers, who had had a row with her boss – a trivial silly story. Milo, ignored in the corner, rose to go. She didn't rise from her chair but said goodnight to him as if he were some casual acquaintance. Her parents glanced at her in surprise as she allowed him to walk out by himself. She fully intended to let him travel home without a sign from her at all but at the last moment her resolution faltered and she rushed out into the yard, knocking two flowerpots over in her haste. He was just turning the car, overcome with depression when the light from the open doorway caused him to look around and he found her in the car beside him. A torrent of relief flowed through him and he kissed her with passion. No words were necessary. His tears met hers. His rapture equalled her rapture. She was in his arms. They left the car which restricted their sense of closeness. Under a great old-fashioned orange blossom tree they embraced. His hunger for her knew no bounds. In the scented air they clung together. Not a word had been said. Her heart beat wildly. How long they stayed there, who could tell? At last she spoke.

'Let's go and tell them we're going to get married,' she whispered and he assented with happiness.

Elated and emotional, they entered the kitchen door. The old couple looked up at them with anticipation. In a voice choked with emotion Milo could hardly get out the words.

'I want to marry your daughter.'

He could go no further. The glow of happiness in Sheila's face told her parents all they needed to know. She stood hand in hand with her dark young man. There was silence for a moment. Mrs Kelly then rose from her chair. First she kissed Sheila. Then she kissed Milo. Then she sat down with tears streaming down her face.

'Say something, Daddy,' she said.

Mr Kelly put his arms around the young couple.

'I...we wish you every happiness. It will bring us all great joy.'

He too sat down overcome by the occasion. Then, mindful of his duties as master of the house, he went into the sitting room. Cupboard doors were opened and out he came with a bottle of Lockes' whiskey and some glasses. He poured four large glasses of whiskey and he toasted the new alliance.

'*Sláinte go saol agat agus go saol agat go léir agat,*' Mrs Kelly protested.

'Oh, Daddy, give us some water in the whiskey. Otherwise 'tis terribly strong.'

Mr Kelly pandered to what he thought was female weakness and he toasted the young couple afresh. As he did so, a car drove into the yard and in came Seamus and four of his friends back from a football practice. Another journey had to be made to the sitting room. One of the young footballers was dispatched for beer to a local pub and there was a hullabaloo of congratulations and cheers. Sheila was kissed on all sides and Milo was clapped on the back and had the hand almost shaken off him.

'Well begod,' shouted Seamus, 'I'll have a lord for a brother-in-law. Wait ' til you see me airs and graces.'

Milo blushed as they good-naturedly ragged him. But the warmth was genuine. Paul Smith, who had gone to the pub for beer, brought back not only a crate but Mooney the fiddler. More cars arrived into the yard as the word spread that Sheila Kelly had got engaged to the young Lord Kilbeggan. The crowds filled the kitchen and over-spilled into the yard where Mooney started to play in the warm night air and there was dancing up and down the yard, and many a sore ankle next morning.

'Come on, Daddy, give us "The Killucan Lady",' urged Mrs Kelly.

This was the romantic local ballad, which Mr Kelly was always persuaded to render on occasions of great importance. As so often happens, it took a half hour of persuasion before the old man reluctantly agreed to sing and then his surprisingly fine tenor voice rang over the yard. A bullock bawled loudly in a nearby field, bringing subdued laughing among the young people but he carried on with the famous old song, which was sung to the air of "The Old Orange Flute".

> Now I'll tell you a story
> A legend I'll tell
> Of a fine Westmeath lady
> Her name it was Nell.
> She came from Killucan
> A borough of note
> And she bought a fine shift
> From a tailor in Moate.
>
> *Chorus*
> And she bought a fine shift
> From a tailor in Moate.
>
> Now Pride was her downfall
> for travelling one day
> To fodder her cows
> wid a parcel of hay.
> She laid down her finery

for cleanness and thrift
When a young tinker man
He ran off with her shift.

Chorus
When a young tinker man
He ran off with her shift.

She left all her cattle
She left all her stock
She put her old Daddy
in charge of the clock.
She gave her old mammy
a pig as a gift
And off she went travelling
in search of her shift.

Chorus
And off she went traveling
in search of her shift.

O Tinker Lad, Tinker Lad
Danger it calls
There's a girl from Killucan
will cut off your . . .

Here Mrs Kelly blushed at the coarseness. Mr Kelly had once sung it at a wedding in front of three parish priests. She had been mortified. The only consolation was that Granny Kelly was deaf and didn't hear it. She made him promise to leave out this verse in future but sometimes he forgot.

'Ah Daddy,' she said reprovingly.

The song went on –

He fled on his piebald
From Drum to Kilcrift
And divil a sign could she find
Of her shift.

167

Verse after verse followed until the climax came. Nell caught up with the tinker at last.

> His dark eyes grew sad
> When he saw her distress
> He put his arms round her
> And gave her a kiss.
> Shure she leapt on his piebald
> You've now got my drift.
> And she married the tinker
> And brought back her shift.

Shouts of applause followed the song. Mr Kelly sat down feeling pleased. It was like his annual swim in Lough Ennel. It was damned hard to start but you enjoyed it once you'd started. Milo and Sheila sat at one in their happiness. Around them the party continued. The fiddler played and somebody sang 'The Boatman of Lough Lene'. The old people retired into the kitchen. Young Buckley walked on the dog's tail and caused a pitiable bark from the theatrical collie. The moonlight lit up the yard. A vixen was spotted crossing the meadow by the road. An argument started about what team was runner-up in the World Cup in 1994. Mrs Kelly was describing to a neighbour how a niece of hers by marriage, a daughter of the Maguires of Rathcroghan, had got engaged to an American who owned his own business and had a wonderful house with two deep freezes – one for meat and one for fish. Sandwiches were made and young Buckley made friends with the collie by offering her a compensatory crust. O'Shea fell off the chair with the drink. More singing started, mainly one verse songs with only the chorus being familiar. Teevan got mixed up in the words of 'The Rose of Tralee'. Kevin Mulligan started on his jokes.

'Did you hear the one about the girl who sat on the jockey's lap? She got a hot tip.'

An old bachelor neighbour, Bertie O'Neill, started on a long story but couldn't remember the details and had to give up. Young Reynolds and Kavanagh asked Milo if the castle was haunted and when he denied it, they told him long stories about ghosts that had been seen there. Milo was now so exhausted that he almost lay asleep in Sheila's arms. It had been an extraordinarily long day with rows and reconciliations culminating in emotional and mental contentment. He couldn't have cared less if there were poltergeists or phantom coachmen or ghosts of crying children flying around his castle. He roused himself up, went inside and kissed Mrs Kelly goodnight. She was almost as tired as himself. He got a shake of hands from Mr Kelly that almost took his own hands off him.

'I'll have to take him home,' said Sheila. 'Else, he'll fall asleep at the wheel.'

Her parents nodded understandingly.

'I might stay the night,' said Sheila and, to her surprise, the old pair did not demur. The party was still going on as they left the yard to a chorus of voices wishing them well.

'Well, I wouldn't stay in that castle if you paid me a hundred pounds, not even a thousand pounds,' said an old man.

Sheila drove carefully through the night, around to the lodge gates with their great stone escutcheons shining in the moonlight. Nor did she pause to think that someday she would be mistress of this ancient place. She drove slowly up to the front steps and helped out her almost comatose passenger. The staircase was hazardous but she eventually got Milo to the bedroom. He lay absolutely exhausted on the bed. She took off his shirt and jeans tenderly, undressed herself quickly and got in beside him. A fierce feeling of pride and possession flowed through her and she hugged the thin body to her breasts. He was aware of warmth and happiness beyond compare and nestled there. Sleep took them both.

21

News travels fast in the countryside. Country people do not need fax machines or other modern gadgets to receive information. Young Buckley had to get a fill of diesel for his tractor early next morning. The garage was open early. Buckley told the garage man who liked chatting with his customers. Sheridan, the milkman, passed the news on to Mr Grant, the postman. Congregations at early church services were soon discussing the news. Relations in Enfield were astonished and rather horrified. Apparently the young couple had only known each other for a few weeks. Repeated telephone calls to the castle brought Mrs Neligan up the stairs. A reporter from a local paper wanted to get more information about the engagement. He thought of selling it to the big Dublin dailies, something on the lines of 'Romance. Handsome Earl to marry childhood sweetheart' or something like that. Mrs Neligan, although flabbergasted at the news, was very curt with the reporter. His lordship was still in bed. She had heard him coming in late and she wouldn't disturb him. He must be tired. Besides, the reporter was wrong. Miss Kelly had only known him for a few weeks. She would pass on the message to his lordship. She then flew down the stairs to tell old Neligan the news. There would be big changes coming. God knows what would happen to the place. Old Neligan dropped his porridge spoon into his cup of tea at the news. What was the world coming to? Farmers' daughters shouldn't be marrying into the gentry. The reporter had sold his first headline to the gossip column of a Dublin paper by this time and it appeared on Sunday.

'Exhausted Earl's Sudden Engagement. Lord Milo Kilbeggan's Speedy Decision.' There followed a flood of vague innuendoes and suggestions, which would cause Mrs Neligan to answer the telephone more circumspectly in the future. Another telephone call was a message for Lord Kilbeggan from Ted Fitzpatrick. It was – 'Tipperary 4.30 Lind's Lobelia'.

As Mrs Neligan put down the telephone she heard the young lord bounding down the staircase.

'A message about flowers from a Mr Fitzpatrick. He's collecting the lobelia at half past four. He spoke from Tipperary.' Milo looked very surprised and astonished. 'And am I right in thinking that congratulations are in order?' continued Mrs Neligan. 'Old Neligan and myself would like to wish you every happiness. I don't know how it will affect our position here. Indeed we have no other home. It's often I've said to old Neligan that he should have put aside money for our old age. I've no wish to lose a roof over our . . .' here she was interrupted by Milo.

'There is no question of you losing the roof over your head while I own this house. Thank you both for your congratulations. I'll pass your good wishes on to Miss Kelly. Perhaps you'd make breakfast for two this morning.'

He bounded up the staircase.

'Sheila, what on earth could Ted Fitzpatrick be ringing for? Something about lobelias at half past four. Surely that's not his line? He's coming up to raid the garden at half four.'

Sheila lay in the bed glowing with happiness and laughing at his puzzlement.

'Let's buy a paper this morning and look up the racing pages,' she suggested.

Snug and contented she was almost reluctant to leave the bed. Not all the cosmetics in the world can produce the glowing appearance that happiness imparts and her face was radiant and beautiful. There was a certain amount of horseplay which might have slowed things up, but he desisted and they were able to descend the staircase later looking pleasantly serious. There was a certain tenseness in the air when Mrs Neligan arrived with the breakfast. She was still apprehensive and shocked and worried about possible changes to come.

'Can I congratulate you on your good fortune, miss? she said primly.

Milo laughed.

'It's me who had the good fortune,' he told her. 'I'm the most fortunate man in the country. We would both like yourself and Mr Neligan to have a drink with us this evening to toast our health and to wish us all many happy years in this house. We'll be away all day as we're going up to Dublin. You might take down any telephone messages on a pad.'

They had decided to drive to Dublin to buy an engagement ring. But first Sheila had to change clothes so they went over to Drumlerry where the household was recovering from the festivities of the night before. Seamus was cleaning up the yard. Mrs Kelly was answering the phone, then darting out to feed the geese which were indignant with their late release, then darting in again to answer the phone.

'That was Cissie Grogan from Grangegeeth, my own third cousin. You remember her. She has sons that work in the Tara Mines, Tosh and Emmet, and they're very good to her. God knows she deserves it after losing poor Tommy early on in the marriage. She was a Bennet from Senshalstown.'

She was halted in her reminiscences as the phone rang again.

'Peter Buckley for you, Dadda,' she shouted and relaxed for a moment in her chair. 'Well, what a night. It's lucky you got away early. Such laughing and dancing and music. Young O'Shea had to be driven home by Seamus. Bertie O'Neill started in to the politics. You'd think he'd leave them at home sometime. And Paul Smith drove out of the yard – you'd think he'd knock down a gate post. What's the sense of driving so fast? And Brigid and Bobby – they're thinking of doing the same thing as yourselves. But it was a great night all the same. God send us a few more like it. Now I've forgotten about food. Are ye half-starved? I'll put the pan

172

on the stove. Well now, Sheila, you'll want to start thinking of feeding the pair of you. Are you certain you won't have a fry? You're going to Dublin, you say. There's perfectly good jewellers in Mullingar or Tullamore. Probably cheaper too. But shure you'll go where you want to. Dadda wants to buy a buckrake from Peter Buckley. You should hear them arguing over the price. They say potatoes are a very poor price this year. I'm glad Seamus never got into them. Dadda, they're going up to Dublin. Do you want any messages? He wants something collected from Lenihan's of Capel Street. They sent word down it was fixed.'

Milo was relieved when Sheila got changed quickly and they drove off with alacrity.

'She's full of excitement,' said Sheila. 'She won't stop talking for days. Not like me. I'm cool, calm and collected.'

'Sometimes,' said Milo.

An hour later they were approaching Dublin.

'Stop,' said Sheila dramatically, as they passed a news-agents. She ran to the shop and bought a morning paper.

'Now let's look at the racing pages. Here we are. The Tipperary Races are being held today. Now let's go down the list. 4.30. Here we are, Lind's Lobelia – owner Mrs Fitzpatrick, Trainer T. Fitzpatrick. Let's see the SP Forecast 8/1. He wasn't calling about flowers. It's a tip. Do you remember he was delighted with the effect of the touch. Drive on until we find a bookmaker. This must be very worthwhile or he wouldn't ring you about it.'

They both got excited as they thought about it. Milo decided that he would place the biggest bet of his life. Previously he had never betted more than a fiver. He had won twenty pounds once at Cheltenham and had a good win at Ascot but he was a naturally cautious person who had seen friends of his losing small fortunes. This was no time for caution he felt. He decided to place a hundred pounds at eight to one in a city centre bookmaker. The car was parked in a supervised car park, as Milo was all too conscious of the attraction to joyriders of the very smart and stylish Porsche. They walked hand in hand down a crowded

O'Connell Street. He placed his bet and then escorted Sheila to a large jewellers where country people had bought their rings for over a century. McDowells has a certain air about it – a mixture of antiquity, taste and luxury. They were escorted upstairs by John McDowell whose youthful appearance belied a profound knowledge of the trade. He showed them trays of diamond rings.

There were trays of solitaires, of three-stone clusters and five-stone clusters. Sheila became absorbed, totally absorbed in the brilliant stones and the elegant designs of their settings. She moved from tray to tray, lifting rings out and placing them on her finger. She hovered over a round brilliant cut diamond, then got enthusiastic over an oval cut. They were shown the international colour grading systems. There was talk of the four c's – cut, colour, clarity and carat-weight. They heard of birthmarks, known as inclusions in diamonds, of loupes, of carat-weight and of the seven most popular shapes. Milo swallowed hard as Sheila enquired the price of a one-carat solitaire to be told that it would cost £3,500. He tried to look unconcerned as she moved on to a three-stone ring of one carat weight. This was a mere £2,200. The next ring, a cluster of one carat, was priced at £1,500. At the bottom range of the market there was a small solitaire set in 18-carat gold costing £395. This quite pretty ring did not look right on Sheila's strong finger. At last she picked a three-stone ring in a collet setting which Milo also admired. This was a splendid and beautiful ring which flashed prettily on her finger.

'Is it possible?' she asked Milo. A consultation revealed the price to be £800 and Milo wrote out a cheque.

'You forgot to write your first name on the cheque,' said the cashier. When she was told it was for Lord Kilbeggan, she enquired if Milo would take the other rings which had been left in for cleaning and had not been collected for years.

Milo and Sheila, astonished, asked to see the rings. After a short delay a box was brought up with the faded inscription 'Lady Cynthia Kilbeggan, Kilbeggan, Co. Westmeath'. Inside the box laid out on velvet lay some unusual jewellery. First they picked out a square emerald ring surrounded by twelve small diamonds mounted in white gold on a gold band. A second ring was an eternity ring of diamonds and emeralds. The third item fascinated them. This was a bar brooch of gold depicting two wolves with brilliant ruby eyes. The bar represented a hand. They turned the brooch over and found the motto *Vinceo quem tango* inscribed on the back. The last item was a large-linked gold charm bracelet with twelve seals, two of which had the family crest. One of the seals held the Kilcock crest and another portrayed an old-fashioned racehorse at the gallop. The bracelet had its own little satin box. The collection surprised and delighted them. Mr McDowell was pleased to have found somebody to take the family jewellery.

'We kept ringing the castle but could get no reply, so the collection has been here for a long time. Could you give me the family solicitor's number so that we can verify your identity. These are very good stones and the items are of great value.'

Milo gave him Mr Kinch's telephone number and they inspected the hoard with delight and interest. What a piece of luck to have come to the one jeweller with whom Lady Cynthia had dealt. Mr McDowell came back having confirmed that this young and rather scruffy man was indeed the Earl of Kilbeggan.

'I believe there is another and rather larger piece in the workshops that we still haven't found a part for. It's a silver centrepiece for a dining room table. There are two wolves rampant separated by a tree which is really a hand. We have been trying to find the right silver to repair two broken fingers on the hand. This is a very valuable piece made about 1775 of Dublin silver and would fetch a huge sum at auction. Phillips sold a somewhat similar piece five years ago and it went for over a hundred thousand pounds with a lot of interest shown. Prices have almost doubled since. If you'd like to leave the other rings here while you do the rest of your shopping, you can take them later on this afternoon.'

175

Sheila kept her pretty engagement ring which she almost preferred to the old-fashioned more valuable rings and they walked out half stunned into the bright light of O'Connell Street.

Dublin, like many an ancient city, can be captivating on a bright sunlit day. They crossed O'Connell Bridge over a bright sparkling Liffey, passed between two great eighteenth-century buildings, Trinity College and the Bank of Ireland with its splendid pillared facade. Grafton Street was full of shoppers and young people like themselves. They had a late luncheon at QV2 where the tipsy cake trifle from an antique recipe made them ask for seconds. She found that Milo had a sweet tooth and he discovered that she found garlic anathema, a fact which was to cause dissension later on in their lives. But today all was unity and happiness. A brass band was playing in Saint Stephen's Green and the gallant airs swelled between the four sides of this lovely Georgian square. Old tunes like 'Clare's Dragoons', 'O'Donnell Abu' and 'The West's Awake' were martial in their dignity. In between, the band played sentimental but haunting songs – the 'Pride of Petravore', 'Long Long Ago in the Woods of Gortnamona', and the 'Mountains of Mourne'. They sat happily amid the flower borders, feet tapping to the music. Afterwards they walked down Dawson Street past the charming mansion house of the Lord Mayor of Dublin. They went into travel offices and collected brochures of holiday places much reduced for winter and spring bookings. They strolled through Temple Bar, Dublin's Left Bank, which was colourful and full of young people, some with predatory intentions. At Lenihan's of Capel Street they collected a pin for a mowing bar for Mr Kelly. Thirsty, they dropped into a pub where they found the racing from Tipperary being televised. Milo had almost forgotten his largest ever bet, so full of happiness and events had the day been. Now the pair of them sat glued to the pub television set as the 4.30 race was previewed. The two commentators could not have been more opposite in their styles. One had a pleasantly plummy voice, relaxed, as if at a party among friends. The second commentator had an excited voice with the 'saucy rough-ness' that Shakespeare had once described. This second blunt commentator felt that Lind's Lobelia had a good chance and felt surprised that the horse stood so far out in the betting. His colleague did not see him being a threat to the favourite and saw his chances as very remote. Milo and Sheila could see the Fitzpatricks in the ring and marked the jaunty step of the young man who had not yet returned to the saddle but who must be close to a recovery.

'The horses are leaving the parade ring.'

They sat back with some excitement to watch the race. Minutes later they were on their feet almost stunned with excitement as Lind's Lobelia flew past the winning post just ahead of the favourite and second favourite. Curious glances from the other customers did not dim their excitement, but the almost instant announcement quelled their sense of victory.

'Stewards' enquiry.'

They had to wait agitatedly. Preparation went ahead for the next race. The disparity between the day's performance by Lind's Lobelia and its previous appearances on the race track had been noted by the stewards. Horses for a five o'clock race appeared in the parade ring. At length an announcement was made – 'Winner all right' and the two young lovers hugged each other to the astonishment of the rather elderly drinkers in the gloomy bar.

'Come on,' said Sheila, 'let's go and collect.' They pushed their way through the evening crowds and collected a cool £900 from the bookmakers. They crossed O'Connell Street to McDowell's and collected the parcel of jewellery and silver. John McDowell took them aside.

'Could I advise you to insure these items immediately. They are extremely valuable and would be difficult to recover if stolen. I can get you immediate cover from my own agent if you would like me to do so. I have just been told that a young man with blond hair came in some time ago and purported to be a member of the Kilbeggan family. He looked disreputable and left immediately when we told

177

him we would have to investigate his credentials. He never returned.'

Sheila looked at Milo and both were thinking the same thoughts. Packy had probably heard of the treasures that were ready for collection.

'A second point, I should mention,' went on Mr McDowell, 'Lady Cynthia on the same day that she brought in the jewellery to us was going on to some picture restorers to have two oil paintings cleaned. I wonder did the same thing happen? She fell ill and never collected the jewellery and our letters were never answered. I wonder are the oil paintings still awaiting collection in some gallery in Dublin. While one admired the lady enormously, it was obvious that she had grown quite eccentric and might well have forgotten the pictures or told the restorers to hold them until they were collected.'

'You may well be right,' said Milo.

They left the shop full of surmise and satisfaction. Milo could not get over the turn in his luck. He had arrived in Dublin apprehensive and wondering if he could afford the price of the engagement ring. His tip from the Fitzpatricks had now paid for the ring and he was carrying home a small fortune in jewellery as well. Besides this, there was the excitement of wondering about the value of the oil paintings that might be retrieved. Snug in the Porsche they set off for home. The motorway had not yet been built. Not even the intolerable traffic jams at Leixlip, the incredible slowness of the evening traffic at Maynooth could dim their sense of elation. Beyond Kilcock ('my uncle's town,' he told her laughingly), he was able to let the superb engine dominate the road and they drove back to Kilbeggan the happiest couple in Ireland.

22

'I thought her ladyship had sold that jewellery,' said Mrs Neligan, looking unimpressed at the superb pieces of silver that Milo laid out on the library table. 'She went off to Dublin with them and they never came back, so I took it that she was short of money. Was it the same time she took away some pictures from the far wall just under the damp spots?' Milo inspected the wall and found three spaces of a different colour to the rest of the wall. 'She took Packy up to Dublin with her that day to help her carry them wherever she was going. I worry about our Packy. Those policemen ought to be out chasing robbers and burglars instead of hounding young people and turning them against the law. I always say that young people need a bit of give and take.'

She was in tired form. The telephone had never stopped ringing all day with enquiries and messages for the young lord. She hadn't known what to say when Miss Baring-Brown had rung up asking her if it was true that Lord Kilbeggan was engaged to Miss Kelly. Fortunately Miss Penelope had taken it well and had seemed quite anxious to find out if Miss Kelly could bring some bags of potatoes to the hunt sale. Mrs Metcalfe had rung up and had seemed quite astonished at the news of the engagement. She had asked if that was the girl accompanying Lord Kilbeggan to the party before the races. Another jockey, a friend of the Fitzpatricks, had rung asking for an appointment – something about strained ligaments that wouldn't heal. There were other calls and some she hadn't been able to answer as she was dressing old Neligan's corns at the time. Indeed the telephone was becoming a bit of a curse – always ringing when you were in the toilet or your hands were greasy from cooking. She hoped Lord Kilbeggan would answer his own

179

calls when he was in the house. Milo calmed her down and also told her that her wages would be increased from now on to help her cope with the increased workload. They asked her to fetch old Neligan up so that they might drink to their future.

An hour later the Neligans had relaxed. Indeed, old Neligan had lost his old retainer's manner and was laughing uproariously at his own jokes. Anecdote after anecdote was told about his employers. He remembered the time Lady Cynthia could not get her hunting boot off. He had tugged and tugged and eventually fell back across Mrs Neligan and had stunned her for a moment. There was the time when the hound puppies had got in the back door and had eaten a skirt belonging to Lady Cynthia and taken one of her shoes out to the yard and it was never found. There was the story of Lady Cynthia getting absent-minded. She had asked the bishop and some of her friends to dinner and had forgotten all about it. The only food in the house was half a game pie and some bread and butter pudding. The bishop didn't mind because it was Lent but the colonel and his lady were not pleased. She had done the same with the hunt, invited them all to a lawn meet and then forgotten about it.

'Who are those people?' she had asked old Neligan peering down the steps at riders and hounds and horse-boxes. But she was a wonderful lady if the truth be told, had a heart of gold. There was no one would say a bad word about her. She had been very good to Packy, indeed had spoilt him and she hadn't said a word to the guards when the silver sugar bowl disappeared. Here Mrs Neligan glared so hard at him that he shut up abruptly and only wished health and prosperity to Sheila and Milo. Mrs Neligan diverted the conversation. She enquired if it would be possible to get 'a branch line of the telephone' down to the kitchen to save her mounting the stairs so often and Milo promised that he would have a line to the kitchen installed and also a line upstairs. He would ring Telecom next day to arrange it. Mr Neligan had restarted his reminiscences about the drinking habits of the old lord and how Lady Cynthia had tried to cope with it by hiding the bottles of whiskey. Once the earl had asked him to take a look at the grand-father clock in the hall which had stopped ringing the hours. Old Neligan had found two bottles of Powers which Lady Cynthia had hidden hastily and then forgotten to remove. They were blocking the works of the clock. Hunting had become a nightmare as the earl set off enthusiastically in the morning but later dropped into some village pub and didn't come home until the small hours. Good hunters were left unfed for hours in a horsebox outside some remote bar. Lady Cynthia would be sitting stately in the dining room at eight o'clock but sat alone as her husband caroused and forgot about dinners. Another time old Neligan recalled when Lord Kilbeggan had stumbled out of some village pub late at night and got into the rear seat of his car by mistake. Failing to find the steering wheel, he had returned to the pub and telephoned the guards in Mullingar to complain that his steering wheel had been stolen. Out came the squad car to investigate the robbery. They had brought his lordship home in the squad car, while one of the guards drove the Kilbeggan car back to the castle. For they were different times then and you could get away with being a bit intoxi-cated even if you were driving. It was the time of a nod and a wink, not like nowadays when they lay waiting for you with the bag ready to test you.

'They say Rochford Bridge is a terror,' old Neligan said almost irrelevantly.

Later, having helped the old man down the stairs, Milo and Sheila sat discussing the revelation about the missing pictures. Could the pictures still be in Dublin awaiting collection? If so, Packy was the only person who would know where they were and this in itself was alarming. They felt it was essential to investigate the whereabouts of the pictures immediately and decided to start the search next day by telephoning some of the well-known Dublin picture restor-ers. Money would be essential to do repairs to the castle and the sale of a couple of valuable paintings might provide the necessary finances. They decided also to place the newly-acquired silver in the bank for safety. Sheila was nearly nodding off by now and Milo drove his sleepy fiancée over to Drumlerry where the yard was full of cars and a fresh number of friends and relations crowded the kitchen hoping to meet and congratulate the young couple. Longing for a quiet intimacy, Milo and Sheila had to face a fresh session of conviviality. Uncle Tim from Stradbally was there, curious to meet Milo.

'Well, as the fellow says, it's great to see a good-looking couple getting hitched.'

Almost every sentence he spoke contained the phrase, 'As the fellow says'. Sheila told Milo afterwards that at Uncle Tim's wedding years ago when the priest asked, 'Wilt thou take this woman to be thy lawful wedded wife?' Uncle Tim was reputed to have answered, 'As the fellow says, I will.' Once again there was a swarm of young people. Milo and Sheila were engulfed in a warm tide of goodwill. There were good-natured jibes about Sheila rising high in social circles.

'Mind she doesn't run off with a duke,' said Bobby Doyle to Milo. There were also jokes about the usefulness of marrying a nurse.

'You'll be safe if you ever get piles,' was one frivolous comment. Many and varied were the remarks about how the Kilbeggan touch was successful with the women. Milo was invited to shoot pheasant with one lot of friends, offered the loan of a tractor by others. A venerable old cousin of Mrs Kelly kept offering him advice about keeping brood mares while another ancient lady told him that religious differences meant nothing to her, that some of her best friends were members of a different religion and not to let these differences worry him. Milo told her that he hadn't even thought of such a thing and this seemed to disappoint her. Mrs Kelly would not let her husband sing 'The Killucan Lady' again after him slipping in the coarse verse the previous night. Instead he sang an enormously complicated old ballad called 'The Boatman of Lough Bawn' which recalled a legend containing many romantic ingredients including a lovelorn maiden fleeing from her tyrannical parents, a great storm rising with a boat in peril, a rescue by a handsome but poverty-stricken swain who himself drowned in the attempt after saving the maiden, one funeral which turned into a double funeral and many other sad moments. The elderly people wiped their eyes as Mr Kelly concluded his song.

> At night if you travel
> Near Lough Bawn's wild strand
> In a drear winter's fog
> Which afflicts all the land.
> Through the mist and the moonlight
> A vision appears
> 'Tis the gallant young boatman
> Still searching with tears.

After this cheerful ditty which silenced the crowd for a while, some of the young people drifted out to the yard and soon 'rickety tickety tin' and other comic and even coarse songs were being sung as the lager consumption added depth and boldness to the voices. Milo and Sheila tried to keep themselves from falling asleep, but eventually he had to slip away before fatigue overcame him completely. Sheila too fell fast asleep in her whitewashed bedroom long before the party below had finished and the yard lay in silence. The young couple dreamt of each other – he in his great high-ceilinged bedroom under the Gothic turrets and she in her simple surroundings.

23

At nine-thirty next morning Milo was awoken by noises of cars and dogs yapping far below him at the front of the castle. Shortly afterwards the Indian gong in the hall sounded sonorously. Not only did Mrs Neligan want to avoid climbing the great staircase but she also was apprehensive about who she might find in the lord's bedroom. Used as she was to the ways of the gentry she still kept her eyes averted from sexual matters. Once a foolish neighbour had suggested to her that Packy might be gay.

'Very much so,' she had replied, 'he's one of the most cheerful gay lads you could find.' She smote the gong a second time but Milo was already descending the staircase wondering who could have called at this hour of the morning. It was about half way through the day for the two Miss Blacks whom Mrs Neligan was entertaining in the small morning room. She had always liked the two Miss Blacks, left high and dry when the brigadier had died so suddenly. If people are said to look like their dogs, then the Blacks could be brought forward to prove the assertion. Voices, sharp movements and thin healthy appearances made them appear like the terriers of the human world. While their late father, the brigadier, might have resembled a boxer or perhaps a basset hound, Di and Ginny were the Jack Russells of County Westmeath.

'We brought over the litter to show you,' shouted Di and Ginny completed, as she always did, her sister's sentence, 'so you can pick the best of the litter. We've been telling Mrs Neligan how to feed it but of course she's had plenty of experience of feeding dogs. It's a lucky dog that has Mrs Neligan to feed it, isn't it, Di?'

Her sister concurred enthusiastically and, in a babble of

noise, Milo was brought down his own steps to be met by an even greater babble as the Blacks opened the tail door of their ancient station-wagon. Milo nearly had the hand taken off him as he mistakenly tried to pat a small masculine head. Young puppies as they were, the whole litter had inherited full terrier instincts, fearless despite their size.

'There, who's a splendid little fighter?' said Ginny, pulling out a small tricoloured bitch which began to lick her frantically.

They were a beautiful bunch, all good-looking and well looked after. Milo decided to have a dog, much less trouble than the bitches in later life or so, mistakenly he thought. He picked a white-faced dog with black ears and a good head.

'Good choice if I may say so,' said Di. 'He's had his tail docked. We don't agree with all this silly modern tomfoolery. It's like getting your tonsils out – you suffer a little but it's good for you afterwards. He's had his injections and we'll let him go to you for a hundred. Really nice to get him into a good home. Thank you, we won't have coffee. We have several other deliveries to make.'

So they had. Every time they sold terriers they paid their bills and were able to take their short holiday in Cork at Castletownsend. This morning they could nearly add something to their prices, telling all the later customers that Lord Kilbeggan had pressed them to sell him a terrier. Naive as they might appear at times, they had developed a strong selling instinct and would have been a great success in a company's marketing department. Milo wrote a cheque for a hundred pounds and lifted his new attractive companion up the steps. He put it down in the hall, where it promptly peed, not on the flagstones but on a rug – a practice it perfected in the coming weeks.

Scarcely was his breakfast over than his day's first patient appeared. Middle-aged and very stiff, he sat down on the sofa before Milo was ready to treat him. He was arthritic. In later months, Milo was to find arthritis a very common ailment among his clients. Whether it was climate or neglect or over-exercise that caused it, the country seemed to be full of arthritic sufferers and many's the pain-racked body Milo was to handle in the coming months. Here the pain afflicted the hips. Once again it appeared to Milo that the pain did not just leave the patient, but it seemed to be transmitted out of the patient via the healer. When he had completed his task, he had to leave the room and sit down exhausted in the library with his face and body sweating profusely. After washing and towelling himself down, he returned to find a grateful patient very much relieved and less fearful of rising and walking and descending the flight of steps. He paid Milo the price of one leg of the terrier and asked for another appointment in a month.

Milo waved goodbye to his visitor and re-entered the house to find puddles everywhere and no pup. Mrs Neligan had found an old rug to bed the terrier but the rug lay empty. Milo called and felt stupid as he had no name for the little dog.

'Here, Puddles, Puddles, Puddles,' he called.

He looked under sofas, armchairs and stools. He searched behind the great gong, behind the military chest, behind the long ancient yew table which stood near the door. No pup appeared and no whimper gave away a hiding place. Frustrated, he set off downstairs and entered the kitchen. Here he found the problem solved. Old Neligan sat by the Aga with the little terrier in his lap sound asleep. Both looked well content.

'He lapped a little milk but he needs company now that he's separated from his family. I'll look after him if you're going out,' said the old man.

This relieved the terrier's new owner, as he had begun to feel that the tiny dog would be absorbing a great deal of his time. He returned upstairs, boxed the silver to take to the bank and set off for Drumlerry.

The farmhouse was full of activity after the second night's revelry. The last of their visitors had not left until three o'clock and the old pair looked a bit worn.

'Thank goodness that's over,' said an exhausted Mrs Kelly.

'But you couldn't put them out when they had come to wish us well. As for that young Hickey, I'm really surprised at him. You'd think his manners would be better than that, considering that his mother was a Miss Glynn from Williamstown that used to look down their nose at everybody. Now here's Sheila,' she said irrelevantly.

Milo didn't find out how young Hickey had blotted his copybook, for Sheila in blue jeans and a figure-hugging T-shirt had come down the stairs. Her hand had been nearly worn off, she said, showing the ring to everybody but she looked fresh and radiant in the morning light. They sat down to mugs of tea and discussed possible names for Milo's new terrier.

'Trixie is a nice name for a terrier,' said Mrs Kelly.

'Ah Mammy, it's a dog,' said Sheila, 'you can't call a dog Trixie.'

Mrs Kelly was shocked at the suggestion that it should be called Puddles. Mr Kelly suggested Dandy. Sheila suggested Agassi after the tennis player whom she thought Milo slightly resembled apart from the uncouth hairstyle. This was too long a name for Milo who wanted a short sharp name befitting a terrier. Seamus suggested Quinn after Niall Quinn, the soccer star who had scored a spectacular recent goal for Ireland. Milo, whose London friends had a habit of calling any terriers by vulgar names like Fart or Blast or Poo, still was not satisfied. Somebody suggested Casey as a name for a good masculine terrier. This reference to a Bishop of Galway did not please Mrs Kelly. McGuigan was suggested after the small terrier-like boxer from Clones. Finally Sheila came up with a brilliant offering.

'Why not call him Touch after the Kilbeggan touch?' she asked and this met with unanimous approval.

So Touch was named and Sheila couldn't wait to see him.

They drove into the town to deposit the silver in the Bank of Ireland. A young assistant was confused by the title.

'Sir Kilbeggan would like to see you,' she told the manager.

The sight of the ancient silver impressed the manager.

This ancient landed family had not been the best of customers in previous times. Overdrafts had gone on for very long periods. Lady Cynthia had seemed to feel that having the manager's wife to tea and view the garden would make up for constant loans. It made it difficult to send harsh letters to the castle, when your wife was enjoying attending committee meetings with Lady Cynthia to set up a hunt sale for money to keep the foxhounds in action. Now and again slightly absurd presents were dropped in at the private door of the bank. Two peaches nestling in slightly dirty cotton wool would be appreciated by the manager's wife.

'How kind of Lady Cynthia. It was only last week that she promised me she'd send me some. They're not very good this year. She said a lot of them got covered in mildew.'

The manager had secretly cursed Lady Cynthia and her mildewed peaches, aware that headquarters in Dublin were pressing him to do something about the overdraft. Then she never called him 'the manager' but always the more traditional title used by the Bank of Ireland.

'How is the Agent?' she would ask his wife and his wife would feel rather flattered at being married to an Agent rather than a manager. Now this new young earl looked better business, even if he did engage in quackery. At last some money was coming in and the Georgian silver showed solid wealth rather than debt and mortgages. He welcomed Milo and Sheila and they discussed some of their plans with him. The renovation of gate lodges and outbuildings would take money, but money he was assured would be coming in. They left the bank with a pleasant feeling.

'Seems quite a nice bloke,' said Milo. 'Funny how banks can lend millions to fraudulent businessmen, whom even simple people could see are quite crooked and yet be very aggressive to the ordinary person if he gets a hundred overdrawn. This chap seems a very decent sort.'

They set off for Mullingar feeling warm and cosy in the Porsche. This close proximity in the cockpit-like comfort of the car inevitably brought on a desire for greater intimacy

188

and they stopped at a lakeside halfway between the two towns to release their feelings.

Later they read the Yellow Pages of the telephone directory to get some information about picture restorers in Dublin. Between the entry pianos-repairing and tuning and the entry pig breeders and dealers there were three entries to do with pictures, all to do with framing and moulding and none with restoration. They turned to the art entries and here between entries for aromatherapy and artificial flowers they struck it lucky. Here were telephone numbers for art centres and art galleries. They rang one of the most prominent private galleries and explained their predicament. They were given a list of names of the more important restoration firms.

'Try Harrisons first,' they were told. 'Just off Merrion Square. They have a long tradition of storing and restoring pictures for county families. If they are not the right people they will probably give you a few suggestions for where the pictures might be held.'

Milo thanked them for their help and looked up the number for Harrisons and dialled straightaway. It was engaged. They sat down and had a cup of coffee and tried again. Engaged. Ten minutes later they tried again, and again the number was engaged. Milo swore. Perhaps this was the end of their good luck.

They drove back to the castle and again inspected the gate lodges with a view to getting them restored quickly and making some money. On the back avenue, lorries were collecting the timber that Hughie Quigley had felled and cut. In the late afternoon sun they brought the little terrier out to the terrace in front of the castle and Sheila almost got broody as it made little chases after stray leaves and began to chew her sandals. She fondled it on her lap and it gave excited little barks and then stayed still while it watched her intensely.

'It's a dote,' she said and kept calling it Touch so that it might become familiar with its name.

189

It fell asleep on her lap. Milo went in and brought back a tray with boiled eggs and brown bread and potato cakes. In great contentment the two lovers sat below the great Gothic castle and discussed their future. Jack Brennan would be home the next day she told him.

'Jack who?' he enquired. He had forgotten about Seamus's friend who she had suggested might restore the gate lodges. They had decided to go up to Dublin again the next day to visit Harrisons and other picture restorers and find out once and for all about the pictures.

'We can see Jack when we get back,' she suggested.

As the terrier shifted in her lap, a hot drip went down the side of her leg. The inevitable had happened. Adoring puppy lovers are never careful enough. Nor can they expect sympathy from their friends. Milo's laugh echoed against the castle walls as the terrier began to play more exciting little games after proudly depositing its liquid burden.

'Language please,' said Milo chuckling as Sheila looked in dismay at her sodden jeans. 'Remember you're a nurse. They're used to everything, aren't they?'

He returned Touch to his bed beside the Aga and took Sheila upstairs to change her clothes.

Two hours later after he had kitted her out in more ways than one, Milo led Sheila back to the library. She was dressed rather smartly in an old pair of shooting trousers that Milo had found in a wardrobe. They hid her superb curves while emphasizing the tightness and revelation of the T-shirt above. Mrs Neligan, entering the room, recognized instantly the darn she had sewn in the crotch where the old earl had nearly split himself while crossing barbed wire. What would he have thought if he were alive today? Mrs Neligan thought sourly that she knew the answer to that only too well. His fondness for an attractive girl had been only too well-known. She had often seen Lady Cynthia pursing her lips when the earl had gone too far in admiration of some leggy youngster.

'You remember that you were talking to me about the pictures only last night. Old Neligan says that he remembers

190

the name of the artist. He was called Whiting and they were pictures of horses. Very dull old pictures and very dark. Lady Cynthia liked them a lot. She said that they were her bank, so dull as they looked, they must have been some value. The firm kept writing after she died and Packy said that he would look after the matter as he had helped her in the first place. They also kept telephoning and Packy answered them each time. So I don't know what's happened to them. Maybe they've gone to some museum. There's people that likes that sort of thing. The old lord preferred pictures of young ladies but Lady Cynthia burnt them after he died. Otherwise I know nothing of the picture scene. It was after the trustees dying and the solicitor being left with all the work. There was great confusion about the furniture and the pictures. Have you seen the grocer's calendar? There's a lovely picture of a little girl with two kittens. I'm going to try to get it framed when the year is up. Would you like a fresh pot of tea?'

She padded off down the stairs after they had thanked her and refused the tea. Milo drove Sheila home but didn't go into the house, because she had spotted a Dublin car in the yard.

'It's cousin Lily from Clontarf,' she said, 'if you'd like to come in and answer a hundred questions you're welcome.'

But Milo could not face a third night running and he drove off, promising to collect her at ten o'clock next morning.

Sheila entered the farmhouse to be smothered with affection by cousin Lily from Clontarf. She had married a civil servant who had endured her questions for half a century before expiring gratefully. His friends had hoped he wouldn't face any more questions on his entrance to the next world.

'Well, here she is,' said cousin Lily. 'How are you and where is himself? Have you got the ring? Where did you buy it?' Disappointed that she was not to meet Milo, she rose to leave after half an hour. 'What's the time. Could you believe it's nearly ten o'clock? Is the clock right? Where on earth does the time go? Did you see the piece in the paper about the crash near Enfield? Will I send it to you? Where on earth are my keys? Did I put them in my coat pocket?'

They escorted her to her car where after a further barrage of interrogation, she drove off into the night.

'Phew,' said Mr Kelly in relief.

He had endured a night of it.

'Now, Dadda,' said Mrs Kelly. 'Don't be at that. Poor Lily is the soul of kindness, she'd do anything for you.'

'Except keep quiet,' said Mr Kelly to Sheila in an aside.

'It's a pity Dublin is such a distance and she doesn't like driving,' said Mrs Kelly. 'Otherwise we might see more of her.'

Mr Kelly thanked Heaven that Dublin was such a distance away and that cousin Lily didn't like driving.

'Maybe she'll give up driving altogether,' he said hopefully.

But cousin Lily's mind was full of more questions as she drove home to Clontarf.

'What on earth was Sheila doing dressing so shabbily? Where had she got that extraordinary old pair of tweed trousers? Had she not noticed the huge darn in the crotch?'

Not until she was stopped at a police check near Maynooth did the questions leave her mind. Then her mind was diverted by asking the two young policemen where did they come from, did they know the Bradys in that part of the country, had the new church been built there yet? They waved her on hurriedly into the night. In this case her questions were studied. She had suddenly remembered her driving licence was out of date.

24

Next morning Sheila received a letter in the post about an interview for a nursing post in Mullingar Hospital. She was to go for an interview to the Midland Health Board in Tullamore on the following week. They discussed it as they crawled up part of the main road. A tractor with a huge trailerful of straw was followed by a bespectacled and very careful lady in a brown Ford Fiesta. She was followed at an interval by a mother with a cargo of babies and young children crawling around the back seat. An elderly farmer in a woeful Cortina drove slowly behind her. Behind them all was Milo who had made several efforts to race past in his powerful machine. As soon as he put his foot to the accelerator, a huge lorry would appear going in the opposite direction and forcing him back into the slow procession. Time and again he prepared to let the Porsche rip past the intolerably slow group of vehicles and each time had to drop down into low gear and crawl behind the others. He fumed with rage.

'Call this a main road? It's mediaeval to be slowed down by farm traffic on a main road. Does nobody teach them to stop in a layby or a gateway and let the traffic by? Does he ever look in his mirror and see a mile of cars held up behind him?'

Sheila massaged his leg to distract him and he nearly drove into the rusty Cortina. Eventually the tractor pulled into a farmyard and Milo was able to roar past the other drivers who were oblivious of the impatient young man behind them.

A long queue of traffic started well before the entrance to Leixlip. Milo was full of frustration at this waste of power. Slowly the long procession eased its way down the hill and into the main street. Heavy lorries edged cautiously towards the traffic lights. A Toyota was double-parked outside a shop while its owner who did not believe in parking stood at the counter inside watching the huge jam he had caused and seeming quite unconcerned.

'What a thick bastard,' spat Milo. 'How do they get away with it? Not a policeman in sight. It seems to be the same everywhere. Mullingar was at a standstill the other day. Do they ever leave the police station or is it purely a sit-down job?'

Sheila reminded him that they had visited him a while previously in connection with the drug scare. The windscreen wipers hissed annoyingly. Even the rain was operating in an irritating way. It poured for a moment, then stopped, then resumed so that you constantly had to stop the wipers and restart them.

'They're building a by-pass,' said Sheila. 'All these towns will be off a motorway in a few weeks.'

At last the flow of traffic speeded up and they drove into the heart of Dublin and parked near the National Gallery. On the far side of Merrion Square they found Harrisons. The large window held only one painting, a large Munnings on an easel. Inside there was a huge variety of paintings, some of them awaiting collection by their owners.

'Is Mr Harrison expecting you?' asked a receptionist. 'He's very busy today and has lots of appointments.'

'Perhaps you'd tell him Lord Kilbeggan would like to speak to him for a moment. I won't keep him long,' said Milo, deciding to use the title for once, if it secured him an entry.

The receptionist, puzzled, went into an inside office and almost instantly an elderly bespectacled gentleman came hurriedly out and stared at the young couple. He brought them into his office, sat them down and again inspected them as he sat behind his desk.

'This is very, very extraordinary," he said. 'I've been told that the line is extinct. The Dutch trustee told me personally that he was to collect the pictures for an estate sale. He's

194

calling this afternoon at three o'clock with the young estate worker who helped to bring them here originally with Lady Cynthia. This is very confusing and most irregular. I shall have to ask you to prove your identity. I smell fraud in the air.'

It took ten minutes involving a telephone call to Mr Kinch's office in Mullingar and another to Kilbeggan Castle where Mrs Neligan was indignant at the suggestion that Milo was not a genuine lord, before Mr Harrison was convinced.

'We shall have to call the gardai in,' he stated. 'This would have been an unbelievable fraud. We kept writing to Kilbeggan asking for the pictures to be collected. A young man answered – the same person who had assisted Lady Cynthia when she brought them to us for restoration. He brought a Dutchman to see them and he said that he had been a friend of the late owner and that he would take the pictures for sale with the rest of the furniture and effects. Fortunately we had not quite finished with the paintings – we had spotted a blemish which was overlooked in the restoration and we told them we would have them ready this afternoon. What a coincidence that you've called today – a lucky coincidence if I may say for you and also for me. I detest this skullduggery in the art world. I shall ring up the fraud squad immediately. We'll have some detectives waiting for this pair of criminals when they arrive this afternoon. Miss Domville, could we have some coffee please for Lord Kilbeggan and Miss . . . oh Miss Kelly. Personally I feel more like a brandy. That was quite a shock to the system. But it's too early in the day. I shall have a couple at my club tonight before going home.'

He puffed slightly and his cheeks reddened. Sheila wondered if she would have to use her professional skills before the day was out.

'What exactly are the paintings?' asked Milo. 'We know they're by an artist called Whiting but apart from that we know nothing.'

'Whiting!' said Mr Harrison, 'who on earth is Whiting? Never head of an artist called Whiting. What your aunt

195

owned and what you presumably now own is a couple of paintings by J.G. Herring the Senior.'

'Wrong fish,' said Sheila to Milo. 'Mr Neligan confused Herring with Whiting. Not bad for the old man.'

'Come along and see them,' said Mr Harrison, not amused or interested.

He brought them into an adjoining studio where they found the restored paintings in their impressive gilt frames. The picture on the left was entitled 'Gustavus, the property of the Lord Viscount Kilcock'. It showed a landscape with figures. A groom held a splendid Arab horse with very glistening eyes while the owner seated in a phaeton inspected the animal. At the rear of the landscape was a lake with a small classical pillared building.

'That's the mausoleum,' said Milo, 'and that must be my wicked great-great-great-uncle.' The painting was signed and dated J.G. Herring 1838. 'He was at the height of his fame then,' said Mr Harrison. 'Lord Kilcock called the horse Gustavus, I believe, to annoy a neighbouring landowner, Gustavus Lambart, whom he detested. Now look at the second painting. It's called 'The Start'. You can see it's a massed start at some unidentified race meeting but Gustavus is clearly seen near the starter, the top-hatted figure with the flag. You can see there are no stands or any of the paraphernalia of a modern race meeting. Lord Kilcock's groom, Ben Doyle, is the same as in the left-hand painting. He was an eccentric, often outspoken yokel, greatly liked by the viscount.'

'Is Herring a famous painter?' asked Milo.

'Yes and no. In racing circles he had always been greatly admired. At the National Racing Museum at Newmarket, he would be one of the most important in the collection together with Sawrey Gilpin and Stubbs. Some of the greatest English sporting families and some Irish ones too commissioned him. Perhaps the most famous Herring is in the Duke of Hamilton's collection. It's called 'The Dirtiest Derby in History'. It's a huge painting and not unlike The Start. It's hung in a National Trust castle in Scotland – Brodick

Castle. Lord Barnard had a famous Herring in Durham – 'Raby Stableyard With Ponies', the Victoria and Albert has a very fine oil called 'Seedtime'. In Ireland there are a couple at Florence Court in Fermanagh and there are several hung in country houses in Meath and County Limerick. On the other hand you could look up many encyclopaedias and art books and not find his works mentioned. You'll find pages devoted to Hockney and this extremely gifted painter is not mentioned. Perhaps this is due to the choice of subject which is very confined but I think it's unjust.

'How valuable is this couple of Herrings?' asked Milo.

'A single Herring Senior sold for £50,000 recently. A pair of course would be more than double that value. Given the provenance, they've always been in your family, and their condition, you would expect competitive bidding. Recently prices have risen sharply; for example, paintings by J.B. Yeats, especially the horse paintings, have soared in value. So we are talking about a great deal of money and a fraud which has very narrowly been averted. If I were you I would insure the pair for £120,000. Now there's the phone. I asked Miss Domville to ring the fraud squad. Hello, inspector, William Harrison here from Harrison Muldoon Restorers. I have a little story that might interest you and that demands urgent attention.'

He spoke for a long while to the inspector explaining the attempted fraud. The inspector asked to speak to Milo and after talking to him said that it was essential that Milo should be at Harrisons a good half hour before the other appointment to help in identifying his property and possibly the thieves. They sat back discussing the extraordinary affair.

'You know, I suppose,' said Mr Harrison, 'about the Munnings at Kilbeggan. Lady Cynthia told me that it was hanging on the back staircase. It's a picture of a circus with animals doing tricks. Munnings was very fond of gypsies and circuses. In fact I think that he travelled around the country working with them and doing drawings while he was young. Lady Cynthia had it in one of the reception rooms but she told me that she was going to hang it on the back staircase for safety after the house was robbed. The old lord apparently bought it for half nothing when he was young and knew Munnings who was very short of cash. That picture must also be worth a small fortune today. Now if you have time before your luncheon, go and see the Yeats pictures in the National Gallery and have a look at their newly discovered Caravaggio.' He rose slowly from the chair. 'The place will be full of detectives when you get back. I hope my blood pressure survives the excitement.'

Milo and Sheila left the gallery and walked through the gardens of Merrion Square. Immaculate lawns and interesting flower beds were dwarfed by thin trees whose tops did not conceal the small Georgian windows on the top storeys of the houses around the square. Office workers on their lunch-hour break crowded on the grass, some with their sandwiches and salad rolls, others with vegetarian titbits. Sheila commented that she could never become a vegetarian, being far too attached to steaks and any kind of beef. Milo told her that he had once gone through a vegetarian period at school. He did not tell her that the reason for this was a nineteen-year-old student with perfect legs, a mouth to dream about, inviting eyes, but a vegetarian 'nutter'. They left the park and crossed the street to the restaurant of the National Gallery of Ireland where they relaxed over lunch and discussed the extraordinary situation.

'Inside a week you have become the owner of valuable silver and famous pictures which you didn't know you possessed. Whatever happens, you will have a large amount of capital to back you up. It's wonderful to have a substantial amount of money to help you and not to have to worry about day-to-day needs. It must represent a great comfort despite all the complications.'

Milo believed that he should sell the pictures which could help greatly in restoring the castle. Sheila was for selling the silver. Although both silver and pictures had historic value and sentimental value, she felt that the Herring pictures were of interest to the county as well as to the family. One thing that the Kilbeggans had always been interested in and been successful at was racing. Their colours had been carried at most of the great Irish meetings and on some of the better-known English courses like Aintree and Cheltenham. They had never won an English Grand National but the fourth earl had been second twice at the Irish Grand National at Fairyhouse. Sheila believed that the racing connection was more important than the retention of the family silver, no matter how handsome this was. All around them tables buzzed with chat about politics and politicians, business and businessmen, the media and media people, weekend parties and social gossip. Dowagers bored each others about grandchildren. A teacher was having some difficulty in controlling a party from a country school up in Dublin to walk the galleries and 'absorb culture'. A few of the more precocious students were planning a quick disappearance and hopefully some adventurous pick-ups. The teacher was wondering why on earth she had allowed Patricia and Margaret up for the trip when she might have known, from long experience, that they had not travelled for cultural reasons. Wearily she assented when they asked if they might go to the toilet and that was the last thing she saw of them until they turned up at the bus hours later complaining that they had got lost. Patricia winked at Milo on her way out. She quite liked an older man. Milo and Sheila watched it all with amusement and some sympathy. After lunch they sat and looked at the Yeats paintings. Milo admired Yeats and loved the distance aspect where you had to observe a painting for some time before understanding came and hills and horses and mountainy men came clear before the eyes. He liked Yeats's use of colour and his handling of impressionist techniques. They went on to view the recently discovered Caravaggio, dark and impressive and not, they thought, very attractive. By this time it was nearly three and they set out to be well in time before the two crooks were to appear on the scene.

The office workers had returned to their desks and it was

mostly tourists who cluttered the pavements. Some Japanese took photographs of the plaque on a corner house recording the fact that Sir William Wilde had lived there – the father of Oscar Fingal O'Flaherty Wills Wilde whose multitude of names had not saved him from a sad and lonely end. Dublin was full of such plaques and statues commemorating the incredible contribution to literature by Irish writers from Swift to James Joyce. From Saint Patrick's Cathedral to the Sandymount Martello Tower, cameras clicked to record historic associations. Sheila was telling Milo that she had once tried to read *Ulysses* and had failed dismally, finding it enormously complicated and difficult to read. As Milo was telling her that he had not even started to try to read the Joycean classics they turned the corner of the square and came face to face with Packy who was talking to a companion.

The unexpected puts us at a disadvantage. Those who have encountered a burglar in the house without any previous suspicion of such an encounter will understand the fatal delay, the hesitation that gives the advantage to the criminal. So it was with Milo and Sheila. They gaped just long enough at Packy and his companion to give time for Packy to take to his heels, and his companion likewise, and disappear down a mews lane behind the tall houses. Milo sprinted down to the entrance of the lane in time to see the pair racing wildly at the far end before they took off down another side alley.

'I'll try and catch them,' shouted Milo. 'You get the police and tell them which direction they've taken.'

She wanted to tell him to be careful but he was off sprinting down the mews lane, confident he was fitter than Packy or any other drug addict. Sheila raced down the street and breathlessly tried to tell Mr Harrison and two waiting detectives what was happening. They took off after being shown the direction where the suspects had fled. Sheila sat down with Mr Harrison who seemed relieved that the activity was not taking place in his gallery. Meanwhile the detectives had contacted a squad car which drove around the neighbouring streets after being given a description of the pair to look out for. Milo had come to a stop after sprinting down a lane which turned out to be a *cul-de-sac*. Here the two detectives caught up with him and were about to hold him on suspicion until he told them who he was. A half-closed coach-house door attracted their attention. They entered a dusty and neglected old building and opened a door at the far end. Beyond was a small neglected yard. The high Georgian house towering over the yard had been converted into offices and a dismayed secretary with a telephone in her hand was about to scream when the detectives produced their identity.

'I'm nearly sick with the fright,' she said. 'Two men just forced the back door open and rushed through, knocking the table over as they went. It's shocking and my mother died only a month ago. I'd only just got over that and now this fright.'

Eventually she stopped talking about her emotional problems and showed them the route the pair had probably taken to the front door. When they opened the front door they found a busy street with a bus-stop right in front of the house.

'Bravo over, suspects believed to be near Pearse Street or else have taken a bus from this street. Looking for thin blond-haired youth with middle-aged man, possibly foreign.'

The detective put down his walkie-talkie and with his colleague did a quick search of the building. Startled accountants peered from their desktops as the search proceeded through the building. Meanwhile Milo was soothing the emotional secretary who was now feeling rather brave and important after the experience. If all detectives were as young and attractive as this one she wouldn't mind being interviewed further. She told Milo that at first she thought it was drug-crazed men who intended to rape her. Dolores had told her she should learn karate to defend herself against sexual attack. Dolores had had a bad experience with a man on the Dun Laoghaire bus, pushing against her and rubbing his leg against hers. Milo had to forgo the end

201

of the story as the detectives returned, took down the secretary's name and telephone number and the three of them departed from the building.

'The birds have flown, I'm afraid. They're probably on a bus somewhere and they'll certainly keep out of circulation for a while.'

The younger detective was disappointed at losing them.

'We should have asked you to keep off the streets for a longer period before they were due to collect the pictures. They were obviously having a recce and a scout around before they made the move. It was most unfortunate that they encountered you first. They're obviously prepared to take a risk, but they were suspicious as well. We'll get the descriptions out to all of the squad cars and guards on the beat and we might have a bit more luck next time.'

They arrived at the Harrison Gallery and sat down with Sheila and Mr Harrison.

'It can be extremely hard to convict,' said the second detective, 'unless we actually found them in possession of the pictures or trying to sell them on. We might find it difficult to get a case that would stick. The young fellow could always say that he was returning the picture to you after helping to bring it up in the first place.'

'There are times,' said his colleague, 'when it seems that the law is almost prejudiced against the police and the victim. The right to silence works well for the criminal. Some of these clever criminals have very experienced law-yers who can defend them so well that the police are almost in despair. Or an eccentric judge may let them off the hook over some technicality. You'll find some judges weighing the evidence so carefully and giving the benefit of the doubt to some appalling and cruel criminal and then others will pass long sentences for minor and almost trivial offences. Then a violent burglar will get a suspended sentence. And any garda will tell you that a summons may disappear on certain occasions. That's when the rumours start. However, to get back to this case, we'll let you know if we get any sightings or any further information. Keep in touch with us.'

They said goodbye and left the gallery.

Milo and Sheila asked Mr Harrison if he would keep the pictures for a while until Milo had decided whether to sell them or not.

'Any of the bigger auctioneers in Dublin would be delighted to sell them for you,' said Mr Harrison. 'If you wanted to go farther afield, the London houses, Sotheby's and Christie's, have offices here. Phillips, off Oxford Street in London, sell quite a few Irish pictures or pictures of Irish interest. Americans, especially the hunting set from Virginia, would be very interested in acquiring Herring paintings. You'll have no shortage of bidders. Although I must say it would please me greatly if the two pictures were to return to Kilbeggan Castle. Let me know if the Munnings is still in the castle. That would fetch you a lot of money and is of no particular Irish interest. In the meantime we'll keep these safe for you.'

They drove home that evening strangely tired after the day in the city and all the excitement. Sheila sank in the comfortable leather seat in the Porsche, fell asleep and her hair fell across his shoulder and her hand gave comfort to his leg. They were just in time to escape the evening rush hour traffic and the splendid engine for once had an opportunity to open up and devour the miles ahead of them.

25

Next morning saw Milo trying to eat his breakfast while Touch tried to eat his socks and his trainers below the breakfast table. Trying to train the pup was proving difficult. Each time it peed on the carpet Milo spoke sternly and took it out of the hall and out onto the steps. This the pup saw not as a lesson but as a type of game. If it peed on the carpet, kind master would bring it out for a walk or a little game. When it was down below in the kitchen, old Neligan never noticed the little pools on the flagged floor and Touch could do much as he pleased. Milo began to realize what many others had found out before him that rearing a pup is no easy matter. Already one of old Neligan's slippers had disappeared and a woollen vest drying on the Aga rail and belonging to either of the Neligans (he wasn't told which) had been pulled down and half-eaten. Milo promised replacements for all these damages. He walked the pup around the gravel sweep dutifully. Touch frisked and frolicked before being brought inside where he immediately spread some liquid turds on the hall carpet. Milo sighed and went off to view the back staircase where he had been told there was a Munnings picture. But the back staircase proved blank except for a series of Spy cartoons hanging on its brown walls. He asked Mrs Neligan. He had not told either of them about the dramatic events concerning Packy, judging that there was little cause to worry them as the robbery bid had been unsuccessful.

'That's not the back staircase,' said Mrs Neligan, 'that's the Tower staircase you've been on. What we call the back staircase is the stairs off the long gallery leading up to the nursery wing.'

She led him up to the long gallery and opened a locked

door. Beyond was a small landing and a short staircase that led up to nursery bedrooms. On the landing wall staring Milo in the face was a large and colourful oil painting with elephants and circus horses and an insolent-looking but attractive girl trainer with a whip. All the fascination of an old-time circus was portrayed in the picture. In the half-darkness behind the ring you could just distinguish country people in their seats with mouths open with astonishment at the strange spectacle. The picture was signed and dated Alfred Munnings, 1932.

'That's just a print that Lady Cynthia thought might be nice for the nursery wing,' said Mrs Neligan, 'although why she wanted to keep this end locked I do not know. There's nothing valuable in it at all. Here, keep the key. I've no cause to be traipsing up to this end of the house.'

She led the way downstairs, reminding Milo that the parish priest of Newtown was coming to be treated by him in half an hour's time.

Milo rang Sheila to wish her well at her interview and to tell her about his discovery of the Munnings painting. She suggested that they remove it from its present position and keep it in a safe place. She would join him after the interview and they were to go into the town later where some of the young people wanted to celebrate their engagement. The arrival of the crippled clergyman put paid to their conversation. Another healing session brought relief to the patient and exhaustion to the healer. Afterwards Milo sat down wearily and waited for Sheila, while Touch slept in his lap, the sweet innocent sleep of a pup. When Sheila arrived, she found them both asleep and was reluctant to disturb Milo whose eyes brightened when he awoke to her kiss. He took her up to see the Munnings picture which he had decided to put on the market rather than the more personal Herring pictures. They also decided to put announcements of their engagement in the Irish and English newspapers. They prepared two slightly different formats – the first for *The Irish Independent* which read – 'Mr and Mrs P.J. Kelly of Drumlerry, Kilbeggan, Co. Westmeath, are delighted to announce the engagement of their daughter, Sheila, to Milo Kilbeggan of Kilbeggan Castle, Co. Westmeath.'

The second announcement was for *The Daily Telegraph*. It read – 'The engagement is announced of the Earl of Kilbeggan of Kilbeggan Castle, Co. Westmeath, Ireland, to Miss Sheila Kelly of Drumlerry, Co. Westmeath.' After this intellectual exercise they decided on certain necessary improvements to the castle which might be put into effect immediately. The ancient lavatory and washroom behind the hall with its leaking cistern and discoloured cracked basin was to be modernized and a shower installed. More important still was the renovation of a bathroom near Milo's bedroom, the installation of hot water units for shower and bath and washbasin and a hot press. Sheila told him immersions were expensive to run but Milo had no wish for such discomfort as he had put up with in the last few weeks.

'I'd never last the winter,' he laughed, 'with only cold water. I'd either pong like a goat or else get pneumonia in this freezing chamber.'

They also decided to buy some duvets and a couple of electric heaters for the bedroom. When winter approached the fading grandeur of the rooms would need a flush of heat or they would be hard to live in. Lady Cynthia had been used to an austere setting; she had been heard to speak disparagingly of this new central heating she had encountered with friends who had descended to bungalow living. Sheila and Milo were determined to have a modicum of comfort in the castle. Later they went down to meet Seamus's friend, Jack Brennan, at the gate lodge. Once again they walked through the shabby rooms treading carefully on dangerous floorboards. Seamus's friend was quite enthusiastic after his preliminary survey.

'It looks worse than it is,' Jack suggested. 'Any house that's left empty gives you a bad impression. But look on the positive side. The stonework is sound. Most of the roof is sound. The guttering has slipped but it can easily be put up again. Electricity and water are available and that means a great saving. The woodwork doesn't need a complete renewal; it needs patching here and there. You've evidence of woodworm and some wet rot, but that can be treated. I'll fix the roof up, get a lot of replastering done, work on the stairs and floorboards and get that great fireplace cleared to heat up the place. You'll see a distinct difference inside a month. I'll kip down in one of the rooms once you've had the electricity reconnected.'

They agreed on details of payment and Milo told him to go ahead ordering supplies of cement and plaster and other necessities. They would get down some essentials from the castle – a bed, chairs, kitchen utensils. Sheila promised to bring Jack over a cat from Drumlerry which was a famous ratter and always deposited a victim at the front door each morning. They had been looking at mouse and rat holes in the skirting boards. He told them that a friend of his would clean and repaint the gates, if they wished, and they agreed to this also. He also suggested getting a tractor and trailer from Seamus to clear out the rubbish and take it to the dump. They all went over to Drumlerry where Mrs Kelly had a huge stew on the stove. There were a great number of letters to be read, mainly notes of congratulations from friends and relations. Mrs Kelly had a rhubarb tart and a bowl of thick cream – a pudding which nearly rendered them all comatose. Later they helped Seamus bring in bales of hay. They stacked them in a tall barn where the wind would get at them but they would remain dry. Afterwards they accompanied Seamus down to the bog where the last cut of turf ('We call it peat,' said Milo) was lying under a plastic sheet ready to be taken in. They filled the trailers with bags of the dark fuel, while enjoying the marvellous air of the bog. There is something very reviving and healthy about the air on a peat bog. Milo was reminded of the passage from his A level *Macbeth* – 'This castle hath a sweet and pleasant air.'

Dusty and happy they climbed up on the trailer and Seamus drove back across the uneven bog roads to Drumlerry where they unloaded and stacked the turf. Milo and Sheila walked down the lane to bring in the cows and loitered purposefully as they drove the herd back for milking.

'Well, you were a quare time collecting cows,' said Seamus with a wink as he marshalled his animals for milking.

After tea they were to meet the young crowd in the town 'for a drink'. When they got there, some were in the Black Kettle, some in the Distillery Inn. First they drove down to the old distillery, where the great water wheel still turned in the foaming water of a cutting from the Brosna river. The grey distillery dominated the little town and had attracted a share of visitors to its museum. At the Black Kettle, they were received with a cheer and many a curious glance was cast at Milo and many a welcoming drink proffered. Some of their friends who worked at a local factory, Powerscreen, suggested that they go on to Mullingar where there was a group playing at a disco called The Final Fence. Sheila agreed to this if Milo allowed her to drive, for she felt that the amount of drinks he was being offered might diminish his capacity to drive safely.

'Nonsense,' he snorted but the majority vote was against him and like many a wise man before him, he agreed to let the woman drive.

So a procession of cars drove to Mullingar and the crowd piled into The Final Fence. Young Hickey found it difficult to mount the stairs but was helped up, being goosed by the girls several times on the way. Here they ate and drank and were happy until the small hours. Toasts were drunk to the engaged couple and a lot of Sheila's girlfriends bumped against Milo looking for a Kilbeggan touch. Sheila and Milo were almost oblivious of them, being lost in their own feelings. Around them the party went on. O'Shea had passed out and his girlfriend was watching over him with a look of exasperation. Reynolds and Kavanagh were deep in a discussion about football. Paul Smith was telling a story about doing a ton down the new motorway at Mullingar and the gardai couldn't catch him in the squad car. Bobby Boyle was telling a story that obliged him to lower his voice at the end, when a burst of male laughter suggested the style of the joke. Eventually Milo and Sheila were allowed to leave the party after thanking everybody for the hospitality and good feeling. A frantic effort to hold them was made with a feeble attempt to sing 'Auld Lang Syne' and 'For He's a Jolly Good Fellow' but they got away into the warm night and drove away home.

26

The embarrassment of human behaviour can discomfort the inexperienced. Not that Milo had intended this when he took her to London to meet his relations.

'I haven't got many but you'd better take a look at them,' he had told her before booking tickets to travel to London. At first she was conscious of nothing but happiness. They sat in the plane, an attractive young couple who drew many an admiring glance. The plane had to circle Heathrow for a half an hour before landing 'owing to a technical delay' and Sheila, who was nervous of flying held Milo's hand and was very glad he was there. The relief of landing overcame the ensuing tedium of delays and long walks to collect their baggage. Heathrow is a huge contrast to smaller airports – a metropolis in size compared to a village. They took the tube into the city and she recognized with some nostalgia the familiar London smell, a compound of diesel and fumes and people and smoke and cooking, which is inseparable from the streets and buildings.

Their first call was to an indescribably squalid flat, bed-room, kitchenette and bathroom, in a mews off Eaton Square.

Milo had warned her 'It may look awful but it's worth a fortune. A flat in this area is very valuable.'

Sheila looked with dismay at the filthy sink, full of a week's accumulation of plates. The unmade bed looked as if the users had been battling all night, dirty socks and underwear were strewn on the floor. A joke plastic 'sick' lay on the floor of the tiny bathroom. The fridge was repulsive. This charming pad belonged to Milo's cousin, Roddy, who galloped up the stairs shortly after them.

'Oh no!' he said in dismay. 'You're very early. I'd meant

to clean up a bit before you came. Emma the witch promised she'd do a sweep-up. The cow's gone off to some polo match. There, let me get you some coffee. Is this the unfortunate girl? Great heavens you're too good-looking for Milo. Have me instead.' He kissed Sheila enthusiastically and then eyed her with appreciation. 'Well Milo, you have done well for yourself. First a title and now somebody to make an honest man of you.' They sat on the unmade bed while he burbled on while making coffee. 'Christ, Emma's left half her clothes here.' He pulled a pair of pants away from the bottom of the bed. 'Aunty Kate is expecting you for lunch at the Lansdowne Club tomorrow. One o'clock sharp, she said. If you're a minute late no wedding present.' Thin, willowy, beautifully dressed, Roddy would have looked more at home in The Ritz than in this upper-class slum. 'At any rate you're welcome to stay here. You take the bed and I'll sleep on a camp-bed in the kitchen. I've often done it before. Have to be up early though. It's Coutts at eight o'clock in the morning. Not like some.'

He reminded Sheila of a puppy she had got as a present long ago. Uncle Tommy from Ballinagar had a poodle which had been covered by a stray spaniel. He had presented a pup to the Kellys who had christened the dog Spoodle. This had developed into a delightful playful and good-looking mongrel which they had all enjoyed, even her father who had first seen it as another mouth to feed. It was a black day for all the household when Spoodle flew across the main road in pursuit of a hare and was killed by a milk tanker. Roddy had the same instant friendliness, the affectionate manner as Spoodle had long ago. He romped around the room, asking them questions, pulling out a not so-clean duvet, asking Sheila why on earth she had accepted his cousin. He fell over his bag of golf clubs twice, knocked down a squash racket, offered Sheila a squashed cigarette.

'Have a drink.' He grabbed some tooth mugs and flushed dead insects out under the tap. 'Damn, there isn't any. Sorry about that.'

211

He listened to their description of Kilbeggan Castle, giving hoots of laughter at their account of the great Gothic pile.

'You don't mean to say that you're keeping it? It'll kill you both. Do you remember Aunty Bobo with the castle in Norfolk? She died of pneumonia. Could only afford one bar of the three-bar fire. The ceilings were thirty feet high, the whole place was sold for scrap later. Some dealers bought the stonework and made it into fountains and arches for suburban gardens. The old floorboards went for a fortune. Why not do the same? Get rid of it and build yourselves a nice comfy house or a small fishing lodge.'

He burbled on, arranging their future for them. Sheila was quite enjoying his good-natured babble. Bertie Wooster was alive and well, living in reduced circumstances off Eaton Square. Her knees touched Milo's as they sat on the squalid bed and a shiver of desire emerged from the touch. They gave the occasional laugh and encouraged Roddy's conversation while enjoying their own glow of proximity.

Presently Roddy said, 'Now it's time to go; all off to Hairy Mary's.'

Sheila looked puzzled but the two men told her about the famous pub. Hairy Mary's was a yuppie haunt near The Boltons. It was a watering hole for Milo's friends, selected for some mysterious reasons when other cleaner, brighter establishments did not attract them. The catering was atrocious and the lavatories often awash, for the upper classes get careless of aim as the night wears on.

'Come on with us and we'll introduce you to Hairy Mary's,' they said.

A taxi dropped them at the corner where a great babble of sound emerged from the crowded pub.

'A bit crowded tonight' said Roddy and they fought their way in through a mass of beautiful girls, baying public school voices, precarious pint glasses wobbling as their owners shouted to be heard and presently an avalanche of acclaim in the second bar where the crowd recognized Milo.

Sheila was almost swallowed in the crowd as Milo was greeted with shouts of laughter and recognition.

'How's the Playboy of the Western World?' 'Hugh Grant, stand aside, Milo's back.' 'Haven't slept since you left, Milo.' 'Be jabers, a hundred thousand welcomes to your lordship.' 'Remember that £50 you owe me, Milo?' 'Watch that coronet, leave it for safety behind the bar.' 'Milo, our baby is longing to see Daddy again.' 'Find a girl for the earl.' 'Milo, that bed is still broken from the night last year.' 'Thought you were in jail. Welcome back to real living.'

Young men and women fought to have a look at the blushing Milo, who was overwhelmed by the welcome and wondered what Sheila would think of it all. She had been in a crowd like this at Twickenham once for an England-Ireland Rugby International. Milo vainly tried to introduce her to everybody.

'Fiancé, nonsense darling, you're all mine. Don't you remember you promised? Don't tell me you forgot the weekend at Daisy's. Oh, you are a tease. You're not engaged at all. I was so looking forward to the tiara. Remember the night after Ascot. God, how he uses those legs of his. Give us a great long kiss, darling. What memories we have together.'

Sheila was nearly swept aside as Milo, blushing and almost desperate, tried to maintain himself and kept introducing her to the swaying throng. Only Roddy, suddenly strong and secure beside her, kept her on her feet until the crowd simmered down. The admiring eyes of the young men focused on her and Milo felt a tinge of jealousy as well as of pride. Sheila felt the young debs assessing her with quizzical looks. Her voice, her dress, her whole ethos was so different from theirs. They could annihilate people with a few words and she felt she might be the victim. They weren't bred for kindness. They had a vocabulary of their own. Centuries of ruling-class connections had left them confident, sophisticated and, she felt, cruel. But by now she was almost smothered in an admiring crowd herself. There was Giles, there was Sebastian, there was Jamie. She began to distinguish faces and to answer their questions.

'Don't tell me that he's fooled you. There isn't a woman

in London would have him. How will you control the bugger? Rope him in at night?'

She replied laughingly to their queries. Her attitude changed. These might be different from the people she usually mixed with, but they grew friendlier by the minute. Some of the girls came to talk to her. They enquired about friends of theirs in Ireland, none of whom she knew.

'Oh, you must know her, she hunts with the Westmeaths sometimes. Oh, you only go out with the harriers. I'm sure they're great fun. I'm sure you know Veronica MacLean. Oh no! Of course she's Scottish.'

They made an effort to find common ground. One of them had tried her hand at nursing but had given up. People they knew fell into two categories – either absolute bastards or very, very sweet. Sheila wondered if they were on a high with cocaine, but she found out afterwards that they spoke like this most of the time. Hence the noise was far louder than in a normal pub where people spoke in quiet almost apologetic tones. At times the din here reached almost manic proportions. There was talk of debagging Milo to celebrate his engagement but this exciting event was postponed for another time. There was talk of visiting Dicky to bring him a bottle of champagne. This too was postponed. Dicky was in prison for drunk driving. He had 'winged' an elderly cyclist who was so unsporting as to call a policeman. Daniel was on duty at the Bank of England together with some other Guards officers, that they knew. Should they surprise him while he was having his dinner? This notion was also rejected. The evening wore on with laughter and gossip. There was nowhere to sit down and Sheila grew very tired on her feet. Milo noticed her exhausted look and grew concerned.

'Come on, darling, we're leaving,' he said.

They left amid a storm of protest at their early departure and promises to lunch with one and drive with a second and have drinks with a third. Milo called a taxi and they returned to Eaton Square, she dozing on his arm. They slipped under

214

the grotty duvet and fell asleep with wonderful contentment in that unlikely setting. They did not hear Roddy return later in the small hours when he dived into an old sleeping bag like a stick insect and snored happily under the kitchen sink. They did not even hear his alarm clock at seven or his frantic search for a striped shirt or his splashes in the cramped bath or his departure with hat and umbrella into the London morning. It was hours later when they awoke to almost perfect sexual arousal and the distant bells from Sloane Square coincided with their own noisy climax.

Sheila had rarely seen Milo in a suit but he was determined to impress Aunty Kate. He had raked around Roddy's wardrobe to find a well-cut tweed suit which nearly fitted him. Nor had Milo often seen Sheila in a dress and he looked happily at the woollen outfit which could not conceal the curves of her superb figure. The bird-like figures of the girls in the pub on the previous night could not compare with Sheila's fresh and lovely body. Who was it who had said, 'You can't be too thin or too rich'? Milo would have disagreed vehemently with the first half of that statement. Many an eye followed them in admiration as they ascended the steps of the Lansdowne Club.

This club had been established many years ago before one sex had started to torment the other with politically correct attitudes. Leaving men to enjoy their own society in their own clubs, the women had taken the sensible attitude and founded their own club, where they enjoyed equal facilities. They allowed in men as guests of the members. The club was as solid and dignified as any of the established male clubs. Those who expected it to have a whimsically female atmosphere were disappointed. It is no more and no less than a well-run club, with an atmosphere rather like a comfortable country house. Oil paintings and stylish old furniture set the tone for a pleasant atmosphere. The food was always well-cooked, probably better than that in other dining rooms. Country members found it a haven in the rather frightening metropolis. Here was serenity, solidity, tradition. Town members used it more frequently. London is often a bewildering and confusing city. One needs an oasis of comfort – a place where one is known and where decent standards prevail.

Here in the library Aunt Kate sat reading magazines which she would never have dreamt of buying. Inside *The Field* she had found a depressing review of a depressing book called *Vanishing Irish Houses.* Photographs of colossal Georgian ruins gaunt against an Irish sky illustrated the article. Why, she wondered, had they ever been built – these monuments to power and arrogance and vanity and good taste? Here in a poverty-stricken countryside had arisen the palazzi of the Anglo-Irish aristocracy. And here across the decent Axminster carpet came her nephew, the successor to such outstanding grandeur and with him a most beautiful and unmistakably Irish girl. The arthritic old lady sat still with pleasure as the very handsome young couple came to greet her. She hoped that old cat Lizzie Tonbridge was watching them too.

'Hello, Aunt Kate,' said Milo and kissed his aunt. 'This is Sheila Kelly, whom I hope to marry shortly.'

Aunt Kate looked up and scrutinized this pleasant-looking country girl. The frank honest face pleased her, as did the slight look of alarm on the girl's face. She had been afraid of her nephew's choice. Milo had brought other girls to see her and she had not approved of his taste in brittle sophisti-cated over-confident little pieces who were obviously bored to be meeting elderly relations. This girl had a diffident charm, wanted the lacquer of sophistication, but was no worse for that. She smiled warmly at Sheila and they sat down, one on each side of her.

'I've just been reading about this frightening book,' she said 'and I thought of the pair of you setting up in Kilbeggan. How on earth will you keep the place in repair? We shut off the basement and the top storey at Kiplin but eventually the bills defeated us. Just to paint the windows cost us thousands. And then that obnoxious little man offered us £2,000,000 and we couldn't refuse. William was having awful trouble trying to climb the stairs. Old Madge died and we couldn't

216

get a maid for love or money. So it was a blessing in its way. We built that very comfortable warm bungalow and a very lovely flat here in London. As you know, I've sold the bungalow and I'm quite happy with my little flat. One grows tired of the country when one is old. All those herbaceous borders, so demanding, and those awful women organizing their sales of work. I send them a cheque now once a year and they're quite satisfied. But here I am again talking about myself – quite the old lady, I'm afraid. Now you two, tell me all about yourselves. I want to hear all your news, Milo, and Sheila, you must tell me all about yourself.'

Milo, who was quite fond of his rather formidable aunt, started to tell her about their plans but was constantly interrupted.

'Old Neligan, still alive?' she asked. 'Very fond of his glass of port, Cynthia used to say.' She had been to Kilbeggan in the old days and still remembered some of the neighbours. 'Don't tell me those curious women are still selling terriers. Do they ever draw breath, I wonder? Molly Tullamore is dead I know. Went to her funeral last year. She was living with a young man I believe. Wish I was her.'

She gave an almighty chuckle and allowed Milo to continue. He told her of his discovery of the healing touch and she grew quite alarmed.

'I know all about it,' she said. 'I know it works very effectively but you'll have to be very careful of the side effects. It's got a most exhausting effect. About three a week, poor Tommy used to say – any more and the body is drained. I remember your great-uncle looking ashen one time. A car load of ill people arrived at the castle and he tried to heal them all. He was in bed for a week after it. It can be quite dangerous. Promise, my dear,' she continued, turning to Sheila, 'promise that you won't let him see more than two people a week. He's so headstrong, you know, and always disregards his old aunt's advice. You'll have to bully him to keep him on the right track. If you're short of money, I'll lend you some now that you're starting to be sensible. My dear Sheila, he was a very wild young man. Talk about

217

wild oats. Keep a tight rein on him. The Kilbeggans always needed a strong woman or they went haywire.'

She stopped and laughed and Sheila smiled back, pleased at the old lady's obvious acceptance of her.

'We gals,' said Aunt Kate, rising from her chair, 'must keep each other informed.'

They walked slowly into the dining room. The slow progress included brief stops to meet some other elderly dowagers. 'My nephew, Milo Kilbeggan and his fiancée Sheila Kelly.' She introduced them, 'Lady MacDonald and Mrs Cholomondely-Mainwaring.'

Sheila felt herself being inspected. Good breeding stock? Sensible-looking girl? Not terribly smart, a trifle rustic?

The dining room was nearly full with plenty of professional people and country people up for the day.

By the end of the luncheon, Aunt Kate had found out everything about Sheila that she wanted to know. She had induced Sheila to talk about her family, her career and even her views on topics like contraception, religion, politics, finances. She had been a little apprehensive. Milo had been notoriously prone to fatal attractions. The Moroccan girl had been very hard to get rid of, once the attraction had worn off. That politician's daughter had been quite loopy, although fascinating and beautiful; she had been locked up before harm was done. No reason for alarm here. This girl was obviously hard-working, honest, glowing with good health (and perhaps something else). Not quite our type, of course, but times had changed and she was probably quite acceptable. She had a sense of humour and, thank God, no chip on the shoulder about the obvious matters. The only difficulty would probably be in the fact that she might be hurt.

'I must talk to Milo when I get him to myself,' she decided and she settled her approval on Sheila.

'Now tell me, Milo, what do you want?' she demanded. 'You never come near me unless you're short and want something, absolute rascal.' She turned to Sheila. 'Ignores me totally until he runs short.'

Milo protested that this was unfair. He was always

218

delighted to see Aunt Kate. But she insisted, 'Now I want you two to be happy and if my instincts are correct you'll have a darned good chance. If I can help out in any way, let me know. Money is always short at your age and you have that albatross of a house to keep up. I am going to give you a cheque to help support you for the time being.'

She fumbled in a creased leather bag which contained a very odd collection including a broken biscuit. She extracted a shabby jeweller's box and passed it over to Sheila, who opened it with curiosity. Inside the Garrads box lay an exquisite brooch.

'This, my dear, is for you. It's a vote of confidence in you. It was made for Milo's great-great-great grandmother and given to her by her husband when he was our ambassador to Vienna. I have no doubt that it will look as lovely on you as it did on her. I have her portrait showing her wearing the brooch. When you visit my little flat I'll show it to you.' Sheila gazed with delight at the wonderful jewels. It was a peacock brooch, with exquisite antique sapphire, emerald and diamond feathers. 'Boucheron made them famous. The rest seem to have gone to America. But do insure it, my dear. It's a wicked, wicked world I'm afraid.' Sheila's obvious delight in the brooch was sufficient thanks to Aunt Kate. Sheila kissed the old lady and tried to express her pleasure at the gift. 'Don't say a word more. I hate these embarrassing moments. Just wear it and be happy. I still have it insured but do please take my advice and insure it yourself.'

She mentioned a sum which startled Sheila. Kate then passed an envelope to Milo.

'Be sensible with this. I'll be furious if I hear that you've bought a silly car or something. Now it's time for my afternoon lie-down.'

She rose from her chair and they left the Lansdowne Club, each one satisfied and happy. They got Kate into a taxi and she smiled as they waved good-bye to her.

'Wow,' said Milo, 'you've made a hit. She's never been like this before. Let's see what's in the envelope. Have a guess. Twenty, fifty, a hundred?'

219

He opened the envelope and peered inside. There lay a cheque for £5,000. They hugged each other with delight. Passers-by looked enviously. It was rare to see young people looking so pleased – not with drugs or drink – and so filled with affection. They linked arms and set off walking down the street. Two Arab men waiting for a taxi gazed appreciatively at the pair of them.

The afternoon held more mundane pleasures. Sheila went to see her friends at the hospital and over cups of coffee exchanged news and gossip. When she confessed that her fiancé was a lord, that they intended to live in an ancestral castle, there was astonishment, congratulations and in one case a whiff of envy. One sour staff nurse when she heard the news seemed almost affronted.

'What would she know of the high life?' she sniffed. 'She'll probably use the wrong knives and forks. Now she'll be all airs and graces. That sort of thing never works out. Class will always tell. It's like the royal family. Just think of the mess Fergie made with her marriage.' But the rest of the nurses were delighted.

'When are we going to see him? Come on, you can't disappoint us. He probably has some good-looking friends,' they said hopefully.

Sheila arranged to meet them later at the The King's Head. She left the hospital with congratulations ringing in her ears.

Cards were sent to her parents, views of St Paul's and Westminster Cathedral, and to her friends rather more saucy ones. She picked a colourful view of Buckingham Palace for Mr and Mrs Neligan. Then, rather tired, she took a taxi back to Eaton Square where she found Roddy making a sporting effort to tidy his flat up – clothes being flung into drawers, books on shelves and glasses in cupboards. They settled down to a quiet cup of tea and discussed his Aunt Kate and also his Uncle Bertram whom they were to see next day in Brighton.

'Rum sort,' said Roddy. 'Never got married, travels to London once a month, says that keeps him going. He's a very smart dresser – thinks we're a very shabby lot. You should see his shoes, bought before the last World War – Hitler's war he calls it. He plays a lot of bridge with some pompous old women – brigadiers' widows and the like. Likes to keep fit – geriatric tennis and very fast walks, hard to keep up with. You'll like him if you can keep his hands off you. Make sure that you admire his Stubbs – he's very proud of it.'

Sheila laughed at this description of Uncle Bertie. When Milo arrived back, having had 'a few drinks' with some friends in a club off Shaftesbury Avenue, they all decided to have a meal out before meeting their joint sets of friends at the pub. Milo and Sheila changed from their formal clothes to more comfortable outfits. Together they set out to find some pub grub.

Sheila was somewhat worried about the two sets of friends. Would they mix or would it be awkward? Class distinctions in England have a greater impact than they do in Ireland. A man's accent can make him a figure of ridicule to others if he finds himself in an alien group. 'She stood in tears amid the alien corn' does not refer to crops but to a hostile environment. In the event, her fears were groundless. At the start it was rather boisterous. Giles in particular was attracted to the notion of nursing.

'Come and feel me, nurse,' he kept shouting. 'I've an awful pain down here.'

Sebastian urged Sheila's very pretty friend, Emma, to inspect a thigh muscle which he alleged he had pulled playing squash with Jamie.

'Don't bother, Emma,' shouted his friends, 'there's only one thing he pulls in that area.'

One staff nurse they christened 'Matron'.

Shouts of 'A double gin for Matron' rose in the air.

'Remove the Nuciform sac,' shouted another. 'The blood pressure is in danger.'

Sheila's friends, instead of resenting the horseplay, took to it with pleasure and gave as good as they got. Emma, instead of inspecting Sebastian's thigh, asked him questions about his bowel movements.

'The thigh,' she told him, 'is often affected by irregular bowel movements. Tell me, when did you last have a sound movement? Are you watching your food and drink habits. I'd advise you to have a check-up.'

They advised Giles to have his prostate looked at. Giles, who had a weak bladder, was somewhat embarrassed by this turn in the conversation.

'Matron' made Jeremy say, 'Ah' fifteen times and told him not to strain his throat with too many shouts.

Sheila was relieved that both sets of friends took to each other so well. She introduced Milo to friend after friend. Off-duty nurses kept arriving to be introduced. Round after round of drink was consumed. Debs and nurses and young men mingled together in a hugely successful party. The noise level increased. Milo stayed by Sheila and she felt his strong hand around her waist. A hundred people promised that they were coming to the wedding. There was talk of chartering Concorde.

'London-Dublin in ten minutes,' said Roddy. 'No good, I want to get drunk on the plane.'

They ended up inviting half the pub to come over to Kilbeggan – the only stipulation being to bring a sleeping bag.

'Here's to lots of little hons.'

Sebastian gave a toast and they all raised their glasses to wish the happy couple long life together. Singing started in the corner despite admonishment from behind the bar.

Soon great choruses came swinging down the crowded room—

> Swing, swing together
> With your body between your knees
> And we'll all swing together
> And drink to the best of schools.

Words were confused and mixed up. A friend of Milo's called Harry sang interminable verses of 'The Ball of Kirriemuir'. 'The Good Ship Venus' echoed out over the darkening square. Soon two songs were being sung at the same time, as different groups started to out-rival each other. 'John Peel' and 'Abide With Me' fought hard for space and hearing, sometimes almost joining. So you heard the sadness of 'Now he has gone far away, far Away', while the opposition sang the equally sad 'Change and decay in all about I see', any serious singer was drowned when a great bawdy chorus would come surging from one end of the bar to the other. 'Danny Boy' was overwhelmed in its turn by the Harrow song sung in a mock melancholy way—

Forty years on, growing older and older
Shorter of breath if in memory long
Feeble of foot and rheumatic of shoulder
What shall it help you that once you were strong.

Eventually last drinks were being called and the drunken and now homogeneous mob spilled out onto the pavement. Despite mighty efforts to drag them off to further revelry, Milo and Sheila hailed a taxi and escaped from their friends who were reluctant to let them go. They snuggled together in the back of the taxi bringing them back to Eaton Square, which now seemed like an old familiar neighbourhood to them. They dragged up the stairs and Milo sat on the narrow bed reading the evening paper in a desultory way while Sheila brushed her teeth in the narrow bathroom.

Suddenly she heard him call out excitedly, 'Sheila, just look at this.'

She came out, toothbrush in hand, and peered over his shoulder to see what had excited him. He was looking at the social column where several columns were devoted to the fabulously wealthy divorcee, Mrs John Perke III, who was photographed arriving at the Lanesborough Hotel after lunching at the Manoir Aux Quat' Saisons with her new toyboy companion, a young man in a superb Armani suit and immaculate blond hair. This, the evening paper, stated was the young man about town, Mr Patrick Milligan. Milligan or Neligan, the face smiling patronizingly at the camera was undoubtedly that of Packy Neligan.

27

The next morning Sheila awoke just early enough to catch Roddy tip-toeing out on his way to the bank. She asked him to take the brooch to Coutts and place it in a deposit box because she was terrified of losing it to a pickpocket or mislaying her handbag with such a valuable piece inside it. With Roddy out the door, she snuggled back beside her sleeping lover and held him as if afraid of losing him. She dozed uncomfortably for thin as he was, he held the centre of the narrow bed. A faded drawing by the side of the bed caught her attention. It showed a handsome English country house surrounded by tall trees. By its side stood a square towered church. A clock tower over a farmyard could be seen on the other side of the house. Milo stirred awake and followed her gaze. 'It was Roddy's home,' he told her. 'The National Trust have taken it over. The family have six rooms at the back.'

The newspaper that they had seen on the previous night lay on the floor and they examined it again. Yes, it was clearly Packy, suave, sophisticated, arrogant-looking, who was squiring one of the richest women in the world. 'Where on earth could she have picked him up?' said Milo.

A few days ago Packy had been on the run, a small-time drugs dealer and learner crook. Now he seemed to be near the top of café society.

'From rags to riches,' said Sheila wonderingly. 'Should somebody not tell her?'

'That woman,' said Milo witheringly, 'has picked up more young men than we've had hot dinners. She's been married several times with that condition understood. Most of the husbands couldn't bear her behaviour but she's always managed to take them to the cleaners rather than the reverse. She'd have a waiter in Rome or a young sailor in Marbella, pick them up, dress them in the best shops, take them into places they'd only seen from the outside. Mind you, she's supposed to drop them as swiftly as she picks them up. Packy may be on a roll at the moment but he'll be lucky if it lasts for long. Funny, I never thought that he was really gay, just trying everything that would be an advantage to him. Well, let's get moving. I want to drop into Sotheby's in Bond Street and enquire about the Munnings.'

The tiny squalid bathroom was almost too small for the pair of them but they managed to sponge each other and remove some of the London grime. As usual, seriousness did not last long and the sponge found itself being used as a playful weapon. She gave Milo a vigorous tweak which made him jerk into the ancient cistern high over the lavatory and almost bring it down. In revenge he flew after her with the bathbrush and caught her on the narrow bed where he spanked her with enthusiasm. The Munnings and Uncle Bertram were forgotten for the next half hour.

Sheila was surprised later that morning to find out how unglamorous Sotheby's offices were. Milo asked if he could speak to somebody about a Munnings. After a short delay a rather pompous young man arrived to interview them.

'Yes, lots of people think they have a Munnings. You're certain it's a genuine picture? Could I ask how you come to be in possession of it? Provenance is all-important.'

'A relation of mine bought it from Munnings,' said Milo, 'Kilbeggan was the name.'

The pompous young man did some instant research in a sheaf of notes he was carrying.

'I'm afraid there must be a mistake here. No picture of Munnings went to a Mr Kilbeggan. I have the provenance of all the circus pictures here. Could it be a print that you have?'

Milo was not going to accept a brush-off.

'Just show me those notes for a moment,' he said. Reluctantly the pompous young man gave him the typed lists. 'There it is,' said Milo triumphantly, 'owned by the Viscount

Kilcock. He bought it before he inherited the earldom. 1932 that's the right date. It must be the same picture.'

'Could I enquire your own name?' asked the auctioneer's agent. 'Well if this is the same picture, I must say that I envy you. Munnings was at the height of his power during this period. His pictures were full of power and colour and enjoyment. He was a very physical painter, wonderfully attracted to animals. He rode very well himself, much preferred the horse to the car. He also knew his anatomy. Some of the Impressionists you feel paint in a vague blurred way to avoid accurate description. But Munnings knew every vein in a horse's neck. The hunt and circus enthralled him.'

He continued talking with huge interest about the painter. Sheila and Milo listened with curiosity.

'What about selling the picture?' asked Milo.

'Well, no shortage of buyers. The last sporting sale contained a small oil painting of a gipsy girl looking out from a caravan. Not a large picture for a Munnings. It went to Virginia for £80,000. He is now recognized as a first-rate painter and you'll find plenty of buyers both private and public who are anxious to obtain a Munnings. I'll tell you what I can do. We have some of our people travelling to Ireland to look up some pictures for our Irish sale in June. We have a major Irish sale then. We are selling some very important Irish works. You've heard of the Prospect of Stradbally Hall. It's coming up for sale and there are some other very interesting pictures, an Orpen, an O'Conor and some of those lovely Irish watercolours – Rose Barton and Mildred Butler. I'll ask one of our men to bring over your Munnings, if you could arrange to leave it in the Dublin office with Anne Dillon. We can discuss probable prices once I have had a look at it. Now if you are interested in other antiquities, we have a sale of Egyptian artefacts in our gallery around the corner. You can view these artefacts at the moment; the sale does not start until this afternoon.'

Milo and Sheila declined the offer and made their way down to Victoria to catch a train for Brighton. Soon they were aboard a rather dirty train through whose smeared windows they were soon able to view Clapham Junction station for at least five minutes and other unattractive and unexplained stopping places. It was a relief to leave the urban grot behind and eventually to chug through a pleasant green landscape. How neat it was, thought Sheila, compared to the untidy Irish landscape. Milo nuzzled her neck in the empty carriage as they stared out at the pleasing countryside.

The railway station in Brighton was alive with foreign students and English families with sunburnt children. Heavy London teenagers devoured crisps and chips and were not too fastidious about the cartons afterwards. Milo received a large sticky wet substance on his shirt as a feeding youth pressed hastily by him. He emerged soiled from the station into brilliant sunlight. They took a taxi down into the town centre, passed Prinny's oriental palace and drove along the coast road towards Shoreham where they stopped at the substantial bungalow called Simla Lodge. Having paid off the taxi, they walked up the gravelled path. A red and suspicious face looked out from the bay windows when they rang the bell. It scrutinized them carefully before it disappeared. At length the rattle of bolts and clanking of chains gave notice that the front door was being opened. Then a dapper old gentleman appeared.

'Come in, my dear fellow. Don't be put out by all these alarms and precautions. We've all been robbed around here, silver gone here, furniture stolen there. Not just at night. Cheeky buggers in plain daylight. Marjorie Hoddle went to the library last week. Just half an hour. Her miniatures were gone when she got back. They took a sledgehammer to the door. Police absolutely useless. Have to defend yourself nowadays; I'll use the shotgun if necessary. Not on you, my dear young lady.' He swung towards Sheila and kissed her warmly on the mouth. 'Very sweet, very sweet. You're a lucky young man, Milo.'

Sheila felt the ancient hand descend her back and press warmly against her bottom as Uncle Bertram pretended to be escorting her into the sitting room.

'It's rarely I have a young woman in the house. Used to have a nice young woman come in to clean but there was an unfortunate misunderstanding. Now I've only Mrs Williams and I'm not too sure about her, I miss things. Went up to London for the VE celebrations. There was a saucepan missing when I got back. Handy little pan – useful for boiling an egg. I put it up to Mrs Williams, "Where's that little green saucepan?" I said. She made up some cock and bull story about a hole in it and she'd put it in the bin. But I asked the bin men on their next round had they by any chance spotted a small green saucepan when they were emptying my bin a week ago. A rather impertinent young man told me that he'd seen lots of green things but not a green saucepan. So I just keep an eye on Mrs Williams. The Welsh you know – they're not reliable, now let me get you a drink. Sun over the yardarm. Just a mineral for you, eh? You can't be Irish at all. A beer, Milo?'

Uncle Bertram went out to the dining room where he kept the drinks and the young couple smiled at each other although Sheila resolved to keep at arm's length from Uncle Bertram's roving fingers. They looked around the old-fashioned room. Some small side tables held silver-framed photographs of regimental groups. Uncle Bertram, younger and quite handsome, appeared in photographs of polo matches. A portrait showed him in front of a pleasant country house with a dark-haired young man.

'Who's that with him?' asked Sheila. 'It's my father,' replied Milo.

Other family groups showed Milo's mother and father with Kate looking sweetly innocent as a bridesmaid. Brass was everywhere. Trays, ornaments, ashtrays, statues jostled for space. A couple of Nelson tables held photographs of Indian hill stations. A splendid tiger's-head rug yawned behind the sofa. Over the open doorway kudu horns were hung. The large marble clock had been presented by some fellow officers on his retirement.

Back came Uncle Bertram with the drinks clanking on yet another brass tray. He took his own very large gin and tonic and handed them each their drink. He toasted their future and started to examine Sheila on her background. 'Any relation to old Toby Kelly?' he enquired. 'I soldiered with him in Ceylon years ago. A very good shot. Had a place in Roscommon I believe. No, no relation. What about the Rochfort-Kellys? You know with the boy at Gordonstoun who nearly drowned. Absolute miracle they say. His long hair saved him. Caught on a broken spar. Well, they're probably distant relations of yours. Not as good-looking as you I'm afraid, although Muriel had her day.' He paused sentimentally, possibly thinking of some bygone adventure.

'Well Milo, behaving yourself I hope. You'll have to change your ways now. Awful rogue he used to be, Sheila; you'll have a lot on your plate.'

Milo blushed. He was finding these constant warnings to Sheila a trifle irritating, especially a warning from Uncle Bertie. Talk about the kettle calling the pot black, or green in Bertie's case. But the old man rambled on. He enquired closely about Kilbeggan Castle and told them several stories about his visits there in the old days. Cynthia had been rather strange at times, although her husband was very generous with the drink, almost too generous. Did they know that the old lord kept a supply of drink in the boathouse that Cynthia did not know about. Going fishing was a constant pursuit of his. When Cynthia grew suspicious of his visits to the boathouse, he shifted his cache to the mausoleum. He removed several bricks to make a drinks' cupboard. The dead would not steal his drink. He supposed the secret cupboard was still there. Milo and Sheila exchanged glances thinking of more recent users of the hidey-hole.

'Well,' said Bertie, 'we'll have a bite to eat and then we'll run down to Shoreham and get a blow of air. I've got to keep the exercise up.'

'There was a cold meal waiting in the dining room. A small side of rare beef had a strong salad beside it. The dining room was cold, obviously only used for visitors. Several family portraits lined the walls, but one outstanding picture hung over the sideboard. A dark-faced bucolic groom held an Arab horse in some English parkland. It was not a large painting but marvellously impressive.

'Do you like my little Stubbs?' said Uncle Bertie. 'Thank God, the thieves around here wouldn't recognize it. I never tell anybody it's a Stubbs. I'll probably have to sell it, if ever I go into a nursing home. Do you know they cost £400 a week. Mags Parker is in a place down the road and they charge her £350 a week. She hardly eats anything, so they must be making a hell of a profit. That's what you should do with Kilbeggan. You could kill them off with the steps, when you'd got them to sign over their money to you.'

He chuckled at the idea. They explained to him their ideas for making an income out of the castle. He was delighted to hear that it was not going to go the way of other great houses.

'Mind you, it alters the character, living in a big house,' he said. '*Folie de grandeur* the French call it. You begin to have notions about yourself. Think of that politician fellow Clark whose father bought Saltwood Castle. You'd think he came from five hundred years of feudal ancestors the way he talks about it. Still, very comic fellow. Got his diaries for my birthday. Mostly around here it's spivs and profiteers who keep the big places going. You'd be surprised – all flash cars and never go to church.' Milo coloured again at the statement which might refer to himself. 'The sleaze factor,' said Bertie. 'That's what they call it over here. Chaps want to make millions in a few months. The country's full of crooked buggers nowadays. The straight bat has gone. Everything went down since national service was abolished. And then getting rid of the cane in the schools. What madness. It was the only way of controlling these people. Here, have some cheese to finish off. There's biscuits somewhere. Mrs Williams doesn't like them, so they never disappear. Old Mosley had some right ideas although they did him down in the end. Jack's as good as his master nowadays. I've no port. In any event it's not good for you in the middle of the day. You see it's no use pretending we're the same as them. We're not and that's it. They can't even be bothered to polish their shoes. You look round Brighton. You'll hardly see a pair of decently polished shoes.' Milo stuck his feet further under the table. Sheila had worn highly-polished brogues for the outing so did not feel uncomfortable. 'When you think of quite decent people and then see how their descendants carry on, you feel pessimistic. Think of Blandford. Every time you open *The Telegraph*, you see him entering or leaving a courtroom. Young Thatcher is really unspeakable and as for Winston Churchill what a pity he carries the same name. Is there anybody left whom you can look up to? Even in my own old trade, there's a lot of them making fools of themselves, spending fortunes on curtains for army houses. But I like the cut of that General Rose. Brave chap in the old-fashioned style. What do you think?'

He stared suddenly at Sheila.

'Was it all roses in the old days?' she asked.

'No my dear, you're quite right. It wasn't all roses. But I'm damned sure it was better than nowadays. I'm going to get the car out and I'll drive you over to Shoreham. I'll show you the karzy first, if you want to use it.'

Cartoons of military life hung in the lavatory and there was a small library of slightly salacious novels. Taps were polished and paintwork was gleaming. Despite this, it smelt slightly of old man – a smell not unfamiliar to Sheila from her hospital experience.

They waited at the front of Simla Lodge while bolts were bolted, locks were locked and alarms were set.

'One good terrier would be better than this lot,' said Uncle Bertie glumly, 'but I've had three terriers run over by speeding cars, and I grew depressed at risking their lives. No matter what you did they got out on the road and some selfish bastard would run over them. Now would you like to get into the front, my dear?' he said to Sheila, his eyes brightening. She declined the offer to his disappointment and Milo took her place. They drove carefully and took the road to Shoreham. 'Much nicer there,' said Bertie, 'I like to get away from Brighton. There's a lot of dreadful people there in the summer. That's Molly Partridge's house there with the walnut tree in front. She's one of our bridge four. Funny old thing but a splendid cook. You'd nearly take her for her cooking. Milo do you remember the Barretts – friends of your mother's? They sold their place and they've bought that very flat-looking bungalow. He's got MS poor fellow. Finding it hard to get around, I'm afraid. Just look at that for bad driving.' He sounded his horn fiercely at a car which had pulled out ahead of them. Traffic began to slow down. 'There's a very good mechanic in that garage there. Served in the Durham Light Infantry he told me. I always go to him to get it serviced. You can't trust the younger fellows. Always charges me a reasonable price.' Traffic was suddenly down to a crawl. 'Must be an accident.' Patience was called for and Uncle Bertie did not seem to have a large supply of this virtue. 'Stupid woman, she doesn't have to go that slow. Look, she's letting them in.' The driver in front had stopped to let other cars in from a side road. She waved them in ahead of her courteously, while behind her Uncle Bertie's blood pressure rose steadily. 'That's right, let the whole bloody country in ahead of us. Don't think of the cars behind you.'

He could bear it no longer and sounded his horn furiously. In response the young woman driver ahead of them stuck her hand out of the window and gave Uncle Bertie a prolonged V sign.

All the miseries connected with traffic jams now made themselves felt. Ahead of them a mile of cars, buses, lorries and vans stayed static and then for a moment of relief drove another five yards and stopped. Heat mounted in family cars; children grew impatient, noisy and sticky. The impatient driver felt blood pressure rise. A few switched off their engines and then almost immediately had to restart them as traffic made a slight advance. A few drivers had to keep revving, terrified that their ancient engines might stop permanently and leave them exposed and vulnerable, holding up the rest of the traffic. Elderly radiators began to boil. So did Uncle Bertie. He looked with distaste at the three children in the back seat of a red Escort ahead of him. Their waving and sticking out of tongues did not amuse him while

232

his passengers had to conceal their mirth. All are made equal in a traffic jam. The Jaguar which purrs richly past lower breeds of car is stuck side by side with inferior vehicles where ice cream is dripped on cheap upholstery. Important people full of self-satisfaction have to endure the humiliation of sitting a few feet away from the unmoneyed and shabby whom they would normally avoid like the plague. The long traffic jam is a leveller that is not appreciated, especially by those whose great advantage in financial possessions renders them normally immune from such contacts. Even chairmen of public utilities, the new gods of civilization, have to endure the closeness of their customers. Almost imperceptibly this hold-up began to ease and gradually they drew close to Shoreham where the cause of the traffic jam became apparent. A considerable crowd, alive with self-righteousness, was protesting against animal exports. Uncle Bertie drove slowly past tweedy women waving placards, new age travellers ready to die for a sheep and sensitive souls agonizing over the discomfort of animal travel.

'A fat lot they care about the discomfort of human travel,' snorted Uncle Bertie.

'Go home,' he shouted, 'and look after your family.'

This was directed at respectable looking middle-aged women but it was responded to by an antagonistic group which was just waiting for such criticism. Uncle Bertie's beautifully polished car was thumped and kicked. Furiously he tried to open his door to confront them but the car was being rocked. A sudden rush of policemen scattered the attackers and Uncle Bertie was told to drive on immediately and leave the area.

'Go home, grandad,' shouted one of his tormentors, with an extra string of abuse.

Uncle Bertie's face grew purple with rage, Sheila from the rear seat saw the colour spread across his balding head and a vein in his neck swell ominously.

'Country's in a state of anarchy,' he snorted. 'Impertinent young puppy. Somebody will have to take a stand. Come on Milo, let's face the ruffians.'

Milo tried to restrain him but it was too late. Bertie was out of the car door. He had faced savage mobs as a young man. The fire still ran strong in his blood. Milo jumped out to try to avert disaster. The police were holding back the demonstrators and several of the more serious demonstrators were trying to steward their unwelcomed allies. But disaster struck. Bertie suddenly changed colour again and collapsed. A claw-like hand clutched Milo but he sank to the ground, supported by his nephew. Sheila ran to help and took over quickly.

'Looks like a heart attack,' she told Milo. 'We need an ambulance immediately.'

Bertie now lay prone on the ground absolutely still. A bluish colour tinged his face and froth emerged from the mouth. While Milo used police walkie-talkies to summon an ambulance, Sheila went through her emergency drill, pumping the chest and using mouth-to-mouth resuscitation. At first she feared the worst. Breathing seemed to have stopped and the heartbeat was incredibly faint. But life persisted and the old man was not about to yield. Almost imperceptibly, the breathing became easier and she was able to relax her urgent attentions. The police held onlookers at bay and eventually the ambulance arrived. Uncle Bertie was connected to the emergency equipment. Sheila decided to accompany him to hospital, leaving Milo to retrieve the car and deal with police and media. Journalists, photographers and television crews jostled to interview him. The aggressive demonstrators who had been responsible for the attack had melted from the scene and were probably on the way back to London. Question after question was hurled at Milo. Was his uncle an exporter of calves? Was he an opponent of the animal lovers' lobby? Why had he got involved then in the demonstration? What age was he? What relation was he to Milo? Names were taken down and the journalists gradually eased off their questions, having established a superficial view of the affair. Several lorries had taken advantage of the diversion to bring their loads of calves to the docks. The demonstrators realized what had happened and ran off to obstruct the following lorries. The cries of abuse and the shouts faded in the distance and the media hoping for a fresh sensation followed the crowd. Milo was left with a smeared and scratched little car and a solitary policeman who took down the details. But the cameras had been elsewhere during the scene and the search for the attackers proved futile.

Milo got into the car and drove it slowly out of the town and back along the coast road to Uncle Bertie's bungalow. Fortunately the house keys were on the bunch of car keys. He found the right keys and entered the deserted house. A quick telephone call to Worthing hospital brought news that the ambulance had arrived, that tests were being carried out but that it did not appear that any serious damage had been caused to Uncle Bertie. For safety's sake they would hold him overnight and possibly for a few days. He asked to speak to Sheila and was reassured by her calm voice. Bertie had rallied strongly in the ambulance. Sheila had been obliged to bully him slightly and warn him that indulging in bad temper could bring on a really serious attack, that he had been very lucky and that calm and tranquillity were essential. The old man was frightened enough to comply. What Swift had called *saeva indignatio* must be avoided at all costs. This for a peppery old gentleman was a difficult task. He had held Sheila's hand throughout the ambulance ride and had given up complaining about the state of anarchy the country was in. There was nothing more that Sheila could do for him but she had promised that they would stay in the bungalow overnight and visit him in the morning. Milo cursed at this disturbance to their arrangements. He drove over to collect Sheila and they drove back to Simla Lodge and sat down to discuss this sudden upset to their plans.

'He recovered remarkably quickly,' said Sheila. 'I thought he was nearly goners at first or that sight or hearing or some nervous injury would have occurred. Another person would be dead by now or be paralysed or have brain damage. He is like a terrier that has been winded by a sudden collision. I doubt if he'd survive a repeat performance. They'll have to

235

keep him very quiet. Sedatives and no stimulation from now on. Getting mad at the world or getting excited by pinching some girl's bottom could be fatal for him. He's worried about the house so we had better stick around.'

They sat arm in arm on the sofa and eventually dropped off warm and sleepy. When they awoke it was dusk. Milo switched the early evening news on the television to find a picture of himself confronting them. There were pictures of the excited crowds, of Uncle Bertie being carried into the ambulance. The commentator had got Milo's name wrong and had exaggerated all the events. Only for Lord Kilbacon's intervention, his aged uncle would have died. The Irish peer's fiancée, Miss Kelly, had saved the old gentleman. Public sympathy had now swung against the demonstrators who were being criticized for their violence. 'Is all this worth a human life?' asked a member of Parliament who said that he would ask the Home Secretary to order more police to the area. There were suggestions of sinister organizations which wished to infiltrate lawful protesters for their own ends. The journalists had found Uncle Bertie's tobacconist who gave a fascinating account of the old gentleman and told the press that he had been a war hero. 'Is this the way to treat our heroes?' asked a journalist rhetorically.

Milo and Sheila watched fascinated to find themselves the centre of such unwanted attention. Five minutes later, the telephone rang and the doorbell sounded at the same time. Sheila answered the telephone and Milo went to the hall door. Journalists from a local paper were at the hall door. Local radio were on the telephone. Would Lord Kilbricken like to describe the incident to their listeners? If not, could Miss Kelly tell their listeners about the famous war hero and his aristocratic nephew? Outside on the gravel drive photographers snapped close-up pictures of the slightly battered car.

'Had Uncle Bertie taken part in the VE Day celebrations? Could they have a picture of Lord Kilbucket and Miss Kelly together. Closer please. Could they move much closer please?'

'Lord Kilbucket please place your arm around Miss Kelly. Is Lord Kilbucket any relation of the royal family?'

More telephone calls. A string of obscene abuse was directed at anybody who helped animals to travel to their doom.

Milo shouted, 'Fuck off,' angrily into the phone, only to discover that it was Roddy ringing from London. He had seen the television news and took the comic view. No sooner had he rung off than more calls followed.

Milo and Sheila spent a breathless couple of hours, trying to play down the excitement of the media which in a dull couple of days were inclined to sensationalize the event. The bungalow was photographed again and again. 'The little country cottage where a war hero hoped to end his days in peace.' They described roses around the door, a more human touch than the clematis which was really there. Milo mistakenly allowed one photographer into the house who immediately snapped 'the humble kitchen where the war hero prepared his simple repast. A simple boiled egg and toast satisfied his elderly needs.' They kept the snapper out of the bedrooms and eventually persuaded him to leave. 'Aristocratic couple pose in simple setting.'

More telephone calls came. Mr and Mrs Kelly had seen it on the Irish television news and were anxious. Sheila asked them to reassure their friends and to ring Mrs Neligan in case she was anxious. There was very little sympathy in the Irish countryside for any interference in animal exports. The Irish farmers exported huge numbers of cattle and sheep to the Continent. Milo and his uncle rose rapidly in esteem as a result. Congratulatory calls exceeded abusive calls. A few very odd calls came that evening including one from a crying lady who hoped God would forgive them, for he had created animals and nobody had any right to abuse the animals and they would suffer the torments of the damned for their sympathy with such cruel practices. It was useless trying to explain that all they were doing was driving to Shoreham on a social visit. Nobody wanted to know the real circumstances. The media was the message and everything was distorted. Eventually disgusted, they took the telephone off the hook and did not answer the doorbell. Sheila cooked supper from the fragments in the fridge. They found the guest room and dropped into bed exhausted. Sheila had the most vivid dream where crowds of savage youths and girls were attacking the car she was travelling in. As they rocked and tried to overturn the car she clung to Milo who was dreaming in a somewhat similar vein. He kissed her tenderly and held her firmly until she dropped off again. But it was an uneasy night and it wasn't until the early dawn set birds singing on the branches outside that the young couple caught a few hours of relaxed sleep.

As they sat eating breakfast, disturbances started again. *Hello* magazine would like a photograph of Milo and Sheila. A tabloid wondered if they would be going for a swim as it was such a hot day. Their photographer might perhaps take a photograph of the young couple in swimming togs. A neighbour arrived with a few tomatoes and a huge marrow to prepare the larder for Uncle Bertie's return. A message of goodwill from the British Legion. A message of goodwill from the local Conservative Association. A cross telephone call from Aunt Kate. What on earth were they all up to? Really Bertie should be ashamed of himself. He was always flying off the hoop. Milo shouldn't let him behave so wildly. Do keep themselves out of the newspapers in future. Kate sounded so indignant that Milo began to laugh and she grew even further annoyed. The arrival of a police superintendent at the front door saved him from a lengthy lecture. The officer, an intelligent and understanding person, was as concerned as Milo over the hype and exaggeration of the media. Milo told him that there was no intention to press any charges. A telephone call to the hospital in Worthing confirmed that Uncle Bertie was well and had recovered remarkably. The doctors, while issuing strong warnings about any emotional upsets, were nevertheless impressed by his resilience. When all tests were completed they would release him, probably the next morning.

'The whole thing,' said Milo to the superintendent, 'is

unwelcome to us and has been blown out of all proportion. We would like to resume our normal lifestyle and get out of the limelight.'

The superintendent agreed, for the police had been under fire from all sides and he was tired of his force being the filling in the sandwich. He suggested that they issue a public statement to cover all public enquiries. The hospital had already done so. They drew up a harmless formula thanking everybody for their interest and confirming that no injuries had been received by Uncle Bertie. At this stage they had a piece of luck, and public attention was diverted elsewhere. An early morning jogger running with his dog on Tooting Common had stumbled on the naked body of a beautiful young woman with a single stab wound to the throat. Publicity had connected her with a pop singer. A search of a flat in Primrose Hill revealed the pop singer unconscious and suffering from an overdose of drugs. The tabloids switched all their attentions back to London and the sad face of the dead woman filled the evening newspapers later. Uncle Bertie was suddenly deserted by the media. The telephone calls ceased. As quickly as the newspapers had focused on them, so suddenly were they deserted by them. Apart from a few local enquiries, there was peace at Simla Lodge. Milo brought out some cleaners and did his best to restore Uncle Bertie's car to its shining appearance. A firm application of wax left the little vehicle in more impressive condition ready for its owner's inspection.

They drove to the hospital where Uncle Bertie, having endured the humiliation of medical tests, was now resting in a day ward. His only pain lay in having to listen to other patients' opinions. He was trying not to listen to them in case the blood pressure rose again. Sheila sat down and gave a lecture to the old man. Slowly she made him understand that stress was his real enemy. Tantrums and irritations were inclined to increase with age and the 'short fuse' had seen off many a good man. Bertie must avoid the causes of umbrage, must not get ruffled over opinions or actions he disapproved of. If you bristled every time you listened to the news, it would shorten your life or make it miserable in other ways. A combination of alcohol and exasperation was dangerous. Uncle Bertie, who flew into a rage most mornings as he read his *Daily Telegraph*, was risking his life if he did not change his lifestyle.

'You cannot change the world,' Sheila told him. 'It's better to ignore all the sore subjects and avoid the fits of explosiveness. Ignore the things that you cannot change.'

Suddenly the old man looked pathetic as he lay on the hospital pillows. It's difficult to change the habits of a lifetime. He had always enjoyed being the character he was. His friends always expected him to be tetchy, had often introduced a sore subject into a conversation to provoke him into a rage. He had almost begun to enjoy it himself, to become the cartoon-type retired colonel. Uncle Bertie with eyes flashing was a splendid spectacle. The members of his club almost expected to see Bertie in flying form, damning this ruffian and that as he heard the latest news of his countrymen. To change from being a snappish, testy old man to a benevolent, tolerant person was going to be difficult and Bertie realized this all too well. Slowly Sheila convinced him that the change would be worthwhile and she gave him some practical advice about avoiding the causes of anger and ignoring the many petty irritations. Her nurse's training and her inherited common sense made her a powerful advocate. Now Bertie was worrying about his house and his Stubbs. Sheila went off to see the specialist in charge of him, while Milo described to the old man all their intended changes at Kilbeggan.

Sheila was kept waiting for a short while outside the great man's office. Like all hospital personnel he was run off his feet and looked weary and stressed himself when Sheila was invited in to see him. Mr Mohommed Mubarrac, a thin Egyptian, gave her encouraging news about Bertie.

'I hope that I'll be as fit and as healthy when I'm the same age,' he said, 'but precautions are essential. If he keeps getting provoked into a passion over minor things, he will inevitably end up in a serious condition and with a crippling

240

disablement. He should not drive a car; he is probably a danger to others as well as himself. He should have a nurse within call and somebody to keep an eye on him. If all goes well, we will release him tomorrow morning. As you must know, we don't detain patients unnecessarily. In fact it's almost the opposite. So collect him tomorrow and keep talking to him about ways to avoid flying into an excitement at every opportunity. I think possibly a sedative at times. I'll leave that to you as you are a relation.'

Sheila blinked. Here she was being claimed as a relation of an elderly man she had known for a very short time and drawn into responsibilities for him. She walked back to the ward and told Bertie the good news. They left him with a promise to collect him the next morning and they gave instructions at the hospital reception area that no media enquiries were to be answered about the old man, except for the news that he was no worse off for the Shoreham experience.

'Come on,' said Milo. 'Let's get off to the beach for the rest of the day.'

They drove off to the beach at Portslade and basked in the sun.

Next day, the publicity had all but evaporated. No journalists or media people appeared at the house. A few telephone calls enquiring about Bertie's health seemed to signal the end of the interest in the old man. Another Conservative sex scandal was rocking the government and the newspaper hacks were besieging an MP's house near Victoria. 'Beat me, cried politician' was the new tabloid sensation. Milo and Sheila were relieved to be left in obscurity. At eleven, they drove over to the hospital to collect Uncle Bertie. The pretty young nurse who had attended him was pleased to see them arrive. Uncle Bertie had seemed to believe that being touched in soft places would please the hospital staff. She had tried to keep out of reach of his agile old hands. She had warned him there could be a relapse if his fingers produced new excitements for him. 'Girls always enjoy a bit of fun' had been his motto as a dashing young soldier. But age changes the desirability of sexual attention. An approach from a wrinkled and balding old gentleman with bad breath was an irritation and a nuisance. So Uncle Bertie was waved out of the ward with relief. They placed him in the back seat of the car and drove back to Shoreham.

Now came the difficulty of trying to arrange for the old man to be looked after. He was independent enough to resent the idea of a nurse in the house, much as he might enjoy the excitement of it if she were young. In any event, most of the supply nurses were elderly or middle-aged widows supplementing their pensions. What he really needed was somebody 'to look in', to see that he was all right. They sat down trying to resolve the problem when a sudden thought crossed the old man's mind.

'Now I'm going to suggest something to you which might suit all of us,' he said. 'How about it, if I came over to Kilbeggan with you. I'd help you by putting some money in the place in return for accommodation. I'm sure that strapping young Mrs Neligan could look after me a bit, arrange my washing and so on.'

They had to inform him that Mrs Neligan was no longer a vigorous young woman but a rather tired elderly dame. Sheila caught Milo's eye and signalled 'no' to the suggestion.

'The steps would be too much for you,' she said to Uncle Bertie. 'They're bad enough for young people but they'd be dangerous for you. And the basement is far too damp.'

This idea was now abandoned and they thought again. Suddenly Milo had an idea.

'What about the front gate lodge?' he said to Sheila. 'If Jack makes that comfortable and we put in some storage heaters or central heating wouldn't that be ideal for Uncle Bertie? We could drop in on him each day and I'm sure Mrs Neligan would cycle down to him and help out with the washing and the chores. It's big enough to have a bedroom on the ground floor.'

This idea appealed to Sheila more. She had no wish to start off married life with an elderly relation of her husband in the house. But the gate lodge was at a sufficient distance for both parties to preserve their independence. They discussed the proposal and Uncle Bertie got enthusiastic.

'I always liked Ireland,' he said. 'Is there a bridge club in the town? Would you mind storing the rest of my furniture? I don't want to sell it – you can have it completely when I'm gone.'

He fired off question after question at them. Could he get a driver, somebody to take him into the town now and then? He might like the odd day in Dublin, was the Kildare Street Club still open? He mentioned names of country figures, long since dead. He used to play cards with J.D. Guille and his missis. Both dead! My word, what about Belvedere? Open to the public, owned by the County Council? Good God, lots of changes. Still, he'd give it a try, quite sure it would work out. Now what about money? He mentioned a figure to pay for renting the gate lodge, which made Milo almost jump at its generosity. If they looked after him, well he'd look after them. Have to leave a few bob to Roddy of course, but he'd be glad to feel that his money was restoring some of the family property. He grew quite sentimental. They talked about the plan. Uncle Bertie would put Simla Lodge up for sale. In fact he mightn't have to. Olive Emerson's brother had been looking for a house near them. This would save auctioneers' fees and all the hoo-ha with strangers walking around the house and no doubt talking sarcastically about it later. He'd ring Olive. Not now, she'd be at the physiotherapist's, terrible problems with her hips. The Stubbs would travel with him. He wouldn't let it out of his sight.

With all the discussions about the future, they had to remind themselves about the present. Milo made a few telephone calls to Bertie's friends who promised to help out. They would give lifts to bridge games and to the town. They gave Milo names and numbers of retired nurses who might help out for the present. He took down a list of names and addresses and began to ring around. He struck lucky almost immediately. Mrs Benson from Wavecrest Villas would be willing to come in for a couple of hours each evening. She was a retired nurse, had her own car and emphasized that it was not the money that attracted her but an outside interest.

'My late husband, as you probably know, was a retired chemist,' she told Milo. 'You know Benson and Green's Pharmacy just off Cliff Walk. He left me comfortably off but I like to keep my hand in, for the right sort of people of course.'

Milo gulped at the Freudian imagery and wondered how long she would last with Uncle Bertie. She would arrive that afternoon. He hinted as delicately as he could to Bertie that he should keep his hands to himself. Sheila put it more bluntly. She spoke of a groper who had suffered a heart attack when he was gratifying his desires and was now confined to a wheelchair.

'By all means admire the view,' she advised him 'but try to restrain yourself.'

But it turned out that there was no necessity for the warning. Mrs Benson, when she arrived, was of a spectacular plainness. Few hands had ever wished to caress that mighty rump. Hattie Jacques could have been replaced by Mrs Benson in the Carry On films.

'You can call me Doreen,' she told them with a touch of condescension. Uncle Bertie, who disliked the modern trend to call patients by their Christian names, addressed her firmly as Mrs Benson. 'Well, we must keep an eye on you,' she boomed, 'mustn't let you do anything silly.'

Sheila showed her the layout of the house while Bertie looked thunderstruck and rebellious at this intervention in his life. Milo tried to console him by telling him it would only last for a few weeks and that he would be free of this interference within a month. Mrs Benson returned to the sitting room and demanded a spare key to Simla Lodge. When Uncle Bertie told her that he thought this would be unnecessary, she brushed aside his protest. Bertie, who had once commanded a regiment of brown-skinned warriors, was now treated like a new recruit in his former regiment. Milo and Sheila were entertained by the arrival of the autocratic nurse. They almost expected Sid James to walk up the garden path. Mrs Benson finally left, promising to keep a regular eye on the patient.

'My God,' said Bertie, 'what an ugly woman. What have you done to me? Will I ever last out a month with that gorgon? You don't think she'll try to bath me or anything?'

He eventually began to chuckle, until all three of them sat back laughing while tears rolled down their faces.

'Call me Doreen,' said Bertie. 'What impertinence. I'll call her something else if she doesn't watch out. No wonder her poor husband died. Probably crushed in the bed.'

Bertie shook with laughter at the thought. When they had all recovered from the bouts of chuckling Milo and Sheila prepared to return to London. Bertie made them promise firmly to get the gate lodge ready for him quickly and to ask Roddy to come and see him so that he might make some of the arrangements.

28

'I feel like a holiday now,' said Sheila as they waited in the departure lounge at Heathrow.

What she had anticipated as a quiet few days in London with meetings of old friends and relations had turned out to be active and tiring. London had been full of diversions and she had enjoyed the high spirits and the sportiveness of Milo's friends. But the couple of days in Shoreham had been disagreeable – the unpleasant face of England. She had sympathized previously to some little extent with the protests of the self-called animal lovers but meeting them in the flesh had changed her views. Milo had quoted to her a saying that his grandfather had copied down from Samuel Butler –

> Compound for sins we feel inclin'd to
> By damning those we have no mind to.

She had begun to feel outraged that the protesters, the majority of whom enjoyed eating meat and fish and fowl, should feel entitled to criticize farmers and livestock exporters. As for those who attacked hunting, she had no sympathy at all. She had seen the result of the fox's cruelty in her mother's hen-run – a mass of blood and feathers and torn flesh. Mrs Kelly had lost a hen with nine chicks and a brace of ducks in the last savage attack on her poultry. A few days later, when the Westmeath Hunt met nearby, she had nearly exploded with anger to see a crowd of self-righteous young people from Mullingar arrive to picket the hunt. They had brought supporters to gain publicity – a famous writer who never stopped writing about eating lobsters and roast lamb and a member of Parliament whose political correctness did not inhibit him from eating beef sandwiches. This crowd

246

had marched up and down with posters accusing the farmers of cruelty. Mr Kelly had been obliged to restrain his wife.

'God forgive me,' she had said, 'I'd like to see them suffer like my poor ducks did.'

Priggish and smug, the protesters waved their posters, unconscious of the fact that the people they were attacking were the real lovers of wildlife and had hundreds of years of traditions of animal husbandry in their very bloodstream. Mr Kelly had sat up many a night with a sick calf. Mrs Kelly had brought back sick lambs from the edge of death, had shared her kitchen with weakly or crippled animals. To a great extent they had given their lives to the care of animals. Now they were being shouted at and abused by young people, ignorant of animal husbandry and brainwashed by the media campaigns for 'animal liberation'. Hounds were frightened, horses upset, until the new tormentors of the countryside eventually drove away satisfied with their own outrageous conduct and leaving shaken and distressed countryfolk behind them. These blinded people were an affront to a peaceful land. But in England they had become dangerous as well. They had blown up a dairy, for 'exploiting cows'. They sent letter bombs to butchers' shops. Fanatical and sinister, they attracted the 'bleeding heart' types who were often of genuine if misled views. Media sympathy often portrayed them as heroes and their opponents as arrogant upper-class snobs.

England being full of urban constituencies, the MPs were lobbied and harried into promoting bills to prohibit hunting. They kept their attitude to fishing hidden for the time being, as this sport practised very widely by rich and poor alike would be a more difficult nut to crack. All their energy was concentrated in the attacks on hunting and animal transport. Sheila wished that they would take up badminton or table tennis or synchronized swimming or some innocent pursuit instead of harrying their fellow men. She shivered at the memory of the hate-filled eyes and was glad to board the Ryanair plane to Dublin.

Ryanair is the puritanical face of business. Their flights

247

are efficient, punctual and well-run. They have no superficial frills or pretence of grandeur or luxury. As a result, their costs are kept to a minimum and tickets are so cheap that millions avail of them. The affectation of serving a three-course dinner on a one-hour flight has inflated the prices of other airline tickets but Ryanair are content with giving old-fashioned value. A cup of coffee or a drink is really all you need on such a short flight. Sheila held on to Milo's hand as the plane circled around the Hill of Howth and began its short approach to the Dublin airport runway. She closed her eyes as the plane came lower and lower. The initial bump alarmed her and she clung tighter to her man's hand. The sudden engine hissing and the brake noises kept her on tenterhooks but the calm voice of the air hostess reassured her and a surprisingly large number of other nervous passengers. Milo, who enjoyed a certain amount of tension in a car or boat or aircraft, squeezed her with a loving show of protectiveness. There was much sound of bottle clinking as the bags of duty-free spirits were withdrawn from the recesses overhead, and then a general air of impatience before the doors were opened and they could commence the long walk to the carousel. Dublin airport would not set a record for slowness of luggage being emptied from the plane, but the passengers seemed to spend the usual tedious interval staring at the empty carousel as it drove past them repeatedly. Some stared as if mesmerized at the hole in the wall which would eventually yield their possessions. The first few cases to appear brought a surge of activity and a certain amount of ill-mannered elbowing.

'Bloody foreigners,' said Milo as a large German lady pushed ahead of him and left him in the second row.

They got their cases eventually and made their way with their trolley through the awaiting crowds outside. Here stood families scanning the arrivals for the dreaded foreign student. Large country families strained forward to greet their youngster back from America. A brace of nuns awaited the arrival of Sister Bernadette who had spent a whole year in Zambia. Couriers with signs held aloft tried to attract the attention of their arriving clients. Kisses competed with awkwardness as families were reunited. Milo and Sheila dodged through the crowds, nearly ran down a low baby carriage with their trolley and finally emerged into the familiar drizzle of Ireland.

It is always a relief to find your car still parked where you left it. In the case of a Porsche owner, the relief is more pronounced. They emptied out the trolley and sat inside the low luxury of the Porsche. She kissed him with affection and with relief at landing after the flight. She felt secure on land and on land only; both the air and the sea presented her with fears. Safety and confidence she associated with the ground.

They drove off towards Dublin, windscreen wipers working speedily against the driving rain. Reaching the quays, they turned west past the classical handsomeness of Heuston Station and they were soon on the dual carriageway. After Lucan, Milo found to his delight that the new motorway had opened and the splendid open road lay before them. Three towns had been by-passed. Leixlip, with its narrow bridge over the Liffey and the mediaeval castle on its rock, can scarcely be seen from the motorway, although at one time it had been the most traffic-congested town on the road to the west. But the new road had opened up other views. The Conolly Folly, a 1740 obelisk, can be seen through the trees. So too can The Wonderful Barn, another eighteenth-century oddity. Some distance along, the tall spire of Maynooth College chapel arises gracefully among the meadows. Milo welcomed the speed of the Porsche, let the great engine take up a challenge at last. The car surged forward almost effortlessly passing lorries and tankers and other cars without strain. Sheila snuggled back listening to a Christy Moore tape and the faint hiss of the wet road. The needle crept around the speedometer. Kilcok lay to their right as the engine clocked 130 on the speedometer. Milo at last was enjoying driving his car in Ireland. Sheila began to fall asleep, lulled by Christy Moore's innocuous ramblings and the faint purring of the powerful car.

The motorway came to an end and they were back on to the old road taking them on towards Enfield. Milo still had his foot down, passing cars with ease, forgetful that motorway speed is dangerous on the ordinary main road. He glanced down with fondness at his sleeping fiancée and so missed sight of the cow breaking through a hedge and ambling across the road fifty yards ahead. When he spotted the beast, it was too late. He jerked violently at the wheel to avoid the collision, and the car, responding, skidded on gravel by the roadside and hit a telephone pole some yards ahead. The impact on the passenger side was fearsome. Pole and fractured metal and cracked glass and blood were mixed inextricably. A rear wheel lifted up in the air revolved madly in space. Milo had been flung out on the verge by the force of the impact. Sheila lay somewhere in the tangled metal heap. Steam hissed somewhere. The cow continued on its way and grazed contentedly on the verge on the far side. A few seconds' silence lay on the scene; then came the rumble of vans and trucks. The horrifying accident lay in full view. Brakes screeched, cars pulled to a halt.

'O my God, is there somebody still inside the car?'

Lorry drivers of sinister, almost criminal, appearance suddenly became ministering angels. But little could be done. To move Milo would be dangerous. Bones were obviously broken and he was unconscious. Timber and metal were prised apart to reveal the maimed body of a girl.

'Still breathing – very slowly,' said an elderly man, almost weeping.

A salesman with a mobile telephone rang for ambulance and police. A doctor appeared. He injected both with painkillers and rang Beaumont Hospital warning them what to expect. Milo suddenly moaned. Tears came to eyes at the piteous spectacle. The back wheel had now stopped revolving. On the far side of the roadway the cow tried to break into the adjoining field. The assortment of bystanders, frustrated at not being able to help further, guessed inaccurately what had caused the accident. At last, at long last came the siren of the ambulance and, with infinite care, Sheila

250

was lifted out still breathing and placed gently inside the ambulance. Milo was also lifted by the paramedics and laid down on the opposite stretcher. The police examined the car, took out the crushed luggage and tried to find some evidence of who the victims were. It was an English registration; possibly the couple were English tourists. They examined the roadway further back and the first signs of the brake marks. What had caused the driver to brake? There was no sign of another car or cyclist or pedestrian. It was not until the next day that the gap in the hedge gave them a clue. They uncovered the speedometer stuck at 107 m.p.h. A young garda found Sheila's bag flung into the wreckage of the back of the car. A letter to Miss Sheila Kelly of Drumlerry gave them the first information of the identity of the victims.

The siren on the ambulance wailed as it speeded back to Dublin carrying its tragic burden. Through the dense rush-hour traffic the urgent message of the ambulance cleared a path. Through red lights and across main roads the ambulance was driven, causing old men apprehension and old women to bless themselves. The two young lovers in the ambulance heard nothing and saw nothing. Already evening newspapers were altering their front pages to accommodate the latest news. 'Carnage on Galway Road,' the new headlines were to proclaim. 'English tourists in horror crash.' As the ambulance raced towards Beaumont Hospital, medical staff were hastening into action preparing to help the victims of yet another speeding disaster.

Back in Drumlerry, Mrs Kelly was feeding her hens and changing the water in the containers. She was in a state of rare contentment. Mr Kelly's cows had all passed the test that morning. She looked forward to the return of the young couple. She had almost adopted Milo already into the family; different as he was from them, she sensed the sincerity and the straightness of the young lad. Her intuition told her that his love for Sheila was genuine. Happiness filled her thoughts. A fine apple tart was in the oven to help feed the couple on their return. She hummed 'The Rose of Tralee' –

251

It was not her beauty alone
That won me.
Oh no! 'twas the truth in her eyes
Ever beaming
That made me love Mary,
The Rose of Tralee.

The hens were laying well. Even the little bantams, the rogues of the poultry world, were laying in the nettles and she had retrieved some of their eggs, being careful to leave one in each nest to keep them laying in the same place. The sun shone through the gnarled old Bramleys in the little orchard.

'Bad cess to you,' she said to the greedy cock that had almost knocked the feeding tray over. 'That's a blackguard,' she told Mr Kelly who was coming up behind her on the path. Then she noticed his face drawn with worry. 'What is it, Dadda?' she said instantly. 'Is it the mare?'

He sat her down on the wall by the hen-run almost unable to speak. He put his arm around her shoulders. An egg fell out from her apron pocket.

'What is, Dadda?' she said again, this time with an impending sense of dread. He could scarcely answer her. 'Is it the aeroplane?' she whispered. 'Holy Lord, is it the aeroplane?'

He tried to tell her the bad news.

'There's been a car crash,' he said hoarsely. 'I've just had a telephone call from the gardai station, Milo and Sheila have had a bad smash. They've been brought to Beaumont Hospital.'

She sat almost paralysed, unable to move, almost unable to speak.

'Ah Dadda,' she whispered and the tears came flowing. 'Is it bad? Are they alive?'

The sunny world had got dark all of a sudden.

Prayers ran through her head.

'This vale of tears, O mother of the Word incarnate,

252

despise not my petition but in Thy clemency hear and answer me.'

He supported her to the house and sat her down again while he tried to contact the hospital. Engaged. He kept ringing, maltreating the telephone in his impatience. Mrs Kelly was praying in the chair. At last he got through, was cut off, then put through again, then finally got a sister on the phone. The news was not comforting. Sheila had multiple injuries, crushed limbs, loss of blood, what head injuries they did not know. Milo was seriously injured, with possible spinal damage. Both were in intensive care. Hours on the operating table might reveal more information. The sister could not promise anything. It had been a frightful smash, one of the worst they had ever had to deal with. Mr Kelly reeled at the appalling report.

'I'm afraid,' said the nurse, 'that you had better be prepared for the worst. At the moment the chances are only fifty-fifty.'

Mr Kelly sat down in the chair beside the telephone and covered his face with his hands. Tears trickled through his fingers, although he tried to hide them from his wife. Outside in the yard Shep barked at some imagined invader. The kitchen clock ticked loudly and sadly. A gust of wind in the yard slammed a shed door shut. Inside the kitchen, the tormented old couple tried to regain their thoughts and composure.

Seamus it was who brought back a touch of normality to the stunned household. He took charge of the situation, made a lot of telephone calls, called on their friends for assistance. Paul Smith, full of concern, raced over to help and nearly caused an accident on the lane skidding to avoid the goslings crossing. He promised to organize some of the lads to look after the milking. Young Buckley, O'Shea and himself would look after anything that needed doing in the yard. Brigid Horan would look after the house; she would take a few days off work and get a temporary secretary in for Bobby Doyle, to replace her. They rang Mrs Neligan at the castle. Some elderly neighbours were trying to console Mrs

Kelly. They rang cousin Lily in Clontarf who would give them a bed, as there was only herself in quite a big house in Styles Road. They cut off her numerous questions and then rang Dr McNeece to see if he could find out more information from the hospital.

'Still on the operating table,' he reported back to them.

He didn't tell them the rest of the facts he had discovered.

'Little hope of recovery,' he had been told. 'If there is recovery, she will be an invalid all her life – possibly a vegetable.'

More cars poured into the yard bringing neighbours to sympathize. They took Mrs Kelly upstairs, helped her to change and packed a bag for her.

'Sure God is good,' they told her. 'She's a great healthy girl. She'll recover. They do miracles nowadays in these big hospitals.'

Bertie O'Neill had a cousin nursing in the Adelaide Hospital, a young Gibson girl, who would give any help she could.

They were settled into their own car and Seamus drove out of the yard for the journey to Dublin.

'I'll not forget our neighbours, no matter what happens,' said Mrs Kelly. 'We have the kindest neighbours in the country.'

Mrs Kelly seemed to have shrunk physically in the last couple of hours. She wept into the back seat. They drove through Tyrell's Pass and Rochfort Bridge and joined the Sligo-Dublin road at Kinnegad. On the far side of Enfield, cars were parked by the side of the road and crowds gathered looking at something. Too late, Seamus realized what it was, as he spotted the tangled mass of metal embedded on the almost horizontal telegraph pole. Mrs Kelly was too distraught to notice anything and Mr Kelly kept silence as they drove past the horrifying sight. Seamus closed the car windows in case his mother heard any of the bystanders' comments on the wreckage. Shaken, Seamus drove on and eventually as dusk descended they arrived at Beaumont Hospital.

The old couple were awed by the great size of this modern hospital, which was like a small town; crowds were thronging in for the evening visiting hour. They were instructed where to go, but lost their way several times through corridors and passages and up steps and down stairs. Mrs Kelly had to stop and rest several times. Eventually they found the right lift which deposited them at the entrance to the intensive care department. White-faced relations awaited news from other patients. A child had fallen down a cliff in Howth. Joyriders had driven over an old man in Cabra. The proximity of these other disasters made Mrs Kelly even more shaky. She trembled in the chair awaiting news. Mr Kelly had never felt so awful in his life. Seamus, supporting both parents and trying to keep their spirits steady, was full of anguish under a calm exterior. They waited and eventually a nurse came out who told them the surgeon wanted to see them.

'See if you can get hold of a counsellor for them, nurse,' he had suggested to her. 'They will need more than courage to face this.'

They were brought in to a side room where the small unimpressive grey-haired surgeon came to tell them his news. Their daughter had suffered multiple injuries; the first operation had really been to keep her alive and breathing despite the crushing to chest bone and ribcage. She was unconscious and would not be conscious for some time. There was absolutely no point in asking if they could see her. They would keep her as comfortable as possible, but he could not disguise the fact that her condition was grave. She would need further operations in the morning, if she was thought able to bear the treatment. It all depended.

'Depended on what?' asked Mr Kelly.

'On her reaction to treatment,' replied the surgeon.

She was of course on a life-support machine. At this news Mrs Kelly fainted and was looked after by a young nurse.

'She would have had to know, some time,' said the surgeon.

There were some hopeful features. The patient was young and had obviously been used to a healthy lifestyle. Against that, internal bleeding and multiple injuries were very hard on the body. He regretted very much having to tell them such difficult news. They would do all they could possibly do to save Miss Kelly. Seamus's heart sank as he watched his father's grieving.

Mr Kilbeggan, said the surgeon, was also on a life-support machine. If he regained consciousness, it would help them cope with the spinal injuries. X-rays and examinations had not given them sufficient information to say anything definite. They should have more news by the morning. They would like to notify his relations. Could the Kellys inform them of an address? Could the hospital also have the telephone number of their accommodation in Dublin, in case of emergency or sudden deterioration? Otherwise, would they contact the ward the next day at eleven o'clock? Again he offered them sympathy and advised a sleeping pill for Mrs Kelly and perhaps also for Mr Kelly. Mrs Kelly had recovered by now and shakily they made their way out of the hospital.

'She's in God's hands,' said Mr Kelly.

They drove to Styles Road where for once cousin Lily was almost speechless. She rose to the occasion, fed them or tried to make them eat, gave Mrs Kelly her sleeping tablets and Mr Kelly a large glass of Paddy.

'Ah, Dadda!' said Mrs Kelly, 'what will we do?'

They got her off to bed and then Mr Kelly and Seamus went upstairs too, before Cousin Lily got back into her normal questioning ways.

29

The following days were like nightmares. A sense of dread and unspoken apprehension filled the minds of the old couple. Seamus had to leave them to go home and look after the place, promising them to come immediately if there was any change for the worse. Even cousin Lily was stilled by the catastrophe. She ferried them each day to the hospital where they sat numbly waiting for news and fearing the worst. They were not alone. Relations of other victims of other crashes sat timidly, petrified by their anxieties. An accident sends out so many ripples that it affects far more than the people involved. Those who love or even like the victims are hurt. The professionals, the doctors and nurses and ward staff are worked often through the barriers of nerve and tiredness. Which of us would take the risk or press the accelerator for thrills if we could see the devastation we cause? The white hairs on Mr Kelly's head seemed to go silver as they waited. All happiness had left Mrs Kelly's eyes and the lines had deepened on her face. They heard bulletins from surgeon and doctors. At least Sheila was still alive. The heart was strong even if the injuries were fearsome. Mrs Kelly fell into a fit of trembling each time a surgeon came through a door. Mr Kelly felt that he might lose the two women in his family and a black despair invaded his mind.

The radio in the waiting room played the latest of pop tunes as they waited through the day. RTE disc jockeys and personalities put on affected voices to jolly their programmes. News after news brought almost infinite repetition. The radio newscaster seemed only interested in politicians or spokesmen for various pressure groups. Again and again banal questions received dreary banal answers.

'Spokesmen' for organizations were skilled at evading any questions they did not want to answer. The boring inconclusive drivel seemed the only interest to the newscasters. A bishop was spoken to about some religious topic. He too triumphed in his evasiveness – unctious, paternalistic, plausible. Country matters were scarcely spoken about. RTE called the countryside 'the rural area'. It was only mentioned if they wished to discuss a murder or a pederast priest. Outside the capital, millions continued their ordinary or extraordinary lives. Boats throbbed up the Shannon, foreign tourists revelled in the south and west, farmers worked and grumbled and watched the sky, race meetings were held, sports and festivities occurred, a nation engaged in work and play. But RTE seemed only interested in politics and especially in the politics of the North of Ireland – who had said what to whom, who could they get to reply to that. A whole edifice of false publicity received keen attention. Specious argument succeeded outrageously false declaration. Then came the pop music again, aimed at an ambiguous audience.

Even offers of cups of tea were refused by Mrs Kelly as she sat hunched with misery and the radio programmes passed over her. Information was minimal. Nurses coming out smiled kindly at her. Somebody brought her a magazine. Liz Hurley and Hugh Grant were on the cover. Photographers had crouched on tree branches to obtain this 'exclusive' photograph of the famous couple. Their misery could be as nothing compared with hers. Mr Kelly turned the pages of a newspaper. The pages could have been upside down as far as he was concerned. Famous English politicians told the readers how they had no interest whatever in the premiership. Their lies were unheeded by Mr Kelly, tormented by his own sadness.

Some families seem untouched by unhappiness in their lives. The ambulance never comes to their door. The fire brigade is never called to their house. They are the lucky ones. Other families seem to be perpetual victims of misfortune. Their children are prey to every ill. Their lumps turn

258

out to be malignant. Their talk is of nothing but hospitals and doctors and of unorthodox cures they heard about on the Gerry Ryan show. The Kellys were in the first category. A few knocks playing football had bothered Seamus, but only occasionally. His last accident had been about the only occasion that had given worry to the family. They had always been a healthy family living a healthy life. Fresh air, plenty of hard work and wise cooking by Mrs Kelly had left them unscathed by any but commonplace ailments. Sheila had scarcely ever missed a day at school. Mr Kelly had the odd twitch of arthritis, nothing to talk about. So this blow, when it had suddenly arrived, struck them with almost savage intensity. Hospital, especially a Dublin hospital was an alien land to them; not all the courtesies of staff, the sympathy of others, could console them in their distress. It was their Tenebrae, their veiling of statues. Instinctively they turned to religion. Side by side and unknown to each other they asked God's help in the calamity. With the deep faith of the elderly, prayer was their consolation. What had appeared 'vain repetition' and mumbo-jumbo to the reformers was their natural refuge. The Almighty was stormed with invocation.

The day wore on. Nurses went off duty and were succeeded by other nurses. New faces appeared. A couple of strange surgeons walked through. One consultant came out. A conference took place at the other end of the hall.

At length it broke up and a surgeon called out, 'Mr and Mrs Kelly, can you come into this room please.'

Mr Kelly felt Mrs Kelly trembling as he helped her to her feet. Her eyes were red. They made their way slowly into the side room and the surgeon motioned to them to sit down. This was the hardest part of his duties. There was happiness in announcing good news to relations and to watch worry change into elation. He hated this part. Sheila was still alive, he told them, but only just. They had been able to relieve pressure on her chest and breathing. There had been blood transfusions to replace the great loss she had suffered. There had been no return to consciousness. If she grew any

259

stronger, they would discuss the possibilities of operating. Everything was being done that could be done. Only time would tell. Another doctor came to tell them about Milo. It was a miracle how Mr Kilbeggan had survived. Being thrown out of the car had been an extraordinary piece of luck for him. Spinal tests had disclosed no breakages. There were multiple lacerations, a broken wrist, a fractured cheekbone, but they were fairly confident of a successful recovery. He had not fully regained consciousness. Both doctors told them that they would telephone immediately if there was any change in Sheila's condition. They understood Sheila had been a nurse. The words 'had been' sounded ominously in Mr Kelly's ears. He left Mrs Kelly in the charge of a nurse while he went to telephone Lily and ask her to collect them in her car. They walked the long length of the hospital, two shattered elderly people. They passed banks and restaurants and flower shops and card shops in this ultra-modern hospital and emerged into the car park with sinking hearts. Nothing could relieve the pressure of their own feeling, as they drove sadly out of the grounds, leaving the broken body of their daughter, scarcely alive within the hospital.

The night-time seemed full of telephone calls. Seamus of course was waiting for news and half of the town of Kilbeggan sent their sympathy through him. Mrs Neligan rang to say that on the day of the accident, the terrier Touch, sitting on old Neligan's lap, had suddenly let out a terrible howl which had alarmed and frightened them, because dogs seem to know that disasters are about to happen. Mr Kelly was about to say that they should worm the pup but decided to leave them to their fancy. The captain, as Mrs Neligan called Uncle Bertie, had rung the castle and Master Roddy was going to come over as soon as he could. Mr Kinch had asked to be given Cousin Lily's number and would like to speak to Mr Kelly. The nuns were praying for Sheila. The Misses Thomson had asked where to send a get well card. Hughie Quigley had asked something about tree cutting that Mrs Neligan didn't understand. Mr Kelly was distracted by the number of calls and passed on messages to Mrs Kelly who was slumped in an armchair, but her mind was too distracted to take it all in.

'They're very good,' she kept murmuring. 'We have the best of neighbours. But it's hard to think straight.'

Cousin Lily's efforts to feed them were unsuccessful. Their appetites had vanished. A glass of whiskey sat in front of Mr Kelly all night and had later to be poured down the sink. Cousin Lily turned on the television and they watched a chat show, where the audience, packed in more senses than one, unanimously cheered extremist views. The next programme was hosted by a lascivious comedian who specialized in double meanings. Every time he talked about a famous tennis star playing with his opponent's balls he winked and the audience fell about with laughter. Not so Cousin Lily, who changed channels with disapproval. She was very religious. To Mr and Mrs Kelly it was like shadows on the wall. Their minds were centred on the intensive care wards in Beaumont Hospital.

The following day, after a sleepless night, they resumed their vigil in the hospital. There was no change and no fresh news about Sheila. Milo had regained consciousness but had no notion of what had occurred. He was still in a deep state of shock. He had been in theatre and had been operated on for wrist and jaw-bone. He would recover and they would be allowed to see him later for a few moments as they understood that the Kellys were his nearest connections in Ireland. Wasn't it strange that he was in a ward of the same name as himself? When the Richmond Hospital had been absorbed into the huge new Beaumont complex they had kept the names of the wards and brought the plaques which had distinguished them. The Kilbeggan Ward in the Richmond has originally been endowed by the sixth earl of Kilbeggan with the proviso that one bed was always to be kept for a Westmeath patient, so the bright administrator told the old couple, hoping to draw their thoughts away from the tragedy. The effort was in vain. They waited nodding politely and thanking the staff but their thoughts were elsewhere.

The day progressed. Patients recovering from operations

made slow stately journeys along the corridors. Visitors came laden with flowers of psychedelic hue which had certainly never emerged from an Irish garden. Sad damaged children with questioning eyes were visited by distraught parents. Stretchers with anonymous passengers were wheeled through double swing-doors. Mr Kelly bought a morning paper. He handed it to Mrs Kelly who held it upside down.

A pop singer on the radio sang overwhelmingly silly words to some monotonous tune –

> Press – ess – ess me. Please press – ess – ess me
> I need someone to press – ess – ess me.
> Nobod – edy will press – ess me
> I need a friend to press – ess me.

On and on the song went.

'Beautiful,' commented the DJ reverently. 'They don't write them like that nowadays.'

There were requests from listeners to be remembered to Uncle Mattie in Swinford and the O'Toole family in Tallaght. A competition was held to answer the greatest number of questions. Was Amsterdam a city in France or Holland? Was *The Messiah* the name of a sports car or a piece of music? The singer from Donegal called O'Donnell – his first name, was it Daniel or Stuart? The Grand National was a race for greyhounds or horses? Vatican City was in Italy or Finland? Albert Reynolds was the name of a previous prime minister or an Arsenal player? After a number of unsuccessful attempts, the competition was won by an ecstatic listener from Santry. She won the prize of a hairdryer outright and a place in another competition where the prize was a week in the Isle of Man. News bulletins came and went. More politicians were interviewed about Northern Ireland. A Cork nun's first cousin had been injured in an explosion in Bosnia. A shopowner in Bray had been convicted of wounding a burglar who had attacked him while robbing his premises. There was a report from the 'rural area' about a farmer who was so biased that he did not want a large encampment of

262

tinkers on his land. The reporters went to town accusing him
of intolerance and racism. We must appreciate a thing called
'the culture' of these people. A number of English politicians
denounced any suggestions that they were interested in
replacing their prime minister. They evaded statements that
their pressure groups were making arrangements for campaigns. A bishop was interviewed about declining numbers
of vocations to the priesthood. He denounced the media
which undoubtedly had a double agenda containing secular
values. Farms along the Shannon were now short of water.
The weather would remain dry but windy. Somebody tuned
in to a different station.

Mrs Kelly started to tremble when she saw a surgeon walk
past them. Eventually the familiar surgeon came through
the swing-doors and invited them into a side room. What he
told them did not console them but it brought a certain
small note of hope. Sheila was now off a ventilator and able
to breathe on her own. They had operated to relieve
pressure on the brain and to treat head injuries. They felt
the patient was easier but it was going to be a long process
and they were unable to guarantee what the final result
would be. The patient was still unconscious and heavily
drugged with painkillers and other medicines. They would
be allowed to visit her the next day. Perhaps the sound of
their voices might produce a reaction in the patient. He
repeated that she was getting all the treatment that would
be beneficial to her. He suggested that they now go and see
her fiancé who was sleepy but recovering.

Milo had been removed from intensive care and was in a
ward at the far end of the hospital. Almost all the beds had
clusters of visitors around them but one was conspicuously
bare. The dark hair and pale face of Milo contrasted with
the bandage across his cheek. He was still somewhat drowsy
and puzzled as to why he was there. Mrs Kelly leaned over
and kissed him, leaving a tear on his cheek. Far from
blaming him for the crash, she felt her heart go out to him
for the news he was about to hear. They tried to diminish
the effect of the blow. They told him that Sheila was in

hospital too and was having treatment for her injuries. Their intention was somewhat undermined when Mrs Kelly felt tears flooding into her eyes as they spoke of Sheila. She had to turn aside as Mr Kelly spoke to Milo.

'Please give her my love,' said Milo. 'As soon as they allow me, I'll go up to talk to her. She's probably as worried about me as I am about her. What frightful luck. I've never had more than a broken headlamp before this. I'll have to get a replacement to drive her home.'

Mrs Kelly felt her heart sink at the suggestion. Would that drive ever take place? Milo asked them to get messages through to his relations that he was recovering and would be as right as rain soon. It would be silly for Roddy to come over to see him. He suddenly got sleepy again and they left him.

Back in Styles Road, they felt that there would be no end to the sadness and torment which had suddenly attacked their lives. Mrs Kelly again sat sighing in the armchair. Seamus rang up with the idea of distracting her.

'Mam, where did you put that white shirt, the one I bought in Bermingham's last month?'

She who knew where every sock lay in a drawer could not recollect where she had placed the shirt. It distressed her to think that her interest in her laundry was gone. The Marren hen, Seamus told her, the one that laid the deep mahogany-brown eggs, had walked out of the bushes before dinner time with seven chicks around her. This news would normally have given great excitement to Mrs Kelly who felt a sense of achievement with every arrival of chicks.

'Look after them, Seamus, look after them,' was all she said.

The new part had arrived for the milking machine, Seamus told his father.

'Ah yes,' said Mr Kelly and fell silent.

Peter Buckley had rung up about the buckrake. Mr Kelly told Seamus to leave it for the moment; he would contact Peter when things improved. Altogether it was a wasted phone call.

Seamus told Brigid and Bobby, who were sitting with him in the kitchen, 'They're in the depths and who can blame them?'

He had not slept himself the last two nights with the sense of impending doom that afflicted his mind.

At eight o'clock that night a telephone call came through to Styles Road. It was from the sister in charge of the intensive care unit at Beaumont. She would like Mr and Mrs Kelly to come over to the hospital immediately. She would explain why when she met them. Mrs Kelly had practically to be lifted to the car with Cousin Lily on one side and her husband on the other. They drove in sombre silence through the suburban roads where children's voices echoed happily in their late evening games. There was a golden sunset which nearly blinded them as they drove up the hospital avenue. Up the steps they walked and into the now familiar entrance. As Mr Kelly looked back, the outside world looked so inviting; he did not know that this is a familiar experience to those entering hospitals. A few minutes later they met the sister at the door of the intensive care department. They prepared for the worst.

'I'm afraid there's been a relapse,' she told them. 'We thought you had better come in case she is sinking. Breathing and heartbeats seem to be getting more difficult for her. Come this way, please.'

She led them towards a bed where at first it was difficult to tell that it was their daughter lying there with the mass of bandages and wires and connections to blood bags. Mrs Kelly felt for the hand and held it.

'Sheila asthore,' she whispered. 'Don't die on us. You're going to live. Sweet Jesus, keep you alive and safe.'

On the far side of the bed, Mr Kelly sat bleakly. There was no reaction from their wounded child. They sat there praying while a nurse waited quietly behind them.

'Talk to her,' she urged Mrs Kelly. 'Keep on talking, you don't know what effect it will have.'

Mrs Kelly continued to say non-consequential words to her daughter.

'Milo is only a short distance away. He is hoping to come and see you soon. He's recovering well and he'll bring you home when he's better. And Seamus rang us up to say that the Marren hen has had chicks. Do you remember that you brought some of her eggs to London and gave them to friends of yours at the hospital and they thought that you were playing a trick on them? The eggs were coloured like an old piece of mahogany. And Owen Kavanagh has won the car in the football draw. He's never been at the driving wheel of anything but a tractor. The lads are all trying to enter young O'Shea for the Mullingar Bachelor Festival – the shyest lad in the county. Mrs Horan has had terrible trouble with the new washing machine. It nearly shook itself off the floor the first time she used it. And Dadda's very upset about a calf. He'll tell you himself about it. Won't you, Dadda?'

She stared purposefully at Mr Kelly who took up the recital. A deep sigh came from the patient, and was it imagination or did the breathing seem to improve? A doctor came in and made a short inspection.

'Just keep on as you are,' he whispered to Mrs Kelly. 'There's a definite recovery taking place.'

For the first time in days Mrs Kelly felt a lift herself. For several hours they sat there talking to the silent Sheila until they had almost run out of small-talk. They gossiped about relations and friends; they gave her news of football matches; they described the building of a new wing to the hospital in Mullingar. They told her what was happening in her favourite television soaps. Mrs Kelly spoke to her of the failed wedding in *Coronation Street*. Mr Kelly told her how a friend of his, Ned Fitzpatrick, had been to the Dublin Show and had met Stephen from *Glenroe* – a very nice gentleman and not stand-offish at all for such a famous actor. Half the country seemed to be travelling next week-end to see Boyzone at the Equestrian Centre. Goodness knows if the place would hold them all. Cissie Grogan had brought them a present of a tub of Haagan-Dazs, the new ice cream. There were young ones from Wexford selling

266

strawberries in all the towns. The new age travellers were being moved on by the guardai. Desperately they tried to remember any pieces of news or information. They had no idea if she heard any of their talk but the doctor might be right that the mere sound of familiar voices could have a benign effect. And gradually it seemed that this might be so, for the nurse told them that pulse and temperature had almost normalized and Sheila seemed to have overcome this crisis.

'Well done,' she told them. 'I think that we could let you go and get some sleep.'

They kissed Sheila gently and held her hand again. The nurse gave Mrs Kelly a sleeping tablet that she recommended.

'We'll be in touch,' she told them. 'We'll see you in the morning.'

It was now past midnight and Cousin Lily was asleep in the chair in the waiting room. The hospital was quieter now, although the accident department was getting busy with its quota of fighting drunks and berserk drug addicts ready to attack even the staff trying to help them. They avoided these scenes and travelled back along the peaceful corridors to the entrance. Cousin Lily drove them back and Mrs Kelly, now exhausted mentally and physically, slept the sleep of the just. They did not awaken until ten o'clock the next morning, feeling rested but slightly guilty.

To Cousin Lily's surprise they ate a large breakfast the next day – a contrast to the nibbles that had been their sustenance for the previous few days. Mrs Kelly even ate a fried egg, after examining its pale texture suspiciously.

'What shall we do about Lily?' she had asked Mr Kelly in the bedroom. 'We had better do something. She's been very good to us and all that driving.'

Mr Kelly had almost had a row at the petrol station. He had tried to pay for a fill of petrol for Lily's car but she would not hear of it.

'When Sheila improves,' she said hopefully, 'we'll arrange some little token for everything that she has done for us. She's certainly been very good to us.'

He felt a little guilty. He had always found cousin Lily and her constant questioning and gossip a bit of a strain. He had privately had his little joke about Lily's long-dead husband having passed to an easier place. But she turned up trumps in this crisis. She had been the soul of kindness – sympathetic without being overwhelming. He had warmed to her in these last few days. Now she took them once more up to the hospital.

To their great surprise they found a tall very thin young Englishman asking the sister about Sheila's progress.

'I'm Roddy,' he told them, 'a cousin of Milo's. Sheila and Milo stayed with me in London. I'm so awfully sorry that this has happened. You must be very upset.'

He had been to see Milo, who was going to be allowed out of bed for a short while – he was on the mend. The three of them heard that Sheila's injuries were healing slowly – she was definitely improving. They would be able to say shortly that she was off the danger list. But the worrying thing was that she had not regained consciousness yet; however recovery sometimes proceeded like this. They would welcome Mr and Mrs Kelly, and indeed this young man if he was a friend, to go and talk beside Sheila's bed. To talk to her as if she was wide awake. They passed into the ward and her parents kissed the bruised face of their daughter and held her hand. Golden hair escaped out of the bandages and lay across the pillow. Mrs Kelly sighed deeply and so did this strange young man, who seemed inexplicably like one of their own. When Mr Kelly dried up after speaking for ten minutes, Roddy took over. Sheila was breathing easily but bore no sign of receiving their messages.

Roddy started to tell Sheila about the young crowd she had met in London. He told her amusing stories of Uncle Bertie's problems with his new minder, Mrs Benson. Bertie was running a daily battle with the nurse, or 'The Tank' as he called her. She had hidden some of his drink and tried

268

to re-arrange his habits. She kept repeating silly children's rhymes to him –

Early to bed, early to rise,
Will make us all healthy, wealthy and wise

was repeated to Bertie as she told him that early bedtimes were essential in his condition. She addressed him as 'we'. She would say things like, 'Now we mustn't be a naughty boy; we must eat our Complan,' or 'How are our bowels working today then?' Even Mrs Kelly began to laugh as Roddy described Mrs Benson and her imperious ways. Uncle Bertie had been forced to take 'syrup of figs'. Mrs Benson had begun to answer the telephone, ordering callers not to spend too long on the line to Bertie, as it might tire him out. By now Mrs Kelly had almost forgotten her great sorrow over Sheila and tears of laughter replaced tears of sadness. But she still held hands with Sheila and they waited anxiously for signs of recognition.

It was agreed among them that Milo should not be brought down to see Sheila, as it would possibly slow his own recovery. His heaviness of heart had increased with his own physical improvement. To injure a person you love beyond measure must bring an onset of grief. Like most young men, he had not believed that a fatal or near-fatal accident could occur to him. He was far too efficient a driver. He and his friends had laughed about 'prangs'. They were masters of their machines. They could gauge to within a second how long it would take them to stop. What they could not forecast was the unknown – the stray dog, the excited child, the irrational event. How many parents lie awake at night, waiting for their teenagers to return safely and hoping that if there is an accident it will not be a fatal one? But hospitals are filled with young men like Milo who find out too late. So there was little comfort for Milo as the realization dawned that he had caused pain and fearsome injuries to the woman he loved. The Kellys had to try and comfort him, when they felt little comfort themselves.

30

A week later much had changed. Milo, vastly improved but still shaken, had left hospital and was staying in a B & B near the hospital. He spent all the time he was allowed at the bedside of Sheila. She had continued to impress the surgeons by her quick physical recovery – the wounds and abrasions alike healing soundly. She had come through the operations unscathed. Lungs and heart gave no cause for concern. But she had not recovered consciousness and lay in apparent coma. The medical staff were puzzled and concerned; they could see no reason why Sheila could not be communicating by now. Tests and brain scans gave no indications of an injury that should leave her with no sign of mental activity. As each day passed, the worry increased. Mr Kelly had gone home for a few days to help Seamus on the farm and it was Mrs Kelly and Milo who kept vigil at the bedside. They were encouraged all the time by the nurses to behave normally and to talk to each other and the sleeping Sheila. They would meet in the morning and sit in the waiting room while the nurses changed Sheila and gave her the treatment she required. The morning radio shows poured out their inanities to the nation as the life-saving work of the hospital went on all around them. News bulletins sent out their depressing views of the world. Riots took place in the north and a politician kept repeating that these were only 'symptoms' – once you understood that they were only 'symptoms' all would be well. Two teenagers had died from an overdose of Ecstasy tablets; they had apparently been very bored. The government was blamed for almost everything. The soccer team had lost again but a Clare athlete had been in a dead heat for third place at a European athletic meeting. Teenagers in Neilstown had been burning cars;

this time it was the police who were being blamed for daring to arrest one of them for a suspected mugging. A Red Indian, or Native American, had been walking in a march to commemorate the Famine. He told journalists he was doing this to show solidarity with oppressed peoples everywhere. On a lighter note, he liked Guinness. A cabinet minister in London might have to resign for a sexual offence which a popular tabloid had unearthed by paying £50,000 to a drag artist. And the weather – by some strange quirk, it was going to be beautifully sunny with a fresh westerly airstream. Next came the advertisements and it was time for Milo and Mrs Kelly to start their daily vigil.

Sheila lay pale but serene-looking. Head wounds were healing and bandages were being removed to allow the wounds to heal naturally. They kissed her and held her hand and wished her good morning. By lunchtime they would have run out of small-talk. They told her that Roddy had returned to London to work and that he had sent his love to her. Brigid Horan was coming up to Dublin for the weekend and would stay with Sheila while Mrs Kelly had a break. Touch had killed his first rat and wouldn't let Mrs Neligan take it from him. She was afraid that he might have hidden it in Packy's room. There were hints in the English newspapers that Packy and his American patroness might be getting married – she for the fifth time and Packy certainly for the first. The whole affair was inexplicable to old Neligan and Mrs Neligan; they kept getting postcards with friendly messages from Gleneagles, from Nice and even from the Isle of Man. Mrs Kelly's bunion was troubling her but she'd wait until she got home to Kilbeggan before she'd have anything done with it. There was a great chiropodist in Tullamore whom she had full trust in. She told Sheila that she was looking much better and they'd soon have her in action again. But Shelia still lay there giving no sign that she was hearing any of their forced conversation. When their gossip dried up, Milo started to read the newspapers out loud to her. There was a long article about Prozac and some famous people who were said to have used it. A picture of Princess

Di accompanied the article. Several famous tennis stars were said to depend on the drug. Mrs John Perke III had now ceased using it, since she had started to live with her young Irish toyboy. Not a sign of interest crossed Sheila's face as Milo read out this item of gossip. He went on to read paragraphs from *Hello* magazine. The Prince of Asturias was said to be friendly with a daughter of the Grand Duke of Luxembourg. Would Roddie Doyle get engaged to Princess Irma von Thurn und Taxis? The Pope had received in private audience the Archduke Otto von Hapsburg. Pete Sampras was to make a film about an international tennis player who falls in love with a peasant girl. Elizabeth Hurley was said to be considering the part of the peasant girl. Senator Edward Kennedy was said to be going into a nursing home for treatment. No reason was given for this but a spokesman for the clinic confirmed that they would issue a bulletin shortly.

As days passed by, all the bandages were removed. The long golden hair covered the marks of stitches and abrasions. Sheila lay strikingly lovely again, a sleeping beauty. No pain seemed to mar her serenity. Colour returned to her skin. But the eyes did not open and no response came to the continuous presence of her mother and her lover. Staff, who had told them that it would take time, began to question themselves. Mrs Kelly did not admit to herself the dreaded thoughts that also tormented Milo's mind. The word 'vegetable' is sometimes used about those who have recovered physically but whose intellectual functions are seriously impaired.

Sheila's friends came convinced that she would soon be speaking to them again. Brigid spent Saturday and Sunday desperately trying to evoke a reaction from her friend but all was in vain. She left on Sunday night, trying to hide her tears and her disappointment from Mrs Kelly.

Seamus came up one night with a crowd of his friends – young Buckley, O'Shea, Eddy Kavanagh and the happy-go-lucky young Hickey. He had instructed them to act normally and talk and joke as if they were at The Halfway House. Shocked as they were at Sheila's comatose state, they did as they were told and soon the atmosphere became almost rowdy. Hickey's approach to one of the nurses was rejected; O'Shea was told twice not to light up until he was outside the hospital. Kavanagh told the story of his uncle's greyhound. The animal had been trained for months to win a race at the Clones Dog Track. They got a great price, 4 to 1, and the dog was in superlative condition. The race started and the Kavanagh dog led from the first bend. Coming around the last bend, the dog was four yards ahead of the field and the money was almost in their pockets.

'Well, what do you think could happen?' asked Kavanagh and answered the question himself. 'Didn't the fucking electricity fail, the electric hare stopped and the race was declared void. When the race was restarted the bookies would only give even money on our dog. The uncle lost a packet and indeed I lost a few bob myself. That power failure saved the bookies a sight of money.'

The lads sympathized with Kavanagh and other stories and jokes were passed around. But no smile or even a slight reaction crossed Sheila's face and Seamus eventually kissed his sister's cheek and left the hospital with his disappointed team. The thoughts were unspoken with respect to Seamus but his friends were wondering if Sheila's condition would remain permanent. They had a few stops on the road home and spirits were raised somewhat but the message they took back to Kilbeggan was a sombre one.

'God help Milo. What a thing to have on his conscience. What a blow for the Kellys. What did they do to earn this tragedy?'

It was on the night after the young people had travelled to see Sheila that the idea first occurred to Mrs Kelly. By now she had grown used to hiding her despondency, but she felt herself in a cave of despair. She kept trying to encourage Milo to bear up but now and again she caught sight of his grim face across the still body of the patient and her eyes moistened at their common affliction. She waited until the next morning and as they resumed their positions on each side of Sheila, she made her suggestion.

'What about the 'touch'?' she asked. 'The Kilbeggan Touch. Surely we should be exploring every method to see if we can bring Sheila back from . . .' She stopped. She had nearly said, 'The Dead.' He stared at her with surprise. The thought had not occurred to him. 'Surely,' said Mrs Kelly, 'if the touch has worked for others and you have felt a power inside you, surely it would be worthwhile even trying it on Sheila?'

Milo saw the hope in her eyes and knew that he could not refuse. Not that he wanted to refuse but he hated to think of what further disappointment failure might bring to Mrs Kelly or what further afflictions to himself. He nodded his agreement to her and a light lit up her face. A new ray of hope filled her mind.

'We'll have to ask them,' she whispered. 'We could not do it without the approval of the doctors.'

The sister at first thought that it was a joke.

'Get a quack,' she said. 'That's a good one. We've never had one inside this unit. I don't think the surgeons would approval of that. I think all that crowd is after is the money. People are so gullible. They should trust in orthodox medicine.'

She went away scarcely considering the suggestion.

When the surgeon made his round later that morning, Mrs Kelly asked if she could speak to him for five minutes. It took him a while to consider the suggestion seriously.

'It's Lord Kilbeggan,' she told him, 'not Mr Kilbeggan. It's a gift that's been in his family for hundreds of years. He has inherited the gift and I know he has used it to help people. Surely it must be worthwhile to try to use it on Sheila. It can hardly do her any harm. Even doctors themselves used to ask the old lord to help them, when they grew old and crippled themselves. I'm not asking you to approve of it but I'd like you to talk to Milo and perhaps he could just try to help bring Sheila out of her coma.'

'You're pressing an open door,' answered the surgeon. 'I don't belive in any form of quackery, except manipulation, and I'm afraid I couldn't consider manipulation in this case.

274

But if it's merely a question of touching the patient, I don't see any difficulty. I'll talk to Lord Kilbeggan and find out what exactly he intends to do. If I give the go-ahead, it is essential that a nurse stay in the room and stop the treatment if she considers it is doing harm. It will be completely at your own risk. I shall not hold myself responsible for any reaction that may occur. I shall ask you, as her nearest relative, to sign a short note taking complete responsibility. Now I'll just talk to this young man and find out what it's all about.'

The young man was on the telephone in the waiting room and having a most uncomfortable conversation with Uncle Bertie, if trying to interrupt Uncle Bertie's monologue could be called a conversation.

'Now at last I've got hold of you,' Uncle Bertie was saying. 'I must have an answer from you about coming over to Kilbeggan. When will the lodge be ready? Mrs Neligan does not know a blind thing about it. I've got a good offer for Simla Lodge and if I don't accept, I mightn't get another. The market for houses over here is dreadful. Prices have gone down the Swanee. Olive Emerson's brother wants to buy it. He's been generous with his offer but I can't keep him waiting. There's a heap of hags along the coast all wanting to sell their houses and go into nursing homes. He could get better places cheaper. But he wants to live close to Olive. She's bad with her hips, you know. Now I'll accept his offer if you can guarantee to have the lodge ready for me inside a month. I hear your young lady's had an accident. Tell her I hope it doesn't spoil her looks. Damned fine-looking girl. Now what about it? What do you say?'

Bertie paused, Milo shot in an answer.

'Yes,' he replied quickly, intent on getting his uncle off the phone.

'Right,' said Bertie, 'I'll tell the bloody Tank her days are numbered. Ring me later and tell me all about it.'

Milo released the telephone with such a look of relief that the surgeon and Mrs Kelly stared at him in surprise. They sat down to discuss Mrs Kelly's proposal. The surgeon would agree to a laying on of hands but no pressure must be exerted. A gentle contact would be permitted. Lesions had been healing nicely and any force could damage the process. The surgeon would have preferred a healer who waved his hands near the patient and had no body contact. But Mrs Kelly told him that traditionally it was called the Kilbeggan Touch and there must be some bodily contact.

'If it goes beyond that,' said the surgeon, 'there will be serious danger of a physical relapse.'

Milo promised that he would use only the gentlest of movements.

The surgeon left them and a nurse appeared to tell them that she would be with them the next day for this 'unortho-dox treatment'. They resumed their vigil by Sheila's bed; she still lay serene on the pillows with nothing to suggest that she might not reawake at any moment and reward them for their long wait. In the background, the radio chat shows continued. You could get a Continental holiday if you imitated Rhett Butler and Scarlett O'Hara in some dialogue from *Gone With The Wind*. The news bulletins concentrated on Northern Ireland. The south did not exist. Another bishop was interviewed. Some very rich executives of a public company had made themselves richer still. Their 'bonus payments' had increased by 70% while their company losses had only risen by 49% – a very good year. There had been another country house robbery. A very valuable Sheraton card table and some exquisite chairs had been stolen by a gang. The police had taken down the particulars and warned the owners it could happen again. Pop music succeeded chat programmes. The day wore on.

Mrs Kelly slept well that night. She trusted Milo and had faith in his influence. Milo, on the other hand, scarcely slept at all. His mind was haunted by visions of failure. He would doze off for a short while and then awaken in a panic. He was scarcely able to respond to his landlady's questions at break-fast. She told him if he had time after visiting the hospital that he should visit the casino in Clontarf which was a lovely old Norman building. There was a great concert coming up

276

at Clontarf Castle which was a really beautiful place, very old-fashioned but modernized. He should take his young lady there when she was improved – lift her out of herself.

It was a rainy day. Cousin Lily collected him and he sat answering her questions in the little car. Were his digs comfortable? Was his landlady a Cavan lady? Did she have grown-up children? What did her husband do? She told him that he would be very welcome to come and stay with her in poor Dan's room. He refused politely, wondering what had happened to poor Dan. The hospital, as ever, seemed frantic with activity. Milo felt as if he were re-entering the hospital for an operation himself. An older nurse sat near Sheila's bed. She was to keep an eye on this strange unconventional treatment and halt proceedings if she felt any mishap could occur. Milo explained to Mrs Kelly that he would prefer to have her outside while he made an effort with Sheila. The nurse sat looking disapprovingly and Mrs Kelly left to sit down anxiously outside.

Now came the focus of Milo's endeavour. Failure now would mean depression for life, not just for him but for many others also. He placed both hands gently on Sheila, touching her neck, feeling her body with affection after many weeks' separation. A shudder ran through his hands and down his body. He began to sweat. He left his hands for a short while along her and then moved them to her darling breasts. A surge of feeling ran through him as his fingers made contact. No response of any kind came from the patient below him. He willed any power he had to enter her and revive her. Sweat now poured off him and he had to stop and wipe his brow. The grey-haired nurse was looking curiously at him; she was already thinking of her story for the nurses' staffroom. Milo resumed his effort, holding Sheila's elbow. Again, no signal appeared in the patient of any acknowledgement of his actions. Milo tried to remember the order of things – neck, chest and elbow followed by knee, leg and buttock. He pulled down the sheet and touched the knee tenderly. It was still almost entirely covered by bandages but he laid his hand on a bare patch

277

of skin and left it there. Next he laid both hands gently on the leg and resumed his careful quest.

Once again prayers from an earlier experience poured back into his mind and he muttered some phrases aloud –

Yea, though I walk through death's dark vale
Yet shall I fear none ill.
For Thou art with me and Thy rod
And staff me comfort still.

As the nurse listened with astonishment, she too felt her lips moving and willing that the strange young man's ritual would reward his efforts. Lastly, Milo fearful of disturbing Sheila's body too much, could not shift her to touch her buttocks but he slid his fingers in under the familiar flesh and, with heart and soul determined, prayed that she would make some response.

She did not.

With sweat pouring down him, he could bear it no longer. Tears poured down his face as he abandoned the still prone body and pushed his way blindly out of the room. His face told everything to Mrs Kelly. She did not need to ask. The result was a failure. But one memory had stayed with her. She fumbled in her bag and took out a £20 note. She pushed it into Milo's hands and dropped bag, purses and keys on to the tiled floor. As they bent down to retrieve the articles, there was a cry through the open door. The nurse with excited face was pointing to the bed. Sheila's face had changed, had become animated.

'The present for Mammy, Milo, did I put it in the boot?'

She spoke hoarsely but with a measure of excitement. Her eyes opened and she smiled at them. Mrs Kelly gripped the chair and the nurse guided her into the seat. Milo leant over, still with tears flowing down his face, and kissed Sheila. Mrs Kelly held her hand.

'Why are you crying Milo?' asked Sheila. She looked at her mother. 'You're both upset,' she whispered. 'I'm very tired. I'll just nod off for a little while.'

She turned her head on the pillows and dozed off. The three people in the room looked at each other as if a miracle had occurred. Milo went round the bed and sat beside Mrs Kelly and she kissed him fondly.

'Thank God,' she said, 'I never doubted you. That's the second of my children you've cured. Please God, we won't need any more treatment again. Will you ring Dadda for me and tell him the good news?'

The elderly nurse had brought in some of the regular staff. The doctor checked Sheila.

'Now she needs real rest,' he said. 'What a change.'

He ushered them out of the room, too professional to congratulate or acknowledge an activity which he had been taught to treat with disdain.

Milo rang Drumlerry with the good news and urged them not to come up until next day, to allow Sheila a different chance to recuperate. But he felt weak at the knees suddenly and had almost to be lifted to the door where they hailed a taxi. Mrs Kelly was dropped off, still very emotional, at Cousin Lily's, while Milo went back to his digs where he slept solidly until the next morning.

'We are survivors,' he said to Sheila as, suffused with happiness, he sat beside her bed long before the official visiting hours next morning.

She had remembered little and the intervening weeks had to be described to her in their horrifying details. A telephone was brought to them and installed beside the bed. They rang Drumlerry, where Mr Kelly almost dropped the phone when he answered it and heard the words, 'Daddy, it's Sheila.'

Cows were milked quickly that morning at Drumlerry.

'Aunty Lily, could I speak to Mammy, please?' left her Clontarf relation almost speechless.

They rang everybody they knew, and in Westmeath the message travelled by postman and milk lorry, by digger, tractor and bread van, until a countryside rejoiced.

Mrs Kelly, for her part, felt as Lazarus's mother must have felt. She sat by the bed all day while carloads of country

279

people arrived and the room was filled with farmers and flowers, with young people and old.

'Rejoice and make merry / Set sadness aside,' run the ancient lines.

They had crossed the dangerous river but returned safely.